Les Misérables

Les Misérables

by Victor Hugo

TRANSLATED FROM THE FRENCH
BY CHARLES E. WILBOUR

ABRIDGED
WITH AN INTRODUCTION
BY JAMES K. ROBINSON
ASSOCIATE PROFESSOR OF ENGLISH
UNIVERSITY OF CINCINNATI

Fawcett Premier • *New York*

LES MISÉRABLES

A FAWCETT-PREMIER ABRIDGMENT

PUBLISHED BY FAWCETT PREMIER BOOKS, A UNIT OF CBS
PUBLICATIONS, THE CONSUMER PUBLISHING DIVISION OF CBS INC.

ISBN: 0-449-30835-9

PRINTED IN THE UNITED STATES OF AMERICA.

29   28   27   26   25   24   23   22   21   20

Contents

SAINT DENIS

JEAN VALJEAN

Introduction

THE AUTHOR of *Les Misérables*, Victor-Marie Hugo, born in 1802, was at the age of thirty already a recognized master of the arts of poetry, drama and fiction. A political figure as well, he was banished to the Channel Island of Guernsey for opposing Louis Napoleon's coup of 1851. During his twenty-year exile he wrote a number of novels, the most notable being *Les Misérables*, published in 1862. After his death in Paris in 1885 he lay in state beneath the Arc de Triomphe and was buried in the Pantheon among France's greatest men.

Les Misérables, Hugo's best and most famous novel, is essentially the story of Jean Valjean and those who profoundly influenced him. The novel opens on Jean just after he has been released from the galleys, to which he had been sent nineteen years before for trying to steal a loaf of bread to feed his sister and her starving children. His yellow passport, signifying him as an ex-convict, closes all doors to him except that of the Bishop of D—— who, by his Christian charity and faith in Jean's best nature, starts him on a new career as a good man. As M. Madeleine, Jean becomes a thriving manufacturer and mayor of M—— sur M——, though he is under the suspicion of a tenacious police inspector, Javert. Jean's public career ends suddenly when he is forced by conscience to expose himself to prevent the conviction of an innocent man for a crime which Jean had committed.

The remaining four parts of the novel show us Jean Valjean in Paris, whither he fled after escaping from the galleys. In a succession of houses and under a number of assumed names, Jean brings up a little girl, Cosette, in fulfilment of his promise to her dying mother, Fantine. In Paris Jean is again hounded by Javert, whom he once eludes after a thrilling manhunt, another time after an ambush. Meanwhile, Cosette becomes a beautiful young lady wooed secretly by the youthful idealist, Marius. Faced with the loss of the one person he loves, Jean nevertheless rescues the gravely-wounded Marius from a revolutionary barricade, carries him to safety through the terrifying sewers of Paris, and insures his marriage to Cosette. Not until he is on his deathbed does Jean Valjean feel the unrestrained love of Cosette and Marius and release from his painful past.

This summary may suggest that the novel is sheer melodrama, a sensational adventure story about a man who triumphs over the evil in himself and in others. It is much more than that. It is a great humanitarian novel which shows how a man can be redeemed by accepting suffering, by doing the duty his conscience directs him to, by sacrificing himself lovingly.

It is a novel about a real, recognizable world, the France of the post-Napoleonic age. It accurately reflects the inhumane treatment of convicts and ex-convicts, the violent political upheavals of the times, the character of Paris. The chief characters had actual models. The bishop of D—— was patterned on Monsignore Miolles of Digne, who helped a real criminal as Jean Valjean was helped. The Baron Pontmercy resembled General Hugo, the author's father. Young Marius Pontmercy, the political idealist, recalled young Victor Hugo, and his courtship of Cosette was like Hugo's of Adèle Foucher, who became Madame Hugo.

From the moment of its publication Les Misérables created a great stir. Among French readers its sales were so great that Hugo was guaranteed a good income for life. In America it was a favorite of Civil War soldiers. Though some critics, especially English critics, attacked the book for its sensationalism, indecency and hollowness, others defended it memorably. The Frenchman, Gautier, impressed with the novel's vigor, said it was "no handiwork of man but a phenomenon of natural forces." Among English admirers, Tennyson, recalling the account of Jean's death, called Hugo "lord of human tears." George Meredith considered Les Misérables the "masterwork of fiction of this century," and Walter Pater classed it with such other great works of art at Dante's Divine Comedy, Milton's Paradise Lost and the Holy Bible.

A century after its triumphant publication Les Misérables may not take us by storm, but it can hardly fail to move us with its convincing characterizations, its vivid presentation of nineteenth-century problems, beliefs and events, its animating human sympathy, its moving treatment of the struggle for existence and the supernatural power of love. It is hard to think of a novel which has more memorable characters: the Bishop, Jean Valjean, Javert, Cosette, Marius. Jean Valjean, at least, belongs in that gallery of unforgettable fictional characters beside Flaubert's Madame Bovary, Melville's Captain Ahab, Dickens' Abel Magwitch. Hugo's characters reveal themselves in adventures which, if hair-raising, are nevertheless appropriate. *Les Misérables* successfully conveys important moral ideas through an exciting story.

The abridgement of *Les Misérables* which follows is inevitably different from the complete novel. What is chiefly lost is the novel of ideas, the novel which treats a number of the central problems and interests of nineteenth-century France. What remains is a novel of character and action seen in much clearer outline. Even when the novel was first published discerning critics noted that for all the novel's power it was diffuse and wordy. They saw that too much philosophizing slowed down the movement of the narrative and that digressions of various sorts were often so lengthy that the narrative thread was sometimes lost. Digressions on the glass industry, on the Picpus Convent, on money, on Paris slang, on revolutionary thought, on the use of sewage as fertilizer have little to do with the central action. Accounts of the Battle of Waterloo and the Insurrection of 1832 are interesting, even brilliant, but they are only remotely relevant.

It has therefore been desirable and possible to abridge the novel, to dispense with numerous lengthy digressions and to eliminate many a phrase, a sentence, a paragraph. By means of such cutting there emerges more clearly the moving, heroic life of a simple and good man.

JAMES K. ROBINSON

University of Cincinnati

Author's Preface

So long as there shall exist, by reason of law and custom, a social condemnation, which, in the face of civilization, artificially creates hells on earth, and complicates a destiny that is divine, with human fatality; so long as the three problems of the age—the degradation of man by poverty, the ruin of woman by starvation, and the dwarfing of childhood by physical and spiritual night—are not solved; so long as, in certain regions, social asphyxia shall be possible; in other words, and from a yet more extended point of view, so long as ignorance and misery remain on earth, books like this cannot be useless.

Hauteville House, 1862.

FANTINE

The Fall

An hour before sunset, on the evening of a day in the beginning of October, 1815, a man travelling afoot entered the
little town of D——. The few persons who at this time were
at their windows or their doors, regarded this traveller with a
sort of distrust. It would have been hard to find a passer-by
more wretched in appearance. He was a man of middle height,
stout and hardy, in the strength of maturity; he might have
been forty-six or seven. A slouched leather cap half hid his
face, bronzed by the sun and wind, and dripping with sweat.
His shaggy breast was seen through the coarse yellow shirt
which at the neck was fastened by a small silver anchor; he
wore a cravat twisted like a rope; coarse blue trousers, worn
and shabby, white on one knee, and with holes in the other;
an old ragged gray blouse, patched on one side with a piece
of green cloth sewed with twine: upon his back was a well-
filled knapsack, strongly buckled and quite new. In his hand
he carried an enormous knotted stick; his stockingless feet
were in hobnailed shoes; his hair was cropped and his beard
long.

The sweat, the heat, his long walk, and the dust, added an
indescribable meanness to his tattered appearance.

His hair was shorn, but bristly, for it had begun to grow a
little, and seemingly had not been cut for some time. Nobody
knew him; he was evidently a traveller. Whence had he come?
From the south—perhaps from the sea; for he was making his
entrance into D—— by the same road by which, seven
months before, the Emperor Napoleon went from Cannes to
Paris. This man must have walked all day long; for he appeared very weary. Some women of the old city, which is at
the lower part of the town, had seen him stop under the trees
of the Boulevard Gassendi and drink at the fountain which
is at the end of the promenade. He must have been very
thirsty, for some children who followed him, saw him stop

not two hundred steps further on and drink again at the fountain in the market-place.

When he reached the corner of the Rue Poichevert he turned to the left and went towards the mayor's office. He went in, and a quarter of an hour afterwards he came out.

The man raised his cap humbly and saluted a gendarme who was seated near the door, upon the stone bench which General Drouot mounted on the fourth of March, to read to the terrified inhabitants of D—— the proclamation of the *Golfe Juan.*

Without returning his salutation, the gendarme looked at him attentively, watched him for some distance, and then went into the city hall.

There was then in D——, a good inn called *La Croix de Colbas;* its host was named Jacquin Labarre, a man held in some consideration in the town on account of his relationship with another Labarre, who kept an inn at Grenoble called *Trois Dauphins,* and who had served in the Guides.

The traveller turned his steps towards this inn, which was the best in the place, and went at once into the kitchen, which opened out of the street.

The host, hearing the door open, and a new-comer enter, said, without raising his eyes from his ranges—

"What will monsieur have?"

"Something to eat and lodging."

"Nothing more easy," said mine host, but on turning his head and taking an observation of the traveller, he added, "for pay."

The man drew from his pocket a large leather purse, and answered,

"I have money."

"Then," said mine host, "I am at your service."

The man put his purse back into his pocket, took off his knapsack and put it down hard by the door, and holding his stick in his hand, sat down on a low stool by the fire. D—— being in the mountains, the evenings of October are cold there.

However, as the host passed backwards and forwards, he kept a careful eye on the traveller.

"Is dinner almost ready?" said the man.

"Directly," said mine host.

While the new-comer was warming himself with his back turned, the worthy innkeeper, Jacquin Labarre, took a pencil from his pocket, and then tore off the corner of an old paper which he pulled from a little table near the window. On the margin he wrote a line or two, folded it, and handed the scrap of paper to a child, who appeared to serve him as lackey and scullion at the same time. The innkeeper whispered a word to the boy and he ran off in the direction of the mayor's office.

The traveller saw nothing of this.

He asked a second time: "Is dinner ready?"

"Yes; in a few moments," said the host.

The boy came back with the paper. The host unfolded it hurriedly, as one who is expecting an answer. He seemed to read with attention, then throwing his head on one side, thought for a moment. Then he took a step towards the traveller, who seemed drowned in troublous thought.

"Monsieur," said he, "I cannot receive you."

The traveller half rose from his seat.

"Why? Are you afraid I shall not pay you, or do you want me to pay in advance? I have money, I tell you."

"It is not that."

"What then?"

"You have money—"

"Yes," said the man.

"And I," said the host; "I have no room."

"Well, put me in the stable," quietly replied the man.

"I cannot."

"Why?"

"Because the horses take all the room."

"Well," responded the man, "a corner in the garret; a truss of straw: we will see about that after dinner."

"I cannot give you any dinner."

This declaration, made in a measured but firm tone, appeared serious to the traveller. He got up.

"Ah, bah! but I am dying with hunger. I have walked since sunrise; I have travelled twelve leagues. I will pay, and I want something to eat."

"I have nothing," said the host.

The man burst into a laugh, and turned towards the fireplace and the ranges.

"Nothing! and all that?"

"All that is engaged."

"By whom?"

"By those persons, the wagoners."

"How many are there of them?"

"Twelve."

"There is enough there for twenty."

"They have engaged and paid for it all in advance."

The man sat down again and said, without raising his voice: "I am at an inn. I am hungry, and I shall stay."

The host bent down his ear, and said in a voice which made him tremble:

"Go away!"

At these words the traveller, who was bent over, poking some embers in the fire with the iron-shod end of his stick, turned suddenly around, and opened his mouth, as if to reply, when the host, looking steadily at him, added in the same low tone: "Stop, no more of that. Shall I tell you your name? Your name is Jean Valjean; now shall I tell you *who* you are? When I saw you enter, I suspected something. I sent to the mayor's office, and here is the reply. Can you read?" So saying, he held towards him the open paper, which had just come from the mayor. The man cast a look upon it; the inn-keeper, after a short silence, said: "It is my custom to be polite to all: Go!"

The man bowed his head, picked up his knapsack, and went out.

The good inn was closed against him: he sought some humble tavern, some poor cellar.

Just then a light shone at the end of the street; he saw a pine branch, hanging by an iron bracket, against the white sky of the twilight. He went thither.

It was a tavern in the Rue Chaffaut.

The traveller did not dare to enter by the street door; he slipped into the court, stopped again, then timidly raised the latch, and pushed open the door.

"Who is it?" said the host.

"One who wants supper and a bed."

"All right: here you can sup and sleep."

He seated himself near the fireplace and stretched his feet out towards the fire, half dead with fatigue: an inviting odor came from the pot. All that could be seen of his face under his slouched cap assumed a vague appearance of comfort, which tempered the sorrowful aspect given him by a long-continued suffering.

However, one of the men at the table was a fisherman who had put up his horse at the stable of Labarre's inn before entering the tavern of the Rue de Chaffaut. It so happened that he had met, that same morning, this suspicious-looking stranger travelling between Bras d'Asse and—I forget the place, I think it is Escoublon. Now, on meeting him, the man, who seemed already very much fatigued, had asked him to take him on behind, to which the fisherman responded only by doubling his pace. The fisherman, half an hour before, had been one of the throng about Jacquin Labarre, and had himself related his unpleasant meeting with him to the people of the *Croix de Colbas*. He beckoned to the tavern-keeper to come to him, which he did. They exchanged a few words in a low voice; the traveller had again relapsed into thought.

The tavern-keeper returned to the fire, and laying his hand roughly on his shoulder, said harshly:

"You are going to clear out from here!"

The stranger turned round and said mildly,

"Ah! Do you know?"

"Yes."

"They sent me away from the other inn."

"And we turn you out of this."

"Where would you have me go?"

"Somewhere else."

The man took up his stick and knapsack, and went off. As he went out, some children who had followed him from the *Croix de Colbas*, and seemed to be waiting for him, threw stones at him. He turned angrily and threatened them with his stick, and they scattered like a flock of birds.

He passed the prison: an iron chain hung from the door attached to a bell. He rang.

The grating opened.

"Monsieur Turnkey," said he, taking off his cap respectfully, "will you open and let me stay here to-night?"

A voice answered:

"A prison is not a tavern: get yourself arrested and we will open."

The grating closed.

He went into a small street where there are many gardens; some of them are enclosed only by hedges, which enliven the street. Among them he saw a pretty little one-story house, where there was a light in the window. He looked in as he had done at the tavern. It was a large whitewashed room, with a bed draped with calico, and a cradle in the corner, some wooden chairs, and a double-barrelled gun

hung against the wall. A table was set in the centre of the
room; a brass lamp lighted the coarse white table-cloth; a
tin mug full of wine shone like silver, and the brown soup-
dish was smoking. At this table sat a man about forty years
old, with a joyous, open countenance, who was trotting a
little child upon his knee. Near by him a young woman
was suckling another child; the father was laughing, the
child was laughing, and the mother was smiling.

He rapped faintly on the window.

No one heard him.

He rapped a second time.

He heard the woman say, "Husband, I think I hear some
one rap."

"No," replied the husband.

He rapped a third time. The husband got up, took the
lamp, and opened the door.

"Monsieur," said the traveller, "I beg your pardon; for
pay can you give me a plate of soup and a corner of the shed
in your garden to sleep in? Tell me; can you, for pay?"

"Who are you?" demanded the master of the house.

The man replied: "I have come from Puy-Moisson; I have
walked all day; I have come twelve leagues. Can you, if I
pay?"

"I wouldn't refuse to lodge any proper person who would
pay," said the peasant; "but why do you not go to the inn?"

"There is no room."

"Bah! That is not possible. It is neither a fair nor a market-
day. Have you been to Labarre's house?"

"Yes."

"Well?"

The traveller replied hesitatingly: "I don't know; he didn't
take me."

"Have you been to that place in the Rue Chaffaut?"

The embarrassment of the stranger increased; he stammered: "They didn't take me either."

The peasant's face assumed an expression of distrust: he
looked over the new-comer from head to foot, and suddenly exclaimed, with a sort of shudder: "Are you the man!"

He looked again at the stranger, stepped back, put the lamp
on the table, and took down his gun.

His wife, on hearing the words, *are you the man,* started
up, and, clasping her two children, precipitately took refuge
behind her husband; she looked at the stranger with affright,

her neck bare, her eyes dilated, murmuring in a low tone: *"Tso maraude!"* [1]

All this happened in less time than it takes to read it; after examining the man for a moment, as one would a viper, the man advanced to the door and said:

"Get out!"

"For pity's sake, a glass of water," said the man.

"A gun shot," said the peasant, and then he closed the door violently, and the man heard two heavy bolts drawn. A moment afterwards the window-shutters were shut, and noisily barred.

Night came on apace; the cold Alpine winds were blowing; by the light of the expiring day the stranger perceived in one of the gardens which fronted the street a kind of hut which seemed to be made of turf; he boldly cleared a wooden fence and found himself in the garden. He neared the hut; its door was a narrow, low entrance; it resembled, in its construction, the shanties which the road-laborers put up for their temporary accommodation. He got down and crawled into the hut. It was warm there and he found a good bed of straw. He rested a moment upon his bed motionless from fatigue; then, as his knapsack on his back troubled him, and it would make a good pillow, he began to unbuckle the straps. Just then he heard a ferocious growling and looking up saw the head of an enormous bull-dog at the opening of the hut.

It was a dog-kennel!

He was himself vigorous and formidable; seizing his stick, he made a shield of his knapsack, and got out of the hut as best he could, but not without enlarging the rents of his already tattered garments.

When he had, not without difficulty, got over the fence, he again found himself alone in the street without lodging, roof, or shelter, driven even from the straw bed of the wretched dog-kennel. He threw himself rather than seated himself on a stone, and it appears that some one who was passing heard him exclaim, "I am not even a dog!"

Then he arose, and began to tramp again, taking his way out of the town, hoping to find some tree or haystack beneath which he could shelter himself. He walked on for some time, his head bowed down. When he thought he was far away

---

[1] Patois of the French Alps, "Chat de maraude."

from all human habitation he raised his eyes, and looked about him inquiringly. He was in a field: before him was a low hillock covered with stubble, which after the harvest looks like a shaved head.

The earth was then lighter than the sky, which produced a peculiarly sinister effect, and the hill, poor and mean in contour, loomed out dim and pale upon the gloomy horizon: the whole prospect was hideous, mean, lugubrious, and insignificant. There was nothing in the field nor upon the hill but one ugly tree, a few steps from the traveller, which seemed to be twisting and contorting itself.

He retraced his steps; the gates of D—— were closed. D——, which sustained sieges in the religious wars, was still surrounded, in 1815, by old walls flanked by square towers, since demolished. He passed through a breach and entered the town.

It was about eight o'clock in the evening: as he did not know the streets, he walked at hazard.

So he came to the prefecture, then to the seminary; on passing by the Cathedral square, he shook his fist at the church.

At the corner of this square stands a printing-office; there were first printed the proclamations of the emperor, and the Imperial Guard to the army, brought from the island of Elba, and dictated by Napoleon himself.

Exhausted with fatigue, and hoping for nothing better, he lay down on a stone bench in front of this printing-office.

Just then an old woman came out of the church. She saw the man lying there in the dark and said:

"What are you doing there, my friend?"

He replied harshly, and with anger in his tone:

"You see, my good woman, I am going to sleep."

The good woman, who really merited the name, was Madame la Marquise de R——.

"Upon the bench?" said she.

"For nineteen years I have had a wooden mattress," said the man; "to-night I have a stone one."

"You have been a soldier?"

"Yes, my good woman, a soldier."

"Why don't you go to the inn?"

"Because I have no money."

"Alas!" said Madame de R——, "I have only four sous in my purse."

"Give them then." The man took the four sous, and Madame de R—— continued:

"You cannot find lodging for so little in an inn. But have you tried? You cannot pass the night so. You must be cold and hungry. They should give you lodging for charity."

"I have knocked at every door."

"Well, what then?"

"Everybody has driven me away."

The good woman touched the man's arm and pointed out to him, on the other side of the square, a little low house beside the bishop's palace.

"You have knocked at every door?" she asked.

"Yes."

"Have you knocked at that one there?"

"No."

"Knock there."

PRUDENCE COMMENDED TO WISDOM

THAT evening, after his walk in the town, the Bishop of D—— remained quite late in his room. He was busy with his great work on Duty, which unfortunately is left incomplete. He carefully dissected all that the Fathers and Doctors have said on this serious topic. He collated with much labor these injunctions into a harmonious whole, which he wished to offer to souls.

At eight o'clock he was still at work, writing with some inconvenience on little slips of paper, with a large book open on his knees, when Madame Magloire, as usual, came in to take the silver from the panel near the bed. A moment after, the bishop, knowing that the table was laid, and that his sister was perhaps waiting, closed his book and went into the dining room.

Madame Magloire had just finished placing the plates.

While she was arranging the table, she was talking with Mademoiselle Baptistine.

The lamp was on the table, which was near the fireplace, where a good fire was burning.

Mademoiselle Baptistine has so often related what occurred at the bishop's house that evening, that many persons are still living who can recall the minutest details.

Just as the bishop entered, Madame Magloire was speaking with some warmth. She was talking to *Mademoiselle* upon a familiar subject, and one to which the bishop was quite accustomed. It was a discussion on the means of fastening the front door.

It seems that while Madame Magloire was out making provision for supper, she had heard the news in sundry places. There was talk that an ill-favored runaway, a suspicious vagabond, had arrived and was lurking somewhere in the town, and that some unpleasant adventures might befall those who should come home late that night; besides, that the police was very bad, as the prefect and the mayor did not like one another, and were hoping to injure each other by untoward events; that it was the part of wise people to be their own police, and to protect their own persons; and that every one ought to be careful to shut up, bolt, and bar his house properly, and *secure his door thoroughly*.

Madame Magloire dwelt upon these last words; but the bishop having come from a cold room, seated himself before the fire and began to warm himself, and then, he was thinking of something else. He did not hear a word of what was let fall by Madame Magloire, and she repeated it. Then Mademoiselle Baptistine, endeavoring to satisfy Madame Magloire without displeasing her brother, ventured to say timidly:

"Brother, do you hear what Madame Magloire says?"

"I heard something of it indistinctly," said the bishop. Then turning his chair half round, putting his hands on his knees, and raising towards the old servant his cordial and good-humored face, which the firelight shone upon, he said: "Well, well! what is the matter? Are we in any great danger?"

This readiness to question her encouraged Madame Magloire; it seemed to indicate that the bishop was really well-nigh alarmed. She continued triumphantly: "Yes, monseigneur; it is true. There will something happen to-night in the town: everybody says so. The police are so badly organized" (a convenient repetition). "To live in this mountainous country, and not even to have street lamps! If one goes out, it is dark as a pocket. And I say, monseigneur, and mademoiselle says also—"

"Me?" interrupted the sister; "I say nothing. Whatever my brother does is well done."

Madame Magloire went on as if she had not heard this protestation:

"We say that this house is not safe at all; and if monseigneur will permit me, I will go and tell Paulin Musebois, the locksmith, to come and put the old bolts in the door again; they are there, and it will take but a minute. I say we must have bolts, were it only for to-night; for I say that a door which opens by a latch on the outside to the first comer, nothing could be more horrible: and then monseigneur has the habit of always saying 'Come in,' even at midnight. But, my goodness! there is no need even to ask leave—"

At this moment there was a violent knock on the door.

"Come in!" said the bishop.

THE HEROISM OF PASSIVE OBEDIENCE

THE door opened.

It opened quickly, quite wide, as if pushed by some one boldly and with energy.

A man entered.

He came in, took one step, and paused, leaving the door open behind him. He had his knapsack on his back, his stick in his hand, and a rough, hard, tired, and fierce look in his eyes, as seen by the firelight. He was hideous. It was an apparition of ill omen.

Madame Magloire had not even the strength to scream. She stood trembling with her mouth open.

Mademoiselle Baptistine turned, saw the man enter, and started up half alarmed; then, slowly turning back again towards the fire she looked at her brother, and her face resumed its usual calmness and serenity.

The bishop looked upon the man with a tranquil eye.

As he was opening his mouth to speak, doubtless to ask the stranger what he wanted, the man, leaning with both hands on his club, glanced from one to another in turn, and without waiting for the bishop to speak, said in a loud voice:

"See here! My name is Jean Valjean. I am a convict; I have been nineteen years in the galleys. Four days ago I was set free, and started for Pontarlier, which is my destination; during those four days I have walked from Toulon. To-day I have walked twelve leagues. When I reached this place this evening I went to an inn, and they sent me away on account of my yellow passport, which I had shown at the mayor's office, as was necessary. I went to another inn; they said: 'Get out!' It was the same with one as with another; nobody would have me. I went to the prison, and the turnkey

would not let me in. I crept into a dog-kennel, the dog bit
me, and drove me away as if he had been a man; you would
have said that he knew who I was. I went into the fields to
sleep beneath the stars: there were no stars; I thought it would
rain, and there was no good God to stop the drops, so I
came back to the town to get the shelter of some doorway.
There in the square I lay down upon a stone; a good woman
showed me your house, and said: 'Knock there!' I have
knocked. What is this place? Are you an inn? I have money;
my savings, one hundred and nine francs and fifteen sous
which I have earned in the galleys by my work for nineteen
years. I will pay. What do I care? I have money. I am
very tired—twelve leagues on foot, and I am so hungry.
Can I stay?"

"Madame Magloire," said the bishop, "put on another
plate."

The man took three steps, and came near the lamp which
stood on the table. "Stop," he exclaimed; as if he had not
been understood, "not that, did you understand me? I am a
galley-slave—a convict—I am just from the galleys." He drew
from his pocket a large sheet of yellow paper, which he unfolded. "There is my passport, yellow as you see. That is
enough to have me kicked out wherever I go. Will you read it?
I know how to read, I do. I learned in the galleys. There is a
school there for those who care for it. See, here is what they
have put in the passport: 'Jean Valjean, a liberated convict,
native of ——,' you don't care for that, 'has been nineteen
years in the galleys; five years for burglary; fourteen years
for having attempted four times to escape. This man is very
dangerous.' There you have it! Everybody has thrust me out;
will you receive me? Is this an inn? Can you give me something to eat, and a place to sleep? Have you a stable?"

"Madame Magloire," said the bishop, "put some sheets on
the bed in the alcove."

Madame Magloire went out to fulfil her orders.

The bishop turned to the man:

"Monsieur, sit down and warm yourself: we are going to
take supper presently, and your bed will be made ready while
you sup."

At last the man quite understood; his face, the expression
of which till then had been gloomy and hard, now expressed
stupefaction, doubt, and joy, and became absolutely wonderful. He began to stutter like a madman.

"True? What! You will keep me? you won't drive me away?

a convict! You call me *Monsieur* and don't say 'Get out, dog!'
as everybody else does. I thought that you would send me
away, so I told first off who I am. Oh! the fine woman who
sent me here! I shall have a supper! a bed like other people
with mattress and sheets—a bed! It is nineteen years that I
have not slept on a bed. You are really willing that I should
stay? You are good people! Besides I have money: I will
pay well. I beg your pardon, Monsieur Innkeeper, what is
your name? I will pay all you say. You are a fine man. You
are an innkeeper, an't you?"

"I am a priest who lives here," said the bishop.

"A priest," said the man. "Oh, noble priest! Then you do
not ask any money? You are the curé, an't you? the curé
of this big church? Yes, that's it. How stupid I am; I didn't
notice your cap."

While speaking, he had deposited his knapsack and stick in
the corner, replaced his passport in his pocket, and sat down.
Mademoiselle Baptistine looked at him pleasantly. He continued:

"You are humane, Monsieur Curé; you don't despise me.
A good priest is a good thing. Then you don't want me to
pay?"

"No," said the bishop, "keep your money. How much
have you? You said a hundred and nine francs, I think."

"And fifteen sous," added the man.

"One hundred and nine francs and fifteen sous. And how
long did it take you to earn that?"

"Nineteen years."

"Nineteen years!"

The bishop sighed deeply.

Madame Magloire brought in a plate and set it on the
table.

"Madame Magloire," said the bishop, "put this plate as
near the fire as you can." Then turning towards his guest,
he added: "The night wind is raw in the Alps; you must be
cold, monsieur."

Every time he said this word monsieur, with his gently
solemn, and heartily hospitable voice, the man's countenance
lighted up. *Monsieur* to a convict is a glass of water to a
man dying of thirst at sea. Ignominy thirsts for respect.

"The lamp," said the bishop, "gives a very poor light."

Madame Magloire understood him, and going to his bed-
chamber, took from the mantel the two silver candlesticks,
lighted the candles, and placed them on the table.

"Monsieur Curé," said the man, "you are good; you don't despise me. You take me into your house; you light your candles for me, and I hav'n't hid from you where I come from, and how miserable I am."

The bishop, who was sitting near him, touched his hand gently and said: "You need not tell me who you are. This is not my house; it is the house of Christ. It does not ask any comer whether he has a name, but whether he has an affliction. You are suffering; you are hungry and thirsty; be welcome. And do not thank me; do not tell me that I take you into my house. This is the home of no man, except him who needs an asylum. I tell you, who are a traveller, that you are more at home here than I; whatever is here is yours. What need have I to know your name? Besides, before you told me, I knew it."

The man opened his eyes in astonishment:

"Really? You knew my name?"

"Yes," answered the bishop, "your name is my brother."

"Stop, stop, Monsieur Curé," exclaimed the man. "I was famished when I came in, but you are so kind that now I don't know what I am; that is all gone."

The bishop looked at him again and said:

"You have seen much suffering?"

"Oh, the red blouse, the ball and chain, the plank to sleep on, the heat, the cold, the galley's crew, the lash, the double chain for nothing, the dungeon for a word,—even when sick in bed, the chain. The dogs, the dogs are happier! nineteen years! and I am forty-six, and now a yellow passport. That is all."

"Yes," answered the bishop, "you have left a place of suffering. But listen, there will be more joy in heaven over the tears of a repentant sinner than over the white robes of a hundred good men. If you are leaving that sorrowful place with hate and anger against men, you are worthy of compassion; if you leave it with goodwill, gentleness, and peace, you are better than any of us."

Meantime Madame Magloire had served up supper; it consisted of soup made of water, oil, bread, and salt, a little pork, a scrap of mutton, a few figs, a green cheese, and a large loaf of rye bread. She had, without asking, added to the usual dinner of the bishop a bottle of fine old Mauves wine.

The bishop's countenance was lighted up with this expression of pleasure, peculiar to hospitable natures. "To supper!" he said briskly, as was his habit when he had a guest. He seated the man at his right. Mademoiselle Baptistine, perfectly quiet and natural, took her place at his left.

The bishop said the blessing, and then served the soup himself, according to his usual custom. The man fell to, eating greedily.

TRANQUILITY

AFTER having said good-night to his sister, Monseigneur Bienvenu took one of the silver candlesticks from the table, handed the other to his guest, and said to him:

"Monsieur, I will show you to your room."

The man followed him.

The house was so arranged that one could reach the alcove in the oratory only by passing through the bishop's sleeping chamber. Just as they were passing through this room Madame Magloire was putting up the silver in the cupboard at the head of the bed. It was the last thing she did every night before going to bed.

The bishop left his guest in the alcove, before a clean white bed. The man set down the candlestick upon a small table.

"Come," said the bishop, "a good night's rest to you: to-morrow morning, before you go, you shall have a cup of warm milk from our cows."

"Thank you, Monsieur l'Abbé," said the man.

Scarcely had he pronounced these words of peace, when suddenly he made a singular motion which would have chilled the two good women of the house with horror, had they witnessed it. Even now it is hard for us to understand what impulse he obeyed at that moment. Did he intend to give a warning or to throw out a menace? Or was he simply obeying a sort of instinctive impulse, obscure ever to himself? He turned abruptly towards the old man, crossed his arms, and casting a wild look upon his host, exclaimed in a harsh voice:

"Ah, now, indeed! You lodge me in your house, as near you as that!"

He checked himself, and added, with a laugh, in which there was something horrible:

"Have you reflected upon it? Who tells you that I am not a murderer?"

The bishop responded:

"God will take care of that."

Then with gravity, moving his lips like one praying or talking to himself, he raised two fingers of his right hand and blessed the man, who, however, did not bow; and without turning his head or looking behind him, went into his chamber.

When the alcove was occupied, a heavy serge curtain was drawn in the oratory, concealing the altar. Before this curtain the bishop knelt as he passed out, and offered a short prayer.

As to the man, he was so completely exhausted that he did not even avail himself of the clean white sheets; he blew out the candle with his nostril, after the manner of convicts, and fell on the bed, dressed as he was, into a sound sleep.

Midnight struck as the bishop came back to his chamber. A few moments afterwards all in the little house slept.

JEAN VALJEAN

TOWARDS the middle of the night, Jean Valjean awoke.

Jean Valjean was born of a poor peasant family of Brie. In his childhood he had not been taught to read: when he was grown up, he chose the occupation of a pruner at Faverolles. His mother's name was Jeanne Mathieu, his father's Jean Valjean or Vlajean, probably a nickname, a contraction of *Voilà Jean*.

Jean Valjean was of a thoughtful disposition, but not sad, which is characteristic of affectionate natures. Upon the whole, however, there was something torpid and insignificant, in the appearance at least, of Jean Valjean. He had lost his parents when very young. His mother died of malpractice in a milkfever: his father, a pruner before him, was killed by a fall from a tree. Jean Valjean now had but one relative left, his sister, a widow with seven children, girls and boys. This sister had brought up Jean Valjean, and, as long as her husband lived, she had taken care of her younger brother. Her husband died, leaving the eldest of these children eight, the youngest one year old. Jean Valjean had just reached his twenty-fifth year: he took the father's place, and, in his turn, supported the sister who reared him. This he did naturally, as a duty, and even with a sort of moroseness on his part.

His youth was spent in rough and ill-recompensed labour: he never was known to have a sweetheart; he had not time to be in love.

He earned in the pruning season eighteen sous a day: after that he hired out as a reaper, workman, teamster, or laborer. He did whatever he could find to do. His sister worked also, but what could she do with seven little children? It was a sad group, which misery was grasping and closing upon, little by little. There was a very severe winter; Jean had no work, the family had no bread; literally, no bread, and seven children.

One Sunday night, Maubert Isabeau, the baker on the Place de l'Eglise, in Faverolles, was just going to bed when he heard a violent blow against the barred window of his shop. He got down in time to see an arm thrust through the aperture made by the blow of a fist on the glass. The arm seized a loaf of bread and took it out. Isabeau rushed out; the thief used his legs valiantly; Isabeau pursued him and caught him. The thief had thrown away the bread, but his arm was still bleeding. It was Jean Valjean.

All that happened in 1795. Jean Valjean was brought before the tribunals of the time for "burglary at night, in an inhabited house." He had a gun which he used as well as any marksman in the world, and was something of a poacher, which hurt him, there being a natural prejudice against poachers. Jean Valjean was found guilty: the terms of the code were explicit. Jean Valjean was sentenced to five years in the galleys.

On the 22nd of April, 1796, there was announced in Paris the victory of Montenotte, achieved by the commanding-general of the army of Italy, whom the message of the directory, to the Five Hundred, of the 2nd Floréal, year IV., called Buonaparte; that same day a great chain was riveted at the Bicêtre. Jean Valjean was a part of this chain. While they were with heavy hammer-strokes behind his head riveting the bolt of his iron collar, he was weeping. The tears choked his words, and he only succeeded in saying from time to time: "*I was a pruner at Faverolles.*" Then sobbing as he was, he raised his right hand and lowered it seven times, as if he was touching seven heads of unequal height, and at this gesture one could guess that whatever he had done had been to feed and clothe seven little children.

He was taken to Toulon, at which place he arrived after a

journey of twenty-seven days, on a cart, the chain still about
his neck. At Toulon he was dressed in a red blouse, all his
past life was effaced, even to his name. He was no longer
Jean Valjean: he was Number 24,601.

Near the end of his fourth year, his chance of liberty
came to Jean Valjean. His comrades helped him as they always do in that dreary place, and he escaped. During the
evening of the second day he was retaken; he had neither
eaten nor slept for thirty-six hours. The maritime tribunal
extended his sentence three years for this attempt, which
made eight. In the sixth year his turn of escape came again;
he tried it, but failed again. He did not answer at roll-call
and the alarm cannon was fired. At night the people of the
vicinity discovered him hidden beneath the keel of a vessel
on the stocks; he resisted the galley guard which seized him.
Escape and resistance. This the provisions of the special
code punished by an addition of five years, two with the
double chain, thirteen years. The tenth year his turn came
round again; he made another attempt with no better success. Three years for this new attempt. Sixteen years. And
finally, I think it was in the thirteenth year, he made yet
another, and was retaken after an absence of only four
hours. Three years for these four hours. Nineteen years. In
October, 1815, he was set at large: he had entered in 1796 for
having broken a pane of glass, and taken a loaf of bread.

Jean Valjean entered the galleys sobbing and shuddering:
he went out hardened; he entered in despair: he went out
sullen.

NEW GRIEFS

WHEN the time for leaving the galleys came, and when there
were sounded in the ear of Jean Valjean the strange words:
You are free! the moment seemed improbable and unreal; a
ray of living light, a ray of the true light of living men, suddenly penetrated his soul. But this ray quickly faded away.
Jean Valjean had been dazzled with the idea of liberty. He
had believed in a new life. He soon saw what sort of liberty
that is which has a yellow passport.

The day after his liberation, he saw before the door of an
orange flower distillery at Grasse, some men who were un-

loading bags. He offered his services. They were in need of
help and accepted them. He set at work. He was intelligent,
robust, and handy; he did his best; the foreman appeared to
be satisfied. While he was at work, a gendarme passed, noticed him, and asked for his papers. He was compelled to show
the yellow passport. That done, Jean Valjean resumed his
work. A little while before, he had asked one of the labourers
how much they were paid per day for this work, and the
reply was: *thirty sous*. At night, as he was obliged to leave
the town next morning, he went to the foreman of the distillery, and asked for his pay. The foreman did not say a
word, but handed him fifteen sous. He remonstrated. The
man replied: *"That is good enough for you."* He insisted.
The foreman looked him in the eyes and said: *"Look out for
the lock-up!"*

There again he thought himself robbed.

Society, the state, in reducing his savings, had robbed him
by wholesale. Now it was the turn of the individual, who
was robbing him by retail.

Liberation is not deliverance. A convict may leave the galleys behind, but not his condemnation.

This was what befell him at Grasse. We have seen how he
was received at D——.

THE MAN AWAKES

As the cathedral clock struck two, Jean Valjean awoke.

What awakened him was, too good a bed. For nearly
twenty years he had not slept in a bed, and, although he had
not undressed, the sensation was too novel not to disturb his
sleep.

Many thoughts came to him, but there was one which
continually presented itself, and which drove away all others.
What that thought was, we shall tell directly. He had noticed
the six silver plates and the large ladle that Madame Magloire had put on the table.

His mind wavered a whole hour, and a long one, in fluctu-
ation and in struggle. The clock struck three. He opened his
eyes, rose up hastily in bed, reached out his arm and felt his
haversack, which he had put into the corner of the alcove,
then he thrust out his legs and placed his feet on the ground,

and found himself, he knew not how, seated on his bed.

He continued in this situation, and would perhaps have remained there until daybreak, if the clock had not struck the quarter or the half-hour. The clock seemed to say to him: "Come along!"

He rose to his feet, hesitated for a moment longer, and listened; all was still in the house: he walked straight and cautiously towards the window, which he could discern. The night was not very dark; there was a full moon, across which large clouds were driving before the wind. This produced alternations of light and shade, out-of-doors eclipses and illuminations, and in-doors a kind of glimmer. This glimmer, enough to enable him to find his way, changing with the passing clouds, resembled that sort of livid light, which falls through the window of a dungeon before which men are passing and repassing. On reaching the window, Jean Valjean examined it. It had no bars, opened into the garden, and was fastened, according to the fashion of the country, with a little wedge only. He opened it; but as the cold, keen air rushed into the room, he closed it again immediately. He looked into the garden with that absorbed look which studies rather than sees. The garden was enclosed with a white wall, quite low, and readily scaled. Beyond, against the sky, he distinguished the tops of trees at equal distances apart, which showed that this wall separated the garden from an avenue or a lane planted with trees.

When he had taken this observation, he turned like a man whose mind is made up, went to his alcove, took his haversack, opened it, fumbled in it, took out something which he laid upon the bed, put his shoes into one of his pockets, tied up his bundle, swung it upon his shoulders, put on his cap, and pulled the visor down over his eyes, felt for his stick, and went and put it in the corner of the window, then returned to the bed, and resolutely took up the object which he had laid on it. It looked like a short iron bar, pointed at one end like a spear.

It would have been hard to distinguish in the darkness for what use this piece of iron had been made. Could it be a lever? Could it be a club?

In the day-time, it would have been seen to be nothing but a miner's drill. At that time, the convicts were sometimes employed in quarrying stone on the high hills that surround Toulon, and they often had miners' tools in their possession. Miners' drills are of solid iron, terminating at the lower end in a point, by means of which they are sunk into the rock.

He took the drill in his right hand and, holding his breath, with stealthy steps, he moved towards the door of the next room, which was the bishop's, as we know. On reaching the door, he found it unlatched. The bishop had not closed it.

WHAT HE DOES

JEAN VALJEAN listened. Not a sound. He pushed the door.

He pushed it lightly with the end of his finger, with the stealthy and timorous carefulness of a cat. The door yielded to the pressure with a silent, imperceptible movement, which made the opening a little wider.

He waited a moment, and then pushed the door again more boldly.

It yielded gradually and silently. The opening was now wide enough for him to pass through; but there was a small table near the door which with it formed a troublesome angle, and which barred the entrance.

Jean Valjean saw the obstacle. At all hazards the opening must be made still wider.

He so determined, and pushed the door a third time, harder than before. This time a rusty hinge suddenly sent out into the darkness a harsh and prolonged creak.

Jean Valjean shivered. The noise of this hinge sounded in his ears as clear and terrible as the trumpet of the Judgment Day.

He stood still, petrified like the pillar of salt, not daring to stir. Some minutes passed. The door was wide open; he ventured a look into the room. Nothing had moved. He listened. Nothing was stirring in the house. The noise of the rusty hinge had wakened nobody.

Suddenly he stopped: he was near the bed, he had reached it sooner than he thought.

Nature sometimes joins her effects and her appearances to our acts with a sort of serious and intelligent appropriateness, as if she would compel us to reflect. For nearly a half hour a great cloud had darkened the sky. At the moment when Jean Valjean paused before the bed the cloud broke as if purposely, and a ray of moonlight crossing the high window, suddenly lighted up the bishop's pale face. He slept tranquilly. He was almost entirely dressed, though in bed, on account of the cold nights of the lower Alps, with a dark woolen garment which covered his arms to the wrists. His head had fallen on the pillow in the unstudied attitude of slumber; over the side of the bed hung his hand, ornamented with the pastoral ring, and which had done so many good deeds, so many pious acts. His entire countenance was lit up with a vague expression of content, hope, and happiness. It was more than a smile and almost a radiance.

Jean Valjean was in the shadow with the iron drill in his hand, erect, motionless, terrified, at this radiant figure. He had never seen anything comparable to it. This confidence filled him with fear. The moral world has no greater spectacle than this; a troubled and restless conscience on the verge of committing an evil deed, contemplating the sleep of a good man.

He did not remove his eyes from the old man. The only thing which was plain from his attitude and his countenance was a strange indecision. You would have said he was hesitating between two realms, that of the doomed and that of the saved. He appeared ready either to cleave this skull, or kiss this hand.

In a few moments he raised his left hand slowly to his forehead and took off his hat: then, letting his hand fall with the same slowness, Jean Valjean resumed his contemplations, his cap in his left hand, his club in his right, and his hair bristling on his fierce-looking head.

Under this frightful gaze the bishop still slept in profoundest peace.

The crucifix above the mantelpiece was dimly visible in the moonlight, apparently extending its arms towards both, with a benediction for one and a pardon for the other.

Suddenly Jean Valjean put on his cap, then passed quickly, without looking at the bishop, along the bed, straight to the cupboard which he perceived near its head; he raised the drill to force the lock; the key was in it; he opened it; the first thing he saw was the basket of silver, he took it, crossed the room with hasty stride, careless of noise, reached the door, entered the oratory, took his stick, stepped out, put the silver in his knapsack, threw away the basket, ran across the garden, leaped over the wall like a tiger, and fled.

THE BISHOP AT WORK

THE next day at sunrise, Monseigneur Bienvenu was walking in the garden. Madame Magloire ran towards him quite beside herself.

"Monseigneur, monseigneur," cried she, "does your greatness know where the silver basket is?"

"Yes," said the bishop.

"God be praised!" said she, "I did not know what had become of it."

The bishop had just found the basket on a flower-bed. He gave it to Madame Magloire and said: "There it is."

"Yes," said she, "but there is nothing in it. The silver?"

"Ah!" said the bishop, "it is the silver then that troubles you. I do not know where that is."

"Good heavens! it is stolen. That man who came last night stole it."

And in the twinkling of an eye, with all the agility of which her age was capable, Madame Magloire ran to the oratory, went into the alcove, and came back to the bishop. The bishop was bending with some sadness over a cochlearia des Guillons, which the basket had broken in falling. He looked up at Madame Magloire's cry:

"Monseigneur, the man has gone! the silver is stolen!"

While she was uttering this exclamation her eyes fell on an angle of the garden where she saw traces of an escalade. A capstone of the wall had been thrown down.

"See, there is where he got out; he jumped into Cochefilet lane. The abominable fellow! he has stolen our silver!"

The bishop was silent for a moment, then raising his serious eyes, he said mildly to Madame Magloire:

"Now first, did this silver belong to us?"

Madame Magloire did not answer; after a moment the bishop continued:

"Madame Magloire, I have for a long time wrongfully withheld this silver; it belonged to the poor. Who was this man? A poor man evidently."

In a few minutes he was breakfasting at the same table at which Jean Valjean sat the night before. While breakfasting, Monseigneur Bienvenu pleasantly remarked to his sister who said nothing, and Madame Magloire who was grumbling to herself, that there was really no need even of a wooden spoon or fork to dip a piece of bread into a cup of milk.

Just as the brother and sister were rising from the table, there was a knock at the door.

"Come in," said the bishop.

The door opened. A strange, fierce group appeared on the threshold. Three men were holding a fourth by the collar. The three men were gendarmes; the fourth Jean Valjean.

A brigadier of gendarmes, who appeared to head the group, was near the door. He advanced towards the bishop, giving a military salute.

"Monseigneur," said he—

At this word Jean Valjean, who was sullen and seemed entirely cast down, raised his head with a stupefied air—

"Monseigneur!" he murmured, "then it is not the curé!"

"Silence!" said a gendarme, "it is monseigneur, the bishop."

In the meantime Monseigneur Bienvenu had approached as quickly as his great age permitted:

"Ah, there you are!" said he, looking towards Jean Valjean, "I am glad to see you. But! I gave you the candlesticks also, which are silver like the rest, and would bring two hundred francs. Why did you not take them along with your plates?"

Jean Valjean opened his eyes and looked at the bishop with an expression which no human tongue could describe.

"Monseigneur," said the brigadier, "then what this man said was true? We met him. He was going like a man who was running away, and we arrested him in order to see. He had this silver."

"And he told you," interrupted the bishop, with a smile, "that it had been given him by a good old priest with whom he had passed the night. I see it all. And you brought him back here? It is all a mistake."

"If that is so," said the brigadier, "we can let him go."

"Certainly," replied the bishop.

The gendarmes released Jean Valjean, who shrank back—

"Is it true that they let me go?" he said in a voice almost

inarticulate, as if he were speaking in his sleep.

"Yes! you can go. Do you not understand?" said a gendarme.

"My friend," said the bishop, "before you go away, here are your candlesticks; take them."

He went to the mantelpiece, took the two candlesticks, and brought them to Jean Valjean. The two women beheld the action without a word, or gesture, or look, that might disturb the bishop.

Jean Valjean was trembling in every limb. He took the two candlesticks mechanically, and with a wild appearance.

"Now," said the bishop, "go in peace. By the way, my friend, when you come again, you need not come through the garden. You can always come in and go out by the front door. It is closed only with a latch, day or night."

Then turning to the gendarmes, he said:

"Messieurs, you can retire." The gendarmes withdrew.

Jean Valjean felt like a man who is just about to faint.

The bishop approached him, and said, in a low voice:

"Forget not, never forget that you have promised me to use this silver to become an honest man."

Jean Valjean, who had no recollection of this promise, stood confounded. The bishop had laid much stress upon these words as he uttered them. He continued, solemnly:

"Jean Valjean, my brother: you belong no longer to evil, but to good. It is your soul that I am buying for you. I withdraw it from dark thoughts and from the spirit of perdition, and I give it to God!"

PETIT GERVAIS

JEAN VALJEAN went out of the city as if he were escaping. He made all haste to get into the open country, taking the first lanes and by-paths that offered, without noticing that he was every moment retracing his steps. He wandered thus all the morning. He had eaten nothing, but he felt no hunger. He was the prey of a multitude of new sensations.

As the sun was sinking towards the horizon, lengthening the shadow on the ground of the smallest pebble, Jean Valjean was seated behind a thicket in a large reddish plain, an absolute desert. There was no horizon but the Alps.

Not even the steeple of a village church. Jean Valjean might have been three leagues from D——. A by-path which crossed the plain passed a few steps from the thicket.

In the midst of this meditation, which would have heightened not a little the frightful effect of his rags to any one who might have met him, he heard a joyous sound.

He turned his head, and saw coming along the path a little Savoyard, a dozen years old, singing, with his hurdy-gurdy at his side, and his marmot box on his back.

One of those pleasant and gay youngsters who go from place to place, with their knees sticking through their trousers.

Always singing, the boy stopped from time to time, and played at tossing up some pieces of money that he had in his hand, probably his whole fortune. Among them there was one forty-sous piece.

The boy stopped by the side of the thicket without seeing Jean Valjean, and tossed up his handful of sous; until this time he had skilfully caught the whole of them upon the back of his hand.

This time the forty-sous piece escaped him, and rolled towards the thicket, near Jean Valjean.

Jean Valjean put his foot upon it.

The boy, however, had followed the piece with his eye, and had seen where it went.

He was not frightened, and walked straight to the man.

It was an entirely solitary place. Far as the eye could reach there was no one on the plain or in the path. Nothing could be heard, but the faint cries of a flock of birds of passage, that were flying across the sky at an immense height. The child turned his back to the sun, which made his hair like threads of gold, and flushed the savage face of Jean Valjean with a lurid glow.

"Monsieur," said the little Savoyard, with that childish confidence which is made up of ignorance and innocence, "my piece?"

"What is your name?" said Jean Valjean.

"Petit Gervais, monsieur."

"Get out," said Jean Valjean.

"Monsieur," continued the boy, "give me my piece."

Jean Valjean dropped his head and did not answer.

The child began again:

"My piece, monsieur!"

Jean Valjean's eye remained fixed on the ground.

"My piece!" exclaimed the boy, "my white piece! my silver!"

Jean Valjean did not appear to understand. The boy took him by the collar of his blouse and shook him. And at the same time he made an effort to move the big, iron-soled shoe which was placed upon his treasure.

"I want my piece! my forty-sous piece!"

The child began to cry. Jean Valjean raised his head. He still kept his seat. His look was troubled. He looked upon the boy with an air of wonder, then reached out his hand towards his stick, and exclaimed in a terrible voice: "Who is there?"

"Me, monsieur," answered the boy. "Petit Gervais! me! me! give me my forty sous, if you please! Take away your foot, monsieur, if you please!" Then becoming angry, small as he was, and almost threatening:

"Come, now, will you take away your foot? Why don't you take away your foot?"

"Ah! you here yet!" said Jean Valjean, and rising hastily to his feet, without releasing the piece of money, he added: "You'd better take care of yourself!"

The boy looked at him in terror, then began to tremble from head to foot, and after a few seconds of stupor, took to flight and ran with all his might without daring to turn his head or to utter a cry.

At a little distance, however, he stopped for want of breath, and Jean Valjean in his reverie heard him sobbing.

In a few minutes the boy was gone.

The sun had gone down.

The shadows were deepening around Jean Valjean. He had not eaten during the day; probably he had some fever.

He had remained standing, and had not changed his attitude since the child fled. His breathing was at long and unequal intervals. His eyes were fixed on a spot ten or twelve steps before him, and seemed to be studying with profound attention the form of an old piece of blue crockery that was lying in the grass. All at once he shivered; he began to feel the cold night air.

He pulled his cap down over his forehead, sought mechanically to fold and button his blouse around him, stepped forward and stooped to pick up his stick.

At that instant he perceived the forty-sous piece which his foot had half buried in the ground, and which glistened among the pebbles. It was like an electric shock. "What is that?" said he, between his teeth. He drew back a step or two, then stopped without the power to withdraw his gaze from this point which his foot had covered the instant before, as if the thing that glistened there in the obscurity had been an open eye fixed upon him.

After a few minutes, he sprang convulsively towards the piece of money, seized it, and, rising, looked away over the plain, straining his eyes towards all points of the horizon, standing and trembling like a frightened deer which is seeking a place of refuge.

He saw nothing. Night was falling, the plain was cold and bare, thick purple mists were rising in the glimmering twilight.

He said: "Oh!" and began to walk rapidly in the direction in which the child had gone. After some thirty steps, he stopped, looked about, and saw nothing.

Then he called with all his might "Petit Gervais! Petit Gervais!"

And then he listened.

There was no answer.

He met a priest on horseback. He went up to him and said: "Monsieur curé, have you seen a child go by?"

"No," said the priest.

"Petit Gervais was his name?"

"I have seen nobody."

He took two five-franc pieces from his bag, and gave them to the priest.

"Monsieur curé, this is for your poor. Monsieur curé, he is a little fellow, about ten years old, with a marmot, I think, and a hurdy-gurdy. He went this way. One of these Savoyards, you know?"

"I have not seen him."

"Petit Gervais? is his village near here? can you tell me?"

"If it be as you say, my friend, the little fellow is a foreigner. They roam about this country. Nobody knows them."

Jean Valjean hastily took out two more five-franc pieces, and gave them to the priest.

"For your poor," said he.

Then he added wildly:

"Monsieur abbé, have me arrested. I am a robber."

The priest put spurs to his horse, and fled in great fear.

Jean Valjean began to run again in the direction which he had first taken.

He went on in this wise for a considerable distance, looking around, calling and shouting, but met nobody else. Two or three times he left the path to look at what seemed to be somebody lying down or crouching; it was only low bushes or rocks. Finally, at a place where three paths met, he stopped. The moon had risen. He strained his eyes in the distance, and called out once more "Petit Gervais! Petit Gervais! Petit Gervais!" His cries died away into the mist, without even awakening an echo. Again he murmured: "Petit Gervais!" but with a feeble, and almost inarticulate voice. That was his last effort; his knees suddenly bent under him, as if an invisible power overwhelmed him at a blow, with the weight of his bad conscience; he fell exhausted upon a great stone, his hands clenched in his hair, and his face on his knees, and exclaimed: "What a wretch I am!"

Then his heart swelled, and he burst into tears. It was the first time he had wept for nineteen years.

While he wept, the light grew brighter and brighter in his mind—an extraordinary light, a light at once transporting and terrible. His past life, his first offence, his long expiation, his brutal exterior, his hardened interior, his release made glad by so many schemes of vengeance, what had happened to him at the bishop's, his last action, this theft of forty sous from a child, a crime meaner and the more monstrous that it came after the bishop's pardon, all this returned and appeared to him, clearly, but in a light that he had never seen before. He beheld his life, and it seemed to him horrible; his soul, and it seemed to him frightful. There was, however, a softened light upon that life and upon that soul. It seemed to him that he was looking upon Satan by the light of Paradise.

How long did he weep thus? What did he do after weeping? Where did he go? Nobody ever knew. It is known simply that, on that very night, the stage-driver who drove at that time on the Grenoble route, and arrived at D—— about three o'clock in the morning, saw, as he passed through the bishop's street, a man in the attitude of prayer, kneel upon the pavement in the shadow, before the door of Monseigneur Bienvenu.

To Entrust Is
Sometimes to Abandon

ONE MOTHER MEETS ANOTHER

THERE was, during the first quarter of the present century, at Montfermeil, near Paris, a sort of chop-house; it is not there now. It was kept by a man and his wife, named Thénardier, and was situated in the Lane Boulanger. Above the door, nailed flat against the wall, was a board, upon which something was painted that looked like a man carrying on his back another man wearing the heavy epaulettes of a general, gilt and with large silver stars; red blotches typified blood; the remainder of the picture was smoke, and probably represented a battle. Beneath was this inscription: TO THE SERGEANT OF WATERLOO.

Nothing is commoner than a cart or wagon before the door of an inn; nevertheless the vehicle, or more properly speaking, the fragment of a vehicle which obstructed the street in front of the Sergeant of Waterloo one evening in the spring of 1815, certainly would have attracted by its bulk the attention of any painter who might have been passing.

It was the fore-carriage of one of those drays for carrying heavy articles, used in wooded countries for transporting joists and trunks of trees: it consisted of a massive iron axle-tree with a pivot to which a heavy pole was attached, and which was supported by two enormous wheels. As a whole, it was squat, crushing, and misshapen: it might have been fancied a gigantic gun-carriage.

Under the axle-tree hung festooned a huge chain fit for a Goliath of the galleys.

The middle of the chain was hanging quite near the ground, under the axle; and upon the bend, as on a swinging rope, two little girls were seated that evening in exquisite grouping, the smaller, eighteen months old, in the lap of the larger, who was two years and a half old.

The mother, a woman whose appearance was rather forbidding, but touching at this moment, was seated on the sill of the inn, swinging the two children by a long string, while she brooded them with her eyes for fear of accident with that animal but heavenly expression peculiar to maternity. At each vibration the hideous links uttered a creaking noise like an angry cry; the little ones were in ecstasies, the setting sun mingled in the joy, and nothing could be more charming than this caprice of chance which made of a Titan's chain a swing for cherubim.

A woman was before her at a little distance; she also had a child, which she bore in her arms.

She was carrying in addition a large carpet-bag, which seemed heavy.

This woman's child was one of the divinest beings that can be imagined: a little girl of two or three years. She might have entered the lists with the other little ones for coquetry of attire; she wore a head-dress of fine linen; ribbons at her shoulders and Valenciennes lace on her cap. The folds of her skirt were raised enough to show her plump fine white leg; she was charmingly rosy and healthful. The pretty little creature gave one a desire to bite her cherry cheeks. We can say nothing of her eyes except that they must have been very large, and were fringed with superb lashes. She was asleep.

The two women began to talk together.

"My name is Madame Thénardier," said the mother of the two girls: "we keep this inn."

This Madame Thénardier was a red-haired, brawny, angular woman, of the soldier's wife type in all its horror, and, singularly enough, she had a lolling air which she had gained from novel-reading. She was a masculine lackadaisicalness. Old romances impressed on the imaginations of mistresses of chop-houses have such effects. She was still young, scarcely thirty years old. If this woman, who was seated stooping, had been upright, perhaps her towering form and her broad shoulders, those of a movable colossus, fit for a market-woman, would have dismayed the traveller, disturbed her confidence, and prevented what we have to relate. A person seated instead of standing; fate hangs on such a thread as that.

The traveller told her story, a little modified.

She said she was a working woman, and her husband was dead. Not being able to procure work in Paris she was going in search of it elsewhere; in her own province; that she had left Paris that morning on foot; that carrying her child she had become tired, and meeting the Villemomble stage had got in; that from Villemomble she had come on foot to Montfermeil; that the child had walked a little, but not much, she was so young; that she was compelled to carry her, and the jewel had fallen asleep.

And at these words she gave her daughter a passionate kiss, which wakened her. The child opened its large blue eyes, like its mother's, and saw—what? Nothing, everything, with that serious and sometimes severe air of little children, which is one of the mysteries of their shining innocence before our shadowy virtues. One would say that they felt themselves to be angels, and knew us to be human. Then the child began to laugh, and, although the mother restrained her, slipped to the ground, with the indomitable energy of a little one that wants to run about. All at once she perceived the two others in their swing, stopped short, and put out her tongue in token of admiration.

Mother Thénardier untied the children and took them from the swing saying, "Play together, all three of you."

At that age acquaintance is easy, and in a moment the little Thénardiers were playing with the new-comer, making holes in the ground to their intense delight.

This new-comer was very sprightly: the goodness of the mother is written in the gaiety of the child; she had taken a splinter of wood, which she used as a spade, and was stoutly digging a hole fit for a fly. The gravedigger's work is charming when done by a child. The two women continued to chat.

"What do you call your brat?"

"Cosette."

"How old is she?"

"She is going on three years."

"The age of my oldest."

The three girls were grouped in an attitude of deep anxiety and bliss; a great event had occurred; a large worm had come out of the ground; they were afraid of it, and yet in ecstasies over it. Their bright foreheads touched each other: three heads in one halo of glory.

"Children," exclaimed the Thénardier mother; "how soon they know one another. See them! one would swear they were three sisters."

These words were the spark which the other mother was probably awaiting. She seized the hand of Madame Thénardier and said, "Will you keep my child for me?"

Madame Thénardier made a motion of surprise, which was neither consent nor refusal.

Cosette's mother continued:

"You see I cannot take my child into the country. Work forbids it. With a child I could not find a place there; they are so absurd in that district. It is God who has led me before your inn. The sight of your little ones, so pretty, and clean, and happy, has overwhelmed me. I said: there is a good mother; they will be like three sisters, and then it will not be long before I come back. Will you keep her for me?"

"I must think over it," said Thénardier.

"I will give six francs a month."

Here a man's voice was heard from within:

"Not less than seven francs, and six months paid in advance."

"Six times seven are forty-two," said Madame Thénardier.

"I will give it," said the mother.

"And fifteen francs extra for the first expenses," added the man.

"That's fifty-seven francs," said Madame Thénardier.

"I will give it," said the mother; "I have eighty francs. That will leave me enough to go into the country if I walk. I will earn some money there, and as soon as I have I will come for my little love."

The man's voice returned, "Has the child a wardrobe?"

"That is my husband," said Madame Thénardier.

"Certainly she has, the poor darling. I knew it was your husband. And a fine wardrobe it is, too, an extravagant wardrobe, everything in dozens, and silk dresses like a lady. They are there in my carpet-bag."

"You must leave that here," put in the man's voice.

"Of course I shall give it to you," said the mother; "it would be strange if I should leave my child naked."

The face of the master appeared.

"It is all right," said he.

The bargain was concluded. The mother passed the night at the inn, gave her money and left her child, fastened again her carpet-bag, diminished by her child's wardrobe, and very light now, and set off next morning, expecting soon to return. These partings are arranged tranquilly, but they are full of despair.

A neighbor of the Thénardiers met this mother on her way, and came in, saying:

"I have just met a woman in the street, who was crying as if her heart would break."

When Cosette's mother had gone, the man said to his wife:

"That will do me for my note of 110 francs which falls due tomorrow; I was fifty francs short. Do you know I should have had a sheriff and a protest? You have proved a good mousetrap with your little ones."

"Without knowing it," said the woman.

FIRST SKETCH OF TWO EQUIVOCAL FACES

THE captured mouse was a very puny one, but the cat exulted even over a lean mouse. What were the Thénardiers? We will say but a word just here; by-and-by the sketch shall be completed.

They belonged to that bastard class formed of low people who have risen, and intelligent people who have fallen, which lies between the classes called middle and lower, and which unites some of the faults of the latter with nearly all the vices of the former, without possessing the generous impulses of the workman, or the respectability of the bourgeois.

This Thénardier, if we may believe him, had been a soldier, a sergeant he said; he probably had made the campaign of 1815, and had even borne himself bravely according to all that appeared. We shall see hereafter in what his bravery consisted. The sign of his inn was an allusion to one of his feats of arms. He had painted it himself, for he knew how to do a little of everything—badly.

THE LARK

To be wicked does not insure prosperity—for the inn did not succeed well.

Thanks to Fantine's fifty-seven francs. Thénardier had been able to avoid a protest and to honor his signature. The next month they were still in need of money, and the woman carried Cosette's wardrobe to Paris and pawned it for sixty francs. When this sum was spent, the Thénardiers began to look upon the little girl as a child which they sheltered for charity, and treated her as such. Her clothes being gone, they dressed her in the cast-off garments of the little Thénardiers, that is in rags. They fed her on the odds and ends, a little better than the dog, and a little worse than the cat. The dog and cat were her messmates.

Cosette ate with them under the table in a wooden dish.

Her mother, as we shall see hereafter, who had found a place at M—— sur M—— wrote, or rather had some one write for her, every month, inquiring news of her child. The Thénardiers replied invariably:

"Cosette is doing wonderfully well."

The six months passed away: the mother sent seven francs for the seventh month, and continued to send this sum regularly month after month. The year was not ended before Thénardier said: "A pretty price that is. What does she expect us to do for her seven francs?" And he wrote demanding twelve francs. The mother, whom he persuaded that her child was happy and doing well, assented, and forwarded the twelve francs.

The woman was unkind to Cosette; Eponine and Azelma were unkind also. Children at that age are only copies of the mother: the size is reduced, that is all.

A year passed and then another. People used to say: "What good people these Thénardiers are! They are not rich, and yet they bring up a poor child."

They thought Cosette was forgotten by her mother.

Meantime Thénardier, having learned in some obscure way that the child was probably illegitimate, and that its mother could not acknowledge it, demanded fifteen francs a month, saying "that the 'creature' was growing and eating," and threatening to send her away. "She won't humbug me," he exclaimed, "I will confound her with the brat in the midst of her concealment. I must have more money." The mother paid the fifteen francs.

From year to year the child grew, and her misery also.

So long as Cosette was very small, she was the scapegoat of the two other children; as soon as she began to grow a little, that is too say, before she was five years old, she became the servant of the house.

It was a harrowing sight to see in the winter time the poor child, not yet six years old, shivering under the tatters of what was once a calico dress, sweeping the street before daylight with an enormous broom in her little red hands and tears in her large eyes.

In the place she was called The Lark. People like figurative names and were pleased thus to name this little being, not larger than a bird, trembling, frightened, and shivering, awake every morning first of all in the house and the village.

Only the poor lark never sang.

The Descent

HISTORY OF AN IMPROVEMENT IN JET-WORK

WHAT had become of this mother, in the meanwhile, who, according to the people of Montfermeil, seemed to have abandoned her child? where was she? what was she doing?

After leaving her little Cosette with the Thénardiers, she went on her way and arrived at M—— sur M——.

This, it will be remembered, was in 1818.

Fantine had left the province some twelve years before, and M—— sur M—— had greatly changed in appearance. While Fantine had been slowly sinking deeper and deeper into misery, her native village had been prosperous.

Within about two years there had been accomplished there one of those industrial changes which are the great events of small communities.

From time immemorial the special occupation of the inhabitants of M—— sur M—— had been the imitation of English jets and German black glass trinkets. The business had always been dull in consequence of the high price of the raw material, which reacted upon the manufacture. At the time of Fantine's return to M—— sur M—— an entire transformation had been effected in the production of these "black goods." Towards the end of the year 1815, an unknown man had established himself in the city, and had conceived the idea of substituting gum-lac for resin in the manufacture; and for bracelets, in particular, he made the clasps by simply bending the ends of the metal together instead of soldering them.

This very slight change had worked a revolution.

This very slight change had in fact reduced the price of the raw material enormously, and this had rendered it possible, first, to raise the wages of the laborer—a benefit to the country—secondly, to improve the quality of the goods—an advantage for the consumer—and thirdly, to sell them at a lower price even while making three times the profit—a gain for the manufacturer.

Thus we have three results from one idea.

In less than three years the inventor of this process had become rich, which was well, and had made all around him rich, which was better. He was a stranger in the Department. Nothing was known of his birth, and but little of his early history.

The story went that he came to the city with very little money, a few hundred francs at most.

From this slender capital, under the inspiration of an ingenious idea, made fruitful by order and care, he had drawn a fortune for himself, and a fortune for the whole region.

On his arrival at M—— sur M—— he had the dress, the manners, and the language of a laborer only.

It seems that the very day on which he thus obscurely entered the little city of M—— sur M——, just at dusk on a December evening, with his bundle on his back, and a thorn stick in his hand, a great fire had broken out in the town-house. This man rushed into the fire, and saved, at the peril of his life, two children, who proved to be those of the captain of the gendarmerie, and in the hurry and gratitude of the moment no one thought to ask him for his passport. He was known from that time by the name of Father Madeleine.

MADELEINE

HE was a man of about fifty, who always appeared to be preoccupied in mind, and who was good-natured; this was all that could be said about him.

Father Madeleine employed everybody; he had only one condition, "Be an honest man!" "Be an honest woman!"

As we have said, in the midst of this activity, of which he was the cause and the pivot, Father Madeleine had made his fortune, but, very strangely for a mere man of business, that did not appear to be his principal care. It seemed that he thought much for others, and little for himself. In 1820, it was known that he had six hundred and thirty thousand francs standing to his credit in the banking-house of Laffitte; but before setting aside this six hundred and thirty thousand francs for himself, he had expended more than a million for the city and for the poor.

At first, when he began to attract the public attention, the good people would say: "This is a fellow who wishes to get rich." When they saw him enrich the country before he enriched himself, the same good people said: "This man is ambitious." This seemed the more probable, since he was religious and observed the forms of the church, to a certain extent, a thing much approved in those days. He went regularly to hear mass every Sunday.

At length, in 1819, it was reported in the city one morning, that upon the recommendation of the prefect, and in consideration of the services he had rendered to the country, Father Madeleine had been appointed by the king, Mayor of M—— sur M——. Those who had pronounced the newcomer "an ambitious man," eagerly seized this opportunity, which all men desire, to exclaim:

"There! what did I tell you?"

M—— sur M—— was filled with the rumour, and the report proved to be well founded, for, a few days afterwards, the nomination appeared in the *Moniteur*. The next day Father Madeleine declined.

In the same year, 1819, the results of the new process invented by Madeleine had a place in the Industrial Exhibition, and upon the report of the jury, the king named the inventor a Chevalier of the Legion of Honor. Here was a new rumour for the little city. "Well! it was the Cross of the Legion of Honor that he wanted." Father Madeleine declined the Cross.

Decidedly this man was an enigma, and the good people gave up the field, saying, "After all, he is a sort of an adventurer."

As we have seen, the country owed a great deal to this man, and the poor owed him everything; he was so useful that all were compelled to honor him, and so kind that none could help loving him; his workmen in particular adored him, and he received their adoration with a sort of melancholy gravity. After he became rich, those who constituted "society" bowed to him as they met, and, in the city, he began to be called Monsieur Madeleine;—but his workmen and the children continued to call him *Father Madeleine*, and at that name his face always wore a smile. As his wealth increased, invitations rained in on him. "Society" claimed him. The little exclusive parlors of M—— sur M——, which were carefully guarded, and in earlier days, of course, had been closed to the artisan, opened wide their doors to the millionaire. A thousand advances were made to him, but he refused them all.

And again the gossips were at no loss. "He is an ignorant man, and of poor education. No one knows where he came from. He does not know how to conduct himself in good society, and it is by no means certain that he knows how to read."

When they saw him making money, they said, "He is a merchant." When they saw the way in which he scattered his money, they said, "He is ambitious." When they saw him refuse to accept honors, they said, "He is an adventurer." When they saw him repel the advances of the fashionable, they said, "He is a brute."

In 1820, five years after his arrival at M—— sur M——, the services that he had rendered to the region were so brilliant, and the wish of the whole population was so unanimous, that the king again appointed him mayor of the city. He refused again; but the prefect resisted his determination, the principal citizens came and urged him to accept, and the people in the streets begged him to do so; all insisted so strongly that at last he yielded. It was remarked that what appeared most of all to bring him to this determination, was the almost angry exclamation of an old woman belonging to the poorer class, who cried out to him from her door-stone, with some temper:

"A good mayor is a good thing. Are you afraid of the good you can do?"

This was the third step in his ascent. Father Madeleine had become Monsieur Madeleine, and Monsieur Madeleine now became Monsieur the Mayor.

MONEYS DEPOSITED WITH LAFFITTE

NEVERTHELESS he remained as simple as at first. He had grey hair, a serious eye, the brown complexion of a laborer, and the thoughtful countenance of a philosopher. He usually wore a hat with a wide brim, and a long coat of coarse cloth, buttoned to the chin. He fulfilled his duties as mayor, but beyond that his life was isolated. He talked with very few persons. He shrank from compliments, and with a touch of the hat walked on rapidly; he smiled to avoid talking, and gave to avoid smiling. The women said of him: "What a good bear!" His pleasure was to walk in the fields.

He always took his meals alone with a book open before him in which he read. His library was small but well selected. He loved books; books are cold but sure friends. As his growing fortune gave him more leisure, it seemed that he profited by it to cultivate his mind. Since he had been at M—— sur M——, it was remarked from year to year that his language became more polished, choicer, and more gentle.

Although he was no longer young, it was reported that he was of prodigious strength. He would offer a helping hand to any one who needed it, help up a fallen horse, push at a stalled wheel, or seize by the horns a bull that had broken loose. He always had his pockets full of money when he went out, and empty when he returned. When he passed through a village the ragged little youngsters would run after him with joy, and surround him like a swarm of flies.

He did a multitude of good deeds as secretly as bad ones are usually done. He would steal into houses in the evening, and furtively mount the stairs. A poor devil, on returning to his garret, would find that his door had been opened, sometimes even forced, during his absence. The poor man would cry out: "Some thief has been here!" When he got in, the first thing that he would see would be a piece of gold lying on the table. "The thief" who had been there was Father Madeleine.

He was affable and sad. The people used to say: "There is a rich man who does not show pride. There is a fortunate man who does not appear contented."

Some pretended that he was a mysterious personage, and declared that no one ever went into his room, which was a true anchorite's cell furnished with hour-glasses, and enlivened with death's heads and cross-bones. So much was said of this kind that some of the more mischievous of the elegant young ladies of M—— sur M—— called on him one day and said: "Monsieur Mayor, will you show us your room? We have heard that it is a grotto." He smiled, and introduced them on the spot to this "grotto." They were well punished for their curiosity. It was a room very well fitted up with mahogany furniture, ugly as all furniture of that kind is, and the walls covered with shilling paper. They could see nothing but two candlesticks of antique form that stood on the mantle, and appeared to be silver, "for they were marked," a remark full of the spirit of these little towns.

But none the less did it continue to be said that nobody ever went into that chamber, and that it was a hermit's cave, a place of dreams, a hole, a tomb.

It was also whispered that he had "immense" sums deposited with Laffitte, with the special condition that they were always at his immediate command, in such a way, it was added, that Monsieur Madeleine might arrive in the morning at Laffitte's, sign a receipt and carry away his two or three millions in ten minutes. In reality these "two or three millions" dwindled down, as we have said, to six hundred and thirty or forty thousand francs.

MONSIEUR MADELEINE IN MOURNING

NEAR the beginning of the year 1821, the journals announced the decease of Monsieur Myriel, Bishop of D——, "surnamed *Monseigneur Bienvenu*," who died in the odor of sanctity at the age of eighty-two years.

The announcement of his death was reproduced in the local paper of M—— sur M——. Monsieur Madeleine appeared next morning dressed in black with crape on his hat.

This mourning was noticed and talked about all over the town. It appeared to throw some light upon the origin of Monsieur Madeleine. The conclusion was that he was in some way related to the venerable bishop. *"He wears black for the Bishop of D——,"* was the talk of the drawing-rooms; it elevated Monsieur Madeleine very much, and gave him suddenly, and in a trice, marked consideration in the noble world of M—— sur M——. The microscopic Faubourg Saint Germain of the little place thought of raising the quarantine for Monsieur Madeleine, the probable relative of a bishop. Monsieur Madeleine perceived the advancement that he had obtained, by the greater reverence of the old ladies, and the more frequent smiles of the young ladies. One evening, one of the dowagers of that little great world, curious by right of age, ventured to ask him: "The mayor is doubtless a relative of the late Bishop of D——?"

He said: "No, madame."

"But," the dowager persisted, "you wear mourning for him?"

He answered: "In my youth I was a servant in his family."

It was also remarked that whenever there passed through the city a young Savoyard who was tramping about the country in search of chimneys to sweep, the mayor would send for him, ask his name and give him money. The little Savoyards told each other, and many of them passed that way.

VAGUE FLASHES IN THE HORIZON

LITTLE by little in the lapse of time all opposition had ceased. At first there had been, as always happens with those who rise by their own efforts, slanders and calumnies against Monsieur Madeleine, soon this was reduced to satire, then it was only wit, then it vanished entirely; respect became complete, unanimous, cordial, and there came a moment, about 1821, when the words Monsieur the Mayor were pronounced at M—— sur M—— with almost the same accent as the words Monseigneur the Bishop at D—— in 1815. People came from thirty miles around to consult Monsieur Madeleine. He settled differences, he prevented lawsuits, he reconciled enemies. Everybody, of his own will, chose him for judge. He seemed to have the book of the natural law by heart. A contagion of veneration had, in the course of six or seven years, step by step, spread over the whole country.

One man alone, in the city and its neighborhood, held himself entirely clear from this contagion, and, whatever Father Madeleine did, he remained indifferent, as if a sort of instinct, unchangeable and imperturbable, kept him awake and on the watch. It would seem, indeed, that there is in certain men the veritable instinct of a beast, pure and complete like all instinct, which creates antipathies and sympathies, which separates one nature from another for ever, which never hesitates, never is perturbed, never keeps silent, and never admits itself to be in the wrong; clear in its obscurity, infallible, imperious, refractory under all the counsels of intelligence, and all the solvents of reason, and which, whatever may be their destinies, secretly warns the dog-man of the presence of the cat-man and the fox-man of the presence of the lion-man.

Often, when Monsieur Madeleine passed along the street, calm, affectionate, followed by the benedictions of all, it happened that a tall man, wearing a flat hat and an iron-grey coat, and armed with a stout cane, would turn around abruptly behind him, and follow him with his eyes until he disappeared, crossing his arms, slowly shaking his head, and pushing his upper with his under lip up to his nose, a sort of significant grimace which might be rendered by: "But what is that man? I am sure I have seen him somewhere. At all events, I at least am not his dupe."

This personage, grave with an almost threatening gravity, was one of those who, even in a hurried interview, command the attention of the observer.

His name was Javert, and he was one of the police.

He exercised at M—— sur M—— the unpleasant, but useful, function of inspector. He was not there at the date of Madeleine's arrival. Javert owed his position to the protection of Monsieur Chabouillet, the secretary of the Minister of State, Count Anglès, then prefect of police at Paris. When Javert arrived at M—— sur M—— the fortune of the great manufacturer had been made already, and Father Madeleine had become Monsieur Madeleine.

It will be easily understood that Javert was the terror of all that class which the annual statistics of the Minister of Justice include under the heading: *People without a fixed abode*. To speak the name of Javert would put all such to flight; the face of Javert petrified them.

Such was this formidable man.

Javert was like an eye always fixed on Monsieur Madeleine; an eye full of suspicion and conjecture. Monsieur Madeleine finally noticed it, but seemed to consider it of no consequence. He asked no question of Javert, he neither sought him nor shunned him, he endured this unpleasant and annoying stare without appearing to pay any attention to it. He treated Javert as he did everybody else, at ease and with kindness.

Javert was evidently somewhat disconcerted by the completely natural air and the tranquility of Monsieur Madeleine.

One day, however, his strange manner appeared to make an impression upon Monsieur Madeleine. The occasion was this:

MONSIEUR MADELEINE was walking one morning along one of the unpaved alleys of M—— sur M——; he heard a shouting and saw a crowd at a little distance. He went to the spot. An old man, named Father Fauchelevent, had fallen under his cart, his horse being thrown down.

This Fauchelevent was one of the few who were still enemies of Monsieur Madeleine at this time. When Madeleine arrived in the place, the business of Fauchelevent, who was a notary of long-standing, and very well-read for a rustic, was beginning to decline. Fauchelevent had seen this mere artisan grow rich, while he himself, a professional man, had been going to ruin. This had filled him with jealousy, and he had done what he could on all occasions to injure Madeleine. Then came bankruptcy, and the old man, having nothing but a horse and cart, as he was without family, and without children, was compelled to earn his living as a carman.

The horse had his thighs broken, and could not stir. The old man was caught between the wheels. Unluckily he had fallen so that the whole weight rested upon his breast. The cart was heavily loaded. Father Fauchelevent was uttering doleful groans. They had tried to pull him out, but in vain. An unlucky effort, inexpert help, a false push, might crush him. It was impossible to extricate him otherwise than by raising the wagon from beneath. Javert, who came up at the moment of the accident, had sent for a jack.

Monsieur Madeleine came. The crowd fell back with respect.

"Help," cried old Fauchelevent. "Who is a good fellow to save an old man?"

Monsieur Madeleine turned towards the bystanders: "Has anybody a jack?"

"They have gone for one," replied a peasant.

"How soon will it be here?"

"We sent to the nearest place, to Flachot Place, where there is a blacksmith; but it will take a good quarter of an hour at least."

"A quarter of an hour!" exclaimed Madeleine.

It had rained the night before, the road was soft, the cart was sinking deeper every moment, and pressing more and more on the breast of the old carman. It was evident that in less than five minutes his ribs would be crushed.

"We cannot wait a quarter of an hour," said Madeleine to the peasants who were looking on.

"We must!"

"But it will be too late! Don't you see that the wagon is sinking all the while?"

"It can't be helped."

"Listen," resumed Madeleine, "there is room enough still under the wagon for a man to crawl in, and lift it with his back. In half a minute we will have the poor man out. Is there nobody here who has strength and courage? Five louis d'ors for him!"

Nobody stirred in the crowd.

"Ten louis," said Madeleine.

The bystanders dropped their eyes. One of them muttered: "He'd have to be devilish stout. And then he would risk getting crushed."

"Come," said Madeleine, "twenty louis."

The same silence.

"It is not willingness which they lack," said a voice.

Monsieur Madeleine turned and saw Javert. He had not noticed him when he came.

Javert continued:

"It is strength. He must be a terrible man who can raise a wagon like that on his back."

Then, looking fixedly at Monsieur Madeleine, he went on, emphasizing ever word that he uttered:

"Monsieur Madeleine, I have known but one man capable of doing what you call for."

Madeleine shuddered.

Javert added, with an air of indifference, but without taking his eyes from Madeleine:

"He was a convict."

"Ah!" said Madeleine.

"In the galleys at Toulon."

Madeleine became pale.

Meanwhile the cart was slowly settling down. Father Fauchelevent roared and screamed:

"I am dying! my ribs are breaking! a jack! anything! oh!"

Madeleine looked around him:

"Is there nobody, then, who wants to earn twenty louis and save this poor old man's life?"

None of the bystanders moved. Javert resumed:

"I have known but one man who could take the place of a jack; that was that convict."

"Oh! how it crushes me!" cried the old man.

Madeleine raised his head, met the falcon eye of Javert still fixed upon him, looked at the immovable peasants, and smiled sadly. Then, without saying a word, he fell on his knees, and even before the crowd had time to utter a cry, he was under the cart.

There was an awful moment of suspense and of silence.

All at once the enormous mass started, the cart rose slowly, the wheels came half out of the ruts. A smothered voice was heard, crying: "Quick! help!" It was Madeleine, who had just made a final effort.

They all rushed to the work. The devotion of one man had given strength and courage to all. The cart was lifted by twenty arms. Old Fauchelevent was safe.

FAUCHELEVENT BECOMES A GARDENER AT PARIS

FAUCHELEVENT had broken his knee-pan in his fall. Father Madeleine had him carried to an infirmary that he had established for his workmen in the same building with his factory, which was attended by two sisters of charity. The next morning the old man found a thousand franc bill upon the stand by the side of the bed, with this note in the handwriting of Father Madeleine: *I have purchased your horse and cart.* The cart was broken and the horse was dead. Fauchelevent got well, but he had a stiff knee. Monsieur Madeleine, through the recommendations of the sisters and the curé, got the old man a place as gardener at a convent in the Quartier Saint Antoine at Paris.

Some time afterwards Monsieur Madeleine was appointed mayor. The first time that Javert saw Monsieur Madeleine

clothed with the scarf which gave him full authority over
the city, he felt the same sort of shudder which a bull-dog
would feel who should scent a wolf in his master's clothes.
From that time he avoided him as much as he could. When
the necessities of the service imperiously demanded it, and he
could not do otherwise than come in contact with the mayor,
he spoke to him with profound respect.

The prosperity which Father Madeleine had created at
M—— sur M——, in addition to the visible signs that we
have pointed out, had another symptom which, although
not visible, was not the less significant. This never fails.
When the population is suffering, when there is lack of work,
when trade falls off, the tax-payer, constrained by poverty,
resists taxation, exhausts and overruns the delays allowed
by law, and the government is forced to incur large expenditures in the costs of levy and collection. When work is
abundant, when the country is rich and happy, the tax is
easily paid and costs the state but little to collect. It may be
said that poverty and public wealth have an infallible ther-
mometer in the cost of the collection of the taxes. In seven
years, the cost of the collection of the taxes had been reduced three-quarters in the district of M—— sur M——, so
that that district was frequently referred to especially by
Monsieur de Villèle, then Minister of Finance.

Such was the situation of the country when Fantine returned. No one remembered her. Luckily the door of M.
Madeleine's factory was like the face of a friend. She presented herself there, and was admitted into the workshop for
women. The business was entirely new to Fantine; she
could not be very expert in it, and consequently did not
receive much for her day's work; but that little was enough,
the problem was solved; she was earning her living.

Javert

HOW JEAN CAN BECOME CHAMP

ONE morning Monsieur Madeleine was in his office arranging for some pressing business of the mayoralty, when he was informed that Javert, the inspector of police wished to speak with him. On hearing this name spoken, Monsieur Madeleine could not repress a disagreeable impression.

"Let him come in," said he.

Javert entered.

Monsieur Madeleine remained seated near the fire, looking over a bundle of papers upon which he was making notes, and which contained the returns of the police patrol. He did not disturb himself at all for Javert: he could not but think of poor Fantine, and it was fitting that he should receive him very coldly.

Javert respectfully saluted the mayor, who had his back towards him. The mayor did not look up, but continued to make notes on the papers.

Javert advanced a few steps, and paused without breaking silence.

At last the mayor laid down his pen and turned partly round:

"Well, what is it? What is the matter, Javert?"

Javert remained silent a moment as if collecting himself; then raised his voice with a sad solemnity which did not, however, exclude simplicity: "There has been a criminal act committed, Monsieur Mayor."

"What act?"

"An inferior agent of the government has been wanting in respect to a magistrate, in the gravest manner. I come, as is my duty, to bring the fact to your knowledge."

"Who is this agent?" asked Monsieur Madeleine.

"I," said Javert.

"You?"

"I."

"And who is the magistrate who has to complain of this agent?"

"You, Monsieur Mayor."

Monsieur Madeleine straightened himself in his chair. Javert continued, with serious looks and eyes still cast down.

"Monsieur Mayor, I come to ask you to be so kind as to make charges and procure my dismissal."

Monsieur Madeleine, amazed, opened his mouth. Javert interrupted him:

"You will say that I might tender my resignation, but that is not enough. To resign is honorable; I have done wrong. I ought to be punished. I must be dismissed."

And after a pause he added:

"Monsieur Mayor, you were severe to me the other day, unjustly. Be justly so to-day."

"Ah, indeed! why? What is all this nonsense? What does it all mean? What is the criminal act committed by you against me? What have you done to me? How have you wronged me? You accuse yourself: do you wish to be relieved?"

"Dismissed," said Javert.

"Dismissed it is then. It is very strange. I do not understand you."

"You will understand, Monsieur Mayor," Javert sighed deeply, and continued sadly and coldly:

"Monsieur Mayor, six weeks ago, I was enraged and I denounced you."

"Denounced me?"

"To the Prefecture of Police at Paris."

Monsieur Madeleine, who did not laugh much oftener than Javert, began to laugh:

"As a mayor having encroached upon the police?"

"As a former convict."

The mayor became livid.

Javert, who had not raised his eyes, continued:

"I believed it. For a long while I had had suspicions. A resemblance, information you obtained at Faverolles, your immense strength; the affair of old Fauchelevent; your skill as a marksman; your leg which drags a little—and in fact I don't know what other stupidities; but at last I took you for a man named Jean Valjean."

"Named what? How did you call that name?"

"Jean Valjean. He was a convict I saw twenty years ago, when I was adjutant of the galley guard at Toulon. After leaving the galleys this Valjean, it appears, robbed a bishop's palace, then he committed another robbery with weapons in his hands, in a highway, on a little Savoyard. For eight years his whereabouts have been unknown, and search has been made for him. I fancied—in short, I have done this thing. Anger determined me, and I denounced you to the prefect."

M. Madeleine, who had taken up the file of papers again, a few moments before, said with a tone of perfect indifference: "And what answer did you get?"

"That I was crazy."

"Well!"

"Well; they were right."

"It is fortunate that you think so!"

"It must be so, for the real Jean Valjean has been found."

The paper that M. Madeleine held fell from his hand; he raised his head, looked steadily at Javert, and said in an inexpressible tone:

"Ah!"

Javert continued:

"I will tell you how it is, Monsieur Mayor. There was, it appears, in the country, near Ailly-le-Haut Clocher, a simple sort of fellow who was called Father Champmathieu. He was very poor. Nobody paid any attention to him. Such folks live, one hardly knows how. Finally, this last fall, Father Champmathieu was arrested for stealing cider apples from ——, but that is of no consequence. There was a theft, a wall scaled, branches of trees broken. Our Champmathieu was arrested; he had even then a branch of an apple-tree in his hand. The rogue was caged. So far, it was nothing more than a penitentiary matter. But here comes in the hand of Providence. The jail being in a bad condition, the police justice thought it best to take him to Arras, where the prison of the department is. In this prison at Arras there was a former convict named Brevet, who is there for some trifle, and who, for his good conduct, has been made turnkey. No sooner was Champmathieu set down, than Brevet cried out: 'Ha, ha! I know that man. He is a *fagot*.' [1]

[1] Former convict.

" 'Look up here, my good man. You are Jean Valjean.'
'Jean Valjean, who is Jean Valjean?' Champmathieu plays off
the astonished. 'Don't play ignorance,' said Brevet. 'You
are Jean Valjean; you were in the galleys at Toulon. It is
twenty years ago. We were there together.' Champmathieu
denied it all. Faith! you understand; they fathomed it. The
case was worked up and this was what they found. This
Champmathieu thirty years ago was a pruner in divers
places, particularly in Faverolles. There we lose trace of him.
A long time afterwards we find him at Auvergne; then at
Paris, where he is said to have been a wheelwright and to
have had a daughter—a washerwoman, but that is not prov-
en, and finally in this part of the country. Now before
going to the galleys for burglary, what was Jean Valjean? A
pruner. Where? At Faverolles. Another fact. This Valjean's
baptismal name was Jean; his mother's family name, Mathieu. Nothing could be more natural, on leaving the galleys,
than to take his mother's name to disguise himself; then he
would be called Jean Mathieu. He goes to Auvergne, the
pronunciation of that region would make *Chan* of *Jean*
—they would call him Chan Mathieu. Our man adopts it,
and now you have him transformed into Champmathieu. You
follow me, do you not? Search has been made at Faverolles;
the family of Jean Valjean are no longer there. Nobody knows
where they are. You know in such classes these disappear-
ances of families often occur. You search, but can find nothing. Such people, when they are not mud, are dust. And
then as the commencement of this story dates back thirty
years, there is nobody now at Faverolles who knew Jean Valjean. But search has been made at Toulon. Besides Brevet
there are only two convicts who have seen Jean Valjean.
They are convicts for life; their names are Cochepaille and
Chenildieu. These men were brought from the galleys and
confronted with the pretended Champmathieu. They did not
hesitate. To them as well as to Brevet it was Jean Valjean.
Same age; fifty-four years old; same height; same appearance, in fact the same man; it is he. At this time it was
that I sent my denunciation to the Prefecture at Paris. They
replied that I was out of my mind, and that Jean Valjean
was at Arras in the hands of justice. You may imagine
how that astonished me; I who believed that I had here the
same Jean Valjean. I wrote to the justice; he sent for me and
brought Champmathieu before me."

"Well," interrupted Monsieur Madeleine.

Javert replied, with an incorruptible and sad face:

"Monsieur Mayor, truth is truth. I am sorry for it, but that man is Jean Valjean. I recognised him also."

Monsieur Madeleine had turned again to his desk, and was quietly looking over his papers, reading and writing alternately, like a man pressed with business. He turned again towards Javert:

"That will do, Javert. Indeed all these details interest me very little. We are wasting time, and we have urgent business, Javert go at once to the house of the good woman Buseaupied, who sell herbs at the corner of Rue Saint Saulve; tell her to make her complaint against the carman Pierre Chesnelong. He is a brutal fellow, he almost crushed this woman and her child. He must be punished. Then you will go to Monsieur Charcellay, Rue Montre-de-Champigny. He complains that the gutter of the next house when it rains throws water upon his house, and is undermining the foundation. Then you will inquire into the offenses that have been reported to me, at the widow Doris's, Rue Guibourg, and Madame Renée le Bossé's, Rue du Garraud Blanc, and make out reports. But I am giving you too much to do. Did you not tell me you were going to Arras in eight or ten days on this matter?"

"Sooner than that, Monsieur Mayor."

"What day then?"

"I think I told monsieur that the case would be tried to-morrow, and that I should leave by the diligence to-night."

Monsieur Madeleine made an imperceptible motion.

"And how long will the matter last?"

"One day at longest. Sentence will be pronounced at latest to-morrow evening. But I shall not wait for the sentence, which is certain; as soon as my testimony is given I shall return here."

"Very well," said Monsieur Madeleine.

And he dismissed him with a wave of his hand.

Javert did not go.

"Your pardon, monsieur," said he.

"What more is there?" asked Monsieur Madeleine.

"Monsieur Mayor, there is one thing more to which I desire to call your attention."

"What is it?"

"It is that I ought to be dismissed."

Monsieur Madeleine arose.

"Javert, you are a man of honor and I esteem you. You exaggerate your fault. Besides, this is an offence which concerns me. You are worthy of promotion rather than disgrace. I desire you to keep your place."

Javert looked at Monsieur Madeleine with his calm eyes, in whose depths it seemed that one beheld his conscience, unenlightened, but stern and pure, and said in a tranquil voice:

"Monsieur Mayor, I cannot agree to that."

"I repeat," said Monsieur Madeleine, "that this matter concerns me."

But Javert, with his one idea, continued:

"As to exaggerating, I do not exaggerate. This is the way I reason. I have unjustly suspected you. That is nothing. It is our province to suspect, although it may be an abuse of our right to suspect our superiors. But without proofs and in a fit of anger, with revenge as my aim, I denounced you as a convict—you, a respectable man, a mayor, and a magistrate. This is a serious matter, very serious. I have committed an offence against authority in your person, I, who am the agent of authority. If one of my subordinates had done what I have, I would have pronounced him unworthy of the service, and sent him away. Well, listen a moment, Monsieur Mayor; I have often been severe in my life towards others. It was just. I did right. Now if I were not severe towards myself, all I have justly done would become injustice. Should I spare myself more than others? No. What! if I should be prompt only to punish others and not myself, I should be a wretch indeed! They who say: 'That blackguard, Javert,' would be right. Monsieur Mayor, I do not wish you to treat me with kindness. Your kindness, when it was for others, enraged me; I do not wish it for myself. That kindness which consists in defending a woman of the town against a citizen, a police agent against the mayor, the inferior against the superior, that is what I call ill-judged kindness. Such kindness disorganizes society. Good God, it is easy to be kind, the difficulty is to be just. Had you been what I thought, I should not have been kind to you; not I. You would have seen, Monsieur Mayor. I ought to treat myself as I would treat anybody else. When I put down malefactors, when I rigorously brought up offenders, I often said to myself: "You, if you ever trip; if ever I catch you

doing wrong, look out!' I have tripped, I have caught myself doing wrong. So much the worse! I must be sent
away, broken, dismissed, that is right. I have hands: I can
till the ground. It is all the same to me. Monsieur Mayor,
the good of the service demands an example. I simply ask
the dismissal of Inspector Javert."

All this was said in a tone of proud humility, a desperate
and resolute tone, which gave an indescribably whimsical
grandeur to this oddly honest man.

"We will see," said Monsieur Madeleine.

And he held out his hand to him.

Javert started back, and said fiercely:

"Pardon, Monsieur Mayor, that should not be. A mayor
does not give his hand to a spy."

He added between his teeth:

"Spy, yes; from the moment I abused the power of my
position, I have been nothing better than a spy!"

Then he bowed profoundly, and went towards the door.
There he turned around: his eyes yet downcast.

"Monsieur Mayor, I will continue in the service until I
am relieved."

He went out. Monsieur Madeleine sat musing, listening to
his firm and resolute step as it died away along the corridor.

doing wrong, look out! I have tripped, I have caught
self doing wrong. So much the worse! I must be
away, broken, dismissed ... did I have hear ... I
still the mayor? ...

The Champmathieu Affair

A TEMPEST IN A BRAIN

THE reader has doubtless divined that Monsieur Madeleine
is none other than Jean Valjean.

We have but little to add to what the reader already
knows, concerning what had happened to Jean Valjean, since
his adventure with Petit Gervais. From that moment, we have
seen, he was another man. What the bishop had desired to
do with him, that he had executed. It was more than a transformation—it was a transfiguration.

He succeeded in escaping from sight, sold the bishop's
silver, keeping only the candlesticks as souvenirs, glided
quietly from city to city across France, came to M—— sur
M——, conceived the idea that we have described, accomplished what we have related, gained the point of making
himself unassailable and inaccessible, and thence forward,
established at M—— sur M——, happy to feel his conscience
saddened by his past, and the last half of his existence giving
the lie to the first, he lived peaceable, reassured, and hopeful,
having but two thoughts: to conceal his name, and to
sanctify his life; to escape from men and to return to God.

These two thoughts were associated so closely in his mind,
that they formed but a single one; they were both equally
absorbing and imperious, and ruled his slightest actions.
Ordinarily they were in harmony in the regulation of the
conduct of his life; they turned him towards the dark side
of life; they made him benevolent and simple-hearted; they
counselled him to the same things. Sometimes, however, there
was a conflict between them. In such cases, it will be remembered, the man, whom all the country around M——
sur M—— called Monsieur Madeleine, did not waver in
sacrificing the first to the second, his security to his virtue.
Thus, in despite of all reserve and of all prudence, he had
kept the bishop's candlesticks, worn mourning for him,
called and questioned all the little Savoyards who passed

by, gathered information concerning the families at Faverolles, and saved the life of old Fauchelevent, in spite of the
disquieting insinuations of Javert. It would seem, we have already remarked, that he thought, following the example
of all who have been wise, holy, and just, that his highest
duty was not towards himself.

But of all these occasions, it must be said, none had ever
been anything like that which was now presented.

Independently of the severe and religious aim that his actions had in view, all that he had done up to this day was
only a hole that he was digging in which to bury his name.
What he had always most dreaded, in his hours of self-
communion, in his sleepless nights, was the thought of ever
hearing that name pronounced; he felt that would be for him
the end of all; that the day on which that name should reappear would see vanish from around him his new life, and,
who knows, even perhaps his new soul from within him.
He shuddered at the bare thought that it was possible.
Surely, if any one had told him at such moments that an
hour would come when that name would resound in his ear,
when that hideous word, Jean Valjean, would start forth
suddenly from the night and stand before him; when this fearful glare, destined to dissipate the mystery in which he had
wrapped himself, would flash suddenly upon his head, and
that this name would not menace him, and that this glare
would only make his obscurity the deeper, that this rending
of the veil would increase the mystery, that this earth-
quake would consolidate his edifice, that this prodigious event
would have no other result, if it seemed good to him, to
himself alone, than to render his existence at once more
brilliant and more impenetrable, and that, from his encounter
with the phantom of Jean Valjean, the good and worthy
citizen, Monsieur Madeleine, would come forth more honored, more peaceful and more respected than ever—if any
one had said this to him, he would have shaken his head
and looked upon the words as nonsense. Well! precisely that
had happened; all this grouping of the impossible was now
a fact, and God had permitted these absurdities to become
real things!

His musings continued to grow clearer. He was getting a
wider and wider view of his position.

He continued to question himself. He sternly asked himself
what he had understood by this: "My object is attained." He

declared that his life, in truth, did have an object. But what object? to conceal his name? to deceive the police? was it for so petty a thing that he had done all that he had done? had he no other object, which was the great one, which was the true one? to save, not his body, but his soul. To become honest and good again. To be an upright man! was it not that above all, that alone, which he had always wished, and which the bishop had enjoined upon him! To close the door on his past? But he was not closing it, great God! he was reopening it by committing an infamous act! for he became a robber again, and the most odious of robbers! he robbed another of his existence, his life, his peace, his place in the world, he became an assassin! he murdered, he murdered in a moral sense a wretched man, he inflicted upon him that frightful life in death, that living burial, which is called the galleys! on the contrary, to deliver himself up, to save this man stricken by so ghastly a mistake, to reassume his name, to become again from duty the convict Jean Valjean; that was really to achieve his resurrection, and to close for ever the hell from whence he had emerged! to fall back into it in appearance, was to emerge in reality! he must do that! all he had done was nothing, if he did not do that! all his life was useless, all his suffering was lost. He had only to ask the question: "What is the use?" He felt that the bishop was there, that the bishop was present all the more that he was dead, that the bishop was looking fixedly at him, that henceforth Mayor Madeleine with all his virtues would be abominable to him, and the galley slave, Jean Valjean, would be admirable and pure in his sight. That men saw his mask, but the bishop saw his face. That men saw his life, but the bishop saw his conscience. He must then go to Arras, deliver the wrong Jean Valjean, denounce the right one. Alas! that was the greatest of sacrifices, the most poignant of victories, the final step to be taken, but he must do it. Mournful destiny! he could only enter into sanctity in the eyes of God, by returning into infamy in the eyes of men!

"Well," said he, "let us take this course! let us do our duty! Let us save this man!" He pronounced these words in a loud voice, without perceiving that he was speaking aloud.

He took his books, verified them, and put them in order. He threw into the fire a package of notes which he held against needy small traders. He wrote a letter, which he sealed, and upon the envelope of which might have been read, if there had been any one in the room at the time: *Monsieur Laffitte, banker, Rue d'Artois, Paris.*

He drew from a secretary a pocket-book containing some banknotes and the passport that he had used that same year in going to the elections.

The letter to Monsieur Laffitte finished, he put it in his pocket as well as the pocket-book, and began to walk again.

Do what he might, he always fell back upon this sharp dilemma which was at the bottom of his thought. To remain in paradise and there become a demon! To re-enter into hell and there become an angel!

The torment from which he had emerged with so much difficulty, broke loose anew within him. His ideas again began to become confused. They took that indescribable, stupefied, and mechanical shape, which is peculiar to despair. The name of Romainville returned constantly to his mind, with two lines of a song he had formerly heard. He thought that Romainville is a little wood near Paris, where young lovers go to gather lilacs in the month of April.

He staggered without as well as within. He walked like a little child that is just allowed to go alone.

ADMISSION BY FAVOR

WITHOUT himself suspecting it, the Mayor of M—— sur M—— had a certain celebrity. For seven years the reputation of his virtue had been extending throughout Bas-Boulonnais; it had finally crossed the boundaries of the little county, and had spread into the two or three neighboring departments. Besides the considerable service that he had rendered to the chief town by reviving the manufacture of jet-work, there was not one of the hundred and forty-one communes of the district of M—— sur M—— which was not indebted to him for some benefit. He had even in case of need aided and quickened the business of the other districts. Thus he had, in time of need, sustained with his credit and with his own funds the tulle factory at Boulogne, the flax-spinning factory at Frévent, and the linen factory at Boubers-sur-Canche. Everywhere the name of Monsieur Madeleine was spoken with veneration. Arras and Douai envied the lucky little city of M—— sur M—— its mayor.

The Judge of the Royal Court of Douai, who was holding this term of the assizes at Arras, was familiar, as well as everybody else, with this name so profoundly and so universally honored. When the officer, quietly opening the door which led from the counsel chamber to the court room, bent behind the judge's chair and handed him the paper, on which was written this line: *"The gentleman desires to witness the trial,"* the judge made a hasty movement of deference, seized a pen, wrote a few words at the bottom of the paper and handed it back to the officer, saying to him: "Let him enter."

The unhappy man, whose history we are relating, had remained near the door of the hall, in the same place and the same attitude as when the officer left him. He heard, through his thoughts, some one saying to him: "Will monsieur do me the honor to follow me?" It was the same officer who had turned his back upon him the minute before, and who now bowed to the earth before him. The officer at the same time handed him the paper. He unfolded it, and, as he happened to be near the lamp, he could read:

"The Judge of the Court of Assizes presents his respects to Monsieur Madeleine."

He crushed the paper in his hands, as if those few words had left some strange and bitter taste behind.

He followed the officer.

In a few minutes he found himself alone in a kind of panelled cabinet, of a severe appearance, lighted by two wax candles placed upon a table covered with green cloth. The last words of the officer who had left him still rang in his ear: "Monsieur, you are now in the counsel chamber; you have but to turn the brass knob of that door and you will find yourself in the court room, behind the judge's chair." These words were associated in his thoughts with a vague remembrance of the narrow corridors and dark stairways through which he had just passed.

The officer had left him alone. The decisive moment had arrived. He endeavored to collect his thoughts, but did not succeed. At those hours especially when we have sorest need of grasping the sharp realities of life do the threads of thought snap off in the brain. He was in the very place where the judges deliberate and decide. He beheld with a stupid tranquility that silent and formidable room where so many existences had been terminated, where his own name would be heard so soon, and which his destiny was crossing at this moment. He looked at the walls, then he looked at himself, astonished that this could be this chamber, and that this could be he.

Suddenly, without himself knowing how, he found himself near the door, he seized the knob convulsively; the door opened. He was in the court room.

A PLACE FOR ARRIVING AT CONVICTIONS

HE took a step, closed the door behind him, mechanically, and remained standing, noting what he saw.

It was a large hall, dimly lighted, and noisy and silent by turns, where all the machinery of a criminal trial was exhibited, with its petty, yet solemn gravity, before the multitude. At one end of the hall, that at which he found himself, heedless judges, in threadbare robes, were biting their finger-nails, or closing their eyelids; at the other end was a ragged rabble; there were lawyers in all sorts of attitudes; soldiers with honest and hard faces; old, stained wainscoting, a dirty ceiling, tables covered with serge, which was more nearly yellow than green; doors blackened by finger-marks; tavern lamps, giving more smoke than light, on nails in the panelling; candles, in brass candlesticks, on the tables; everywhere obscurity, unsightliness, and gloom; and from all this there arose an austere and august impression; for men felt therein the presence of that great human thing which is called law, and that great divine thing which is called justice.

No man in this multitude paid any attention to him. All eyes converged on a single point, a wooden bench placed against a little door, along the wall at the left hand of the judge. Upon this bench, which was lighted by several candles, was a man between two gendarmes. This was the man.

He did not look for him, he saw him. His eyes went towards him naturally, as if they had known in advance where he was.

He thought he saw himself, older, doubtless, not precisely the same in features, but alike in attitude and appearance, with that bristling hair, with those wild and restless eyeballs, with that blouse—just as he was on the day he entered D——, full of hatred, and concealing in his soul that hideous hoard of frightful thoughts which he had spent nineteen years in gathering upon the floor of the galleys.

He said to himself, with a shudder: "Great God! shall I again come to this?"

This being appeared at least sixty years old. There was something indescribably rough, stupid, and terrified in his appearance.

At the sound of the door, people had stood aside to make room. The judge had turned his head, and supposing the person who entered to be the mayor of M—— sur M——, greeted him with a bow. The prosecuting attorney, who had seen Madeleine at M—— sur M——, whither he had been called more than once by the duties of his office, recognized him and bowed likewise. He scarcely perceived them. He gazed about him, a prey to a sort of hallucination.

Judges, clerk, gendarmes, a throng of heads, cruelly curious—he had seen all these once before, twenty-seven years ago. He had fallen again upon these fearful things; they were before him, they moved, they had being; it was no longer an effort of his memory, a mirage of his fancy, but real gendarmes and real judges, a real throng, and real men of flesh and bone. It was done; he saw reappearing and living again around him, with all the frightfulness of reality, the monstrous visions of the past.

All this was yawning before him.

Stricken with horror, he closed his eyes, and exclaimed from the depths of his soul: "Never!"

And by a tragic sport of destiny, which was agitating all his ideas and rendering him almost insane, it was another self before him. This man on trial was called by all around him, Jean Valjean!

He had before his eyes an unheard-of vision, a sort of representation of the most horrible moment of his life, played by his shadow.

All, everything was there—the same paraphernalia, the same hour of the night—almost the same faces, judge and assistant judges, soldiers and spectators. But above the head of the judge was a crucifix, a thing which did not appear in court rooms at the time of his sentence. When he was tried, God was not there.

A chair was behind him; he sank into it, terrified at the idea that he might be observed. When seated, he took advantage of a pile of papers on the judge's desk to hide his face from the whole room. He could now see without being seen. He entered fully into the spirit of the reality; by degrees he recovered his composure, and arrived at that degree of calmness at which it is possible to listen.

He looked for Javert, but did not see him. The witnesses' seat was hidden from him by the clerk's table. And then, as we have just said, the hall was very dimly lighted.

At the moment of his entrance, the counsel for the prisoner was finishing his plea. The attention of all was excited to the highest degree; the trial had been in progress for three hours. During these three hours, the spectators had seen a man, an unknown, wretched being, thoroughly stupid or thoroughly artful, gradually bending beneath the weight of a terrible probability. This man, as is already known, was a vagrant who had been found in a field, carrying off a branch, laden with ripe apples, which had been broken from a tree in a neighboring close called the Pierron enclosure. Who was this man? An examination had been held, witnesses had been heard, they had been unanimous, light had been elicited from every portion of the trial. The prosecution said: "We have here not merely a fruit thief, a marauder; we have here, in our hands, a bandit, an outlaw who has broken his ban, an old convict, a most dangerous wretch, a malefactor, called Jean Valjean, of whom justice has been long in pursuit, and who, eight years ago, on leaving the galleys at Toulon, committed a highway robbery, with force and arms, upon the person of a youth of Savoy, Petit Gervais by name, a crime which is specified in Article 383 of the Penal Code, and for which we reserve the right of further prosecution when his identity shall be judicially established. He has now committed a new theft. It is a case of second offence. Convict him for the new crime; he will be tried hereafter for the previous one." Before this accusation, before the unanimity of the witnesses, the principal emotion evinced by the accused was astonishment. He made gestures and signs which signified denial, or he gazed at the ceiling. He spoke with difficulty, and answered with embarrassment, but from head to foot his whole person denied the charge.

THE SYSTEM OF DENEGATIONS

THE time had come for closing the case. The judge commanded the accused to rise, and put the usual question: "Have you anything to add to your defense?"

The man, standing, and twirling in his hands a hideous cap which he had, seemed not to hear.

The judge repeated the question.

This time the man heard, and appeared to comprehend. He started like one awaking from sleep, cast his eyes around him, looked at the spectators, the gendarmes, his counsel, the jurors, and the court, placed his huge fists on the bar before him, looked around again, and suddenly fixing his eyes upon the prosecuting attorney, began to speak. It was like an eruption. It seemed from the manner in which the words escaped his lips, incoherent, impetuous, jostling each other pell-mell, as if they were all eager to find vent at the same time. He said:

"I have this to say: That I have been a wheelwright at Paris; that it was at M. Baloup's too. It is a hard life to be a wheelwright, you always work out-doors, in yards, under sheds when you have good bosses, never in shops, because you must have room, you see. In the winter, it is so cold that you thresh your arms to warm them; but the bosses won't allow that; they say it is a waste of time. It is tough work to handle iron when there is ice on the pavements. It wears a man out quick. You get old when you are young at this trade. A man is used up by forty. I was fifty-three; I was sick a good deal. And then the workmen are so bad! When a poor fellow isn't young, they always call you old bird, and old beast! I earned only thirty sous a day, they paid me as little as they could—the bosses took advantage of my age. Then I had my daughter, who was a washerwoman at the river. She earned a little for herself; between us two, we got on; she had hard work too. All day long up to the

77

waist in a tub, in rain, in snow, with wind that cuts your face when it freezes, it is all the same, the washing must be done; there are folks who haven't much linen and are waiting for it; if you don't wash you lose your customers. The planks are not well matched, and the water falls on you everywhere. You get your clothes wet through and through; that strikes in. She washed too in the laundry of the Enfants-Rouges, where the water comes in through pipes. There you are not in the tub. You wash before you under the pipe, and rinse behind you in the trough. This is under cover, and you are not so cold. But there is a hot lye that is terrible and ruins your eyes. She would come home at seven o'clock at night, and go to bed right away, she was so tired. Her husband used to beat her. She is dead. We wasn't very happy. She was a good girl; she never went to balls, and was very quiet. I remember one Shrove Tuesday she went to bed at eight o'clock. Look here, I am telling the truth. You have only to ask if 'tisn't so. Ask! how stupid I am! Paris is a gulf. Who is there that knows Father Champmathieu? But there is M. Baloup. Go and see M. Baloup. I don't know what more you want of me."

The man ceased speaking, but did not sit down. He had uttered these sentences in a loud, rapid, hoarse, harsh, and gutteral tone, with a sort of angry and savage simplicity. Once, he stopped to bow to somebody in the crowd. The sort of affirmations which he seemed to fling out haphazard, came from him like hiccoughs, and he added to each the gesture of a man chopping wood. When he had finished, the auditory burst into laughter. He looked at them, and seeing them laughing and not knowing why, began to laugh himself.

The judge, considerate and kindly man, raised his voice:

He reminded "gentlemen of the jury" that M. Baloup, the former master wheelwright by whom the prisoner said he had been employed, had been summoned, but had not appeared. He had become bankrupt, and could not be found. Then, turning to the accused, he adjured him to listen to what he was about to say, and added: "You are in a position which demands reflection. The gravest presumptions are weighing against you, and may lead to fatal results. Prisoner, on your own behalf, I question you a second time, explain yourself clearly on these two points. First, did you or did you not climb the wall of the Pierron close, break off the branch and steal the apples, that is to say, commit the crime of theft, with the addition of breaking into an enclosure? Secondly, are you or are you not the discharged convict, Jean Valjean?"

The prisoner shook his head with a knowing look, like a man who understands perfectly, and knows what he is going to say. He opened his mouth, turned towards the presiding judge, and said:

"In the first place——" Then he looked at his cap, looked up at the ceiling, and was silent.

"Prisoner," resumed the prosecuting attorney, in an austere tone, "give attention. You have replied to nothing that has been asked you. Your agitation condemns you. It is evident that your name is not Champmathieu, but that you are the convict, Jean Valjean, disguised under the name at first, of Jean Mathieu, which was that of his mother; that you have lived in Auvergne; that you were born at Faverolles, where you were a pruner. It is evident that you have stolen ripe apples from the Pierron close, with the addition of breaking into the enclosure. The gentlemen of the jury will consider this."

The accused had at last resumed his seat; he rose abruptly when the prosecuting attorney had ended, and exclaimed:

"You are a very bad man, you, I mean. This is what I wanted to say. I couldn't think of it first off. I never stole anything. I am a man who don't get something to eat every day. I was coming from Ailly, walking alone after a shower, which had made the ground all yellow with mud, so that the ponds were running over, and you only saw little sprigs of grass sticking out of the sand along the road, and I found a broken branch on the ground with apples on it; and I picked it up not knowing what trouble it would give me. It is three months that I have been in prison, being knocked about. More'n that, I can't tell. You talk against me and tell me 'answer!' The gendarme, who is a good fellow, nudges my elbow, and whispers, 'answer now.' I can't explain myself; I never studied; I am a poor man. You are all wrong not to see that I didn't steal. I picked up off the ground things that was there. You talk about Jean Valjean, Jean Mathieu—I don't know any such people. They must be villagers. I have worked for Monsieur Baloup, Boulevard de l'Hôpital. My name is Champmathieu. You must be very sharp to tell me where I was born. I don't know myself. Everybody can't have houses to be born in; that would be too handy. I think my father and mother were strollers, but I don't know. When

I was a child they called me Little One; now, they call me Old Man. They're my Christian names. Take them as you like. I have been in Auvergne, I have been at Faverolles. Bless me! can't a man have been in Auvergne and Faverolles without having been at the galleys? I tell you I never stole, and that I am Father Champmathieu. I have been at Monsieur Baloup's; I lived in his house. I am tired of your everlasting nonsense. What is everybody after me for like a mad dog?"

The prosecuting attorney was still standing; he addressed the judge:

"Sir, in the presence of the confused but very adroit denegations of the accused, who endeavors to pass for an idiot, but who will not succeed in it—we will prevent him— we request that it may please you and the court to call again within the bar the convicts, Brevet, Cochepaille, and Chenildieu, and the police-inspector Javert, and to submit them to a final interrogation, concerning the identity of the accused with the convict Jean Valjean."

"I must remind the prosecuting attorney," said the presiding judge, "that police-inspector Javert, recalled by his duties to the chief town of a neighboring district, left the hall, and the city also as soon as his testimony was taken. We granted him this permission, with the consent of the prosecuting attorney and the counsel of the accused."

"True," replied the presecuting attorney; "in the absence of Monsieur Javert, I think it a duty to recall to the gentlemen of the jury what he said here a few hours ago. Javert is an estimable man, who does honor to inferior but important functions, by his rigorous and strict probity. These are the terms in which he testified: 'I do not need even moral presumptions and material proofs to contradict the denials of the accused. I recognize him perfectly. This man's name is not Champmatheiu; he is a convict, Jean Valjean, very hard, and much feared. He was liberated at the expiration of his term, but with extreme regret. He served out nineteen years at hard labor for burglary; five or six times he attempted to escape. Besides the Petit Gervais and Pierron robberies, I suspect him also of a robbery committed on his highness, the late Bishop of D——. I often saw him when I was adjutant of the galley guard at Toulon. I repeat it: I recognize him perfectly.' "

This declaration, in terms so precise, appeared to produce

a strong impression upon the public and jury. The prosecuting attorney concluded by insisting that, in the absence of Javert, the three witnesses, Brevet, Chenildieu, and Cochepaille, should be heard anew and solemnly interrogated.

The judge gave an order to an officer, and a moment afterwards the door of the witness-room opened, and the officer, accompanied by a gendarme ready to lend assistance, led in the convict Brevet. The audience was in breathless suspense, and all hearts palpitated as if they contained but a single soul.

The old convict Brevet was clad in the black and grey jacket of the central prisons. Brevet was about sixty years old; he had the face of a man of business, and the air of a rogue. They sometimes go together. He had become something like a turnkey in the prison—to which he had been brought by new misdeeds. He was one of those men of whom their superiors are wont to say, "He tries to make himself useful." The chaplain bore good testimony to his religious habits. It must not be forgotten that this happened under the Restoration.

"Brevet," said the judge, "you have suffered infamous punishment, and cannot take an oath."

Brevet cast down his eyes.

"Nevertheless," continued the judge, "even in the man whom the law had degraded there may remain, if divine justice permit, a sentiment of honor and equity. To that sentiment I appeal in this decisive hour. If it still exist in you, as I hope, reflect before you answer me; consider on the one hand this man, whom a word from you may destroy; on the other hand, justice, which a word from you may enlighten. The moment is a solemn one, and there is still time to retract if you think yourself mistaken. Prisoner, rise. Brevet, look well upon the prisoner; collect your remembrances, and say, on your soul and conscience, whether you still recognise this man as your former comrade in the galleys, Jean Valjean."

Brevet looked at the prisoner, then turned to the court. "Yes, your honor, I was the first to recognize him, and still do so. This man is Jean Valjean, who came to Toulon in 1796, and left in 1815. I left a year after. He looks like a brute now, but he must have grown stupid with age; at the galleys he was sullen. I recognise him now, positively."

"Sit down," said the judge. "Prisoner, remain standing."

Chenildieu was brought in, a convict for life, as was shown

by his red cloak and green cap. He was undergoing his punishment in the galleys of Toulon, whence he had been brought for this occasion. He was a little man, about fifty years old, active, wrinkled, lean, yellow, brazen, restless, with a sort of sickly feebleness in his limbs and whole person, and immense force in his eye. His companions in the galleys had nicknamed him Je-nie-Dieu.

The judge addressed nearly the same words to him as to Brevet. When he reminded him that his infamy had deprived him of the right to take an oath. Chenildieu raised his head and looked the spectators in the face. The judge requested him to collect his thoughts, and asked him as he had Brevet, whether he still recognised the prisoner.

Chenildieu burst out laughing.

"Gad! do I recognise him! we were five years on the same chain. You're sulky with me, are you, old boy?"

"Sit down," said the judge.

The officer brought in Cochepaille; this other convict for life, brought from the galleys and dressed in red like Chenildieu, was a peasant from Lourdes, and a semi-bear of the Pyrenees. He had tended flocks in the mountains, and from shepherd had glided into brigandage. Cochepaille was not less uncouth than the accused, and appeared still more stupid. He was one of those unfortunate men whom nature turns out as wild beasts, and society finishes up into galley slaves.

The judge attempted to move him by a few serious and pathetic words, and asked him, as he had the others, whether he still recognised without hesitation or difficulty the man standing before him.

"It is Jean Valjean," said Cochepaille. "The same they called Jean-the-Jack, he was so strong."

Each of the affirmations of these three men, evidently sincere and in good faith, had excited in the audience a murmur of evil augury for the accused—a murmur which increased in force and continuance, every time a new declaration was added to the preceding one. The prisoner himself listened to them with that astonished countenance which, according to the prosecution, was his principal means of defence. At the first, the gendarmes by his side heard him mutter between his teeth: "Ah, well! there is one of them!" After the second, he said in a louder tone, with an air almost of satisfaction, "Good!" At the third he exclaimed, "Famous!"

The judge addressed him:

"Prisoner, you have listened. What have you to say?"

He replied:

"I say—famous!"

A buzz ran through the crowd and almost invaded the jury. It was evident that the man was lost.

"Officers," said the judge, "enforce order. I am about to sum up the case."

At this moment there was a movement near the judge. A voice was heard exclaiming:

"Brevet, Chenildieu, Cochepaille, look this way!"

So lamentable and terrible was this voice that those who heard it felt their blood run cold. All eyes turned towards the spot whence it came. A man, who had been sitting among the privileged spectators behind the court, had risen, pushed open the low door which separated the tribunal from the bar, and was standing in the center of the hall. The judge, the prosecuting attorney, twenty persons recognised him, and exclaimed at once.

"Monsieur Madeleine!"

CHAMPMATHIEU MORE AND MORE ASTONISHED

IT was he, indeed. The clerk's lamp lighted up his face. He held his hat in hand; there was no disorder in his dress; his overcoat was carefully buttoned. He was very pale, and trembled slightly. His hair, already grey when he came to Arras, was now perfectly white. It had become so during the hour that he had been there. All eyes were strained towards him.

Before even the judge and prosecuting attorney could say a word, before the gendarmes and officers could make a sign, the man, whom all up to this moment had called Monsieur Madeleine, had advanced towards the witnesses, Cochepaille, Brevet, and Chenildieu. "Do you not recognize me?" said he.

All three stood confounded, and indicated by a shake of the head that they did not know him. Cochepaille, intimidated, gave the military salute. Monsieur Madeleine turned towards the jurors and court, and said in a mild voice:

"Gentlemen of the jury, release the accused. Your honor, order my arrest. I am Jean Valjean."

Not a breath stirred. To the first commotion of astonishment had succeeded a sepulchral silence. That species of religious awe was felt in the hall which thrills the multitude at the accomplishment of a grand action.

Nevertheless, the face of the judge was marked with sympathy and sadness; he exchanged glances with the prosecuting attorney, and a few whispered words with the assistant judges. He turned to the spectators and asked in a tone which was understood by all:

"Is there a physician here?"

The prosecuting attorney continued:

"Gentlemen of the jury, the strange and unexpected incident which disturbs the audience, inspires us, as well as yourselves, with a feeling we have no need to express. You all know, at least by reputation, the honorable Monsieur Madeleine, Mayor of M—— sur M——. If there be a physician in the audience, we unite with his honor the judge in entreating him to be kind enough to lend his assistance to Monsieur Madeleine and conduct him to his residence."

Monsieur Madeleine did not permit the prosecuting attorney to finish, but interrupted him with a tone full of gentleness and authority. These are the words he uttered; we give them literally, as they were written down immediately after the trial, by one of the witnesses of the scene—as they still ring in the ears of those who heard them, now nearly forty years ago.

"I thank you, Monsieur Prosecuting Attorney, but I am not mad. You shall see. You were on the point of committing a great mistake; release that man. I am accomplishing a duty; I am the unhappy convict. I am the only one who sees clearly here, and I tell you the truth. What I do at this moment, God beholds from on high, and that is sufficient. You can take me, since I am here. Nevertheless, I have done my best. I have disguised myself under another name, I have become rich, I have become a mayor, I have desired to enter again among honest men. It seems that this cannot be. In short, there are many things which I cannot tell. I shall not relate to you the story of my life: some day you will know it. I did rob Monseigneur the Bishop—that is true; I did rob Petit Gervais—that is true. They were right in telling you that Jean Valjean was a wicked wretch. But all the blame may not belong to him. Listen, your honors; a man so abased as I has no remonstrance to make with Providence, nor advice to give to society; but, mark you, the infamy from which I have sought to rise is pernicious to men. The galleys make the galley-slave. Receive this in kindness, if you will. Before the galleys, I was a poor peasant, unintelligent, a species of idiot; the galley changed me. I was stupid, I became wicked; I was a log, I became a firebrand. Later, I was saved by indulgence and kindness, as I had been lost by severity. But, pardon, you cannot comprehend what I say. You will find in my house, among the ashes of the fireplace, the forty-sous piece of which, seven years ago, I robbed Petit Gervais. I have nothing more to add. Take me. Great God! the prosecuting attorney shakes his head. You say 'Monsieur Madeleine has gone mad'; you do not believe me. This is hard to be borne. Do not condemn that man, at least. What! these men do not know me! Would that Javert were here. He would recognise me!"

Nothing could express the kindly yet terrible melancholy of the tone which accompanied these words.

He turned to the three convicts:

"Well! I recognise you, Brevet, do you remember—"

He paused, hesitated a moment, and said:

"Do you remember those checkered, knit suspenders that you had in the galleys?"

Brevet started as if struck with surprise, and gazed wildly at him from head to foot. He continued:

"Chenildieu, surnamed by yourself Je-nie-Dieu, the whole of your left shoulder has been burned deeply, from laying it one day on a chafing dish full of embers, to efface the three letters T.F.P., which yet are still to be seen there. Answer me, is this true?"

"It is true!" said Chenildieu.

He turned to Cochepaille:

"Cochepaille, you have on your left arm, near where you have been bled, a date put in blue letters with burnt powder. It is the date of the landing of the emperor at Cannes, *March 1st, 1815.* Lift up your sleeve."

Cochepaille lifted up his sleeve; all eyes around him were turned to his naked arm. A gendarme brought a lamp; the date was there.

The unhappy man turned towards the audience and the court with a smile, the thought of which still rends the hearts of those who witnessed it. It was the smile of triumph; it was also the smile of despair.

"You see clearly," said he, "that I am Jean Valjean."

There were no longer either judges, or accusers, or gendarmes in the hall; there were only fixed eyes and beating hearts. Nobody remembered longer the part which he had to play; the prosecuting attorney forgot that he was there to prosecute, the judge that he was there to preside, the counsel for the defense that he was there to defend. Strange to say no question was put, no authority intervened.

It was evident that Jean Valjean was before their eyes. That fact shone forth. The appearance of this man had been enough fully to clear up the case, so obscure a moment before. Without need of any further explanation, the multitude, as by a sort of electric revelation, comprehended instantly, and at a single glance, this simple and magnificent story of a man giving himself up that another might not be condemned in his place. The details, the hesitation, the slight reluctance possible were lost in this immense, luminous fact.

"I will not disturb the proceeding further," continued Jean Valjean. "I am going, since I am not arrested. I have many things to do. Monsieur the prosecuting attorney knows where I am going, and will have me arrested when he chooses."

He walked towards the outer door. Not a voice was raised, not an arm stretched out to prevent him. He passed through the throng with slow steps. It was never known who opened the door, but it is certain that the door was open when he came to it. On reaching it he turned and said:

"Monsieur the Prosecuting Attorney, I remain at your disposal." He then addressed himself to the auditory.

"You all, all who are here, think me worthy of pity, do you not? Great God! when I think of what I have been on the point of doing, I think myself worthy of envy. Still, would that all this had not happened!"

He went out, and the door closed as it had opened, for those who do deeds sovereignly great are always sure of being served by somebody in the multitude.

Less than an hour afterwards, the verdict of the jury discharged from all accusation the said Champmathieu; and Champmathieu, set at liberty forthwith, went his way stupefied, thinking all men mad, and understanding nothing of this vision.

Counter-Stroke

THE CHAMBER OF FANTINE

DAY began to dawn. Fantine had had a feverish and sleepless night, yet full of happy visions; she fell asleep at daybreak. Sister Simplice, who had watched with her, took advantage of this slumber to go and prepare a new potion of quinine. The good sister had been for a few moments in the laboratory of the infirmary, bending over her vials and drugs, looking at them very closely on account of the mist which the dawn casts over all objects, when suddenly she turned her head, and uttered a faint cry. M. Madeleine stood before her. He had just come in silently.

"You, Monsieur the Mayor!" she exclaimed.

"How is the poor woman?" he answered in a low voice.

"Better just now. But we have been very anxious indeed."

She explained what had happened, that Fantine had been very ill the night before, but was now better, because she believed that the mayor had gone to Montfermeil for her child. The sister dared not question the mayor, but she saw clearly from his manner that he had not come from that place.

"That is well," said he. "You did right not to deceive her."

"Yes," returned the sister, "but now, Monsieur the Mayor, when she sees you without her child, what shall we tell her?"

He reflected for a moment, then said:

"God will inspire us."

He asked: "Can I see her?"

"Will not Monsieur the Mayor bring back her child?" asked the sister, scarcely daring to venture a question.

"Certainly, but two or three days are necessary."

"If she does not see Monsieur the Mayor here," continued the sister timidly, "she will not know that he had returned; it will be easy for her to have patience, and when the child comes, she will think naturally that Monsieur the Mayor has just arrived with her. Then we will not have to tell her a falsehood."

Monsieur Madeleine seemed to reflect for a few moments, then said with his calm gravity:

"No, my sister, I must see her. Perhaps I have not much time."

The nun did not seem to notice this "perhaps," which gave an obscure and singular significance to the words of Monsieur the Mayor. She answered, lowering her eyes and voice respectfully:

"In that case, she is asleep, but monsieur can go in."

He made a few remarks about a door that shut with difficulty the noise of which might awaken the sick woman; then entered the chamber of Fantine, approached her bed, and opened the curtains. She was sleeping. Her pallor had become whiteness, and her cheeks were glowing. Her long, fair eyelashes, the only beauty left to her of her maidenhood and youth, quivered as they lay closed upon her cheek. Her whole person trembled as if with the fluttering of wings which were felt, but could not be seen, and which seemed about to unfold and bear her away. To see her thus, no one could have believed that her life was despaired of. She looked more as if about to soar away than to die.

Monsieur Madeleine remained for some time motionless near the bed, looking by turns at the patient and the crucifix, as he had done two months before, on the day when he came for the first time to see her in this asylum. They were still there, both in the same attitude, she sleeping, he praying; only now, after these two months had rolled away, her hair was grey and his was white.

The sister had not entered with him. He stood by the bed, with his finger on his lips, as if there were some one in the room to silence. She opened her eyes, saw him, and said tranquilly, with a smile:

"And Cosette?"

FANTINE HAPPY

She did not start with surprise or joy; she was joy itself. The simple question: "And Cosette?" was asked with such deep faith, with so much certainty, with so complete an absence of disquiet or doubt, that he could find no word in reply. She continued:

"I knew that you were there; I was asleep, but I saw you.

I have seen you for a long time; I have followed you with my eyes the whole night. You were in a halo of glory, and all manner of celestial forms were hovering around you!"

He raised his eyes towards the crucifix.

"But tell me, where is Cosette?" she resumed. "Why not put her on my bed that I might see her the instant I woke?"

He answered something mechanically, which he could never afterwards recall.

Happily, the physician had come and had been apprised of this. He came to the aid of M. Madeleine.

"My child," said he, "be calm, your daughter is here."

The eyes of Fantine beamed with joy, and lighted up her whole countenance. She clasped her hands with an expression full of the most violent and most gentle entreaty:

"Oh!" she exclaimed, "bring her to me!"

Touching illusion of the mother; Cosette was still to her a little child to be carried in the arms.

"Not yet," continued the physician, "not at this moment. You have some fever still. The sight of your child will agitate you, and make you worse. We must cure you first."

She interrupted him impetuously.

"But I am cured! I tell you I am cured! Is this physician a fool? I will see my child!"

"You see how you are carried away!" said the physician. "So long as you are in this state, I cannot let you have your child. It is not enough to see her, you must live for her. When you are reasonable, I will bring her to you myself."

"Sir, I ask your pardon. I sincerely ask your pardon. Once I would not have spoken as I have now, but so many misfortunes have befallen me that sometimes I do not know what I am saying. I understand, you fear excitement: I will wait as long as you wish, but I am sure that it will not harm me to see my daughter. I see her now, I have not taken my eyes from her since last night. Let them bring her to me now, and I will just speak to her very gently. That is all. Is it not very natural that I should wish to see my child, when they have been to Montfermeil on purpose to bring her to me? I am not angry. I know that I am going to be very happy. All night, I saw figures in white, smiling on me. As soon as the doctor pleases, he can bring Cosette. My fever is gone, for I am cured; I feel that there is scarcely anything the matter with me; but I will act as if I were ill, and do not stir so as to please the ladies here. When they see that

I am calm, they will say: 'You must give her the child.'"

M. Madeleine was sitting in a chair by the side of the bed. She turned towards him, and made visible efforts to appear calm and "very good," as she said, in that weakness of disease which resembles childhood, so that, seeing her so peaceful, there should be no objection to bringing her Cosette. Nevertheless, although restraining herself, she could not help addressing a thousand questions to M. Madeleine.

"Did you have a pleasant journey, Monsieur the Mayor? Oh! how good you have been to go for her! Tell me only how she is. Did she bear the journey well? Ah! she will not know me. In all this time, she has forgotten me, poor kitten! Children have no memory. They are like birds. To-day they see one thing, and to-morrow another, and remember nothing. Could they not bring her here for one little moment? they might take her away immediately. Say! you are master here, are you willing?"

He took her hand. "Cosette is beautiful," said he. "Cosette is well; you shall see her soon, but be quiet. You talk too fast; and then you throw your arms out of bed, which makes you cough."

In fact, coughing fits interrupted Fantine at almost every word.

She did not murmur; she feared that by too eager entreaties she had weakened the confidence which she wished to inspire, and began to talk about indifferent subjects.

"Montfermeil is a pretty place, is it not? In summer people go there on pleasure parties. Do the Thénardiers do a good business? Not many great people pass through that country. Their inn is a kind of chop-house."

Monsieur Madeleine still held her hand and looked at her with anxiety. It was evident that he had come to tell her things before which his mind now hesitated. The physician had made his visit and retired. Sister Simplice alone remained with them.

But in the midst of the silence, Fantine cried out:—

"I hear her! Oh, darling! I hear her!"

There was a child playing in the court—the child of the portress or some workwoman. It was one of those chances which are always met with, and which seem to make part of the mysterious representation of tragic events. The child, which was a little girl, was running up and down to keep herself warm, singing and laughing in a loud voice. Alas! with what are not the plays of children mingled! Fantine had heard this little girl singing.

"Oh!" said she, "it is my Cosette! I know her voice!"

The child departed as she had come, and the voice died away. Fantine listened for some time. A shadow came over her face, and Monsieur Madeleine heard her whisper, "How wicked it is of that doctor not to let me see my child! That man has a bad face!"

But yet her happy train of thought returned. With her head on the pillow she continued to talk to herself. "How happy we shall be! We will have a little garden in the first place; Monsieur Madeleine has promised it to me. My child will play in the garden. She must know her letters now. I will teach her to spell. She will chase the butterflies in the grass, and I will watch her.

He had to let go the hand of Fantine. He listened to the words as one listens to the wind that blows, his eyes on the ground, and his mind plunged into unfathomable reflections. Suddenly she ceased speaking and raised her head mechanically. Fantine had become appalling.

She did not speak; she did not breathe; she half-raised herself in the bed, the covering fell from her emaciated shoulders; her countenance, radiant a moment before, became livid, and her eyes, dilated with terror, seemed to fasten on something before her at the other end of the room.

"Good God!" exclaimed he. "What is the matter, Fantine?"

She did not answer; she did not take her eyes from the object which she seemed to see, but touched his arm with one hand, and with the other made a sign to him to look behind him.

He turned, and saw Javert.

AUTHORITY RESUMES ITS SWAY

FANTINE could not endure this hideous face, she felt as if she were dying, she hid her face with both hands, and shrieked in anguish:

"Monsieur Madeleine, save me!"

Jean Valjean, we shall call him by no other name henceforth, had risen. He said to Fantine in his gentlest and calmest tone:

"Be composed: it is not for you that he comes."

He then turned to Javert and said:

"I know what you want."

Javert answered:

"Hurry along."

There was in the manner in which these two words were uttered, an inexpressible something which reminded you of a wild beast and of a madman. Javert did not say "Hurry along!" he said: "Hurr-'long!" No orthography can express the tone in which this was pronounced; it ceased to be human speech; it was a howl.

At the exclamation of Javert, Fantine had opened her eyes again. But the mayor was there, what could she fear?

Javert advanced to the middle of the chamber, exclaiming: "Hey, there; are you coming?"

The unhappy woman looked around her. There was no one but the nun and the mayor. To whom could this contemptuous familiarity be addressed? To herself alone. She shuddered.

Then she saw a mysterious thing, so mysterious that its like had never appeared to her in the darkest delirium of fever.

She saw the spy Javert seize Monsieur the Mayor by the collar; she saw Monsieur the Mayor bow his head. The world seemed vanishing before her sight.

Javert, in fact, had taken Jean Valjean by the collar.

Javert burst into a horrid laugh, displaying all his teeth.

"There is no Monsieur the Mayor here any longer!" said he.

Jean Valjean did not attempt to disturb the hand which grasped the collar of his coat. He said:

"Javert—"

Javert interrupted him: "Call me Monsieur the Inspector!"

"Monsieur," continued Jean Valjean, "I would like to speak a word with you in private."

"Aloud, speak aloud," said Javert, "people speak aloud to me."

Jean Valjean went on, lowering his voice.

"It is a request that I have to make of you—"

"I tell you to speak aloud."

"But this should not be heard by any one but yourself."

"What is that to me? I will not listen."

Jean Valjean turned to him and said rapidly and in a very low tone:

"Give me three days! Three days to go for the child of this unhappy woman! I will pay whatever is necessary. You shall accompany me if you like."

"Are you laughing at me!" cried Javert. "Hey! I did not think you so stupid! You ask for three days to get away, and tell me that you are going for this girl's child! Ha, ha, that's good! That is good!"

Fantine shivered.

"My child!" she exclaimed, "going for my child! Then she is not here! Sister, tell me, where is Cosette? I want my child! Monsieur Madeleine, Monsieur the Mayor!"

Javert stamped his foot.

"There is the other now! Hold your tongue, hussy!"

He gazed steadily at Fantine, and added, grasping anew the cravat, shirt, and coat collar of Jean Valjean:

"I tell you that there is no Monsieur Madeleine, and that there is no Monsieur the Mayor. There is a robber, there is a brigand, there is a convict called Jean Valjean, and I have got him! That is what there is!"

Fantine started upright, supporting herself by her rigid arms and hands; she looked at Jean Valjean, then at Javert, and then at the nun; she opened her mouth as if to speak; a rattle came from her throat, her teeth struck together, she stretched out her arms in anguish, convulsively opening her hands, and groping about her like one who is drowning; then sank suddenly back upon the pillow.

Her head struck the head of the bed and fell forward on her breast, the mouth gaping, the eyes open and glazed.

She was dead.

Jean Valjean put his hand on that of Javert which held him, and opened it as he would have opened the hand of a child; then he said:

"You have killed this woman."

"Have done with this!" cried Javert, furious, "I am not here to listen to sermons; save all that; the guard is below; come right along, or the handcuffs!"

There stood in a corner of the room an old iron bedstead in a dilapidated condition, which the sisters used as a camp-bed when they watched. Jean Valjean went to the bed, wrenched out the rickety head bar—a thing easy for muscles like his—in the twinkling of an eye, and with the bar in his clenched fist, looked at Javert. Javert recoiled towards the door.

Jean Valjean, his iron bar in hand, walked slowly towards the bed of Fantine. On reaching it, he turned and said to Javert in a voice that could scarcely be heard:

"I advise you not to disturb me now."

Nothing is more certain than that Javert trembled.

He had an idea of calling the guard, but Jean Valjean might profit by his absence to escape. He remained, therefore, grasped the bottom of his cane, and leaned against the framework of the door without taking his eyes from Jean Valjean.

Jean Valjean rested his elbow upon the post, and his head upon his hand, and gazed at Fantine, stretched motionless before him. He remained thus, mute and absorbed, evidently lost to everything of this life. His countenance and attitude bespoke nothing but inexpressible pity.

Jean Valjean took Fantine's head in his hands and arranged it on the pillow, as a mother would have done for her child, then fastened the string of her night-dress, and replaced her hair beneath her cap. This done, he closed her eyes.

The face of Fantine, at this instant, seemed strangely illumined.

Death is the entrance into the great light.

Fantine's hand hung over the side of the bed. Jean Valjean knelt before this hand, raised it gently, and kissed it.

Then he rose, and, turning to Javert, said:

"Now, I am at your disposal."

A FITTING TOMB

JAVERT put Jean Valjean in the city prison.

The arrest of Monsieur Madeleine produced a sensation, or rather an extraordinary commotion, at M—— sur M——. We are sorry not to be able to disguise the fact that, on this single sentence *he was a galley slave,* almost everybody abandoned him. Three or four persons alone in the whole city remained faithful to his memory. The old portress who had been his servant was among the number.

On the evening of this same day, the worthy old woman was sitting in her lodge, still quite bewildered and sunk in sad reflections. The factory had been closed all day, the carriage doors were bolted, the street was deserted. There was no one in the house but the two nuns, Sister Perpétue and Sister Simplice, who were watching the corpse of Fantine.

Towards the time when Monsieur Madeleine had been accustomed to return, the honest portress rose mechanically, took the key of his room from a drawer, with the taper-stand that he used at night to light himself up the stairs, then hung the key on a nail from which he had been in the habit of taking it, and placed the taper-stand by its side, as if she were expecting him. She then seated herself again in her chair, and resumed her reflections. The poor old woman had done all this without being conscious of it.

More than two hours had elapsed when she started from her reverie and exclaimed, "Why, bless me! I have hung his key on the nail!"

Just then, the window of her box opened, a hand passed through the opening, took the key and stand, and lighted the taper at the candle which was burning.

The portress raised her eyes; she was transfixed with astonishment; a cry rose to her lips, but she could not give it utterance.

She knew the hand, the arm, the coat-sleeve.

It was M. Madeleine.

She was speechless for some seconds, thunderstruck, as she said herself, afterwards, in giving her account of the affair.

"My God! Monsieur Mayor!" she exclaimed, "I thought you were——"

She stopped; the end of her sentence would not have been respectful to the beginning. To her, Jean Valjean was still Monsieur the Mayor.

He completed her thought.

"In prison," said he. "I was there; I broke a bar from a window, let myself fall from the top of the roof, and here I am. I am going to my room; go for Sister Simplice. She is doubtless beside this poor woman."

The old servant hastily obeyed.

He ascended the staircase which led to his room. On reaching the top, he left his taper-stand on the upper stair, opened his door with little noise, felt his way to the window and closed the shutter, then came back, took his taper, and went into the chamber.

The precaution was not useless; it will be remembered that his window could be seen from the street.

He cast a glance about him, over his table, his chair, his bed, which had not been slept in for three days. There remained no trace of the disorder of the night before the last. The portress had "put the room to rights." Only, she had picked up from the ashes, and laid in order on the table, the ends of the loaded club, and the forty-sous piece, blackened by the fire.

He took a sheet of paper and wrote: *These are the ends of my loaded club and the forty-sous piece stolen from Petit Gervais, of which I spoke at the Court of Assizes;* then placed the two bits of iron and the piece of silver on the sheet in such a way that it would be the first thing perceived on entering the room. He took from a wardrobe an old shirt which he tore into several pieces and in which he packed the two silver candlesticks. In all this there was neither haste nor agitation.

Two gentle taps were heard at the door.

"Come in," said he.

It was Sister Simplice.

She was pale, her eyes were red, and the candle which she held trembled in her hand. The shocks of destiny have this peculiarity; however subdued or disciplined our feelings may be, they draw out the human nature from the depths of our souls, and compel us to exhibit it to others. In the agitation of this day the nun had again become a woman. She had wept, and she was trembling.

Jean Valjean had written a few lines on a piece of paper, which he handed to the nun, saying: "Sister, you will give this to the curé."

The paper was not folded. She cast her eyes on it.

"You may read it," said he.

She read: "I beg Monsieur the Curé to take charge of all that I leave here. He will please defray therefrom the expenses of my trial, and of the burial of the woman who died this morning. The remainder is for the poor."

The sister attempted to speak, but could scarcely stammer out a few inarticulate sounds. She succeeded, however, in saying:

"Does not Monsieur the Mayor wish to see this poor unfortunate again for the last time?"

"No," said he, "I am pursued; I should only be arrested in her chamber; it would disturb her."

He had scarcely finished when there was a loud noise on the staircase. They heard a tumult of steps ascending, and the old portress exclaiming in her loudest and most piercing tones:

"My good sir, I swear to you in the name of God, that nobody has come in here the whole day, and the whole evening; that I have not even once left my door!"

A man replied: "But yet, there is a light in this room."

They recognised the voice of Javert.

The chamber was so arranged that the door in opening covered the corner of the wall to the right. Jean Valjean blew out the taper, and placed himself in this corner.

Sister Simplice fell on her knees near the table.

The door opened.

Javert entered.

The whispering of several men and the protestations of the portress were heard in the hall.

The nun did not raise her eyes. She was praying.

The candle was on the mantle, and gave but a dim light.

Javert perceived the sister and stopped, abashed.

It will be remembered that the very foundation of Javert, his element, the medium in which he breathed, was veneration for all authority. He was perfectly homogeneous, and admitted of no objection, or abridgment. To him, be it understood, ecclesiastical authority was the highest of all; he was devout, superficial, and correct, upon this point as upon all others. In his eyes, a priest was a spirit who was never mistaken, a nun was a being who never sinned. They were souls walled in from this world, with a single door which never opened but for the exit of truth.

On perceiving the sister, his first impulse was to retire. But there was also another duty which held him, and which urged him imperiously in the opposite direction. His second impulse was to remain, and to venture at least one question.

This was the Sister Simplice, who had never lied in her life. Javert knew this, and venerated her especially on account of it.

"Sister," said he, "are you alone in this room?"

There was a fearful instant during which the poor portress felt her limbs falter beneath her. The sister raised her eyes, and replied:

"Yes."

Then continued Javert—"Excuse me if I persist, it is my duty—you have not seen this evening a person, a man—he has escaped, and we are in search of him—Jean Valjean—you have not seen him?"

The sister answered—"No."

She lied. Two lies in succession, one upon another, without hesitation, quickly, as if she were an adept in it.

"Your pardon!" said Javert, and he withdrew, bowing reverently.

The affirmation of the sister was to Javert something so decisive that he did not even notice the singularity of this taper, just blown out, and smoking on the table.

An hour afterwards, a man was walking rapidly in the darkness beneath the trees from M—— sur M—— in the direction of Paris. This man was Jean Valjean. It has been established, by the testimony of two or three wagoners who met him, that he carried a bundle, and was dressed in a blouse. Where did he get this blouse? It was never known. Nevertheless, an old artisan had died in the infirmary of the factory a few days before, leaving nothing but his blouse. This might have been the one.

A last word in regard to Fantine.

We have all one mother—the earth. Fantine was restored to this mother.

COSETTE

The Ship Orion

JEAN VALJEAN had been retaken.

We shall be pardoned for passing rapidly over the painful details. We shall merely reproduce a couple of items published in the newspapers of that day, some few months after the remarkable events that occurred at M—— sur M——.

We copy the first from the *Drapeau Blanc*. It is dated the 25th of July, 1823:

"A district of the Pas-de Calais has just been the scene of an extraordinary occurrence. A stranger in that department, known as Monsieur Madeleine, had, within a few years past, restored, by means of certain new processes, the manufacture of jet and black glass ware—a former local branch of industry. He had made his own fortune by it, and, in fact, that of the entire district. In acknowledgment of his services he had been appointed mayor. The police have discovered that Monsieur Madeleine was none other than an escaped convict, condemned in 1796 for robbery, and named Jean Valjean. This Jean Valjean has been sent back to the galleys. It appears that previous to his arrest, he succeeded in withdrawing from Laffitte's a sum amounting to more than half a million which he had deposited there, and which it is said, by the way, he had very legitimately realised in his business. Since his return to the galleys at Toulon, it has been impossible to discover where Jean Valjean concealed this money."

The second article, is taken from the *Journal de Paris* of the same date:

"An old convict, named Jean Valjean, has recently been brought before the Var Assizes, under circumstances calculated to attract attention. This villain had succeeded in eluding the vigilance of the police; he had changed his name, and had even been adroit enough to procure the appointment of mayor in one of our small towns in the North. He had established in this town a very considerable business, but was, at length, unmasked and arrested, thanks to the indefatigable zeal of the public authorities. This wretch, who is endowed with herculean strength, managed to escape, but, three or four days afterwards, the police retook him, in Paris, just as he was getting into one of the small vehicles that ply between the capital and the village of Montfermeil (Seine-et-Oise). It is said that he had availed himself of the interval of these three or four days of freedom to withdraw a considerable sum deposited by him with one of our principal bankers. The amount is estimated at six or seven hundred thousand francs. According to the minutes of the case, he has concealed it in some place known to himself alone, and it has been impossible to seize it; however that may be, the said Jean Valjean has been brought before the assizes of the Department of the Var under indictment for an assault and robbery on the high road committed *vi et armis* some eight years ago. This bandit attempted no defense. Consequently, Jean Valjean, being found guilty, was condemned to death. The criminal refused to appeal to the higher courts, and the king, in his inexhaustible clemency, deigned to commute his sentence to that of hard labor in prison for life. Jean Valjean was immediately forwarded to the galleys at Toulon."

Jean Valjean changed his number at the galleys. He became 9430.

SHOWING THAT THE CHAIN OF THE IRON RING MUST NEEDS HAVE UNDERGONE A CERTAIN PREPARATION TO BE THUS BROKEN BY ONE BLOW OF THE HAMMER

TOWARDS the end of October, in that same year, 1823, the inhabitants of Toulon saw coming back into their port, in consequence of heavy weather, and in order to repair some damages, the ship *Orion*, which was at a later period employed at Brest as a vessel of instruction, and which then formed a part of the Mediterranean squadron.

Every day, then, from morning till night, the quays, the wharves, and the piers of the port of Toulon were covered with a throng of saunterers and idlers, whose occupation consisted in gazing at the *Orion*. One morning, the throng which was gazing at her witnessed an accident.

The crew was engaged in furling sail. The topman, whose duty it was to take in the starboard upper corner of the main top-sail, lost his balance. He was seen tottering; the dense throng assembled on the wharf of the arsenal uttered a cry, the man's head overbalanced his body, and he whirled over the yard, his arms outstretched towards the deep; as he went over, he grasped the man-ropes, first with one hand, and then with the other, and hung suspended in that manner. The sea lay far below him at a giddy depth. The shock of his fall had given to the man-ropes a violent swinging motion, and the poor fellow hung dangling to and fro at the end of this line, like a stone in a sling.

To go to his aid was to run a frightful risk. None of the crew, who were all fishermen of the coast recently taken into service, dared attempt it. In the meantime, the poor top-man was becoming exhausted; his agony could not be seen in his countenance, but his increasing weakness could be detected in the movements of all his limbs. His arms twisted about in horrible contortions. Every attempt he made to re-ascend only increased the oscillations of the man-ropes.

Suddenly, a man was discovered clambering up the rigging with the agility of a wildcat. This man was clad in red—it was a convict; he wore a green cap—it was a convict for life. As he reached the round top, a gust of wind blew off his cap and revealed a head entirely white: it was not a young man.

In a twinkling he was upon the yard. He paused a few seconds, and seemed to measure it with his glance. At length, the convict raised his eyes to heaven, and took a step forward. The crowd drew a long breath. He was seen to run along the yard. On reaching its extreme tip, he fastened one end of the rope he had with him, and let the other hang at full length. Thereupon, he began to let himself down by his hands along this rope, and then there was an inexpressible sensation of terror; instead of one man, two were seen dangling at that giddy height.

However, the convict had, at length, managed to make his way down to the seaman. The convict firmly secured him to the rope to which he clung with one hand while he worked with the other. Finally, he was seen reascending to the yard, and hauling the sailor after him; he supported him there, for an instant, to let him recover his strength, and then, lifting him in his arms, carried him, as he walked along the yard, to the crosstrees, and from there to the round-top, where he left him in the hands of his mess-mates.

He, however, had made it a point of duty to descend again immediately, and go back to his work. In order to arrive more quickly, he slid down the rigging, and started to run along a lower yard. All eyes were following him. There was a certain moment when every one felt alarmed; whether it was that he felt fatigued, or because his head swam, people thought they saw him hesitate and stagger. Suddenly, the throng uttered a thrilling outcry: the convict had fallen into the sea.

The fall was perilous. The frigate *Algesiras* was moored close to the *Orion,* and the poor convict had plunged between the two ships. It was feared that he would be drawn under one or the other. Four men sprang, at once, into a boat. The man had not again risen to the surface. They sounded and dragged the place. It was in vain. The search was continued until night, but not even the body was found.

The next morning, the *Toulon Journal* published the following lines:—"November 17, 1823. Yesterday, a convict at work on board of the *Orion,* on his return from rescuing a sailor, fell into the sea, and was drowned. His body was not recovered. It is presumed that it has been caught under the piles at the pier-head of the arsenal. This man was registered by the number 9430, and his name was Jean Valjean."

Fulfilment of the
Promise to the Departed

NUMBER 9430 COMES UP AGAIN, AND COSETTE DRAWS IT

JEAN VALJEAN was not dead.

When he fell into the sea, or rather when he threw himself into it, he was, as we have seen, free from his irons. He swam under water to a ship at anchor to which a boat was fastened.

He found means to conceal himself in this boat until evening. At night he betook himself again to the water, and reached the land a short distance from Cape Brun.

There, as he did not lack for money, he could procure clothes. Then Jean Valjean, like all those joyless fugitives who are endeavoring to throw off the track the spy of the law and social fatality, followed an obscure and wandering path. He finally reached Paris.

His first care, on reaching Paris, had been to purchase a mourning dress for a little girl of seven years, then to procure lodgings. That done, he had gone to Montfermeil.

On the evening of the same day that Jean Valjean had rescued Cosette from the clutches of the Thénardiers, he entered Paris again. He entered the city at night-fall, with the child, by the Barrière de Monceaux. There he took a cabriolet, which carried him as far as the esplanade of the Observatory. There he got out, paid the driver, took Cosette by the hand, and both in the darkness of the night, through the deserted streets in the vicinity of l'Ourcine and la Glacière, walked towards the Boulevard de l'Hôpital.

The Old Gorbeau House

FORTY years ago, the solitary pedestrian who ventured into the unknown regions of La Salpêtrière and went up along the Boulevard as far as the Barrière d'Italie, reached certain points where it might be said that Paris disappeared. It was an inhabited place where there was nobody, it was a desert place where there was somebody; it was a boulevard of the great city, a street of Paris, wilder, at night, than a forest, and gloomier, by day, than a graveyard.

It was the old quarter of the Horse Market.

Our pedestrian, if he trusted himself beyond the four tumbling walls of this Horse Market, if willing to go even further than the Rue du Petit Banquier, leaving on his right a courtyard shut in by lofty walls, then a meadow studded with stacks of tanbark that looked like gigantic beaver dams, then an enclosure half filled with lumber and piles of logs, sawdust and shavings, from the top of which a huge dog was baying, then a long, low, ruined wall with a small dark-colored and decrepit gate in it, covered with moss, which was full of flowers in spring-time, then, in the loneliest spot, a frightful broken-down structure on which could be read in large letters: POST NO BILLS; this bold promenader, we say, would reach the corner of the Rue des Vignes-Saint-Marcel, a latitude not much explored. There, near a manufactory and between two garden walls, could be seen at the time of which we speak an old ruined dwelling that, at first sight, seemed as small as a cottage, yet was, in reality, as vast as a cathedral. It stood with its gable end towards the highway, and hence its apparent diminutiveness. Nearly the whole house was hidden. Only the door and one window could be seen. This old dwelling had but one story.

The letter-carriers called the house No. 50-52; but it was known, in the *quartier,* as Gorbeau House.

BEFORE this Gorbeau tenement Jean Valjean stopped. Like the birds of prey, he had chosen this lonely place to make his nest.

He fumbled in his waistcoat and took from it a sort of night-key, opened the door, entered, then carefully closed it again and ascended the stairway, still carrying Cosette.

At the top of the stairway he drew from his pocket another key, with which he opened another door. The chamber which he entered and closed again immediately was a sort of garret, rather spacious, furnished only with a mattress spread on the floor, a table, and a few chairs. A stove containing a fire, the coals of which were visible, stood in one corner. The street lamp of the boulevards shed a dim light through this poor interior. At the further extremity there was a little room containing a cot bed. On this Jean Valjean laid the child without waking her.

He struck a light with a flint and steel and lit a candle, which, with his tinder-box, stood ready, beforehand, on the table; and, as he had done on the preceding evening, he began to gaze upon Cosette with a look of ecstasy, in which the expression of goodness and tenderness went almost to the verge of insanity.

Jean Valjean bent down and kissed the child's hand.

Nine months before, he had kissed the hand of the mother, who also had just fallen asleep.

The same mournful, pious, agonizing feeling now filled his heart.

He knelt down by the bedside of Cosette.

It was broad daylight, and yet the child slept on. A pale ray from the December sun struggled through the garret window and traced upon the ceiling long streaks of light and shade. Suddenly a carrier's wagon, heavily laden, trundled over the cobble-stones of the boulevard, and shook the old building like the rumbling of a tempest, jarring it from cellar to roof-tree.

"Yes, madame!" cried Cosette, starting up out of sleep, "here I am! here I am!"

And she threw herself from the bed, her eyelids still half closed with the weight of slumber, stretching out her hand towards the corner of the wall.

"Oh! what shall I do? Where is my broom?" said she.

By this time her eyes were fully open, and she saw the smiling face of Jean Vajean.

"Oh! yes—so it is!" said the child. "Good morning, monsieur."

Children at once accept joy and happiness with quick familiarity, being themselves naturally all happiness and joy.

It was a frightful hovel, but she felt free.

"Must I sweep?" she continued at length.

"Play!" replied Jean Valjean.

And thus the day passed by. Cosette, without troubling herself with trying to understand anything about it, was inexpressibly happy with her doll and her good friend.

TWO MISFORTUNES MINGLED MAKE HAPPINESS

THE dawn of the next day found Jean Valjean again near the bed of Cosette. He waited there, motionless, to see her wake.

Something new was entering his soul.

Jean Valjean had never loved anything. For twenty-five years he had been alone in the world. He had never been a father, lover, husband, or friend. His sister and her children had left in his memory only a vague and distant impression, which had finally almost entirely vanished. He had made every exertion to find them again, and, not succeeding, had forgotten them.

When he saw Cosette, when he had taken her, carried her away, and rescued her, he felt his heart moved. All that he had of feeling and affection was aroused and vehemently attracted towards this child. He would approach the bed where she slept, and would tremble there with delight; he felt inward yearnings, like a mother, and knew not what they were; for it is something very incomprehensible and very sweet, this grand emotion of a heart in its first love.

But, as he was fifty-five and Cosette was but eight years old, all that he might have felt of love in his entire life melted into a sort of ineffable radiance.

This was the second white vision he had seen. The bishop had caused the dawn of virtue on his horizon; Cosette evoked the dawn of love.

On her part, Cosette, too, unconsciously underwent a change, poor little creature! She was so small when her mother left her, that she could not recollect her now. As all children do, like the young shoots of the vine that cling to everything, she had tried to love. She had not been able to succeed. Everybody had repelled her—the Thénardiers, their children, other children. She had loved the dog; it died, and after that no person and no thing would have aught to do with her. And so, from the very first day, all that thought and felt in her began to love this kind old friend.

Her kind friend no longer impressed her as old and poor. In her eyes Jean Valjean was handsome, just as the garret had seemed pretty.

Jean Valjean had well chosen his hiding-place. He was there in a state of security that seemed to be complete.

The apartment with the side chamber, which he occupied with Cosette, was the one whose window looked out upon the boulevard. This window being the only one in the house, there was no neighbor's prying eye to fear either from that side or opposite.

The upper floor contained, as we have said, several rooms and a few lofts, only one of which was occupied—by an old woman, who was maid of all work to Jean Valjean. All the rest were uninhabited.

It was this old woman, honored with the title of landlady, but, in reality, intrusted with the functions of portress, who had rented him these lodgings on Christmas Day. He had passed himself off to her as a gentleman of means, ruined by the Spanish Bonds, who was going to live there with his grand-daughter.

Weeks rolled by. These two beings led in that wretched shelter a happy life.

From the earliest dawn, Cosette laughed, prattled, and sang. Children have their morning song, like birds.

Jean Valjean had begun to teach her to read. Sometimes, while teaching the child to spell, he would remember that it was with the intention of accomplishing evil that he had learned to read, in the galleys. This intention had now been changed into teaching a child to read. Then the old convict would smile with the pensive smile of angels.

To teach Cosette to read, and to watch her playing, was nearly all Jean Valjean's life. And then, he would talk to her about her mother, and teach her to pray.

She called him *Father*, and knew him by no other name.

He spent hours seeing her dress and undress her doll, and listening to her song and prattle. From that time on, life seemed full of interest to him, men seemed good and just; he no longer, in his thoughts, reproached any one with any wrong; he saw no reason, now, why he should not live to grow very old, since his child loved him.

This is but personal opinion; but in order to express our idea thoroughly, at the point Jean Valjean had reached, when he began to love Cosette, it is not clear to us that he did not require this fresh supply of goodness to enable him to per- severe in the right path. He had seen the wickedness of men and the misery of society under new aspects; he had been sent back to the galleys this time for doing good; new waves of bitterness had overwhelmed him; disgust and weariness had once more resumed their sway; the recollection of the bishop, even, was perhaps eclipsed, sure to reappear after- wards, luminous and triumphant; yet, in fact, this blessed remembrance was growing feebler. Who knows that Jean Valjean was not on the point of becoming discouraged and falling back to evil ways? Love came, and he again grew strong. Alas! he was no less feeble than Cosette. He protected her, and she gave strength to him. Thanks to him, she could walk upright in life; thanks to her, he could persist in vir- tuous deeds. He was the support of this child, and this child was his prop and staff.

WHAT THE LANDLADY DISCOVERED

JEAN VALJEAN was prudent enough never to go out in the day- time. Every evening, however, about twilight, he would walk for an hour or two, sometimes alone, often with Cosette, selecting the most unfrequented side alleys of the boulevards and going into the churches at nightfall.

They lived frugally, always with a little fire in the stove, but like people in embarrassed circumstances. Jean Valjean made no change in the furniture described on the first day, excepting that he caused a solid door to be put up in place of the glass door of Cosette's little bed-chamber.

He still wore his yellow coat, his black pantaloons, and his old hat. On the street he was taken for a beggar. It sometimes happened that kind-hearted dames, in passing, would turn and hand him a penny. Jean Valjean accepted the penny and bowed humbly. It chanced, sometimes, also, that he would meet some wretched creature begging alms, and then, glancing about him to be sure no one was looking, he would stealthily approach the beggar, slip a piece of money, often silver, into his hand, and walk rapidly away. This had its inconveniences. He began to be known in the quarter as *the beggar who gives alms.*

The old landlady, a crabbed creature, fully possessed with that keen observation as to all that concerned her neighbors, which is peculiar to the suburbs, watched Jean Valjean closely without exciting his suspicion. She was a little deaf, which made her talkative. She had questioned Cosette, who, knowing nothing, could tell nothing, further than that she came from Montfermeil. One morning this old female spy saw Jean Valjean go, with an appearance which seemed peculiar to the old busybody, into one of the uninhabited apartments of the building. She followed him with the steps of an old cat, and could see him without herself being seen, through the chink of the door directly opposite. Jean Valjean had, doubtless for greater caution, turned his back towards the door in question. The old woman saw him fumble in his pocket, and take from it a needle case, scissors, and thread, and then proceed to rip open the lining of one lapel of his coat and take from under it a piece of yellowish paper, which he unfolded. The beldame remarked with dismay, that it was a bank bill for a thousand francs. It was the second or third one only that she had ever seen. She ran away very much frightened.

A moment afterwards, Jean Valjean accosted her, and asked her to get this thousand-franc bill changed for him, adding that it was the half-yearly interest on his property which he had received on the previous day. "Where?" thought the old woman. He did not go out until six o'clock, and the government treasury is certainly not open at that hour. The woman changed the note, meanwhile forming her conjectures.

THERE was, in the neighborhood of Saint Médard, a mendicant who sat crouching over the edge of a condemned public well near by, and to whom Jean Valjean often gave alms. He never passed this man without giving him a few pennies. Sometimes he spoke to him.

One evening, as Jean Valjean was passing that way, unaccompanied by Cosette, he noticed the beggar sitting in his usual place, under the street lamp which had just been lighted. The man, according to custom, seemed to be praying and was bent over. Jean Valjean walked up to him, and put a piece of money in his hand, as usual. The beggar suddenly raised his eyes, gazed intently at Jean Valjean, and then quickly dropped his head. This movement was like a flash; Jean Valjean shuddered; it seemed to him that he had just seen, by the light of the street-lamp, not the calm, sanctimonious face of the aged beadle, but a terrible and well-known countenance. He experienced the sensation one would feel on finding himself suddenly face to face, in the gloom, with a tiger. He recoiled, horror-stricken and petrified, daring neither to breathe nor to speak, to stay nor to fly, but gazing upon the beggar who had once more bent down his head, with its tattered covering, and seemed to be no longer conscious of his presence. At this singular moment, an instinct, perhaps the mysterious instinct of self-preservation, prevented Jean Valjean from uttering a word. The beggar had the same form, the same rags, the same general appearance as on every other day. "Pshaw!" said Jean Valjean to himself, "I am mad! I am dreaming! It cannot be!" And he went home, anxious and ill at ease.

He scarcely dared to admit, even to himself, that the countenance he thought he had seen was the face of Javert.

Some days after, it might be eight o'clock in the evening, he was in his room, giving Cosette her spelling lesson, which the child was repeating in a loud voice, when he heard the door of the building open and close again. That seemed odd to him. Jean Valjean remained silent and motionless, his back turned towards the door, still seated on his chair from which he had not moved, and holding his breath in the darkness. After a considerable interval, not hearing anything more, he turned round without making any noise, and as he raised his eyes towards the door of his room, he saw a light through the keyhole. This ray of light was an evil star in the black background of the door and the wall. There was, evidently, somebody outside with a candle who was listening.

A few minutes elapsed, and the light disappeared. But he heard no sound of footsteps, which seemed to indicate that whoever was listening at the door had taken off his shoes.

Jean Valjean threw himself on his bed without undressing, but could not shut his eyes that night.

At daybreak, as he was sinking into slumber from fatigue, he was aroused, again, by the creaking of the door of some room at the end of the hall, and then he heard the same footstep which had ascended the stairs, on the preceding night. The step approached. He started from his bed and placed his eye to the keyhole, which was quite a large one, hoping to get a glimpse of the person, whoever it might be, who had made his way into the building in the night-time and had listened at his door. It was a man, indeed, who passed by Jean Valjean's room, this time without stopping. The hall was still too dark for him to make out his features; but, when the man reached the stairs, a ray of light from without made his figure stand out like a profile, and Jean Valjean had a full view of his back. The man was tall, wore a long frock-coat, and had a cudgel under his arm. It was the redoubtable form of Javert.

At seven in the morning, when the old lady came to clear up the rooms, Jean Valjean eyed her sharply, but asked her no questions. The good dame appeared as usual.

While she was doing her sweeping, she said:—

"Perhaps monsieur heard some one come in, last night?"

At her age and on the boulevard, eight in the evening is the very darkest of the night.

"Ah! yes, by the way, I did," he answered in the most natural tone. "Who was it?"

"It's a new lodger," said the old woman, "who has come into the house."

"And his name——?"

"Well, I hardly recollect now. Dumont or Daumont.—
Some such name as that."

"And what is he—this M. Daumont?"

The old woman studied him, a moment, through her little
foxy eyes, and answered:

"He's a gentleman living on his income like you."

When the old woman was gone, he made a roll of a
hundred francs he had in a drawer and put it into his
pocket. Do what he would to manage this so that the clinking
of the silver should not be heard, a five-franc piece escaped
his grasp and rolled jingling away over the floor.

At dusk, he went to the street-door and looked carefully
up and down the boulevard. No one was to be seen.
The boulevard seemed to be utterly deserted. It is true that
there might have been some one hidden behind a tree.

He went upstairs again.

"Come," said he to Cosette.

He took her by the hand and they both went out.

A Dark Chase
Needs a Silent Hound

GROPING FOR ESCAPE

IN order to understand what follows, it is necessary to form an exact idea of the little Rue Droit Mur, and particularly the corner which it makes at the left as you leave the Rue Polonceau to enter this alley. The little Rue Droit Mur was almost entirely lined on the right, as far as the Petite Rue Picpus, by houses of poor appearance; on the left by a single building of severe outline, composed of several structures which rose gradually a story or two, one above another, as they approached the Petite Rue Picpus, so that the building, very high on the side of the Petite Rue Picpus, was quite low on the side of the Rue Polonceau. There, at the corner of which we have spoken, it became so low as to be nothing more than a wall. This wall did not abut squarely on the corner, which was cut off diagonally, leaving a considerable space that was shielded by the two angles thus formed from observers at a distance in either the Rue Polonceau, or the Rue Droit Mur.

From these two angles of the truncated corner, the wall extended along the Rue Polonceau as far as a house numbered 49, and along the Rue Droit Mur, where its height was much less, to the sombre-looking building of which we have spoken, cutting its gable, and thus making a new reentering angle in the street. This gable had a gloomy aspect; there was but one window to be seen, or rather two shutters covered with a sheet of zinc, and always closed.

This truncated corner was entirely filled by a thing which seemed like a colossal and miserable door. It was a vast shapeless assemblage of perpendicular planks, broader above than below, bound together by long transverse iron bands. At the side there was a porte-cochère of ordinary dimensions, which had evidently been cut in within the last fifty years.

A lime-tree lifted its branches above this corner, and the

wall was covered with ivy towards the Rue Polonceau.

In the imminent peril of Jean Valjean, this sombre building had a solitary and uninhabited appearance which attracted him. He glanced over it rapidly. He thought if he could only succeed in getting into it, he would perhaps be safe. Hope came to him with the idea.

Midway of the front of this building on the Rue Droit Mur, there were at all the windows of the different stories old leaden waste-pipes. The varied branchings of the tubing which was continued from a central conduit to each of these waste-pipes, outlined on the façade a sort of tree. These ramifications of the pipes with their hundred elbows seemed like those old closely-pruned grape-vines which twist about over the front of ancient farm-houses.

This grotesque espalier, with its sheet-iron branches, was the first object which Jean Valjean saw. He seated Cosette with her back against a post, and, telling her to be quiet, ran to the spot where the conduit came to the pavement. Perhaps there was some means of scaling the wall by that and entering the house. But the conduit was dilapidated and out of use, and scarcely held by its fastening. Besides, all the windows of this silent house were protected by thick bars of iron, even the dormer windows. And then the moon shone full upon this façade, and the man who was watching from the end of the street would have seen Jean Valjean making the escalade. And then what should he do with Cosette? How could he raise her to the top of a three-story house?

He gave up climbing by the conduit, and crept along the wall to the Rue Polonceau.

When he reached the flattened corner where he had left Cosette, he noticed that there no one could see him. He escaped, as we have just explained, all observation from every side. Besides, he was in the shade. Then there were two doors. Perhaps they might be forced. The wall, above which he saw the lime and the ivy, evidently surrounded a garden, where he could at least conceal himself, although there were no leaves on the trees yet, and pass the rest of the night.

Time was passing. He must act quickly.

He tried the carriage door, and found at once that it was fastened within and without.

He approached the other large door with more hope. It was frightfully decrepit, its immense size even rendering it less solid; the planks were rotten, the iron fastenings, of which there were three, were rusted. It seemed possible to pierce this worm-eaten structure.

On examining it, he saw that this door was not a door. It had neither hinges, braces, lock, nor crack in the middle. The iron bands crossed from one side to the other without a break. Through the crevices of the planks he saw the rubble-work and stones, roughly cemented, which passers-by could have seen within the last ten years. He was compelled to admit with consternation that this appearance of a door was simply an ornamentation in wood of a wall, upon which it was placed. It was easy to tear off a board, but then he would find himself face to face with a wall.

WHICH WOULD BE IMPOSSIBLE WERE THE STREETS LIGHTED WITH GAS

AT this moment a muffled and regular sound began to make itself heard at some distance. Jean Valjean ventured to thrust his head a little way around the corner of the street. Seven or eight soldiers, formed in platoon, had just turned into the Rue Polonceau. He saw the gleam of their bayonets. They were coming towards him.

The soldiers, at whose head he distinguished the tall form of Javert, advanced slowly and with precaution. They stopped frequently. It was plain they were exploring all the recesses of the walls and all the entrances of doors and alleys.

It was—and here conjecture could not be deceived—some patrol which Javert had met and which he had put in requisition.

Javert's two assistants marched in the ranks.

At the rate at which they were marching, and the stops they were making, it would take them about a quarter of an hour to arrive at the spot where Jean Valjean was. It was a frightful moment. A few minutes separated Jean Valjean from that awful precipice which was opening before him for the third time. And the galleys now were no longer simply the galleys, they were Cosette lost for ever; that is to say, a life in death.

There was now only one thing possible.

Jean Valjean had this peculiarity, that he might be said to

carry two knapsacks; in one he had the thoughts of a saint, in the other the formidable talents of a convict. He helped himself from one or the other as occasion required.

Among other resources, thanks to his numerous escapes from the galleys at Toulon, he had, it will be remembered, become master of that incredible art of raising himself, in the right angle of a wall, if need to be to the height of a sixth story.

Jean Valjean measured with his eyes the wall above which he saw the lime tree. It was about eighteen feet high. The angle that it made with the gable of the great building was filled in its lower part with a pile of masonry of triangular shape, probably intended to preserve this too convenient recess from a too public use. This preventive filling-up of the corners of a wall is very common in Paris.

This pile was about five feet high. From its top the space to climb to get upon the wall was hardly more than fourteen feet.

The wall was capped by a flat stone without any projection.

The difficulty was Cosette. Cosette did not know how to scale a wall. Abandon her? Jean Valjean did not think of it. To carry her was impossible.

He needed a cord. Jean Valjean had none. Truly at that instant, if Jean Valjean had had a kingdom, he would have given it for a rope.

All extreme situations have their flashes which sometimes make us blind, sometimes illuminate us.

The despairing gaze of Jean Valjean encountered the lamp-post in the Cul-de-sac Genrot.

At this epoch there were no gas-lights in the streets of Paris. At nightfall they lighted the street lamps, which were placed at intervals, and were raised and lowered by means of a rope traversing the street from end to end, running through the grooves of posts. The reel on which this rope was wound was inclosed below the lantern in a little iron box, the key of which was kept by the lamp-lighter, and the rope itself was protected by a casing of metal.

Jean Valjean, with the energy of a final struggle, crossed the street at a bound, entered the cul-de-sac, sprang the bolt of the little box with the point of his knife, and an instant after was back at the side of Cosette. He had a rope.

Then, without any haste, but without doing anything a sec-

ond time, with a firm and rapid decision, so much the more
remarkable at such a moment when the patrol and Javert
might come upon him at any instant, he took off his cravat,
passed it around Cosette's body under the arms, taking care
that it should not hurt the child, attached this cravat to an
end of the rope by means of the knot which seamen call a
swallow-knot, took the other end of the rope in his teeth,
took off his shoes and stockings and threw them over the
wall, climbed upon the pile of masonry and began to raise
himself in the angle of the wall and the gable with as much
solidity and certainty as if he had the rounds of a ladder
under his heels and his elbows. Half a minute had not passed
before he was on his knees on the wall.

Cosette watched him, stupefied, without saying a word.
Jean Valjean's charge and the name of the Thénardiers had
made her dumb.

All at once, she heard Jean Valjean's voice calling to her in
a low whisper:

"Put your back against the wall."

She obeyed.

"Don't speak, and don't be afraid," added Jean Valjean.

And she felt herself lifted from the ground.

Before she had time to think where she was, she was at
the top of the wall.

Jean Valjean seized her, put her on his back, took her two
little hands in his left hand, lay down flat and crawled along
the top wall as far as the cut-off corner. As he had supposed, there was a building there, the roof of which
sloped from the top of the wooden casing we have mentioned
very nearly to the ground, with a gentle inclination, and
just reaching to the lime-tree.

A fortunate circumstance, for the wall was much higher on
this side than on the street. Jean Valjean saw the ground beneath him at a great depth.

He had just reached the inclined plane of the roof, and had
not yet left the crest of the wall, when a violent uproar pro-
claimed the arrival of the patrol. He heard the thundering
voice of Javert:

"Search the cul-de-sac! The Rue Droit Mur is guarded, the
Petite Rue Picpus also. I'll answer for it if he is in the cul-de-
sac."

The soldiers rushed into the Cul-de-sac Genrot.

Jean Valjean slid down the roof, keeping hold of Cosette,

reached the lime-tree, and jumped to the ground. Whether from terror, or from courage, Cosette had not uttered a whisper. Her hands were a little scraped.

COMMENCEMENT OF AN ENIGMA

JEAN VALJEAN found himself in a sort of garden, very large and of a singular appearance; one of those gloomy gardens which seem made to be seen in the winter and at night.

Jean Valjean had on one side the building, down the roof of which he had come, a wood-pile, and behind the wood, against the wall, a stone statue, the mutilated face of which was now nothing but a shapeless mask which was seen dimly through the obscurity.

The building was in ruins, but some dismantled rooms could be distinguished in it, one of which was well filled, and appeared to serve as a shed.

Jean Valjean's first care had been to find his shoes, and put them on; then he entered the shed with Cosette. A man trying to escape never thinks himself sufficiently concealed.

Cosette trembled, and pressed closely to his side. They heard the tumultuous clamour of the patrol ransacking the cul-de-sac and the street, the clatter of their muskets against the stones, the calls of Javert to the watchmen he had stationed, and his imprecations mingled with words which they could not distinguish.

At the end of a quarter of an hour it seemed as though this stormy rumbling began to recede. Jean Valjean did not breathe.

He had placed his hand gently upon Cosette's mouth.

But the solitude about him was so strangely calm that that frightful din, so furious and so near, did not even cast over it a shadow of disturbance. It seemed as if these walls were built of the deaf stones spoken of in Scripture.

Suddenly, in the midst of this deep calm, a new sound arose; a celestial, divine, ineffable sound, as ravishing as the other was horrible. It was a hymn which came forth from the darkness, a bewildering mingling of prayer and harmony in the obscure and fearful silence of the night; voices of women, but voices with the pure accents of virgins, and artless accents of children; those voices which are not of earth, and which resemble those that the new-born still hear, and the dying hear already. This song came from the gloomy building which overlooked the garden. At the moment when the uproar of the demons receded, one would have said, it was a choir of angels approaching in the darkness.

Cosette and Jean Valjean fell on their knees.

They knew not what it was; they knew not where they were; but they both felt, the man and the child, the penitent and the innocent, that they ought to be on their knees.

The chant ceased. Perhaps it had lasted a long time. Jean Valjean could not have told.

All had again relapsed into silence. There was nothing more in the street, nothing more in the garden. That which threatened, that which reassured, all had vanished. The wind rattled the dry grass on the top of the wall, which made a low, soft, and mournful noise.

THE ENIGMA CONTINUED

THE night wind had risen, which indicated that it must be between one and two o'clock in the morning. Poor Cosette did not speak.

She was still trembling.

"Are you sleepy?" said Jean Valjean.

"I am very cold," she answered.

The ground was damp, the shed open on all sides, the wind freshened every moment. The good man took off his coat and wrapped Cosette in it. "Are you warmer, so?"

"Oh! yes, father!"

THE ENIGMA REDOUBLES

THE child had laid her head upon a stone and gone to sleep.

He sat down near her and looked at her. Little by little, as he beheld her, he grew calm, and regained possession of his clearness of mind.

He plainly perceived this truth, the basis of his life henceforth, that so long as she should be alive, so long as he should have her with him, he should need nothing except for her,

and fear nothing save on her account. He did not even realize
that he was very cold, having taken off his coat to cover her.

Meanwhile, through the reverie into which he had fallen,
he had heard for some time a singular noise. It sounded like
a little bell that some one was shaking. This noise was in the
garden. It was heard distinctly, though feebly. It resembled
the dimly heard tinkling of cow-bells in the pastures at
night.

This noise made Jean Valjean turn.

He looked, and saw that there was some one in the garden.

Something which resembled a man was walking among
the glass cases of the melon patch, rising up, stooping down,
stopping, with a regular motion, as if he were drawing or
stretching something upon the ground. This being appeared
to limp.

Jean Valjean shuddered with the continual tremor of the
outcast. To them everything is hostile and suspicious. They
distrust the day because it helps to discover them, and the
night because it helps to surprise them. Just now he was
shuddering because the garden was empty, now he shuddered because there was some one in it.

He took the sleeping Cosette gently in his arms and carried her into the furthest corner of the shed behind a heap
of old furniture that was out of use. Cosette did not stir.

From there he watched the strange motions of the man
in the melon patch. It seemed very singular, but the sound
of the bell followed every movement of the man. When the
man approached, the sound approached; when he moved
away, the sound moved away; if he made some sudden motion, a trill accompanied the motion; when he stopped, the
noise ceased. It seemed evident that the bell was fastened to
this man; but then what could that mean? what was this
man to whom a bell was hung as to a ram or a cow?

While he was revolving these questions, he touched
Cosette's hands. They were icy.

"Oh! God!" said he.

He called to her in a low voice:

"Cosette!"

She did not open her eyes.

He shook her smartly.

She did not wake.

"Could she be dead?" said he, and he sprang up, shuddering from head to foot.

Cosette was pallid; she had fallen prostrate on the ground at his feet, making no sign.

He listened for her breathing; she was breathing; but with a respiration that appeared feeble and about to stop.

How should he get her warm again? how rouse her? All else was banished from his thoughts. He rushed desperately out of the ruin. It was absolutely necessary that in less than a quarter of an hour Cosette should be in bed and before a fire.

THE MAN WITH THE BELL

HE walked straight to the man whom he saw in the garden. He had taken in his hand the roll of money which was in his vest-pocket.

This man had his head down, and did not see him coming. A few strides, Jean Valjean was at his side.

Jean Valjean approached him, exclaiming:

"A hundred francs!"

The man started and raised his eyes.

"A hundred francs for you," continued Jean Valjean, "if you will give me refuge to-night."

The moon shone full in Jean Valjean's bewildered face.

"What, it is you, Father Madeleine!" said the man.

This name, thus pronounced, at this dark hour, in this unknown place, by this unknown man, made Jean Valjean start back.

He was ready for anything but that. The speaker was an old man, bent and lame, dressed much like a peasant, who had on his left knee a leather knee-cap from which hung a bell. His face was in the shade, and could not be distinguished.

Meanwhile the good man had taken off his cap, and was exclaiming, tremulously:

"Ah! my God! how did you come here, Father Madeleine? How did you get in, O Lord? Did you fall from the sky? There is no doubt, if you ever do fall, you will fall from there. And what has happened to you? You have no cravat, you have no hat, you have no coat? Do you know that you would have frightened anybody who did not know you? No coat? Merciful heavens! are the saints all crazy now? But how did you get in?"

"Who are you? and what is this house!" asked Jean Valjean.

"Oh! indeed, that is good now," exclaimed the old man. "I am the one you got the place for here, and this house is the one you got me the place in. What! you don't remember me?"

"No," said Jean Valjean. "And how does it happen that you know me?"

"You saved my life," said the man.

He turned, a ray of the moon lighted up his side face, and Jean Valjean recognised old Fauchelevent.

"Ah!" said Jean Valjean, "it is you? yes, I remember you."

"That is very fortunate!" said the old man, in a reproachful tone.

"And what are you doing here?" added Jean Valjean.

"Oh! I am covering my melons."

He continued:

"I said to myself: the moon is bright, there is going to be a frost. Suppose I put their jackets on my melons? And," added he, looking at Jean Valjean, with a loud laugh, "you would have done well to do as much for yourself? but how did you come here?"

Jean Valjean, finding that he was known by this man, at least under his name of Madeleine, went no further with his precautions. He multiplied questions. Oddly enough their parts seemed reversed. It was he, the intruder, who put questions.

"And what is this bell you have on your knee?"

"That!" answered Fauchelevent, "that is so that they may keep away from me."

"How! keep away from you?"

Old Fauchelevent winked in an indescribable manner.

"Ah! Bless me! there's nothing but women in this house; plenty of young girls. It seems that I am dangerous to meet. The bell warns them. When I come they go away."

"What is this house?"

"Why, you know very well."

"No, I don't."

"Why, you got me this place here as gardener."

"Answer me as if I didn't know."

"Well, it is the Convent of the Petit Picpus, then."

Jean Valjean remembered. Chance, that is to say, Providence, had thrown him precisely into this convent of the Quartier Saint Antoine, to which old Fauchelevent, crippled by his fall from his cart, had been admitted, upon his recommendation, two years before. He repeated as if he were talking to himself:

"The Convent of the Petit Picpus!"

"But now, really," resumed Fauchelevent, "how the deuce did you manage to get in, you, Father Madeleine? It is no use for you to be a saint, you are a man; and no men come in here."

"But you are here."

"There is none but me."

"But," resumed Jean Valjean, "I must stay here."

"Oh! my God," exclaimed Fauchelevent.

Jean Valjean approached the old man, and said to him in a grave voice:

"Father Fauchelevent, I saved your life."

"I was first to remember it," answered Fauchelevent.

"Well, you can now do for me what I once did for you."

"What do you want me to do?" he added.

"I will explain. You have a room?"

"I have a solitary shanty, over there, behind the ruins of the old convent, in a corner that nobody ever sees. There are three rooms."

"Very well. But now come with me. We will go for the child."

"Ah!" said Fauchelevent, "there is a child!"

He said not a word more, but followed Jean Valjean as a dog follows his master.

In half an hour Cosette, again become rosy before a good fire, was asleep in the old gardener's bed.

Cemeteries Take
What Is Given Them

WHICH TREATS OF THE MANNER OF ENTERING THE CONVENT

WHEN Cosette had been put to bed, Jean Valjean and Fauchelevent had taken a glass of wine and a piece of cheese before a blazing fire; then, the only bed in the shanty being occupied by Cosette, they had thrown themselves each upon a bundle of straw. Before closing his eyes, Jean Valjean had said: "Henceforth I must remain here." These words were chasing one another through Fauchelevent's head the whole night. To tell the truth, neither of them had slept.

Jean Valjean, feeling that he was discovered and Javert was upon his track, knew full well that he and Cosette were lost should they return into the city. Since the new blast which had burst upon him, had thrown him into this cloister, Jean Valjean had but one thought, to remain there. Now, for one in his unfortunate position, this convent was at once the safest and the most dangerous place; the most dangerous, for, no man being allowed to enter, if he should be discovered, it was a flagrant crime, and Jean Valjean would take but one step from the convent to prison; the safest, for if he succeeded in getting permission to remain, who would come there to look for him? To live in an impossible place; that would be safety.

For his part, Fauchelevent was racking his brains.

He formed his resolution then: to devote himself to Monsieur Madeleine.

SUCCESSFUL EXAMINATION

IN the depth of night, two men and a child stood in front of No. 62, Petite Rue Picpus. The elder of the men lifted the knocker and rapped.

It was Fauchelevent, Jean Valjean, and Cosette.

Fauchelevent belonged to the convent and knew all the passwords. Every door opened before him.

The prioress, rosary in hand, was awaiting them.

The prioress scrutinized Jean Valjean. Nothing scans so carefully as a downcast eye.

Then she proceeded to question:

"You are the brother?"

"Yes, reverend mother," replied Fauchelevent.

"What is your name?"

Fauchelevent replied:

"Ultimus Fauchelevent!"

"From what part of the country are you?"

Fauchelevent answered:

"From Picquigny, near Amiens."

"What is your age?"

Fauchelevent answered:

"Fifty."

"What is your business?"

Fauchelevent answered:

"Gardener."

"Are you a true Christian?"

Fauchelevent answered:

"All of our family are such."

"Is this your little girl?"

Fauchelevent answered:

"Yes, reverend mother."

"You are her father?"

Fauchelevent answered:

"Her grandfather."

The mother said to the prioress in an undertone:

"He answers well."

Jean Valjean had not spoken a word.

The prioress looked at Cosette attentively, and then said, aside to the mother—

"She will be homely."

The two mothers talked together very low for a few minutes in a corner of the parlor, and then the prioress turned and said—

"Father Fauvent, you will have another knee-cap and bell. We need two, now."

So, next morning, two little bells were heard tinkling in the garden, and the nuns could not keep from lifting a corner of their veils. They saw two men digging side by side, in the lower part of the garden under the trees—Fauvent and another. Immense event! The silence was broken, so far as to say—

"It's an assistant-gardener!"

The mothers added:

"He is Father Fauvent's brother."

In fact, Jean Valjean was regularly installed; he had the leather knee-cap and the bell; henceforth he had his commission. His name was Ultimus Fauchelevent.

The strongest recommendation for Cosette's admission had been the remark of the prioress: *She will be homely.*

The prioress having uttered this prediction, immediately took Cosette into her friendship and gave her a place in the school building as a charity pupil.

THE CLOSE

COSETTE, at the convent, still kept silent. She very naturally thought herself Jean Valjean's daughter. Moreover, knowing nothing, there was nothing she could tell, and then, in any case, she would not have told anything. As we have remarked, nothing habituates children to silence like misfortune. Cosette had suffered so much that she was afraid of everything, even to speak, even to breathe.

Cosette, in becoming a pupil at the convent, had to assume the dress of the school girls. Jean Valjean succeeded in having the garments which she laid aside given to him. It was the same mourning suit he had carried for her to put on when she left the Thénardiers. It was not much worn. Jean Valjean rolled up these garments, as well as the woollen stockings and shoes, with much camphor and other aromatic substances of which there is such an abundance in convents, and packed them in a small valise which he managed to procure. He put this valise in a chair near his bed, and always kept the key of it in his pocket.

The convent was to Jean Valjean like an island surrounded by wide waters. These four walls were, henceforth, the world to him. Within them he could see enough of the sky to be calm, and enough of Cosette to be happy.

A very pleasant life began again for him.

Jean Valjean worked every day in the garden, and was very

useful there. He had formerly been a pruner, and now found it quite in his way to be a gardener. It may be remembered that he knew all kinds of receipts and secrets of field-work. These he turned to account. Nearly all the orchard trees were wild stock; he grafted them and made them bear excellent fruit.

Cosette was allowed to come every day, and pass an hour with him. As the sisters were melancholy, and he was kind, the child compared him with them, and worshipped him. Every day, at the hour appointed, she would hurry to the little building. When she entered the old place, she filled it with Paradise. Jean Valjean basked in her presence and felt his own happiness increase by reason of the happiness he conferred on Cosette. At the hours of recreation, Jean Valjean from a distance watched her playing and romping, and he could distinguish her laughter from the laughter of the rest.

When the recreation was over and Cosette went in, Jean Valjean watched the windows of her schoolroom, and, at night, would rise from his bed to take a look at the windows of the room in which she slept.

God has his own ways. The convent contributed, like Cosette, to confirm and complete, in Jean Valjean, the work of the bishop.

Everything around him, this quiet garden, these balmy flowers, these children, shouting with joy, these meek and simple women, this silent cloister, gradually entered into all his being, and, little by little, his soul subsided into silence like this cloister, into fragrance like these flowers, into peace like this garden, into simplicity like these women, into joy like these children. And then he reflected that two houses of God had received him in succession at the two critical moments of his life, the first when every door was closed and human society repelled him; the second, when human society again howled upon his track, and the galleys once more gaped for him; and that, had it not been for the first, he should have fallen back into crime, and had it not been for the second, into punishment.

His whole heart melted in gratitude, and he loved more and more.

Several years passed thus. Cosette was growing.

MARIUS

The Grand Bourgeois

NINETY YEARS OLD AND THIRTY-TWO TEETH

In the Rue Boucherat, Rue de Normandie, and Rue de Saintonge, there still remain a few old inhabitants who preserve a memory of a fine old man named M. Gillenormand, and who like to talk about him.

M. Gillenormand, who was as much alive as any man can be, in 1831, was one of those men who have become curiosities, simply because they have lived a long time; and who are strange, because formerly they were like everybody else, and now they are no longer like anybody else. He was a peculiar old man, and very truly a man of another age—the genuine bourgeois of the eighteenth century, a very perfect specimen, a little haughty, wearing his good old bourgeoisie as marquises wear their Marquisates. He had passed his ninetieth year, walked erect, spoke in a loud voice, saw clearly, drank hard, ate, slept, and snored. He had every one of his thirty-two teeth. He wore glasses only when reading. He had an unmarried daughter over fifty years old, whom he belabored severely when he was angry, and whom he would gladly have horsewhipped. She seemed to him about eight years old. He cuffed his domestics vigorously.

TWO DO NOT MAKE A PAIR

THE two daughters of Monsieur Gillenormand were born ten years apart. In their youth they resembled each other very little; and in character, as well as in countenance, were as far from being sisters as possible. The younger was a cheerful soul, attracted towards everything that is bright, busy with flowers, poetry, and music, carried away into the glories of space, enthusiastic, ethereal, affianced from childhood in the ideal to a dim heroic figure. The elder had also her chimera; in the azure depth she saw a contractor, some good, coarse commissary, very rich, a husband splendidly stupid, a million-made man, or even a prefect; receptions at the prefecture, an usher of the ante-chamber, with the chain on his neck, official balls, harangues at the mayor's, to be *"Madame la préfete,"* this whirled in her imagination. The two sisters wandered thus, each in her own fancy, when they were young girls. Both had wings, one like an angel, the other like a goose.

No ambition is fully realised, here below at least. No paradise becomes terrestrial at the period in which we live. The younger had married the man of her dreams, but she was dead. The elder was not married.

At the moment she makes her entry into the story which we are relating, she was an old piece of virtue, an incombustible prude, one of the sharpest noses and one of the most obtuse minds which could be discovered. A characteristic incident. Outside of the immediate family nobody had ever known her first name. She was called *Mademoiselle Gillenormand the elder.*

In cant, Mademoiselle Gillenormand the elder could have given odds to an English miss. She was immodestly modest. She had one frightful reminiscence in her life: one day a man had seen her garter.

Age had only increased this pitiless modesty. Her dress front was never thick enough, and never rose high enough. She multiplied hooks and pins where nobody thought of looking. The peculiarity of prudery is to multiply sentinels, in proportion as the fortress is less threatened.

However, explain who can these ancient mysteries of innocence, she allowed herself to be kissed without displeasure, by an officer of lancers who was her grand-nephew and whose name was Théodule.

Spite of this favored lancer, the title *Prude,* under which we have classed her, fitted her absolutely. Mademoiselle Gillenormand was a kind of twilight soul. Prudery is half a virtue and half a vice.

To prudery she added bigotry, a suitable lining. She was of the fraternity of the Virgin, wore a white veil on certain feast-days, muttered special prayers, revered "the holy blood," venerated "the sacred heart," remained for hours in contemplation before an old-fashioned Jesuit altar in a chapel closed to the vulgar faithful, and let her soul fly away among the little marble clouds and along the grand rays of gilded wood.

We must say that in growing old, Mademoiselle Gillenormand had rather gained than lost. She was sad with an obscure sadness of which she had not the secret herself. There was in her whole person the stupor of a life ended but never commenced.

She kept her father's house. Monsieur Gillenormand had his daughter with him as we have seen Monseigneur Bienvenu have his sister with him. These households of an old man and an old maid are not rare, and always have the touching aspect of two feeblenesses leaning upon each other.

There was besides in the house, between this old maid and this old man, a child, a little boy, always trembling and mute before M. Gillenormand. M. Gillenormand never spoke to this child but with stern voice, and sometimes with uplifted cane: *"Here! Monsieur—rascal, black-guard, come here! Answer me, rogue! Let me see you, scape-grace!"* etc. etc. He idolized him.

It was his grandson. We shall see this child again.

The Grandfather and the Grandson

WHOEVER, at that day, had passed through the little city of Vernon, and walked over that beautiful monumental bridge which will be very soon replaced, let us hope, by some horrid wire bridge, would have noticed, as his glance fell from the top of the parapet, a man of about fifty, with a leather casque on his head, dressed in pantaloons and waistcoat of coarse grey cloth, to which something yellow was stitched which had been a red ribbon, shod in wooden shoes, browned by the sun, his face almost black and his hair almost white, a large scar upon his forehead extending down his cheek, bent, bowed down, older than his years, walking nearly every day with a spade and a pruning knife in his hand, in one of those walled compartments, in the vicinity of the bridge, which, like a chain of terraces border the left bank of the Seine,— charming enclosures full of flowers of which one would say, if they were much larger, they are gardens, and if they were a little smaller, they are bouquets. All these enclosures are bounded by the river on one side and by a house on the other. The man in the waistcoat and wooden shoes of whom we have just spoken lived, about the year 1817, in the smallest of these enclosures and the humblest of these houses. He lived there solitary and alone, in silence and in poverty, with a woman who was neither young nor old, neither beautiful nor ugly, neither peasant nor bourgeois, who waited upon him. The square of earth which he called his garden was celebrated in the town for the beauty of the flowers which he cultivated in it. Flowers were his occupation.

Whoever, at the same time, had read the military memoirs, the biographies, the *Moniteur*, and the bulletins of the Grand Army, would have been struck by a name which appears rather often, the name of George Pontmercy. When quite young, this George Pontmercy was a soldier in the regiment of Saintonge. The revolution broke out. The regiment of aintonge was in the Army of the Rhine. For the old regiments of the monarchy kept their province names even after he fall of the monarchy, and were not brigaded until 1794. 'ontmercy fought at Spires, at Worms, at Neustadt, at Turkeim, at Alzey, at Mayence where he was one of the two undred who formed Houchard's rear-guard. He with eleven thers held their ground against the Prince of Hesse's corps ehind the old rampart of Andernach, and only fell back pon the bulk of the army when the hostile cannon had ffected a breach from the top of the parapet to the slope of he glacis. He was under Kleber at Marchiennes, and at the attle of Mont Palissel, where he had his arm broken by a musket-ball. Then he passed to the Italian frontier, and he was one of the thirty grenadiers who defended the Col di Tende with Joubert. Joubert was made Adjutant-General, and Pontmercy Second-Lieutenant. Pontmercy was by the side of Berthier in the midst of the storm of balls on that day of Lodi of which Bonaparte said: *Berthier was cannoneer, cavalier, and grenadier*. He saw his old general, Joubert, fall at Novi, at the moment when, with uplifted sword, he was crying: Forward! Being embarked with his company, through the necessities of the campaign, in a pinnace, which was on the way from Genoa to some little port on the coast, he fell into a wasp's-nest of seven or eight English vessels. The Genoese captain wanted to throw the guns into the sea, hide the soldiers in the hold, and slip through in the dark like a merchantman. Pontmercy had the colors seized to the halyards of the ensign-staff, and passed proudly under the guns of the British frigates. Fifty miles further on, his boldness increasing, he attacked with his pinnace and captured a large English transport carrying troops to Sicily, so loaded with men and horses that the vessel was full to the hatches. In 1805, he was in that division of Malher which captured Günzburg from the Archduke Ferdinand. At Weltingen he received in his arms under a shower of balls Colonel Maupetit, who was mortally wounded at the head of the 9th Dragoons. He distinguished himself at Austerlitz in that wonderful march in echelon under the enemy's fire. When the cavalry of the Russian Imperial Guard crushed a battalion of the 4th of the Line, Pontmercy was one of those who revenged the repulse, and overthrew the Guard. The emperor gave him the cross. Pontmercy successively saw Wurmser made prisoner in Mantua, Melas in Alexandria, and Mack in Ulm. He was in the eighth corps, of the Grand Army, which Mortier commanded, and which took Hamburg. Then he passed into the 55th of the Line, which was the old Flanders regiment. At Eylau, he was in the churchyard where the heroic captain Louis Hugo, uncle of the author of this book, sustained alone with his company of eighty-three men, for two hours, the whole effort of the enemy's army. Pontmercy was one of the three who came out of that churchyard alive. He was at Friedland. Then he saw Moscow, then the Beresina, then Lutzen, Bautzen, Dresden, Wachau, Leipsic, and the defiles of Glenhausen, then Montmirail, Chateau-Thierry, Caron, the banks of the Marne, the banks of the Aisne, and the formidable position at Laon. At Arney le Duc, a captain, he sabered ten cossacks, and saved, not his general, but his corporal. He was wounded on that occasion, and twenty-seven splinters were extracted from his left arm alone. Eight days before the capitulation of Paris, he exchanged with a comrade, and entered the cavalry. He had what was called under the old régime *the doublehand,* that is to say, equal skill in managing, as a soldier, the saber or the musket, as an officer, a squadron or a battalion. It is this skill, perfected by military education, which gives rise to certain special arms, the dragoons, for instance, who are both cavalry and infantry. He accompanied Napoleon to the island of Elba. At Waterloo he led a squadron of cuirassiers in Dubois' brigade. He it was who took the colors from the Lunenburg battalion. He carried the colors to the emperor's feet. He was covered with blood. He had received, in seizing the colors, a saber stroke across his face. The emperor, well pleased, cried to him: *You are a Colonel, you are a Baron, you are an Officer of the Legion of Honour!* Pontmercy answered: *Sire, I thank you for my widow.* An hour afterwards, he fell in the ravine of Ohain.

After Waterloo, Pontmercy, drawn out from the sunken road of Ohain, succeeded in regaining the army, and was passed along from ambulance to ambulance to the cantonments of the Loire.

The Restoration put him on half-pay, then sent him to a residence, that is to say under surveillance at Vernon. The king, Louis XVIII, ignoring all that had been done in the Hundred Days, recognized neither his position of officer of the Legion of Honor, nor his rank of colonel, nor his title of baron. He, on his part, neglected no opportunity to sign himself *Colonel Baron Pontmercy*. He had only one old blue coat, and he never went out without putting on the rosette of an officer of the Legion of Honor. The *procureur du roi* notified him that he would be prosecuted for "illegally" wearing this decoration. When this notice was given to him by a friendly intermediary, Pontmercy answered with a bitter smile: "I do not know whether it is that I no longer understand French, or you no longer speak it; but the fact is I do not understand you." Then he went out every day for a week with his rosette. Nobody dared to disturb him. Two or three times the minister of war or the general commanding the department wrote to him with this address: *Monsieur Commandant Pontmercy.* He returned the letters unopened. At the same time, Napoleon at St. Helena was treating Sir Hudson Lowe's missives addressed to *General Bonaparte* in the same way. Pontmercy at last, excuse the word, came to have in his mouth the same saliva as his emperor.

One morning, he met the *procureur du roi* in one of the streets of Vernon, went up to him and said: "Monsieur *procureur du roi*, am I allowed to wear my scar?"

He had nothing but his very scanty half-pay as chief of squadron. He hired the smallest house he could find in Vernon. He lived there alone; how we have just seen. Under the empire, between two wars, he had found time to marry Mademoiselle Gillenormand. The old bourgeois, who really felt outraged, consented with a sigh, saying: *"The greatest families are forced to it."* In 1815, Madame Pontmercy, an admirable woman in every respect, noble and rare, and worthy of her husband, died, leaving a child. This child would have been the colonel's joy in his solitude; but the grandfather had imperiously demanded his grandson, declaring that, unless he were given up to him, he would disinherit him. The father yielded for the sake of the little boy, and not being able to have his child he set about loving flowers.

He had moreover given up everything, making no movement nor conspiring with others. He divided his thoughts between the innocent things he was doing, and the grand things he had done. He passed his time hoping for a pink or remembering Austerlitz.

M. Gillenormand had no intercourse with his son-in-law. The colonel was to him "a bandit," and he was to the colonel "a blockhead." M. Gillenormand never spoke of the colonel, unless sometimes to make mocking allusions to "his barony." It was expressly understood that Pontmercy should never endeavor to see his son or speak to him, under pain of the boy being turned away, and disinherited. To the Gillenormands, Pontmercy was pestiferous. They intended to bring up the child to their liking. The colonel did wrong perhaps to accept these conditions, but he submitted to them, thinking that he was doing right, and sacrificing himself alone.

The inheritance from the grandfather Gillenormand was a small affair, but the inheritance from Mlle. Gillenormand the elder was considerable. This aunt, who had remained single, was very rich from the maternal side, and the son of her sister was her natural heir. The child, whose name was Marius, knew that he had a father, but nothing more. Nobody spoke a word to him about him. However, in the society into which his grandfather took him, the whisperings, the hints, the winks, enlightened the little boy's mind at length; he finally comprehended something of it, and as he naturally imbibed, by a sort of infiltration and slow penetration, the ideas and opinions which formed, so to say, the air he breathed, he came little by little to think of his father only with shame and with a closed heart.

While he was thus growing up, every two or three months the colonel would escape, come furtively to Paris like a fugitive from justice breaking his ban, and go to Saint Sulpice, at the hour when Aunt Gillenormand took Marius to mass. There, trembling lest the aunt should turn round, concealed behind a pillar, motionless, not daring to breathe, he saw his child. The scarred veteran was afraid of the old maid.

From this, in fact, came his connection with the curé of Vernon, Abbé Mabeuf.

This worthy priest was the brother of a warden of Saint Sulpice, who had several times noticed this man gazing upon his child, and the scar on his cheek, and the big tears in his eyes. This man, who had so really the appearance of a man, and who wept like a woman, had attracted the warden's attention. This face remained in his memory. One day, having gone to Vernon to see his brother, he met Colonel Pontmercy on the bridge, and recognized the man of Saint Sulpice. The warden spoke of it to the curé, and the two, under some pretext, made the colonel a visit. This visit led to others. The colonel, who at first was very reserved, finally unbosomed himself, and the curé and the warden came to know the whole story, and how Pontmercy was sacrificing his own happiness to the future of his child. The result was that the curé felt a veneration and tenderness for him, and the colonel, on his part, felt an affection for the curé. And, moreover, when it happens that both are sincere and good, nothing will mix and amalgamate more easily than an old priest and an old soldier. In reality, they are the same kind of man. One has devoted himself to his country upon earth, the other to his country in heaven; there is no other difference.

Twice a year, on the first of January and on St. George's Day, Marius wrote filial letters to his father, which his aunt dictated, and which, one would have said, were copied from some Complete Letter Writer; this was all that M. Gillenormand allowed; and the father answered with very tender letters, which the grandfather thrust into his pocket without reading.

END OF THE BRIGAND

THE completion of Marius' classical studies was coincident with M. Gillenormand's retirement from the world. The old man bade farewell to the Faubourg Saint Germain, and to Madame de T.'s salon, and established himself in the Marais, at his house in the Rue des Filles du Calvaire.

In 1827, Marius had just attained his eighteenth year. On coming in one evening, he saw his grandfather with a letter in his hand.

"Marius," said M. Gillenormand, "you will set out tomorrow for Vernon."

"What for?" said Marius.

"To see your father."

Marius shuddered. He had thought of everything but this, that a day might come when he would have to see his father. Nothing could have been more unlooked for, more surprising, and, we must say, more disagreeable. It was aversion compelled to intimacy. It was not chagrin; no, it was pure drudgery.

Marius, besides his feelings of political antipathy, was convinced that his father, the saberer, as M. Gillenormand called him in the gentler moments, did not love him; that was clear, since he had abandoned him and left him to others. Feeling that he was not loved at all, he had no love. Nothing more natural, said he to himself.

He was so astounded that he did not question M. Gillenormand. The grandfather continued:

"It appears that he is sick. He asks for you."

And after a moment of silence he added:

"Start to-morrow morning. I think there is at the Cour des Fontaines a conveyance which starts at six o'clock and arrives at night. Take it. He says the case is urgent."

Then he crumpled up the letter and put it in his pocket. Marius could have started that evening and been with his father the next morning. A diligence then made the trip to Rouen from the Rue du Bouloi by night passing through Vernon. Neither M. Gillenormand nor Marius thought of inquiring.

The next day at dusk, Marius arrived at Vernon. Candles were just beginning to be lighted. He asked the first person he met for *the house of Monsieur Pontmercy*. For in his feelings he agreed with the Restoration, and he, too, recognised his father neither as baron nor as colonel.

The house was pointed out to him. He rang; a woman came and opened the door with a small lamp in her hand.

"Monsieur Pontmercy?" said Marius.

The woman remained motionless.

"Is it here?" asked Marius.

The woman gave an affirmative nod of the head.

"Can I speak with him?"

The woman gave a negative sign.

"But I am his son!" resumed Marius. "He expects me."

"He expects you no longer," said the woman.

Then he perceived that she was in tears.

She pointed to the door of a low room; he entered.

In this room, which was lighted by a tallow candle on the mantel, there were three men, one of them standing, one on his knees, and one stripped to his shirt and lying at full length upon the floor. The one upon the floor was the colonel.

The two others were a physician and a priest who was praying.

The colonel had been three days before attacked with a brain fever. At the beginning of the sickness, having a presentiment of ill, he had written to Monsieur Gillenormand to ask for his son. He had grown worse. On the very evening of Marius' arrival at Vernon, the colonel had had a fit of delirium; he sprang out of his bed in spite of the servant, crying: "My son has not come! I am going to meet him!"

Then he had gone out of his room and fallen upon the floor of the hall. He had but just died.

The doctor and the curé had been sent for. The doctor had come too late. The son also had come too late.

Marius looked upon this man, whom he saw for the first time, and for the last—this venerable and manly face, these open eyes which saw not, this white hair, these robust limbs upon which he distinguished here and there brown lines which were saber-cuts, and a species of red stars which were bullet-holes. He looked upon that gigantic scar which imprinted heroism upon this face on which God had impressed goodness. He thought that this man was his father and that this man was dead, and he remained unmoved.

At the same time he felt something like remorse, and he despised himself for acting thus. But was it his fault? He did not love his father, indeed!

The colonel left nothing. The sale of his furniture hardly paid for his burial. The servant found a scrap of paper which she handed to Marius. It contained this, in the handwriting of the colonel:

"For my Son.—The emperor made me a baron upon the battlefield of Waterloo. Since the Restoration contests this title which I have bought with my blood, my son will take it and bear it. I need not say that he will be worthy of it." On the back, the colonel had added: "At this same battle of Waterloo, a sergeant saved my life. This man's name is Thénardier. Not long ago, I believe he was keeping a little tavern in a village in the suburbs of Paris, at Chelles or at Montfermeil. If my son meets him, he will do Thénardier all the service he can."

Not from duty towards his father, but on account of that vague respect for death which is always so imperious in the heart of man, Marius took this paper and pressed it.

No trace remained of the colonel. Monsieur Gillenormand had his sword and uniform sold to a second-hand dealer. The neighbors stripped the garden and carried off the rare flowers. The other plants became briery and scraggy, and died.

Marius remained only forty-eight hours at Vernon. After the burial, he returned to Paris and went back to his law, thinking no more of his father than if he had never lived. In two days the colonel had been buried, and in three days forgotten.

Marius wore crepe on his hat. That was all.

MARIUS had preserved the religious habits of his childhood. One Sunday he had gone to hear mass at Saint Sulpice, at this same chapel of the Virgin to which his aunt took him when he was a little boy, and being that day more absent-minded and dreamy than usual, he took his place behind a pillar and knelt down, without noticing it, before a Utrecht velvet chair, on the back of which this name was written: *Monsieur Mabeuf, church-warden.* The mass had hardly commenced when an old man presented himself and said to Marius:

"Monsieur, this is my place."

Marius moved away readily, and the old man took his chair.

After mass, Marius remained absorbed in thought a few steps distant; the old man approached him again and said: "I beg your pardon, monsieur, for having disturbed you a little while ago, and for disturbing you again now; but you must have thought me impertinent, and I must explain myself."

"Monsieur," said Marius, "it is unnecessary."

"Yes!" resumed the old man; "I do not wish you to have a bad opinion of me. You see I think a great deal of that place. It seems to me that the mass is better there. Why? I will tell you. To that place I have seen for ten years, regularly, every two or three months, a poor, brave father come, who had no other opportunity and no other way of seeing his child, being prevented through some family arrangements. He came at the hour when he knew his son was brought to mass. He looked at his child, and wept. This poor man worshipped this little boy. I saw that. This place has become sanctified, as it were, for me, and I have acquired the habit of coming here to hear mass. I prefer it to the bench, where I have a right to be as a warden. I was even acquainted slightly

with this unfortunate gentleman. He had a father-in-law, a
rich aunt, relatives, I do not remember exactly, who threatened to disinherit the child if he, the father, should see him.
He had sacrificed himself that his son might some day be rich
and happy. They were separated by political opinions. Certainly I approve of political opinions, but there are people
who do not know where to stop. Bless me! because a man was
at Waterloo he is not a monster; a father is not separated
from his child for that. He was one of Bonaparte's colonels.
He is dead, I believe. He lived at Vernon, where my brother is
curé, and his name is something like Pontmarie, Montpercy.
He had a handsome sabre cut."

"Pontmercy," said Marius, turning pale.

"Exactly; Pontmercy. Did you know him?"

"Monsieur," said Marius, "he was my father."

The old churchwarden clasped his hands, and exclaimed—

"Ah! you are the child! Yes, that is it; he ought to be a
man now. Well! poor child, you can say that you had a father
who loved you well."

Marius offered his arm to the old man, and walked with
him to his house. Next day he said to Monsieur Gillenormand:—

"We have arranged a hunting party with a few friends.
Will you permit me to be absent for three days?"

"Four," answered the grandfather; "go; amuse yourself."

And, with a wink he whispered to his daughter—

"Some love affair!"

WHAT IT IS TO HAVE MET A CHURCH WARDEN

MARIUS was absent three days, then he returned to Paris,
went straight to the library of the law-school, and asked for
the file of the *Moniteur*.

He read the *Moniteur*; he read all the histories of the republic and the empire; the *Memorial de Sainte-Hélène;* all
the memoirs, journals, bulletins, proclamations; he devoured
everything.

It was a passion, indeed. Marius was on the way to adoration for his father.

As when one has a key, everything opened; he explained to
himself what he had hated, he penetrated what he had ab-

horred; he saw clearly henceforth the providential, divine, and human meaning of the great things which he had been taught to detest, and the great men whom he had been instructed to curse. When he thought of his former opinions, which were only of yesterday, but which seemed so ancient to him already, he became indignant at himself, and he smiled. From the rehabilitation of his father he had naturally passed to the rehabilitation of Napoleon.

When, in this mysterious labor, he had entirely cast off his old Bourbon and ultra skin, when he had shed the aristocrat, the jacobite, and the royalist, when he was fully revolutionary, thoroughly democratic, and almost republican, he went to an engraver on the Quai des Orfévres, and ordered a hundred cards bearing this name: *Baron Marius Pontmercy*.

Marius was absent for a while from time to time.

"Where can he go to?" asked the aunt.

On one of these journeys, which were always very short, he went to Montfermeil in obedience to the injunction which his father had left him, and sought for the former sergeant of Waterloo, the innkeeper Thénardier. Thénardier had failed, the inn was closed, and nobody knew what had become of him. While making these researches, Marius was away from the house four days.

"Decidedly," said the grandfather, "he is going astray."

They thought they noticed that he wore something, upon his breast and under his shirt, hung from his neck by a black ribbon.

SOME PETTICOAT

WE have spoken of a lancer.

He was a grand-nephew of M. Gillenormand's on the paternal side, who passed his life away from his family, and far from all domestic hearths in garrison. Lieutenant Théodule Gillenormand fulfilled all the conditions required for what is called a handsome officer. He came to Paris very rarely, so rarely that Marius had never seen him. Théodule was the favourite of Aunt Gillenormand, who preferred him because she did not see him.

One morning, Mlle. Gillenormand the elder had retired to

her room as much excited as her placidity allowed. Marius
had asked his grandfather again for permission to make a
short journey, adding that he intended to set out that evening. "Go!" the grandfather had answered, and M. Gillenormand had added aside, lifting his eyebrows to the top of
his forehead: "He is getting to be an old offender." Mlle.
Gillenormand had returned to her room very much perplexed.

As a diversion from this curiosity which was giving her
a little more agitation than she allowed herself, she took refuge in her talents, and began to festoon cotton upon cotton,
in one of those embroideries of the time of the empire and
the restoration in which a great many cab wheels appear.
She had been sitting in her chair for some hours when the
door opened. Mlle. Gillenormand raised her eyes; Lieutenant
Théodule was before her making the regulation bow.
She uttered a cry of pleasure.

"You here, Théodule!" exclaimed she.

"On my way, aunt."

"Embrace me then."

"Here goes!" said Théodule.

And he embraced her. Aunt Gillenormand went to her secretary, and opened it.

"You stay with us at least all the week?"

"Aunt, I leave this evening."

"Impossible!"

"Mathematically."

"Stay, my dear Théodule, I beg you."

"The heart says yes, but my orders say no. The story is
simple. Our station is changed; we were at Melun, we are sent
to Gaillon. To go from the old station to the new, we must
pass through Paris. I said: I am going to go and see my
aunt."

"Take this for your pains."

She put ten louis into his hand.

"You mean for my pleasure, dear aunt."

Théodule embraced her a second time, and she had the
happiness of having her neck a little chafed by the braid of
his uniform.

"Do you make the journey on horseback with your regiment?" she asked.

"No, aunt. I wanted to see you. I have a special permit.
My servant takes my horse; I go by the diligence. And, speaking of that, I have a question to ask you."

"What?"

"My cousin, Marius Pontmercy, is travelling also, is he?"

"How do you know that?" exclaimed the aunt, her curiosity suddenly excited to the quick.

"On my arrival, I went to the diligence to secure my place in the coupé."

"Well?"

"A traveller had already secured a place on the impériale. I saw his name on the book."

"What name?"

"Marius Pontmercy."

"The wicked fellow!" exclaimed the aunt. "Ah! your cousin is not a steady boy like you. To think that he is going to spend the night in a diligence."

"Like me."

"But for you, it is from duty; for him, it is from dissipation."

"What is the odds?" said Théodule.

Here, an event occurred in the life of Mademoiselle Gillenormand the elder; she had an idea. If she had been a man, she would have slapped her forehead. She apostrophized Théodule:

"Are you sure that your cousin does not know you?"

"Yes. I have seen him; but he has never deigned to notice me."

"And you are going to travel together so?"

"He on the impériale, I in the coupé."

"Where does this diligence go?"

"To Les Andelys."

"Is there where Marius is going?"

"Unless, like me, he stops on the road. I get off at Vernon to take the branch for Gaillon. I know nothing of Marius' route."

"Marius! what an ugly name! What an idea it was to name him Marius! But you at least—your name is Théodule!"

"I would rather it were Alfred," said the officer.

"Listen, Théodule."

"Yes."

"Well, Marius is often away."

"Eh! eh!"

"He travels."

"Ah! ah!"

"He sleeps away."

"Oh! oh!"

"We want to know what is at the bottom of it."

Théodule answered with the calmness of a man of bronze: "Some petticoat."

And with that stifled chuckle which reveals certainty, he added:

"A lass."

"That is clear," exclaimed the aunt, who thought she heard Monsieur Gillenormand speak, and who felt her conviction spring irresistibly from this word.

She resumed:

"Do us a kindness. Follow Marius a little way. He does not know you, it will be easy for you. Since there is a lass, try to see the lass. You can write us the account. It will amuse grandfather."

Théodule had no excessive taste for this sort of watching; but he was much affected by the ten louis, and he thought he saw a possible succession of them. He accepted the commission and said: "As you please, aunt." And he added aside: "There I am, a duenna."

Mademoiselle Gillenormand embraced him.

Marius, on the evening which followed this dialogue, mounted the diligence without suspecting that he was watched. As to the watchman, the first thing that he did was to fall asleep.

At daybreak, the driver of the diligence shouted: "Vernon! Vernon relay! passengers for Vernon?" And Lieutenant Théodule awoke.

"Good," growled he, half asleep, "here I get off."

Then, his memory clearing up by degrees, an effect of awakening, he remembered his aunt, the ten louis, and the account he was to render of Marius' acts and deeds. It made him laugh.

"Perhaps he has left the coach," thought he, while he buttoned up his undress waistcoat.

At this moment a pair of black pantaloons getting down from the impériale appeared before the window of the coupé.

"Can that be Marius?" said the lieutenant.

It was Marius.

A little peasant girl, beside the coach, among the horses and postillions, was offering flowers to the passengers. "Flowers for your ladies," cried she.

Marius approached her and, bought the most beautiful flowers in her basket.

"Now," said Théodule leaping down from the coach, "there is something that interests me. Who the deuce is he going to carry those flowers to? It ought to be a mighty pretty woman for so fine a bouquet. I would like to see her."

And, no longer now by command, but from personal curiosity, like those dogs who hunt on their own account, he began to follow Marius.

Marius paid no attention to Théodule. Some elegant women got out of the diligence; he did not look at them. He seemed to see nothing about him.

"Is he in love?" thought Théodule.

Marius walked towards the church.

"All right," said Théodule to himself. "The church! that is it. These rendezvous which are spiced with a bit of mass are the best of all. Nothing is so exquisite as an ogle which passes across the good God."

Arriving at the church, Marius did not go in, but went behind the building. He disappeared at the corner of one of the buttresses of the apsis.

"The rendezvous is outside," said Théodule. "Let us see the lass."

And he advanced on tiptoe towards the corner which Marius had turned.

On reaching it, he stopped, astounded.

Marius, his face hid in his hands, was kneeling in the grass, upon a grave. He had scattered his bouquet. At the end of the grave, at an elevation which marked the head, there was a black wooden cross, with this name in white letters: COLONEL BARON PONTMERCY. He heard Marius sobbing.

The lass was a tomb.

MARBLE AGAINST GRANITE

IT was here that Marius had come the first time that he absented himself from Paris. It was here that he returned every time that M. Gillenormand said: he sleeps out.

Lieutenant Théodule was absolutely disconcerted by this unexpected encounter with a sepulcher.

Marius returned from Vernon early in the morning of the

third day, was set down at his grandfather's, and, fatigued by the two nights passed in the diligence, feeling the need of making up for his lack of sleep by an hour at the swimming school, ran quickly up to his room, took only time enough to lay off his travelling coat and the black ribbon which he wore about his neck, and went away to the bath.

M. Gillenormand, who had risen early like all old persons who are in good health, had heard him come in, and hastened as fast as he could with his old legs to climb to the top of the stairs where Marius' room was, that he might embrace him, question him while embracing him, and find out something about where he came from.

But the youth had taken less time to go down than the octogenarian to go up, and when Grandfather Gillenormand entered the garret room, Marius was no longer there.

The bed was not disturbed, and upon the bed were displayed without distrust the coat and the black ribbon.

"I like that better," said M. Gillenormand.

And a moment afterwards he entered the parlor where Mademoiselle Gillenormand the elder was already seated, embroidering her cab wheels.

The entrance was triumphal.

M. Gillenormand held in one hand the coat and in the other the neck ribbon, and cried:

"Victory! We are going to penetrate the mystery! We shall know the end of the end, we shall feel of the libertinism of our trickster! here we are with the romance even. I have the portrait!"

In fact, a black shagreen box, much like to a medallion, was fastened to the ribbon.

The old man took this box and looked at it some time without opening it, with that air of desire, ravishment, and anger, with which a poor, hungry devil sees an excellent dinner pass under his nose, when it is not for him.

"For it is evidently a portrait. I know all about that. This is worn tenderly upon the heart.

"Let us see, father," said the old maid.

The box opened by pressing a spring. They found nothing in it but a piece of paper carefully folded.

"From the same to the same," said M. Gillenormand, bursting with laughter. "I know what that is. A love-letter!"

"Ah! then let us read it!" said the aunt.

And she put on her spectacles. They unfolded the paper and read this:

"*For my son.*—The emperor made me a baron upon the battlefield of Waterloo. Since the Restoration contests this title which I have bought with my blood, my son will take it and bear it. I need not say that he will be worthy of it."

The feelings of the father and daughter cannot be described. They did not exchange a word. M. Gillenormand, however, said in a low voice, and as if talking to himself:

"It is the handwriting of that saberer."

The aunt examined the paper, turned it on all sides, then put it back in the box.

Just at that moment, a little oblong package, wrapped in blue paper, fell from a pocket of the coat. Mademoiselle Gillenormand picked it up and unfolded the blue paper. It was Marius' hundred cards. She passed one of them to M. Gillenormand, who read: *Baron Marius Pontmercy.*

A few minutes afterwards, Marius made his appearance. He came in. Even before crossing the threshold of the parlor, he perceived his grandfather holding one of his cards in his hand, who, on seeing him, exclaimed with his crushing air of sneering, bourgeois superiority:

"Stop! stop! stop! stop! stop! you are a baron now. I present you my compliments. What does this mean?"

Marius colored slightly, and answered:

"It means that I am my father's son."

M. Gillenormand checked his laugh, and said harshly:

"Your father; I am your father."

"My father," resumed Marius with downcast eyes and stern manner, "was a humble and heroic man, who served the republic and France gloriously, who was great in the greatest history that men have ever made, who lived a quarter of a century in the camp, by day under grape and under balls, by night in the snow, in the mud, and in the rain, who captured colors, who received twenty wounds, who died forgotten and abandoned, and who had but one fault; that was in loving too dearly two ingrates, his country and me."

This was more than M. Gillenormand could listen to. At the word, *Republic*, he rose, or rather, sprang to his feet. Every one of the words which Marius had pronounced had produced the effect upon the old royalist's face of a blast from a bellows upon a burning coal. From dark he had become red, from red purple, and from purple, glowing.

"Marius!" exclaimed he, "abominable child! Look you, indeed, you are as much a baron as my slipper! they were all bandits who served Robespierre! all brigands who served B-u-o-naparte! all traitors who betrayed, betrayed, betrayed! their legitimate king! all cowards who ran from the Prussians and English at Waterloo!"

In his turn, Marius now became the coal, and M. Gillenormand the bellows. It was impossible for him to insult his grandfather, and it was equally impossible for him not to avenge his father. On one hand a sacred tomb, on the other white hairs. He was for a few moments dizzy and staggering with all this whirlwind in his head; then he raised his eyes, looked straight at his grandfather, and cried in a thundering voice:

"Down with the Bourbons, and the great hog Louis XVIII!"

Louis XVIII had been dead for four years; but it was all the same to him.

The old man, scarlet as he was, suddenly became whiter than his hair.

"A baron like Monsieur and a bourgeois like me cannot remain under the same roof."

And all at once straightening up, pallid, trembling, terrible, his forehead swelling with the fearful radiance of anger, he stretched his arm towards Marius and cried to him:

"Be off."

Marius left the house.

The next day, M. Gillenormand said to his daughter:

"You will send sixty pistoles every six months to this blood-drinker, and never speak of him to me again."

Having an immense residuum of fury to expend, and not knowing what to do with it, he spoke to his daughter with coldness for more than three months.

Marius, for his part, departed in indignation. A circumstance, which we must mention, had aggravated his exasperation still more. In hurriedly carrying away, at the old man's command, Marius' "things" to his room, Nicolette had, without perceiving it, dropped, probably on the garret stairs, which were dark, the black shagreen medallion which contained the paper written by the colonel. Neither the paper nor the medallion could be found. Marius was convinced that "Monsieur Gillenormand"—from that day forth he never named him otherwise—had thrown "his father's will" into the fire. He knew by heart the few lines written by the colonel, and consequently nothing was lost. But the paper, the writing, that sacred relic, all that was his heart itself. What had been done with it?

Marius went away without saying where he was going, and without knowing where he was going, with thirty francs, his watch, and a few clothes in a carpet bag. He hired a cabriolet by the hour, jumped in, and drove at random towards the Latin quarter.

What was Marius to do?

The Excellence of Misfortune

MARIUS NEEDY

LIFE became stern to Marius. To eat his coats and his watch was nothing. He chewed that inexpressible thing which is called *the cud of bitterness*. A horrible thing, which includes days without bread, nights without sleep, evenings without a candle, a hearth without a fire, weeks without labor, a future without hope, a coat out at the elbows, an old hat which makes young girls laugh, the door found shut against you at night because you have not paid your rent, the insolence of the porter and the landlord, the jibes of neighbors, humiliations, self-respect outraged, any drudgery acceptable, disgust, bitterness, prostration—Marius learned how one swallows down all these things, and how they are often the only things that one has to swallow.

There was a period in Marius' life when he swept his own hall, when he bought a pennyworth of Brie cheese at the market-woman's, when he waited for nightfall to make his way to the baker's and buy a loaf of bread, which he carried furtively to his garret, as if he had stolen it. Sometimes there was seen to glide into the corner meatmarket, in the midst of the jeering cooks who elbowed him, an awkward young man, with books under his arm, who had a timid and frightened appearance, and who, as he entered, took off his hat from his forehead, which was dripping with sweat, made a low bow to the astonished butcher, another bow to the butcher's boy, asked for a mutton cutlet, paid six or seven sous for it, wrapped it up in paper, put it under his arm between two books, and went away. It was Marius. On this cutlet, which he cooked himself, he lived three days.

The first day he ate the meat; the second day he ate the fat; the third day he gnawed the bone. On several occasions, Aunt Gillenormand made overtures, and sent him the sixty pistoles. Marius always sent them back, saying that he had no need of anything.

He was still in mourning for his father when the revolution which we have described was accomplished in his ideas. Since then, he had never left off black clothes. His clothes left him, however. A day came, at last, when he had no coat. His trousers were going also. What was to be done? Courfeyrac, for whom he also had done some good turns, gave him an old coat. For thirty sous, Marius had it turned by some porter or other, and it was a new coat. But this coat was green. Then Marius did not go out till after nightfall. That made his coat black. Desiring always to be in mourning, he clothed himself with night.

Through all this, he procured admission to the bar. He was reputed to occupy Courfeyrac's room, which was decent, and where a certain number of law books, supported and filled out by some odd volumes of novels, made up the library required by the rules.

When Marius had become a lawyer, he informed his grandfather of it, in a letter which was frigid, but full of submission and respect. M. Gillenormand took the letter with trembling hands, read it, and threw it, torn in pieces, into the basket.

MARIUS POOR

It is with misery as with everything else. It gradually becomes endurable.

He had got out of the narrowest place; the pass widened a little before him. By dint of hard work, courage, perseverance, and will, he had succeeded in earning by his labor about seven hundred francs a year. He had learned German and English; thanks to Courfeyrac, who introduced him to his friend the publisher, Marius filled, in the literary department of the book house, the useful rôle of *utility*. He made out prospectuses, translated from the journals, annotated republications, compiled biographies, etc.; net result, year in and year out, seven hundred francs. He lived on this. How? Not badly. We are going to tell.

Marius occupied, at an annual rent of thirty francs, a wretched little room in the Gorbeau tenement, with no fireplace, called a cabinet, in which there was no more furniture than was indispensable. The furniture was his own. He gave three francs a month to the old woman who had charge of the building, for sweeping his room and bringing him every morning a little warm water, a fresh egg, and a penny loaf of bread. On this loaf and this egg he breakfasted. His breakfast varied from two to four sous, as eggs were cheap or dear. At six o'clock in the evening he went down into the Rue Saint Jacques, to dine at Rousseau's, opposite Basset's the print dealer's, at the corner of the Rue des Mathurins. He ate no soup. He took a sixpenny plate of meat, a threepenny half-plate of vegetables, and a threepenny dessert. For three sous, as much bread as he liked. As for wine, he drank water. On paying at the counter, where Madame Rousseau was seated majestically, still plump and fresh also in those days, he gave a sou to the waiter, and Madame Rousseau gave him a smile. Then he went away. For sixteen sous, he had a smile and a dinner.

Thus, breakfast four sous, dinner sixteen sous, his food cost him twenty sous a day, which was three hundred and sixty-five francs a year. Add the thirty francs for his lodging, and the thirty-six francs to the old woman, and a few other trifling expenses, and for four hundred and fifty francs, Marius was fed, lodged, and waited upon. His clothes cost him a hundred francs, his linen fifty francs, his washing fifty francs; the whole did not exceed six hundred and fifty francs. This left him fifty francs. He was rich.

Marius always had two complete suits, one old "for every day," the other quite new, for special occasions. Both were black. He had but three shirts, one he had on, another in the drawer, the third at the washerwoman's. He renewed them as they wore out. They were usually ragged, so he buttoned his coat to his chin.

For Marius to arrive at this flourishing condition had required years. Hard years, and difficult ones; those to get through, these to climb. Marius had never given up for a single day. He had undergone everything, in the shape of privation; he had done everything, except get into debt. Rather than borrow, he did not eat. He had had many days of fasting.

In all his trials he felt encouraged and sometimes even upborne by a secret force within.

By the side of his father's name, another name was engraven upon Marius' heart, the name of Thénardier. Marius, in his enthusiastic yet serious nature, surrounded with a sort of halo the man to whom, as he thought, he owed his father's life, that brave sergeant who had saved the colonel in the midst of the balls and bullets of Waterloo. He never separated the memory of this man from the memory of his father, and he associated them in his veneration. It was a sort of worship with two steps, the high altar for the colonel, the low one for Thénardier. The idea of the misfortune into which he knew that Thénardier had fallen and been engulfed, intensified his feeling of gratitude. Marius had learned at Montfermeil of the ruin and bankruptcy of the unlucky innkeeper. Since then, he had made untold effort to get track of him, and to endeavor to find him, in that dark abyss of misery in which Thénardier had disappeared. Marius blamed and almost hated himself for not succeeding in his researches. This was the only debt which the colonel had left him, and Marius made it a point of honor to pay it. "What," thought he, "when my father lay dying on the field of battle, Thénardier could find him through the smoke and the grape, and bring him off on his shoulders, and yet he owed him nothing; while I, who owe so much to Thénardier, I cannot reach him in that darkness in which he is suffering, and restore him, in my turn, from death to life. Oh! I will find him!"

MARIUS A MAN

MARIUS was now twenty years old. It was three years since he had left his grandfather. They remained on the same terms on both sides, without attempting a reconciliation, and without seeking to meet. And, indeed, what was the use of meeting? to come in conflict?

To tell the truth, Marius was mistaken as to his grandfather's heart. He imagined that M. Gillenormand had never loved him, and that this crusty and harsh yet smiling old man, who swore, screamed, stormed, and lifted his cane, felt for him at most only the affection, at once slight and severe, of the old men of comedy. Marius was deceived. There are fathers who do not love their children; there is no grandfather who does not adore his grandson. In reality, we have said, M. Gillenormand worshipped Marius.

TOWARDS the middle of this year, 1831, the old woman who waited upon Marius told him that his neighbors, the wretched Jondrette family, were to be turned into the street. Marius, who passed almost all his days out of doors, hardly knew that he had any neighbors.

"Why are they turned out?" said he.

"Because they do not pay their rent; they owe for two terms."

"How much is that?"

"Twenty francs," said the old woman.

Marius had thirty francs in reserve in a drawer.

"Here," said he to the old woman. "There are twenty-five francs. Pay for these poor people, give them five francs, and do not tell them that it is from me."

The Conjunction of Two Stars

THE NICKNAME: MODE OF FORMATION OF FAMILY NAMES

MARIUS was now a fine-looking young man, of medium height, with heavy jet black hair, a high intelligent brow, large and passionate nostrils, a frank and calm expression, and an indescribable something beaming from every feature, which was at once lofty, thoughtful and innocent. His manners were reserved, cold, polished, far from free. But as his mouth was very pleasant, his lips the reddest and his teeth the whitest in the world, his smile corrected the severity of his physiognomy. At certain moments there was a strange contrast between this chaste brow and this voluptuous smile.

At the time of his most wretched poverty, he noticed that girls turned when he passed, and with a deathly feeling in his heart he fled or hid himself. He thought they looked at him on account of his old clothes, and that they were laughing at him; the truth is, that they looked at him because of his graceful appearance, and that they dreamed over it.

This wordless misunderstanding between him and the pretty girls he met had rendered him hostile to society. He attached himself to none, for the excellent reason that he fled before all. Thus he lived without aim—like a beast, said Courfeyrac.

Courfeyrac said to him also: "Aspire not to be a sage (they used familiar speech; familiarity of speech is characteristic of youthful friendships). My dear boy, a piece of advice. Read not so much in books, and look a little more upon the Peggies. The little rogues are good for thee, O Marius! By continual flight and blushing thou shalt become a brute."

At other times Courfeyrac met him with: "Good day, Monsieur Abbé."

When Courfeyrac said anything of this kind to him, for the next week Marius avoided women, old as well as young, more than ever, and especially did he avoid the haunts of Courfeyrac.

There were, however, in all the immensity of creation, two women from whom Marius never fled, and whom he did not at all avoid. One was the old woman with the beard, who swept his room, and who gave Courfeyrac an opportunity to say: "As his servant wears her beard, Marius does not wear his." The other was a little girl that he saw very often, and that he never looked at.

For more than a year Marius had noticed in a retired walk of the Luxembourg, the walk which borders the parapet of the Pépinière, a man and a girl quite young, nearly always sitting side by side, on the same seat, at the most retired end of the walk, near the Rue de l'Ouest. The man might be sixty years old; he seemed sad and serious; his whole person presented the robust but wearied appearance of a soldier retired from active service. Had he worn a decoration, Marius would have said: it is an old officer. His expression was kind, but it did not invite approach, and he never returned a look. He wore a blue coat and pantaloons, and a broad-brimmed hat, which always appeared to be new; a black cravat, and Quaker linen, that is to say, brilliantly white, but of coarse texture. A grisette passing near him one day, said: There is a very nice widower. His hair was perfectly white.

The first time the young girl that accompanied him sat down on the seat which they seemed to have adopted, she looked like a girl of about thirteen or fourteen, puny to the extent of being almost ugly, awkward, insignificant, yet promising, perhaps, to have rather fine eyes. But they were always looking about with a disagreeable assurance. She wore the dress, at once aged and childish, peculiar to the convent school-girl, an ill-fitting garment of coarse black merino. They appeared to be father and daughter.

Marius had acquired a sort of mechanical habit of promenading on this walk. He always found them there.

It was usually thus:

Marius would generally reach the walk at the end opposite their seat, promenade the whole length of it, passing before them, then return to the end by which he entered, and so on. He performed this turn five or six times in his promenade, and this promenade five or six times a week, but they and he had never come to exchange bows. This man and this young girl, though they appeared, and perhaps because they appeared, to avoid observation, had naturally excited the attention of the five or six students, who, from time to time, took their promenades along the Pépinière: the studious after their lecture, the others after their game of billiards. Courfeyrac, who belonged to the latter, had noticed them at some time or other, but finding the girl homely, had very quickly and carefully avoided them. He had fled like a Parthian, launching a nickname behind him. Struck especially by the dress of the little girl and the hair of the old man, he had named the daughter *Mademoiselle Lenoire* [*Black*] and the father *Monsieur Leblanc* [*White*]; and so, as nobody knew them otherwise, in the absence of a name, this surname had become fixed. The students said: "Ah! Monsieur Leblanc is at his seat!" and Marius, like the rest, had found it convenient to call this unknown gentleman M. Leblanc.

Marius saw them thus nearly every day at the same hour during the first year. He found the man very much to his liking, but the girl rather disagreeable.

LUX FACTA EST

The second year, at the precise point of this history to which the reader has arrived, it so happened that Marius broke off this habit of going to the Luxembourg, without really knowing why himself, and there were nearly six months during which he did not set foot in his walk. At last he went back there again one day; it was a serene summer morning.

He went straight to "his walk," and as soon as he reached it, he saw, still on the same seat, this well known pair. When he came near them, however, he saw that it was indeed the same man, but it seemed to him that it was no longer the same girl. The woman whom he now saw was a noble, beautiful creature, with all the most bewitching outlines of woman, at the precise moment at which they are yet combined with all the most charming graces of childhood,—that pure and fleeting moment which can only be translated by these two words: sweet fifteen. Beautiful chestnut hair, shaded with veins of gold, a brow which seemed chiselled marble, cheeks which seemed made of roses, a pale incarnadine, a flushed whiteness, an exquisite mouth, whence came a smile like a gleam of sunshine, and a voice like music. And that nothing might be wanting to this ravishing form, the nose was not beautiful, it was pretty; neither straight nor curved, neither Italian nor Greek; it was the Parisian nose; that is, something sprightly, fine, irregular, and pure, the despair of painters and the charm of poets.

At the first instant Marius thought it was another daughter of the same man, a sister doubtless of her whom he had seen before. But when the invariable habit of his promenade led him for the second time near the seat, and he had looked at her attentively, he recognised that she was the same.

She had not only grown; she had become idealized. As three April days are enough for certain trees to put on a covering of flowers, so six months had been enough for her to put on a mantle of beauty.

And then she was no longer the school-girl with her plush hat, her merino dress, her shapeless shoes, and her red hands; taste had come to her with beauty. She was a woman well dressed, with a sort of simple and rich elegance without any particular style. She wore a dress of black damask, a mantle of the same, and a white crape hat. Her white gloves showed the delicacy of her hand which played with the Chinese ivory handle of her parasol, and her silk boot betrayed the smallness of her foot. When you passed near her, her whole toilet exhaled the penetrating fragrance of youth.

As to the man, he was still the same.

The second time that Marius came near her, the young girl raised her eyes; they were of a deep celestial blue, but in this veiled azure was nothing yet beyond the look of a child. She looked at Marius with indifference, as she would have looked at any little monkey playing under the sycamores, or the marble vase which cast its shadow over the bench; and Marius also continued his promenade thinking of something else.

He passed four or five times more by the seat where the young girl was, without even turning his eyes towards her.

On the following days he came as usual to the Luxembourg, as usual he found "the father and daughter" there, but he paid no attention to them. He thought no more of this girl now that she was handsome than he had thought of her when she was homely. He passed very near the bench on which she sat, because that was his habit.

EFFECT OF SPRING

ONE day the air was mild, the Luxembourg was flooded with sunshine and shadow, the sky was as clear as if the angels had washed it in the morning, the sparrows were twittering in the depths of the chestnut trees, Marius had opened his whole soul to nature, he was thinking of nothing, he was living and breathing, he passed near this seat, the young girl raised her eyes, their glances met.

But what was there now in the glance of the young girl? Marius could not have told. There was nothing, and there was everything. It was a strange flash.

She cast down her eyes, and he continued on his way.

At night, on returning to his garret, Marius cast a look upon his dress, and for the first time perceived that he had the slovenliness, the indecency, and the unheard-of stupidity, to promenade in the Luxembourg with his "every day" suit, a hat broken near the band, coarse teamsters' boots, black pantaloons shiny at the knees, and a black coat threadbare at the elbows.

COMMENCEMENT OF A GREAT DISTEMPER

THE next day, at the usual hour, Marius took from his closet his new coat, his new pantaloons, his new hat, and his new boots; he dressed himself in this panoply complete, put on his gloves, prodigious prodigality, and went to the Luxembourg.

On the way, he met Courfeyrac, and pretended not to see him. Courfeyrac, on his return home, said to his friends:

"I have just met Marius' new hat and coat, with Marius inside. Probably he was going to an examination. He looked stupid enough."

On reaching the Luxembourg, Marius took a turn round the fountain and looked at the swans; then he remained for a long time in contemplation before a statue, the head of which was black with moss, and which was minus a hip. Finally, he went towards "his walk" slowly, as if with regret.

When he entered the walk he saw M. Leblanc and the young girl at the other end "on their seat." He buttoned his coat, stretched it down that there might be no wrinkles, noticed with some complaisance the lustre of his pantaloons, and marched upon the seat. There was something of attack in this march, and certainly a desire of conquest. I say, then, he marched upon the seat, as I would say: Hannibal marched upon Rome.

As he drew nearer, his step became slower and slower. At some distance from the seat, long before he had reached the end of the walk, he stopped, and he did not know himself how it happened, but he turned back. He did not even say to himself that he would not go to the end. It was doubtful if the young girl could see him so far off, and notice his fine appearance in his new suit. However, he held himself very straight, so that he might look well, in case anybody who was behind should happen to notice him.

He reached the opposite end and then returned, and this time he approached a little nearer to the seat. He even came to within about three trees of it, but there he felt an indescribable lack of power to go further, and he hesitated. He thought he had seen the young girl's face bent towards him. Still he made a great and manly effort, conquered his hesitation, and continued his advance. In a few seconds, he was passing before the seat, erect and firm, blushing to his ears, without daring to cast a look to the right or the left, and with his hand in his coat like a statesman. At the moment he passed under the guns of the fortress, he felt a frightful palpitation of the heart. She wore, as on the previous day, her damask dress and her crape hat. He heard the sound of an ineffable voice, which might be "her voice." She was talking quietly. She was very pretty. He felt it, though he made no effort to see her.

He made no effort to approach the seat again, he stopped midway of the walk, and sat down there—a thing which he never did—casting many side glances, and thinking, in the most indistinct depths of his mind, that after all it must be difficult for persons whose white hat and black dress he admired, to be absolutely insensible to his glossy pantaloons and his new coat.

At the end of a quarter of an hour, he rose, as if to recommence his walk towards this seat, which was encircled by a halo. He, however, stood silent and motionless.

For the first time, also, he felt a certain irreverence in designating this unknown man, even in the silence of his thought, by the nickname of M. Leblanc.

He remained thus for some minutes with his head down tracing designs on the ground with a little stick which he had in his hand.

Then he turned abruptly away from the seat, away from Monsieur Leblanc and his daughter, and went home.

That day he forgot to go to dinner. At eight o'clock in the evening he discovered it, and as it was too late to go down to the Rue Saint Jacques, "No matter," said he, and he ate a piece of bread.

He did not retire until he had carefully brushed and folded his coat.

SUNDRY THUNDERBOLTS FALL UPON MA'AM BOUGON

NEXT day, Ma'am Bougon,—thus Courfeyrac designated the old portress-landlady of the Gorbeau tenement,—Ma'am Bougon was stupefied with astonishment to see Monsieur Marius go out again with his new coat.

He went again to the Luxembourg, but did not get beyond his seat midway of the walk. He sat down there as on the day previous, gazing from a distance and seeing distinctly the white hat, the black dress, and especially the bluish light. He did not stir from the seat, and did not go home until the gates of the Luxembourg were shut.

The next day, for the third time, Ma'am Bougon was thunderstruck. Marius went out with his new suit. "Three days running!" she exclaimed.

She made an attempt to follow him, but Marius walked briskly and with immense strides; it was a hippopotamus undertaking to catch a chamois. In two minutes she lost sight of him, and came back out of breath, three quarters choked by her asthma, and furious. "The silly fellow," she muttered, "to put on his handsome clothes every day and make people run like that!"

Marius had gone to the Luxembourg.

Thus a fortnight rolled away. Marius went to the Luxembourg, no longer to promenade, but to sit down, always in the same place, and without knowing why. Once there he did not stir.

TAKEN PRISONER

ON one of the last days of the second week, Marius was as usual sitting on his seat, holding in his hand an open book of which he had not turned a leaf for two hours. Suddenly he trembled. A great event was commencing at the end of the walk. Monsieur Leblanc and his daughter had left their seat, the daughter had taken the arm of the father, and they were coming slowly towards the middle of the walk where Marius was. Marius closed his book, then he opened it, then he made an attempt to read. He trembled. The halo was coming straight towards him. "O dear!" thought he, "I shall not have time to take an attitude." However, the man with the white hair and the young girl were advancing. It seemed to him that it would last a century, and that it was only a second. He heard the gentle and measured sound of their steps approaching. He imagined that Monsieur Leblanc was hurling angry looks upon him. "Is he going to speak to me?" thought he. He bowed his head; when he raised it they were quite near him. The young girl passed, and in passing she looked at him. She looked at him steadily, with a sweet and thoughtful look which made Marius tremble from head to foot. It seemed to him that she reproached him for having been so long without coming to her, and that she said: "It is I who come." Marius was bewildered by these eyes full of flashing light and fathomless abysses.

He felt as though his brain were on fire. She had come to him, what happiness! And then, how she had looked at him! She seemed more beautiful than she had ever seemed before. Beautiful with a beauty which combined all of the woman with all of the angel, a beauty which would have made Petrarch sing and Dante kneel. He felt as though he was swimming in the deep blue sky. At the same time he was horribly disconcerted, because he had a little dust on his boots.

He was desperately in love.

He was serious, indeed. Marius was in this first vehement

and fascinating period which the grand passion commences. One glance had done all that.

When the mine is loaded, and the match is ready, nothing is simpler. A glance is a spark.

It was all over with him. Marius loved a woman. His destiny was entering upon the unknown.

ADVENTURES OF THE LETTER U ABANDONED TO CONJECTURE

A WHOLE month passed during which Marius went every day to the Luxembourg. When the hour came, nothing could keep him away. "He is out at service," said Courfeyrac. Marius lived in transports. It is certain that the young girl looked at him.

He finally grew bolder, and approached nearer to the seat. However he passed before it no more, obeying at once the instinct of timidity and the instinct of prudence, peculiar to lovers. He thought it better not to attract the "attention of the father." He formed his combinations of stations behind trees and the pedestals of statues, with consummate art, so as to be seen as much as possible by the young girl and as little as possible by the old gentleman.

We must, however, suppose that M. Leblanc perceived something of this at last, for often when Marius came, he would rise and begin to promenade. He had left their accustomed place, and had taken the seat at the other end of the walk, near the Gladiator, as if to see whether Marius would follow them. Marius did not understand it, and committed that blunder. "The father" began to be less punctual and did not bring "his daughter" every day. Sometimes he came alone. Then Marius did not stay. Another blunder.

Marius took no note of these symptoms. His love grew. He dreamed of her every night. And then there came to him a good fortune for which he had not even hoped, oil upon the fire, double darkness upon his eyes. One night, at dusk, he found on the seat, which "M. Leblanc and his daughter" had just left, a handkerchief, a plain handkerchief without embroidery, but white, fine, and which appeared to him to exhale ineffable odours. He seized it in transport. This handkerchief was marked with the letters U. F.: Marius knew nothing of this beautiful girl, neither her family, nor her name, nor her dwelling; these two letters were the first thing he had caught of her, adorable initials upon which he began straightway to build his castle. It was evidently her first name. Ursula, thought he, what a sweet name! He kissed the handkerchief, inhaled its perfume, put it over his heart, on his flesh in the day-time, and at night went to sleep with it on his lips.

"I feel her whole soul in it!" he exclaimed.

This handkerchief belonged to the old gentleman, who had simply let it fall from his pocket.

AN ECLIPSE

WE have seen how Marius discovered, or thought he discovered, that Her name was Ursula.

Hunger comes with love. To know that her name was Ursula had been much; it was little. In three or four weeks Marius had devoured this piece of good fortune. He desired another. He wished to know where she lived.

He followed "Ursula."

She lived in the Rue de l'Ouest, in the least frequented part of it, in a new three-story house, of modest appearance.

From that moment Marius added to his happiness in seeing her at the Luxembourg, the happiness of following her home.

His hunger increased. He knew her name, her first name, at least, the charming name, the real name of a woman; he knew where she lived; he desired to know who she was.

One night after he had followed them home, and seen them disappear at the porte-cochère, he entered after them, and said boldly to the porter:—

"Is it the gentleman on the first floor who has just come in?"

"No," answered the porter. "It is the gentleman on the third."

Another fact. This success made Marius still bolder.

"In front?" he asked.

"Faith!" said the porter, "the house is only built on the street."

"And what is this gentleman?"

"He lives on his income, monsieur. A very kind man, who does a great deal of good among the poor, though not rich."

"What is his name?" continued Marius.

The porter raised his head, and said:—

"Is monsieur a detective?"

Marius retired, much abashed, but still in great transports. He was getting on.

"Good," thought he. "I know that her name is Ursula, that she is the daughter of a retired gentleman, and that she lives there, in the third story, in the Rue de l'Ouest."

Next day Monsieur Leblanc and his daughter made but a short visit to the Luxembourg; they went away while it was yet broad daylight. Marius followed them into the Rue de l'Ouest, as was his custom. On reaching the porte-cochère, Monsieur Leblanc passed his daughter in, and then stopped, and before entering himself, turned and looked steadily at Marius. The day after that they did not come to the Luxembourg. Marius waited in vain all day.

At nightfall he went to the Rue de l'Ouest, and saw a light in the windows of the third story. He walked beneath these windows until the light was put out.

The next day nobody at the Luxembourg. Marius waited all day, and then went to perform his night duty under the windows. That took him till ten o'clock in the evening.

He passed a week in this way.

On the eighth day when he reached the house, there was no light in the windows. "What!" said he, "the lamp is not yet lighted. But yet it is dark. Or they have gone out?" He waited till ten o'clock. Till midnight. Till one o'clock in the morning. No light appeared in the third story windows, and nobody entered the house. He went away very gloomy.

On the morrow—for he lived only from morrow to morrow; there was no longer any to-day, so to speak, to him—on the morrow he found nobody at the Luxembourg, he waited; at dusk he went to the house. No light in the windows; the blinds were closed; the third story was entirely dark.

Marius knocked at the porte-cochère; went in and said to the porter:—

"The gentleman of the third floor?"

"Moved," answered the porter.

Marius tottered, and said feebly:

"Since when?"

"Yesterday."

"Where does he live now?"

"I don't know anything about it."

The Noxious Poor

MARIUS, LOOKING FOR A GIRL WITH A HAT, MEETS A MAN WITH
A CAP

SUMMER passed, then autumn; winter came. Neither M. Leblanc nor the young girl had set foot in the Luxembourg.
Marius had now but one thought, to see that sweet, that adorable face again. He searched continually; he searched everywhere: he found nothing. He fell into a melancholy. It was
all over with him.

He reproached himself a hundred times. Why did I follow
her? I was so happy in seeing her only! She looked upon me;
was not that infinite? She had the appearance of loving me.
Was not that everything? I desired to have what? There is
nothing more after that. I was a fool. It is my fault, etc., etc.

He lived more and more alone, bewildered, overwhelmed,
given up to his inward anguish, walking to and fro in his
grief like a wolf in a cage, seeking everywhere for the absent,
stupefied with love.

At another time, an accidental meeting produced a singular
effect upon him. In one of the little streets in the neighborhood of the Boulevard des Invalides, he saw a man dressed
like a laborer, wearing a cap with a long visor, from beneath
which escaped a few locks of very white hair. Marius was
struck by the beauty of this white hair, and noticed the man
who was walking with slow steps and seemed absorbed in
painful meditation. Strangely enough, it appeared to him that
he recognized M. Leblanc. It was the same hair, the same
profile, as far as the cap allowed him to see, the same manner, only sadder. But why these working-man's clothes? what
did that mean?

A GIRL who was quite young, was standing in the half-opened door. The little round window through which the light found its way into the garret was exactly opposite the door, and lit up this form with a pallid light. It was a pale, puny, meagre creature, one of those beings who are both feeble and horrible at once, and who make those shudder whom they do not make weep.

Marius arose and gazed with a kind of astonishment upon this being, so much like the shadowy forms which pass across our dreams.

The face was not absolutely unknown to Marius. He thought he remembered having seen it somewhere.

"What do you wish, mademoiselle?" asked he.

The young girl answered with her voice like a drunken galley-slave's:

"Here is a letter for you, Monsieur Marius."

She called Marius by his name; he could not doubt that her business was with him; but what was this girl? how did she know his name?

Without waiting for an invitation, she entered.

She had ready in her hand a letter which she presented to Marius.

Marius, in opening this letter, noticed that the enormously large wafer was still wet. The message could not have come far. He read:

"My amiable neighbor, young man!

"I have lerned your kindness towards me, that you have paid my rent six months ago. I bless you, young man. My eldest daughter will tell you that we have been without a morsel of bread for two days, four persons, and my spouse sick. If I am not desseived by my thoughts, I think I may hope that your generous heart will soften at this exposure and that the desire will subjugate you of being propitious to me by deigning to lavish upon me some light gift.

"I am with the distinguished consideration which is due to the benefactors of humanity,

"JONDRETTE

"P. S. My daughter will await your orders, dear Monsieur Marius."

Meantime, while Marius fixed upon her an astonished and sorrowful look, the young girl was walking to and fro in the room with the boldness of a specter. She bustled about regardless of her nakedness. At times, her chemise, unfastened and torn, fell almost to her waist. She moved the chairs, she disarranged the toilet articles on the bureau, she felt of Marius' clothes, she searched over what there was in the corners.

"Ah," said she, "you have a mirror!"

And she hummed, as if she had been alone, snatches of songs, light refrains which were made dismal by her harsh and guttural voice.

She went to the table.

"Ah!" said she, "books!"

She hastily caught up the book which lay open on the table, and read fluently:

"——General Bauduin received the order to take five battalions of his brigade and carry the château of Hougomont, which is in the middle of the plain of Waterloo——"

She stopped:

"Ah, Waterloo! I know that. It is a battle in old times. My father was there; my father served in the armies. We are jolly good Bonapartists at home, that we are. Against English, Waterloo is."

Then she looked at Marius, put on a strange manner, and said to him:

"Do you know, Monsieur Marius, that you are a very pretty boy?"

And at the same time the same thought occurred to both of them, which made her smile and made him blush.

She went to him, and laid her hand on his shoulder: "You pay no attention to me, but I know you, Monsieur Marius. I meet you here on the stairs, and then I see you visiting a man named Father Mabeuf, who lives out by Austerlitz; some-

times, when I am walking that way. That becomes you very
well, your tangled hair."

Her voice tried to be very soft, but succeeded only in being very low. Some of her words were lost in their passage
from the larynx to the lips, as upon a key-board in which
some notes are missing.

Marius had drawn back quietly.

After a thorough exploration of his pockets, Marius had at
last got together five francs and sixteen sous. This was at
the time all that he had in the world. "That is enough for my
dinner to-day," thought he, "to-morrow we will see." He took
the sixteen sous, and gave the five francs to the young girl.

She took the piece eagerly.

"Good," said she, "there is some sunshine!"

She drew her chemise up over her shoulders, made a low
bow to Marius, then a familiar wave of the hand, and moved
towards the door, saying:

"Good morning, monsieur. It is all the same. I am going to
find my old man."

On her way she saw on the bureau a dry crust of bread
moulding there in the dust; she sprang upon it, and bit it,
muttering:

"That is good! it is hard! it breaks my teeth!"

Then she went out.

THE JUDAS OF PROVIDENCE

For five years Marius had lived in poverty, in privation, in distress even, but he perceived that he had never known real
misery. Real misery he had just seen. In fact, he who has
seen the misery of man only has seen nothing, he must see
the misery of woman; he who has seen the misery of woman
only has seen nothing, he must see the misery of childhood.

Marius almost reproached himself with the fact that he had
been so absorbed in his reveries and passion that he had not
until now cast a glance upon his neighbors. Paying their rent
was a mechanical impulse; everybody would have had that
impulse; but he, Marius, should have done better. Every day
at every moment, he heard them through the wall, walking,
going, coming, talking, and he did not lend his ear! and in
these words there were groans, and he did not even listen,

his thoughts were elsewhere, upon dreams, upon impossible glimmerings, upon loves in the sky, upon infatuations; and all the while human beings, his brothers in Jesus Christ, his brothers in the people, were suffering death agonies beside him! agonising uselessly; he even caused a portion of their suffering, and aggravated it. Undoubtedly they seemed very depraved, very corrupt, very vile, very hateful, even, but those are rare who fall without becoming degraded; there is a point, moreover, at which the unfortunate and the infamous are associated and confounded in a single word, a fatal word, *Les Misérables;* whose fault is it? And then, is it not when the fall is lowest that charity ought to be greatest?

While he thus preached to himself, for there were times when Marius, like all truly honest hearts, was his own monitor, and scolded himself more than he deserved, he looked at the wall which separated him from the Jondrettes, as if he could send his pitying glance through that partition to warn those unfortunate beings. The wall was a thin layer of plaster, upheld by laths and joists, through which, as we have just seen, voices and words could be distinguished perfectly. Almost unconsciously, Marius examined this partition; sometimes reverie examines, observes, and scrutinises, as thought would do. Suddenly he arose, he noticed towards the top, near the ceiling, a triangular hole, where three laths left a space between them. The plaster which should have stopped this hole was gone, and by getting upon the bureau he could see through that hole into the Jondrettes' garret. "Let us see what these people are," thought Marius, "and to what they are reduced."

He climbed upon the bureau, put his eye to the crevice, and looked.

STRATEGY AND TACTICS

THE door of the garret was hastily opened. The eldest daughter appeared upon the threshold. On her feet she had coarse men's shoes, covered with mud, which had been spattered as high as her red ankles, and she was wrapped in a ragged old gown which Marius had not seen upon her an hour before, but which she had probably left at his door that she might inspire the more pity, and which she must have put on upon going out. She came in, pushed the door to behind her, stopped to take breath, for she was quite breathless, then cried with an expression of joy and triumph:

"He is coming!"

The father turned his eyes, the woman turned her head, the younger sister did not stir.

"Who?" asked the father.

"The gentleman!"

"The philanthropist?"

"Yes."

"He is going to come?"

"He is coming in a fiacre."

"In a fiacre. It is Rothschild?"

The father arose.

"How are you sure? if he is coming in a fiacre, how is it that you get here before him? you gave him the address, at least? you told him the last door at the end of the hall on the right? provided he does not make a mistake? you found him at the church then? did he read my letter? what did he say to you?"

"Tut, tut, tut!" said the girl, "how you run on, goodman! I'll tell you: I went into the church, he was at his usual place, I made a curtsey to him, and I gave him the letter, he read it and said to me: Where do you live, my child? I said: Monsieur, I will show you. He said to me: No, give me your address; my daughter has some purchases to make, I am going to take a carriage and I will get to your house as soon as you do. I gave him the address. When I told him the house, he appeared surprised and hesitated an instant, then he said: It is all the same, I will go. When mass was over, I saw him leave the church with his daughter. I saw them get into a fiacre. And I told him plainly the last door at the end of the hall on the right."

"And how do you know that he will come?"

"I just saw the fiacre coming into the Rue du Petit Banquier. That is what made me run."

"How do you know it is the same fiacre?"

"Because I had noticed the number."

"What is the number?"

"Four hundred and forty."

"Good, you are a clever girl."

The man sprang up. There was a sort of illumination on his face.

"Wife!" cried he, "you hear. Here is the philanthropist. Put out the fire."

The astounded woman did not stir.

The father, with the agility of a mountebank, caught a broken pot which stood on the mantle, and threw some water upon the embers.

Then turning to his elder daughter:

"You! unbottom the chair!"

His daughter did not understand him at all.

He seized the chair, and with a kick he ruined the seat. His leg went through it.

As he drew out his leg, he asked his daughter:

"Is it cold?"

"Very cold. It snows."

The father turned towards the younger girl, who was on the pallet near the window, and cried in a thundering voice:

"Quick! off the bed, good-for-nothing! will you never do anything? break a pane of glass!"

The little girl sprang off the bed trembling.

"Break a pane of glass!" said he again.

The child was speechless.

"Do you hear me?" repeated the father, "I tell you to break a pane!"

The child, with a sort of terrified obedience, rose upon tiptoe and struck her fist into a pane. The glass broke and fell with a crash.

The mother, who had not yet said a word, got up and asked in a slow, muffled tone, her words seeming to come out as if curdled:

"Dear, what is it you want to do?"

"Get into bed," answered the man.

His tone admitted of no deliberation. The mother obeyed, and threw herself heavily upon one of the pallets.

Meanwhile a sob was heard in a corner.

"What is that?" cried the father.

The younger daughter, without coming out of the darkness into which she had shrunk, showed her bleeding fist. In breaking the glass she had cut herself; she had gone to her mother's bed, and she was weeping in silence.

It was the mother's turn to rise and cry out.

"You see now! what stupid things you are doing? breaking your glass, she has cut herself!"

"So much the better!" said the man. "I knew she would."

"How! so much the better?" resumed the woman.

"Silence!" replied the father. "I suppress the liberty of the press."

Then tearing the chemise which he had on, he made a bandage with which he hastily wrapped up the little girl's bleeding wrist.

An icy wind whistled at the window and came into the room. The mist from without entered and spread about like a whitish wadding picked apart by invisible fingers. Through the broken pane the falling snow was seen.

"Now," said he, "we can receive the philanthropist."

THE SUNBEAM IN THE HOLE

"Do you know," resumed the father, "that it is as cold as a dog in this devilish garret? If this man should not come! Oh! that is it! he makes us wait for him! he says: Well! they will wait for me! that is what they are for!—Oh! how I hate them, and how I would strangle them with joy and rejoicing, enthusiasm and satisfaction, these rich men! all the rich!

Just then there was a light rap at the door, the man rushed forward and opened it, exclaiming with many low bows and smiles of adoration:

"Come in, monsieur! deign to come in, my noble benefactor, as well as your charming young lady."

A man of mature age and a young girl appeared at the door of the garret.

Marius had not left his place. What he felt at that moment escapes human language.

It was She.

She appeared again in this gloom, in this garret, in this shapeless den, in this horror!

She was still the same, a little paler only; her delicate face was set in a violet velvet hat, her form was hidden under a black satin pelisse, below her long dress he caught a glimpse of her little foot squeezed into a silk buskin.

She was still accompanied by Monsieur Leblanc.

She stepped into the room and laid a large package on the table.

Monsieur Leblanc approached with his kind and com-passionate look, and said to the father:

"Monsieur, you will find in this package some new clothes, some stockings, and some new coverlids."

"Our angelic benefactor overwhelms us," said Jondrette, bowing down to the floor. "Look, my benefactor, no bread, no fire. My poor darlings have no fire! My only chair un-seated! A broken window! in such weather as is this! My spouse in bed! sick!"

"Poor woman!" said Monsieur Leblanc.

"My child injured!" added Jondrette.

The little one uttered loud cries.

The adorable young girl whom Marius in his heart called "his Ursula" went quickly to her:

"Poor, dear child!" said she.

"Look, my beautiful young lady," pursued Jondrette, "her bleeding wrist! It is an accident which happened in working at a machine by which she earned six sous a day. It may be necessary to cut off her arm."

"Indeed!" said the old gentleman alarmed.

The little girl, taking this seriously, began to sob again beautifully. "Alas, yes, my benefactor!" answered the father.

For some moments, Jondrette had been looking at "the philanthropist" in a strange manner. Even while speaking, he seemed to scrutinize him closely as if he were trying to recall some reminiscence. Suddenly, taking advantage of a moment when the newcomers were anxiously questioning the smaller girl about her mutilated hand, he passed over to his wife who was lying in her bed, appearing to be overwhelmed and stupid, and said to her quickly and in a very low tone:

"Notice that man!"

Then turning towards M. Leblanc, and continuing his lam-entation:

"You see, monsieur! my whole dress is nothing but a che-mise of my wife's! and that all torn! in the heart of winter. I cannot go out, for lack of a coat. Well, monsieur, my worthy monsieur, do you know what is going to happen to-morrow? To-morrow is the 4th of February, the fatal day, the last delay that my landlord will give me; if I do not pay him this evening, to-morrow my eldest daughter, myself, my spouse with her fever, my child with her wound, we shall all four be turned out of doors, and driven off into the street, upon the boulevard, without shelter, into the rain, upon the snow. You see, monsieur, I owe four quarters, a year! that is sixty francs."

Jondrette lied. Four quarters would have made but forty francs, and he could not have owed for four, since it was not six months since Marius had paid for two.

M. Leblanc took five francs from his pocket and threw them on the table.

Meantime, M. Leblanc had taken off a large brown over-coat, which he wore over his blue surtout, and hung it over the back of the chair.

"Monsieur Fabantou," said he, "I have only these five francs with me; but I am going to take my daughter home, and I will return this evening; is it not this evening that you have to pay?"

Jondrette's face lighted up with a strange expression. He answered quickly:

"Yes, my noble monsieur. At eight o'clock, I must be at my landlord's."

"I will be here at six o'clock, and I will bring you the sixty francs."

M. Leblanc took the arm of the beautiful young girl, and turned towards the door:

"Till this evening, my friends," said he.

"Six o'clock," said Jondrette.

"Six o'clock precisely."

Just then the overcoat on the chair caught the eye of the elder daughter.

"Monsieur," said she, "you forget your coat."

Jondrette threw a crushing glance at his daughter, accom-panied by a terrible shrug of the shoulders.

M. Leblanc turned and answered with a smile:

"I do not forget it, I leave it."

"O my patron," said Jondrette, "my noble benefactor, I am

melting into tears! Allow me to conduct you to your carriage."

"If you go out," replied M. Leblanc, "put on this overcoat. It is really very cold."

Jondrette did not make him say it twice. He put on the
brown overcoat very quickly.

And they went out all three, Jondrette preceding the two
strangers.

USE OF MARIUS' FIVE-FRANC PIECE

MARIUS judged that the time had come to resume his place
at his observatory. In a twinkling, and with the agility of his
age, he was at the hole in the partition.

He looked in.

The interior of the Jondrette apartment presented a singular appearance. A candle was burning in a verdigrised candlestick, but it was not that which really lighted the room. The
entire den was, as it were, illuminated by the reflection of a
large sheet iron furnace in the fireplace, which was filled with
lighted charcoal. The fire which the female Jondrette had
made ready in the daytime. The charcoal was burning and
the furnace was red hot, a blue flame danced over it and
helped to show the form of the chisel bought by Jondrette in
the Rue Pierre Lombard, which was growing ruddy among
the coals. In a corner near the door, and arranged as if for
anticipated use, were two heaps which appeared to be, one,
a heap of old iron, the other a heap of ropes.

The Jondrette lair was, if the reader remembers what we
have said of the Gorbeau house, admirably chosen for the
theatre of a deed of darkness and violence, and for the concealment of a crime. It was the most retired room of the most
isolated house of the most solitary boulevard in Paris. If
ambuscade had not existed, it would have been invented
there.

Jondrette had lighted his pipe, sat down on the dismantled
chair, and was smoking. His wife was speaking to him in a
low tone.

Suddenly Jondrette raised his voice:

"Do you know? we must have two chairs here."

"What for?"

"To sit in."

Marius felt a shiver run down his back on hearing the woman make this quiet reply:—

"Pardieu! I will get our neighbor's."

And with rapid movement she opened the door of the den, and went out into the hall.

Marius physically had not the time to get down from the bureau, and go and hide himself under the bed.

Marius heard the heavy hand of mother Jondrette groping after his key in the dark. The door opened. He stood nailed to his place by apprehension and stupor.

The woman came in.

The gable window let in a ray of moonlight, between two great sheets of shadow. One of these sheets of shadow entirely covered the wall against which Marius was leaning, so as to conceal him.

The mother Jondrette raised her eyes, did not see Marius, took the two chairs, the only chairs which Marius had, and went out, slamming the door noisily behind her.

She went back into the den.

He arranged the two chairs on the two sides of the table, turned the chisel over in the fire, put an old screen in front of the fireplace, which concealed the furnace, then went to the corner where the heap of ropes was, and stooped down, as if to examine something. Marius then perceived that what he had taken for a shapeless heap, was a rope ladder, very well made, with wooden rounds, and two large hooks to hang it by.

This ladder and a few big tools, actual masses of iron, which were thrown upon the pile of old iron heaped up behind the door, were not in the Jondrette den in the morning, and had evidently been brought there in the afternoon, during Marius' absence.

Jondrette had let his pipe go out—a sure sign that he was intensely absorbed—and had come back and sat down. There were contractions of his brows, and abrupt openings of his right hand, as if he were replying to the last counsels of a dark interior monologue. In one of these obscure replies which he was making to himself, he drew the table drawer out quickly towards him, took out a long carving knife which was hidden there, and tried its edge on his nail. This done, he put the knife back into the drawer, and shut it.

Marius, for his part, grasped the pistol which was in his right fob pocket, took it out, and cocked it.

The pistol in cocking gave a little clear, sharp sound.
Jondrette started, and half rose from his chair.

"Who is there?" cried he.

Marius held his breath; Jondrette listened a moment, then
began to laugh, saying:—

"What a fool I am? It is the partition cracking."

Marius kept the pistol in his hand.

MARIUS' TWO CHAIRS FACE EACH OTHER

JUST then the distant and melancholy vibration of a bell
shook the windows. Six o'clock struck on Saint Médard.

Jondrette marked each stroke with a nod of his head. At
the sixth stroke, he snuffed the candle with his fingers.

Then he began to walk about the room, listened in the
hall, walked, listened again: "Provided he comes!" muttered
he; then he returned to his chair.

He had hardly sat down when the door opened.

The mother Jondrette had opened it, and stood in the
hall making a horrible, amiable grimace, which was lighted
up from beneath by one of the holes of the dark lantern.

"Walk in," said she.

"Walk in, my benefactor," repeated Jondrette, rising precipitately. Monsieur Leblanc appeared.

He had an air of serenity which made him singularly venerable.

He laid four louis upon the table.

"Monsieur Fabantou," said he, "that is for your rent and
your pressing wants. We will see about the rest."

"God reward you, my generous benefactor!" said Jondrette,
and rapidly approaching his wife:

"Send away the fiacre!"

She slipped away, while her husband was lavishing bows
and offering a chair to Monsieur Leblanc. A moment afterwards she came back and whispered in his ear, "It is done."

The snow which had been falling ever since morning, was
so deep that they had not heard the fiacre arrive, and did not
hear it go away.

Meanwhile Monsieur Leblanc had taken a seat.

Jondrette had taken possession of the other chair opposite
Monsieur Leblanc.

No sooner was Monsieur Leblanc seated than he turned his eyes towards the empty pallets.

"How does the poor little injured girl do?" he inquired.

"Badly," answered Jondrette with a doleful yet grateful smile, "very badly, my worthy monsieur. Her eldest sister has taken her to the bourbe to have her arm dressed. You will see them, they will be back directly."

"Madame Fabantou appears to me much better?" resumed Monsieur Leblanc, casting his eyes upon the grotesque accoutrement of the female Jondrette, who, standing between him and the door, as if she were already guarding the exit, was looking at him in a threatening and almost a defiant posture.

"She is dying," said Jondrette. "But you see, monsieur! she has so much courage, that woman!"

While Jondrette was talking, with an apparent disorder which detracted nothing from the crafty and cunning expression of his physiognomy, Marius raised his eyes, and perceived at the back of the room somebody whom he had not before seen. A man had come in so noiselessly that nobody had heard the door turn on its hinges. This man had a knit woollen waistcoat of violet colour, old, worn-out, stained, cut, and showing gaps at all its folds, full trousers of cotton velvet, socks on his feet, no shirt, his neck bare, his arms bare and tattooed, and his face stained black. He sat down in silence and with folded arms on the nearest bed, and as he kept behind the woman, he was distinguished only with difficulty.

That kind of magnetic instinct which warns the eye made M. Leblanc turn almost at the same time with Marius. He could not help a movement of surprise, which did not escape Jondrette:

"Ah! I see!" exclaimed Jondrette, buttoning up his coat

with a complacent air, "you are looking at your overcoat.
It's a fit! my faith! it's a fit!"

"Who is that man?" said M. Leblanc.

"That man?" said Jondrette, "that is a neighbor. Pay no
attention to him."

"Pardon me; what were you saying to me, Monsieur Fabantou?"

"I was telling you, monsieur and dear patron," replied
Jondrette, leaning his elbows on the table, and gazing at M.
Leblanc with fixed and tender eyes, similar to the eyes of a
boa constrictor, "I was telling you that I had a picture to sell."

A slight noise was made at the door. A second man entered, and sat down on the bed behind the female Jondrette.
He had his arms bare, like the first, and a mask of ink or
of soot.

Although this man had, literally, slipped into the room, he
could not prevent M. Leblanc from perceiving him.

"Do not mind them," said Jondrette. "They are people of
the house. I was telling you, then, that I have a valuable
painting left. Here, monsieur, look."

He got up, went to the wall, at the foot of which stood
the panel of which we have spoken, and turned it round, still
leaving it resting against the wall. It was something, in fact,
that resembled a picture, and which the candle scarcely revealed. Marius could make nothing out of it, Jondrette being
between him and the picture; he merely caught a glimpse of
a coarse daub, with a sort of principal personage, colored
in the crude and glaring style of strolling panoramas and
paintings upon screens.

"What is that?" asked M. Leblanc.

Jondrette exclaimed:

"A painting by a master; a picture of great price, my benefactor! I cling to it as to my two daughters, it calls up
memories to me! but I have told you, and I cannot unsay it,
I am so unfortunate that I would part with it."

Whether by chance, or whether there was some beginning
of distrust, while examining the picture, M. Leblanc glanced
towards the back of the room. There were now four men
there, three seated on the bed, one standing near the door-
casing; all four bare-armed, motionless, and with blackened
faces.

Jondrette noticed that M. Leblanc's eye was fixed upon
these men.

"They are friends. They live near by," said he. "They are dark because they work in charcoal. They are chimney doctors. Do not occupy your mind with them, my benefactor, but buy my picture. Take pity on my misery. I shall not sell it to you at a high price. How much do you estimate it worth?"

"But," said M. Leblanc, looking Jondrette full in the face and like a man who puts himself on his guard, "this is some tavern sign, it is worth about three francs."

Jondrette answered calmly:

"Have you your pocket-book here? I will be satisfied with a thousand crowns."

M. Leblanc rose to his feet, placed his back to the wall, and ran his eye rapidly over the room. He had Jondrette at his left on the side towards the window, and his wife and the four men at his right on the side towards the door. The four men did not stir, and had not even the appearance of seeing him; Jondrette had begun again to talk in a plaintive key, with his eyes so wild and his tones so mournful that M. Leblanc might have thought that he had before his eyes nothing more nor less than a man gone crazy from misery.

While speaking Jondrette did not look at M. Leblanc, who was watching him. M. Leblanc's eye was fixed upon Jondrette, and Jondrette's eye upon the door, Marius' breathless attention went from one to the other.

Suddenly his dull eye lighted up with a hideous glare, this little man straightened up and became horrifying, he took a step towards M. Leblanc and cried to him in a voice of thunder:

"But all this is not the question! do you know me?"

THE AMBUSCADE

THE door of the garret had been suddenly flung open, disclosing three men in blue blouses with black paper masks. The first was spare and had a long iron-bound cudgel; the second, who was a sort of colossus, held by the middle of the handle, with the axe down, a butcher's pole-axe. The third, a broad-shouldered man, not so thin as the first, nor so heavy as the second, held in his clenched fist an enormous key stolen from some prison door.

It appeared that it was the arrival of these men for which Jondrette was waiting. A rapid dialogue commenced between him and the man with the cudgel, the spare man.

Jondrette, after his colloquy with the man who had the cudgel, turned again towards M. Leblanc and repeated his question, accompanying it with that low, smothered, and terrible laugh of his:

"You do not recognise me, then?"

M. Leblanc looked him in the face, and answered:

"No."

Then Jondrette came up to the table. He leaned forward over the candle, folding his arms, and pushing his angular and ferocious jaws up towards the calm face of M. Leblanc, as nearly as he could without forcing him to draw back, and in that posture, like a wild beast just about to bite, he cried:

"My name is not Fabantou, my name is not Jondrette, my name is Thénardier! I am the innkeeper of Montfermeil! do you understand me? Thénardier! now do you know me?"

An imperceptible flush passed over M. Leblanc's forehead, and he answered without a tremor or elevation of voice, and with his usual placidness:

"No more than before."

Marius did not hear this answer. When Jondrette had said: *My name is Thénardier,* Marius had trembled in every limb, and supported himself against the wall as if he had felt the chill of a sword-blade through his heart. Then his right arm, which was just ready to fire the signal shot, dropped slowly down, and at the moment that Jondrette had repeated: *Do you understand me, Thénardier?* Marius' nerveless fingers had almost dropped the pistol. Jondrette, in unveiling who he was, had not moved M. Leblanc, but he had completely unnerved Marius. That name of Thénardier, which M. Leblanc did not seem to know, Marius knew. Remember what that name was to him! that name he had worn on his heart, written in his father's will! he carried it in the innermost place of his thoughts, in the holiest spot of his memory, in that sacred command: "A man named Thénardier saved my life. If my son should meet him, he will do him all the good he can." This man, to whom he, Marius, burned to devote himself, was a monster! this deliverer of Colonel Pontmercy was in the actual commission of a crime, the shape of which Marius did not yet see very distinctly, but which looked like an assassination! His father from the depths of his coffin commanded him to do all the good he could to Thénardier; for four years Marius had had no other thought than to acquit this debt of his father, and the moment that he was about to cause a brigand to be seized by justice, in the midst of a crime, destiny called to him: that is Thénardier! his father's life, saved in a storm of grape upon the heroic field of Waterloo, he was at last about to reward this man for, and to reward him with the scaffold! He had resolved, if ever he found this Thénardier, to accost him in no other wise than by throwing himself at his feet, and now he found him, indeed, but to deliver him to the executioner! his father said to him: Aid Thénardier! and he was answering that adored and holy voice by crushing Thénardier! presenting as a spectacle to his father in his tomb, the man who had snatched him from death at the peril of his life, executed in the Place St. Jacques by the act of his son, this Marius to whom he had bequeathed this man! He shuddered. Everything depended upon him. He held in his hand, they all unconscious, those beings who were moving there before his eyes. If he fired the pistol, M. Leblanc was saved and Thénardier was lost; if he did not, M. Leblanc was sacrificed, and, perhaps, Thénardier escaped.

Meanwhile Thénardier was walking to and fro before the table in a sort of bewilderment and frenzied triumph.

"Ha!" cried he, "I have found you again at last, monsieur philanthropist! monsieur threadbare millionaire! monsieur giver of dolls! old marrow-bones! ha! you do not know me? no, it was not you who came to Montfermeil, to my inn, eight years ago, the night of Christmas, 1823! it was not you who took away Fantine's child from my house! the Lark! it was not you who had a yellow coat! no! and a package of clothes in your hand just as you came here this morning! say now, wife! it is his mania it appears, to carry packages of woollen stockings into houses! old benevolence, get out! Are you a hosier, monsieur millionaire? you give the poor your shop sweepings, holy man! what a charlatan! Ha! you do not know me? Well, I knew you! I knew you immediately as soon as you stuck your nose in here. Ah! you are going to find out at last that it is not all roses to go into people's houses like that, under pretext of their being inns, with worn-out clothes, with the appearance of a pauper, to whom anybody would have given a sou, to deceive persons, to act the generous, take their help away, and threaten them in the woods, and that you do not get quit of it by bringing back afterward, when people are ruined, an overcoat that is too large and two paltry hospital coverlids, old beggar, child-stealer!"

"With his honest look!"

Thénardier stopped. He was out of breath.

M. Leblanc did not interrupt him but said when he stopped:

"I do not know what you mean. You are mistaken. I am a very poor man and anything but a millionaire. I do not know you; you mistake me for another."

"Ha!" screamed Thénardier, "good mountebank! You stick to that joke yet! You are in the fog, my old boy! Ah! you do not remember! You do not see who I am!"

"Pardon me, monsieur," answered M. Leblanc, with a tone of politeness which, at such a moment, had a peculiarly strange and powerful effect, "I see that you are a bandit."

"Bandit! Yes, I know that you call us so, you rich people! Yes! It is true I have failed; I am in concealment, I have no bread; I have not a sou, I am a bandit. Monsieur Millionaire! know this:—I have been a man established in business, I have been licensed, I have been an elector, I am a citizen, I am! And you, perhaps, are not one?"

Here Thénardier took a step towards the men who were before the door, and added with a shudder:

"When I think that he dares to come and talk to me, as if I were a cobbler!"

When Thénardier had taken breath he fixed his bloodshot eyes upon Monsieur Leblanc, and said in a low and abrupt tone:

"What have you to say before we begin to dance with you?"

Monsieur Leblanc said nothing.

For some moments, Monsieur Leblanc had seemed to follow and to watch all the movements of Thénardier, who, blinded and bewildered by his own rage, was walking to and fro in the den with the confidence inspired by the feeling that the door was guarded, having armed possession of a disarmed man, and being nine to one, even if the Thénardiess should count but for one man. He turned his back to Monsieur Leblanc.

Monsieur Leblanc seized this opportunity, pushed the chair away with his foot, the table with his hand, and at one bound, with a marvellous agility, before Thénardier had had time to turn around he was at the window. To open it, get up and step through it, was the work of a second. He was half outside when six strong hands seized him, and drew him forcibly back into the room. The three "chimney doctors" had thrown themselves upon him. At the same time the Thénardiess had clutched him by the hair.

At the disturbance which this made, the other bandits ran in from the hall. The old man, who was on the bed, and who seemed overwhelmed with wine, got off the pallet, and came tottering along with a road-mender's hammer in his hand.

One of the "chimney doctors," whose blackened face was lighted up by the candle, raised a sort of loaded club made of a bar of iron with a knob of lead at each end, over Monsieur Leblanc's head.

Marius could not endure this sight. "Father," thought he, "pardon me!" And his finger sought the trigger of the pistol. The shot was just about to be fired, when Thénardier's voice cried:

"Do him no harm!"

This desperate attempt of the victim, far from exasperating Thénardier, had calmed him.

"Do him no harm!" he repeated, and without suspecting it, the first result of this was to stop the pistol which was just ready to go off, and paralyze Marius, to whom the urgency seemed to disappear, and who, in view of this new phase of affairs, saw no impropriety in waiting longer.

A herculean struggle had commenced. With one blow full in the chest M. Leblanc had sent the old man sprawling into the middle of the room, then with two back strokes had knocked down two other assailants, whom he held one under each knee; the wretches screamed under the pressure as if they had been under a granite mill-stone; but the four others had seized the formidable old man by the arms and the back, and held him down over the two prostrate "chimney doctors." Thus, master of the latter and mastered by the former, crushing those below him and suffocating under those above him, vainly endeavoring to shake off all the violence and blows which were heaped upon him, M. Leblanc disappeared under the horrible group of the bandits, like a wild boar under a howling pack of hounds and mastiffs.

They succeeded in throwing him over upon the bed nearest to the window and held him there in awe. The Thénardiess had not let go of his hair.

"Here," said Thénardier, "let it alone. You will tear your shawl."

M. Leblanc seemed to have given up all resistance. They

searched him. There was nothing upon him but a leather purse which contained six francs, and his handkerchief.

Thénardier put the handkerchief in his pocket.

Thénardier went to the corner by the door and took a bundle of ropes which he threw to them.

"Tie him to the foot of the bed," said he.

The brigands bound him firmly, standing, with his feet to the floor, by the bed-post furthest from the window and nearest to the chimney.

When the last knot was tied, Thénardier took a chair and came and sat down nearly in front of M. Leblanc. Thénardier looked no longer like himself, in a few seconds the expression of his face had passed from unbridled violence to tranquil and crafty mildness. Marius hardly recognized in that polite, clerkly smile, the almost beastly mouth which was foaming a moment before.

"Monsieur," said Thénardier.

And with a gesture dismissing the brigands who still had their hands upon M. Leblanc:

"Move off a little, and let me talk with monsieur."

They all retired towards the door. He resumed:

"Monsieur, you were wrong in trying to jump out the window. You might have broken your leg. Now, if you please, we will talk quietly."

Thénardier quietly got up, went to the fireplace, took away the screen which he leaned against the nearest pallet, and thus revealed the furnace full of glowing coals in which the prisoner could plainly see the chisel at a white heat, spotted here and there with little scarlet stars.

Then Thénardier came back and sat down by Monsieur Leblanc.

"I continue," said he. "Now we can come to an understanding. Let us arrange this amicably. I was wrong to fly into a passion just now. My God, rich as you may be, you have your expenses; who does not have them? I do not want to ruin you, I am not a catch-poll, after all. Here, I am willing to go half way and make some sacrifice on my part. I need only two hundred thousand francs."

Monsieur Leblanc did not breathe a word. Thénardier went on:

"You will say: but I have not two hundred thousand francs with me. Oh! I am not exacting. I do not require that. I only ask one thing. Have the goodness to write what I dictate."

Here Thénardier paused, then he added, emphasising each word and casting a smile towards the furnace:

"I give you notice that I shall not admit that you cannot write."

Thénardier pushed the table close up to Monsieur Leblanc, and took the inkstand, a pen, and a sheet of paper from the drawer, which he left partly open, and from which gleamed the long blade of the knife.

He laid the sheet of paper before Monsieur Leblanc.

"Write," said he.

The prisoner spoke at last:

"How do you expect me to write? I am tied."

"That is true, pardon me!" said Thénardier, "you are quite right."

And turning towards Bigrenaille:

"Untie monsieur's right arm."

Panchaud, alias Printanier, alias Bigrenaille, executed Thénardier's order. When the prisoner's right hand was free, Thénardier dipped the pen into the ink, and presented it to him.

"Have the kindness now to write."

"What?" asked the prisoner.

"I will dictate."

M. Leblanc took the pen.

Thénardier began to dictate:

"My daughter—"

The prisoner shuddered and lifted his eyes to Thénardier.

"Come immediately, I have imperative need of you. The person who will give you this note is directed to bring you to me. I am waiting for you."

M. Leblanc had written the whole.

"Now," continued Thénardier, "sign it. What is your name?"

"Urbain Fabre," said the prisoner.

Thénardier, with the movement of a cat, thrust his hand into his pocket and pulled out the handkerchief taken from M. Leblanc. He looked for the mark upon it and held it up to the candle.

"U. F. That is it. Urbain Fabre. Well, sign U. F."

The prisoner signed.

"As it takes two hands to fold the letter, give it to me, will fold it."

This done, Thénardier resumed:

"Put on the address, *Mademoiselle Fabre,* at your house."

The prisoner remained thoughtful for a moment, then he took the pen and wrote:

"Mademoiselle Fabre, at Monsieur Urbain Fabre's, Rue Saint Dominique d'Enfer, No. 17."

Thénardier seized the letter with a sort of feverish convulsive movement. "Wife!" cried he.

The Thénardiess sprang forward.

"Here is the letter. You know what you have to do. There is a fiacre below. Go right away, and come back ditto."

There were now but five bandits left in the den with Thénardier and the prisoner. A gloomy stillness had succeeded the savage tumult which filled the garret a few moments before.

Nearly half an hour passed thus. Thénardier appeared absorbed in a dark meditation, the prisoner did not stir. Nevertheless Marius thought he had heard at intervals and for some moments a little dull noise from the direction of the prisoner.

This fearful situation, which had lasted now for more than an hour, changed its aspect at every moment. Marius had the strength to pass in review successively all the most heartrending conjectures, seeking some hope and finding more. The tumult of his thoughts strangely contrasted with the deathly silence of the den.

In the midst of this silence they heard the sound of the door of the stairway which opened, then closed.

The prisoner made a movement in his bonds.

"Here is the bourgeoise," said Thénardier.

He had hardly said this, when in fact the Thénardiess burst into the room, red, breathless, panting, with glaring eyes, and cried, striking her hands upon her hips both at the same time:

"False address!"

She continued:

"Nobody! Rue Saint Dominique, number seventeen, no Monsieur Urbain Fabre! They do not know who he is!"

Marius breathed. She, Ursula or The Lark, she whom he no longer knew what to call, was safe.

While his exasperated wife was vociferating, Thénardier had seated himself on the table; he sat a few seconds without saying a word, swinging his right leg, which was hanging down, and gazing upon the furnace with a look of savage reverie.

At last he said to the prisoner with a slow and singularly ferocious inflection:

"A false address! what did you hope for by that?"

"To gain time!" cried the prisoner with a ringing voice.

And at the same moment he shook off his bonds; they were cut. The prisoner was no longer fastened to the bed save by one leg.

Before the seven men had had time to recover themselves and spring upon him, he had bent over to the fireplace, reached his hand towards the furnace, then rose up, and now Thénardier, the Thénardiess, and the bandits, thrown by the shock into the back part of the room, beheld him with stupefaction, holding above his head the glowing chisel, from which fell an ominous light, almost free and in a formidable attitude.

Being unable to stoop down for fear of betraying himself, he had not cut the cords on his left leg.

The prisoner now raised his voice:

"You are pitiable, but my life is not worth the trouble of so long a defense. As to your imagining that you could make me speak, that you could make me write what I do not wish to write, that you could make me say what I do not wish to say——"

He pulled up the sleeve of his left arm, and added:

"Here."

At the same time he extended his arm, and laid upon the naked flesh the glowing chisel, which he held in his right hand, by the wooden handle.

They heard the hissing of the burning flesh; the odor peculiar to chambers of torture spread through the den. Marius staggered, lost in horror; the brigands themselves felt a shudder; the face of the wonderful old man hardly contracted, and while the red iron was sinking into the smoking, impassable, and almost august wound, he turned upon Thénardier his fine face, in which there was no hatred, and in which suffering was swallowed up in a serene majesty.

"Wretches," said he, "have no more fear for me than I have of you."

And drawing the chisel out of the wound, he threw it through the window, which was still open; the horrible glowing tool disappeared, whirling into the night, and fell in the distance, and was quenched in the snow.

The prisoner resumed:

"Do with me what you will."

He was disarmed.

"Lay hold of him," said Thénardier.

Two of the brigands laid their hands upon his shoulders, and the masked man with the ventriloquist's voice placed himself in front of him, ready to knock out his brains with a blow of the key, at the least motion.

At the same time Marius heard beneath him, at the foot of the partition, but so near that he could not see those who were talking, this colloquy, exchanged in a low voice:

"There is only one thing more to do."

"To kill him!"

"That is it."

It was the husband and wife who were holding counsel.

Thénardier walked with slow steps towards the table, opened the drawer, and took out the knife.

Marius cast his eyes wildly about him; the last mechanical resource of despair.

Suddenly he started.

At his feet, on the table, a clear ray of the full moon illuminated, and seemed to point out to him a sheet of paper. Upon that sheet he read this line, written in large letters that very morning, by the elder of the Thénardier girls:

"THE COGNES ARE HERE."

An idea, a flash crossed Marius' mind; that was the means which he sought; the solution of this dreadful problem which was torturing him, to spare the assassin and to save the victim. He knelt down upon his bureau, reached out his arm, caught up the sheet of paper, quietly detached a bit of plaster from the partition, wrapped it in the paper, and threw the whole through the crevice into the middle of the den.

It was time. Thénardier had conquered his last fears, or his last scruples, and was moving towards the prisoner.

"Something fell!" cried the Thénardiess.

"What is it?" said the husband.

The woman had sprung forward, and picked up the piece of plaster wrapped in the paper. She handed it to her husband.

"How did this come in?" asked Thénardier.

"Egad!" said the woman, "how do you suppose it got in? It came through the window."

"I saw it pass," said Bigrenaille.

Thénardier hurriedly unfolded the paper, and held it up to the candle.

"It is Eponine's writing. The devil!"

He made a sign to his wife, who approached quickly, and he showed her the line written on the sheet of paper; then he added in a hollow voice:

"Quick! the ladder! leave the meat in the trap, and clear the camp!"

As soon as the ladder was fixed, Thénardier cried:

"Come, bourgeoise!"

And he rushed towards the window.

But as he was stepping out, Bigrenaille seized him roughly by the collar.

"No; say now, old joker! after us."

"After us!" howled the bandits.

"You are children," said Thénardier. "We are losing time. The *railles* are at our heels."

"Well," said one of the bandits, "let us draw lots who shall go out first."

Thénardier exclaimed:

"Are you fools? are you cracked? You are a mess of *jobards!* Losing time, isn't it? Drawing lots, isn't it? with a wet finger! for the short straw! write our names! put them in a cap!——"

"Would you like my hat?" cried a voice from the door.

They all turned round. It was Javert.

He had his hat in his hand, and was holding it out smiling.

THE VICTIMS SHOULD ALWAYS BE ARRESTED FIRST

JAVERT, at nightfall, had posted his men and hid himself behind the trees on the Rue de la Barrière des Gobelins, which fronts the Gorbeau tenement on the other side of the boulevard. The going and coming of the fiacre fretted him greatly. At last, he became impatient, and, *sure that there was a nest there,* sure of being *"in good luck,"* having recognized several of the bandits who had gone in, he finally decided to go up.

He had come at the right time.

Javert put on his hat again, and stepped into the room, his arms folded, his cane under his arm, his sword in its sheath.

"Halt there," said he. "You will not pass out through the window, you will pass out through the door. It is less unwholesome. There are seven of you, fifteen of us."

A squad of sergents de ville with drawn swords, and officers armed with axes and clubs, rushed in at Javert's call. They bound the bandits. This crowd of men, dimly lighted by a candle, filled the den with shadow.

"Handcuffs on all!" cried Javert.

The Thénardiess, completely crushed, looked at her manacled hands and those of her husband, dropped to the floor and exclaimed, with tears in her eyes:

"My daughters!"

"They are provided for," said Javert.

Just then he perceived the prisoner of the bandits, who, since the entrance of the police, had not uttered a word, and had held his head down.

"Untie monsieur!" said Javert, "and let nobody go out."

This said, he sat down with authority before the table, on which the candle and the writing materials still were, drew a stamped sheet from his pocket, and commenced his *procés verbal*.

When he had written the first lines, a part of the formula, which is always the same, he raised his eyes:

"Bring forward the gentleman whom these gentlemen had bound."

The officers looked about them.

"Well," asked Javert, "where is he now?"

The prisoner of the bandits, M. Leblanc, M. Urbain Fabre, the father of Ursula, or The Lark, had disappeared.

SAINT DENIS
AND
IDYL OF THE RUE PLUMET

Eponine

THE FIELD OF THE LARK

MARIUS had seen the unexpected dénouement of the ambuscade; but hardly had Javert left the old ruin, carrying away his prisoners in three coaches, when Marius also slipped out of the house. It was only nine o'clock in the evening. Marius went to Courfeyrac's. Courfeyrac was no longer the imperturbable inhabitant of the Latin Quarter; he had gone to live in the Rue de la Verrerie "for political reasons;" this quarter was one of those in which the insurrection was fond of installing itself in those days.

The next day, by seven o'clock in the morning, Marius went back to the tenement, paid his rent, and what was due to Ma'am Bougon, had his books, bed, table, bureau, and his two chairs loaded upon a hand-cart, and went off without leaving his address.

Ma'am Bougon was convinced that Marius was somehow an accomplice of the robbers seized the night before. "Who would have thought so?" she exclaimed among the portresses of the quarter, "a young man who had so much the appearance of a girl!"

Marius had two reasons for his prompt removal. The first was, that he now had a horror of that house, where he had seen, so near at hand, and in all its most repulsive and most ferocious development, a social deformity perhaps still more hideous than the evil rich man: the evil poor. The second was, that he did not wish to figure in the trial which would probably follow, and be brought forward to testify against Thénardier.

Marius, moreover, was in sore affliction. He had for a moment seen close at hand in that obscurity, the young girl whom he loved, the old man who seemed her father, these unknown beings who were his only interest and his only hope 'n this world; and at the moment he had thought to hold ..em fast, a breath had swept all those shadows away. Not a spark of certainty or truth had escaped even from that most fearful shock. No conjecture was possible. He knew not even the name which he had thought he knew. Certainly it was no longer Ursula.

To crown all, want returned. During all these torments, and now for a long time, he had discontinued his work, and nothing is more dangerous than discontinued labor; it is habit lost. A habit easy to abandon, difficult to resume.

AN APPARITION TO MARIUS

HE lived in the Field of the Lark rather than in Courfeyrac's room. This was his real address: Boulevard de la Santé, seventh tree from the Rue Croulebarbe.

That morning, he had left this seventh tree, and sat down on the bank of the brook of the Gobelins. The bright sun was gleaming through the new and glossy leaves.

He was thinking of "Her!" And his dreaminess, becoming reproachful, fell back upon himself; he thought sorrowfully of the idleness, the paralysis of the soul, which was growing up within him, and of that night which was thickening before him hour by hour so rapidly that he had already ceased to see the sun.

Meanwhile, through this painful evolution of indistinct ideas which were not even a soliloquy, so much had action become enfeebled within him, and he no longer had even strength to develop his grief—through this melancholy distraction, the sensations of the world without reached him. He heard behind and below him, on both banks of the stream, the washerwomen of the Gobelins beating their linen; and over his head, the birds chattering and singing in the elms. On the one hand the sound of liberty, of happy unconcern, of winged leisure; on the other, the sound of labor. A thing which made him muse profoundly, and almost reflect, these two joyous sounds.

All at once, in the midst of his ecstasy of exhaustion, he heard a voice which was known to him, say:

"Ah! there he is!"

He raised his eyes and recognised the unfortunate child who had come to his room one morning, the elder of the Thénardier girls, Eponine; he now knew her name. Singular fact, she had become more wretched and more beautiful, two steps which seemed impossible. She had accomplished a double progress towards the light, and towards distress. She was barefooted and in rags, as on the day when she had so resolutely entered his room, only her rags were two months older; the holes were larger, the tatters dirtier.

And with all this, she was beautiful.

Meantime, she had stopped before Marius, with an expression of pleasure upon her livid face, and something which resembled a smile.

She stood for a few seconds, as if she could not speak.

"I have found you, then?" said she at last. "How I have looked for you? if you only knew? Do you know? I have been in the jug. A fortnight! They have let me out! seeing that there was nothing against me, and then I was not of the age of discernment. It lacked two months. Oh! how I have looked for you! it is six weeks now. You don't live down there any longer?"

"No," said Marius.

"Oh! I understand. On account of the affair. Such scares are disagreeable. You have moved. But tell me, where do you live now?"

Marius did not answer.

"Ah!" she continued, "you have a hole in your shirt. I must mend it for you."

She resumed with an expression which gradually grew darker:

"You don't seem to be glad to see me?"

Marius said nothing; she herself was silent for a moment, then exclaimed: ·

"But if I would, I could easily make you glad!"

"How?" inquired Marius. "What does that mean?"

"Ah! you used to speak more kindly to me!" replied she.

"Well, what is it that you mean?"

She bit her lip; she seemed to hesitate, as if passing through a kind of interior struggle. At last, she appeared to decide upon her course.

"So much the worse, it makes no difference. You look sad, I want you to be glad. But promise me that you will laugh, I want to see you laugh and hear you say: Ah, well! that is good. Poor Monsieur Marius! you know, you promised me that you would give me whatever I should ask—"

"Yes! but tell me!"

She looked into Marius' eyes and said:
"I have the address."

Marius turned pale. All his blood flowed back to his heart.
"What address?"

"The address you asked me for."

She added as if she were making an effort:
"The address—you know well enough!"

"Yes!" stammered Marius.

"Of the young lady!"

Having pronounced this word, she sighed deeply.

Marius sprang up from the bank on which he was sitting, and took her wildly by the hand.

"Oh! come! show me the way, tell me! ask me for whatever you will! Where is it?"

"Come with me," she answered. "I am not sure of the street and the number; it is away on the other side from here, but I know the house very well. I will show you."

After a few steps, she stopped.

"You follow too near me, Monsieur Marius. Let me go forward, and follow me like that, without seeming to. It won't do for a fine young man, like you, to be seen with a woman like me."

The House in the Rue Plumet

TOWARDS the middle of the last century, a velvet-capped president of the Parlement of Paris had *"une petite maison"* built in the Faubourg Saint Germain, in the deserted Rue de Blomet, now called the Rue Plumet.

This was a summer-house of but two stories, the whole fronted by a garden with a large iron grated gate opening on the street. This garden contained about an acre. This was all that the passers-by could see; but in the rear of the house there was a small yard, at the further end of which there was a low building, two rooms only and a cellar, a convenience intended to conceal a child and nurse in case of need. This building communicated, from the rear, by a masked door opening secretly, with a long narrow passage, paved, winding, open to the sky, bordered by two high walls, and which, concealed with wonderful art, and as it were lost between the inclosures of the gardens and fields, all the corners and turnings of which it followed, came to an end at another door, also concealed, which opened a third of a mile away, almost in another *quartier,* upon the unbuilt end of the Rue de Babylone.

In the month of October, 1829, a man of a certain age had appeared and hired the house as it stood, including, of course, the building in the rear, and the passage which ran out to the Rue de Babylone. He had the secret openings of the two doors of this passage repaired. The new tenant had ordered a few repairs, added here and there what was lacking, and finally came and installed himself with a young girl and an aged servant, without any noise, rather like somebody stealing in than like a man who enters his own house. The neighbors did not gossip about it, for the reason that there were no neighbors.

This tenant, to partial extent, was Jean Valjean; the young girl was Cosette. The servant was a spinster named Toussaint, whom Jean Valjean had saved from the hospital and misery, and who was old, stuttering, and a native of a province, three qualities which had determined Jean Valjean to take her with him. He hired the house under the name of Monsieur Fauchelevent, gentleman.

Why had Jean Valjean left the convent of the Petit Picpus? What had happened?

Nothing had happened.

As we remember, Jean Valjean was happy in the convent, so happy that his conscience at last began to be troubled. He saw Cosette every day, he felt paternity springing up and developing within him more and more, he brooded this child with his soul, he said to himself that she was his, that nothing could take her from him, that this would be so indefinitely, that certainly she would become a nun, being every day gently led on towards it, that thus the convent was henceforth the universe to her as well as to him, that he would grow old there and she would grow up there, that she would grow old there and he would die there; that finally, ravishing hope, no separation was possible. In reflecting upon this, he at last began to find difficulties. He questioned himself. He asked himself if all this happiness were really his own, if it were not made up of the happiness of another, of the happiness of this child whom he was appropriating and plundering, he, an old man; if this was not a robbery? He said to himself that this child had a right to know what life was before renouncing it. And who knows but, thinking over all this some day, and being a nun with regret, Cosette might come to hate him? a final thought, which was almost selfish and less heroic than the others, but which was insupportable to him. He resolved to leave the convent.

His determination once formed, he awaited an opportunity. It was not slow to present itself. Old Fauchelevent died.

Jean Valjean asked an audience of the reverend prioress, and told her that having received a small inheritance on the death of his brother, which enabled him to live henceforth without labor, he would leave the service of the convent, and take away his daughter; but that, as it was not just that Cosette, not taking her vows, should have been educated gratuitously, he humbly begged the reverend prioress to allow him to offer the community, as indemnity for the five years which Cosette had passed there, the sum of five thousand francs.

On leaving the convent, he took in his own hands, and would not entrust to any assistant, the little box, the key of which he always had about him. This box puzzled Cosette, on account of the odor of embalming which came from it.

Let us say at once, that henceforth this box never left him more. He always had it in his room. It was the first, and sometimes the only thing that he carried away in his changes of abode. Cosette laughed about it, and called this box *the inseparable,* saying: "I am jealous of it."

Jean Valjean nevertheless did not appear again in the open city without deep anxiety.

He discovered the house in the Rue Plumet, and buried himself in it. He was henceforth in possession of the name of Ultimus Fauchelevent.

At the same time he hired two other lodgings in Paris, in order to attract less attention than if he always remained in the same *quartier,* to be able to change his abode on occasion, at the slightest anxiety which he might feel, and finally, that he might not again find himself in such a strait as on the night when he had so miraculously escaped from Javert. These two lodgings were two very humble dwellings, and of a poor appearance, in two *quartiers* widely distant from each other, one in the Rue de l'Ouest, the other in the Rue de l'Homme Armé.

He went from time to time, now to the Rue de l'Homme Armé, and now to the Rue de l'Ouest, to spend a month or six weeks, with Cosette, without taking Toussaint.

JEAN VALJEAN A NATIONAL GUARD

STILL, properly speaking, he lived in the Rue Plumet, and he had ordered his life there in the following manner:

Cosette with the servant occupied the house. For his part, he lived in the sort of porter's lodge in the back-yard, with a mattress on a cot bedstead, a white wood table, two straw chairs, an earthen water-pitcher, a few books upon a board, his dear box in a corner, never any fire. He dined with Cosette, and there was a black loaf on the table for him. He said to Toussaint, when she entered their service: "Mademoiselle is the mistress of the house." "And you, m-monsieur?" replied Toussaint, astounded. "Me, I am much better than the master, I am the father."

Every day Jean Valjean took Cosette's arm, and went to walk with her. They went to the least frequented walk of the Luxembourg, and every Sunday to mass, always at Saint Jacques du Haut Pas, because it was quite distant. As that is a very poor *quartier,* he gave much alms there. No stranger came into the house in the Rue Plumet. Toussaint brought the provisions, and Jean Valjean himself went after the water to a watering trough which was near by on the boulevard.

There was on the Rue de Babylone door a box for letters and papers; but the three occupants of the summer-house on the Rue Plumet receiving neither papers nor letters, the entire use of the box was now limited to the notices of the receiver of taxes and the Guard warnings. For M. Fauchelevent belonged to the National Guard: he had not been able to escape the close meshes of the enrollment of 1831.

Three or four times a year, Jean Valjean donned his uniform, and performed his duties; very willingly moreover; it was a good disguise for him, which associated him with everybody else while leaving him solitary. Jean Valjean had completed his sixtieth year, the age of legal exemption; but he did not appear more than fifty; moreover, he had no desire to escape from his sergeant-major and to cavil with the Count de Lobau; he had no civil standing; he was concealing his name, he was concealing his identity, he was concealing his age, he was concealing everything; and, we have just said, he was very willingly a National Guard. To resemble the crowd who pay their taxes, this was his whole ambition. This man had for his ideal within, the angel—without, the bourgeois.

Neither Jean Valjean, nor Cosette, nor Toussaint, ever came in or went out except by the gate on the Rue de Babylone. Unless one had seen them through the grated gate of the garden, it would have been difficult to guess that they lived in the Rue Plumet. This gate always remained closed. Jean Valjean had left the garden uncultivated, that it might not attract attention.

In this, he deceived himself, perhaps.

CHANGE OF GRATING

COSETTE had left the convent, still almost a child; she was a little more than fourteen years old.

Her education was finished; that is to say, she had been taught religion, and also, and above all, devotion; then "history," that is, the thing which they call thus in the convent, geography, grammar, the participles, the kings of France, a little music, to draw profiles, etc., but further than this she was ignorant of everything, which is a charm and a peril. To form the mind of a young girl, all the nuns in the world are not equal to one mother.

Cosette had had no mother. She had only had many mothers, in the plural.

As to Jean Valjean, there was indeed within him all manner of tenderness and all manner of solicitude; but he was only an old man who knew nothing at all.

On leaving the convent, Cosette could have found nothing more grateful and more dangerous than the house on the Rue Plumet. It was the continuation of solitude with the beginning of liberty; an enclosed garden, but a sharp, rich, voluptuous, and odorous nature; the same dreams as in the convent, but with glimpses of young men; a grating, but upon the street.

Still, we repeat, when she came there she was but a child. Jean Valjean gave her this uncultivated garden. "Do whatever you like with it," said he to her. It delighted Cosette; she ransacked every thicket and turned over every stone, she sought for "animals;" she played while she dreamed; she loved this garden for the insects which she found in the grass under her feet, while she loved it for the stars which she saw in the branches over her head.

And then she loved her father, that is to say, Jean Valjean, with all her heart, with a frank filial passion which made the good man a welcome and very pleasant companion for her.

This simple man was sufficient for Cosette's thought, even as this wild garden was to her eyes. When she had had a good chase after the butterflies, she would come up to him breathless and say, "Oh! how I have run!" He would kiss her forehead.

Cosette adored the good man. She was always running after him. Where Jean Valjean was, was happiness. As Jean Valjean did not live in the summer-house or the garden, she found more pleasure in the paved back-yard than in the enclosure full of flowers, and in the little bedroom furnished with straw chairs than in the great parlor hung with tapestry, where she could recline on silken armchairs. Jean Valjean sometimes said to her, smiling with the happiness of being teased: "Why don't you go home? why don't you leave me alone?"

Cosette had but vague remembrance of her childhood. She prayed morning and evening for her mother, whom she had never known. The Thénardiers had remained to her like two hideous faces of some dream. She remembered that she had been "one day, at night," sent into a wood after water. She thought that that was very far from Paris. It seemed to her that that she had commenced life in an abyss, and that Jean Valjean had drawn her out of it. Her childhood impressed her as a time when there were only centipedes, spiders, and snakes about her. When she was dozing at night, before going to sleep, as she had no very clear idea of being Jean Valjean's daughter, and that he was her father, she imagined that her mother's soul had passed into this good man and come to live with her.

When he sat down, she would rest her cheek on his white hair and silently drop a tear, saying to herself: "This is perhaps my mother, this man!"

While Cosette was a little girl, Jean Valjean had been fond of talking with her about her mother; when she was a young maiden, this was impossible for him. It seemed to him that he no longer dared. Was this on account of Cosette? was it on account of Fantine? He felt a sort of religious horror at introducing that shade into Cosette's thoughts, and at bringing in the dead as a third sharer of their destiny. The more sacred that shade was to him, the more formidable it seemed to him. He thought of Fantine and felt overwhelmed with silence.

One day Cosette said to him:

"Father, I saw my mother in a dream last night. She had two great wings. My mother must have attained to sanctity in her life."

"Through martyrdom," answered Jean Valjean.

Still, Jean Valjean was happy.

When Cosette went out with him, she leaned upon his arm, proud, happy, in the fulness of her heart. Jean Valjean, at all these marks of a tenderness so exclusive and so fully satisfied with him alone, felt his thought melt into delight. The poor man shuddered, overflowed with an angelic joy; he declared in his transport that this would last through life; he said to himself that he really had not suffered enough to deserve such radiant happiness, and he thanked God, in the depths of his soul, for having permitted that he, a miserable man, should be so loved by this innocent being.

THE ROSE DISCOVERS THAT SHE IS AN ENGINE OF WAR

ONE day Cosette happened to look in her mirror, and she said to herself: "What!" It seemed to her almost that she was pretty. This threw her into strange anxiety. Up to this moment she had never thought of her face. She had seen herself in her glass, but she had not looked at herself. And then, she had often been told that she was homely; Jean Valjean alone would quietly say: "Why, no! why, no!" However that might be, Cosette had always thought herself homely, and had grown up in that idea with the pliant resignation of childhood. And now suddenly her mirror said like Jean Valjean: "Why, no!" She had no sleep that night. "If I were pretty!" thought she, "how funny it would be if I should be pretty!" And she called to mind those of her companions whose beauty had made an impression in the convent, and said: "What! I should be like Mademoiselle Such-a-one!"

In the evening after dinner, she regularly made tapestry or did some convent work in the parlor, while Jean Valjean read by her side. Once, on raising her eyes from her work, she was very much surprised at the anxious way in which her father was looking at her.

At another time, she was passing along the street, and it seemed to her that somebody behind her, whom she did not see, said: "Pretty woman! but badly dressed." "Pshaw!"

thought she, "that is not me. I am well dressed and homely."
She had on at the time her plush hat and merino dress.

At last, she was in the garden one day, and heard poor old
Toussaint saying: "Monsieur, do you notice how pretty mademoiselle is growing?" Cosette did not hear what her father
answered. Toussaint's words threw her into a sort of commotion. She ran out of the garden, went up to her room,
hurried to the glass, it was three months since she had looked
at herself, and uttered a cry. She was dazzled by herself.

She was beautiful and handsome; she could not help being
of Toussaint's and her mirror's opinion. The consciousness of
her beauty came to her entire, in a moment, like broad daylight when it bursts upon us; others noticed it moreover,
Toussaint said so.

For his part, Jean Valjean felt a deep and undefinable
anguish in his heart.

He had in fact, for some time past, been contemplating
with terror that beauty which appeared every day more radiant upon Cosette's sweet face. A dawn, charming to all
others, dreary to him.

Cosette had been beautiful for some time before she perceived it. But, from the first day, this unexpected light which
slowly rose and by degrees enveloped the young girl's whole
person, wounded Jean Valjean's gloomy eyes. He felt that it
was a change in a happy life, so happy that he dared not
stir for fear of disturbing something. This man who had
passed through every distress, who was still all bleeding
from the lacerations of his destiny, who had been almost
evil, and who had become almost holy, who, after having
dragged the chain of the galleys, now dragged the invisible
but heavy chain of indefinite infamy, this man whom the
law had not released, and who might be at any instant retaken, and led back from the obscurity of his virtue to the
broad light of public shame, this man accepted all, excused
all, pardoned all, blessed all, wished well to all, and only
asked of Providence, of men, of the laws, of society, of nature, of the world, this one thing, that Cosette should love
him!

That Cosette should continue to love him! That God
would not prevent the heart of this child from coming to
him, and remaining his! Loved by Cosette, he felt himself
healed, refreshed, soothed, satisfied, rewarded, crowned.
Loved by Cosette, he was content! he asked nothing more.

Whatever might affect this condition, were it only on the surface, made him shudder as if it were the commencement of another.

He said to himself: "How beautiful she is! What will become of me?"

Here, in fact, was the difference between his tenderness and the tenderness of a mother. What he saw with anguish, a mother would have seen with delight.

The first symptoms were not slow to manifest themselves. From the morrow of the day on which she had said: "Really, I am handsome!" Cosette gave attention to her dress. She recalled the words of the passer: "Pretty, but badly dressed," breath of an oracle which had passed by her and vanished after depositing in her heart one of the two germs which must afterwards fill the whole life of the woman, coquetry. Love is the other.

With faith in her beauty, the entire feminine soul blossomed within her. She was horrified at the merino and ashamed of the plush.

In less than a month little Cosette was, in that Thebaid of the Rue de Babylone, not only one of the prettiest women, which is something, but one of "the best dressed" in Paris, which is much more.

The first day that Cosette went out with her dress and mantle of black damask and her white crape hat she came to take Jean Valjean's arm, gay, radiant, rosy, proud, and brilliant. "Father," said she, "how do you like this?" Jean Valjean answered in a voice which resembled the bitter voice of envy: "Charming!" He seemed as usual during the walk. When they came back he asked Cosette:

"Are you not going to wear your dress and hat any more?"

"That disguise!" said she. "Father, what would you have me do with it? Oh! to be sure, no, I shall never wear those horrid things again. With that machine on my head, I look like Madame Mad-dog."

Jean Valjean sighed deeply.

From that day, he noticed that Cosette, who previously was always asking to stay in, saying: "Father, I enjoy myself better here with you," was now always asking to go out. Indeed, what is the use of having a pretty face and a delightful dress, if you do not show them?

It was at this period that Marius, after the lapse of six months, saw her again at the Luxembourg.

COSETTE, in her seclusion, like Marius in his, was all ready to take fire. Destiny, with its mysterious and fatal patience, was slowly bringing these two beings near each other, fully charged and all languishing with the stormy electricities of passion.

The power of a glance has been so much abused in love stories, that it has come to be disbelieved in. Few people dare now to say that two beings have fallen in love because they have looked at each other. Yet it is in this way that love begins, and in this way only.

At that particular moment when Cosette unconsciously looked with this glance which so affected Marius, Marius had no suspicion that he also had a glance which affected Cosette.

She got from him the same harm and the same blessing.

For a long time now she had seen and scrutinized him as young girls scrutinize and see, while looking another way. Marius still thought Cosette ugly, while Cosette already began to think Marius beautiful. But as he paid no attention to her, this young man was quite indifferent to her.

On the day their eyes met and at last said abruptly to both those first obscure and ineffable things which the glance stammers out, Cosette at first did not comprehend. She went back pensively to the house in the Rue de l'Ouest, to which Jean Valjean, according to his custom, had gone to spend six weeks.

Knowing that she was beautiful, she felt thoroughly, although in an indistinct way, that she had a weapon.

We remember Marius' hesitations, his palpitations, his terrors. He remained at his seat and did not approach, which vexed Cosette. One day she said to Jean Valjean: "Father, let us walk a little this way." Seeing that Marius was not coming to her, she went to him. In such a case, every woman resembles Mahomet.

That day Cosette's glance made Marius mad, Marius' glance made Cosette tremble. Marius went away confident, and Cosette anxious. From that day onward, they adored each other.

Cosette did not know what love was. She had never heard the word uttered in its earthly sense. She did not know, therefore, what name to give to what she now experienced. Is one less sick for not knowing the name of the disease?

She loved with so much the more passion as she loved with ignorance. She did not know whether it were good or evil, beneficent or dangerous, necessary or accidental, eternal or transitory, permitted or prohibited: she loved.

It proved that the love which presented itself was precisely that which best suited the condition of her soul. It was a sort of far-off worship, a mute contemplation, a deification by an unknown votary. In this condition, it was not a lover that she needed, it was not even an admirer, it was a vision. She began to adore Marius as something charming, luminous, and impossible.

She waited impatiently every day the hour for her walk, she found Marius there, she felt herself inexpressibly happy, and she sincerely believed that she uttered her whole thought when she said to Jean Valjean: "What a delightful garden the Luxembourg is!"

Marius and Cosette were in the dark in regard to each other. They did not speak, they did not bow, they were not acquainted; they saw each other; and, like the stars in the sky separated by millions of leagues, they lived by gazing upon each other.

TO SADNESS, SADNESS AND A HALF

EVERY condition has its instinct. The old and eternal mother, Nature, silently warned Jean Valjean of the presence of Marius. Jean Valjean shuddered in the darkness of his mind. Marius, also warned, and, according to the deep law of God, by this same mother, Nature, did all that he could to hide himself from the "father." It happened, however, that Jean Valjean sometimes perceived him. Marius' ways were no longer at all natural. He ceased to come near them as formerly; he sat down at a distance, and remained there in an ecstasy; he had a book and pretended to be reading; why did he pretend? Formerly he came with his old coat, now he had his new coat on every day; it was not very certain that he did not curl his hair, he had strange eyes, he wore gloves; in short, Jean Valjean cordially detested this young man.

There was between the taste for dress which had arisen in Cosette and the habit of wearing new coats which had grown upon this unknown man, a parallelism which made Jean Valjean anxious. It was an accident perhaps, doubtless, certainly, but a threatening accident.

He had never opened his mouth to Cosette about the unknown man. One day, however, he could not contain himself, and with that uncertain despair which hastily drops the plummet into its unhappiness, he said to her: "What a pedantic air that young man has!"

Cosette, a year before, an unconcerned little girl, would have answered: "Why no, he is charming." Ten years later, with the love of Marius in her heart, she would have answered: "Pedantic and insupportable to the sight! you are quite right!" At the period of life and of heart in which she then was, she merely answered with supreme calmness: "That young man!"

As if she saw him for the first time in her life.

"How stupid I am!" thought Jean Valjean. "She had not even noticed him. I have shown him to her myself."

O simplicity of the old! depth of the young!

Once only Cosette made a mistake, and startled him. He rose from the seat to go, after sitting there three hours, and she said: "So soon!"

Jean Valjean had not discontinued the promenades in the Luxembourg, not wishing to do anything singular, and above all dreading to excite any suspicion in Cosette; but during those hours so sweet to the two lovers, while Cosette was sending her smile to the intoxicated Marius, who perceived nothing but that, and now saw nothing in the world save one radiant, adored face, Jean Valjean fixed upon Marius glaring and terrible eyes. He who had come to believe that he was no longer capable of a malevolent feeling, had moments in which, when Marius was there, he thought that he was again becoming savage and ferocious, and felt opening and upheaving against this young man those old depths of his soul where there had once been so much wrath. It seemed to him almost as if the unknown craters were forming with him again.

We know the rest. The insanity of Marius continued. One day he followed Cosette to the Rue de l'Ouest. Another day he spoke to the porter: the porter in his turn spoke, and said to Jean Valjean: "Monsieur, who is that curious young man who has been asking for you?" The next day, Jean Valjean cast that glance at Marius which Marius finally perceived. A week after, Jean Valjean had moved. He resolved that he would never set his foot again either in the Luxembourg, or in the Rue de l'Ouest. He returned to the Rue Plumet.

Cosette did not complain, she said nothing, she asked no questions, she did not seek to know any reason; she was already at that point at which one fears discovery and self-betrayal. Jean Valjean had no experience of this misery, the only misery which is charming, and the only misery which he did not know; for this reason, he did not understand the deep significance of Cosette's silence. He noticed only that she had become sad, and he became gloomy. There was on either side an armed inexperience.

Once he made a trial. He asked Cosette:

"Would you like to go to the Luxembourg?"

A light illumined Cosette's pale face.

"Yes," said she.

They went. Three months had passed. Marius went there no longer. Marius was not there.

The next day, Jean Valjean asked Cosette again:

"Would you like to go to the Luxembourg?"

She answered sadly and quietly:

"No!"

Jean Valjean was hurt by this sadness, and harrowed by this gentleness.

For her part, Cosette was languishing. She suffered from the absence of Marius, as she had rejoiced in his presence, in a peculiar way, without really knowing it. When Jean Valjean ceased to take her on their usual walk, her woman's instinct murmured confusedly in the depths of her heart, that she must not appear to cling to the Luxembourg; and that if it were indifferent to her, her father would take her back there. But days, weeks, and months passed away. Jean Valjean had tacitly accepted Cosette's tacit consent. She regretted it. It was too late. The day she returned to the Luxembourg, Marius was no longer there. Marius then had disappeared; it was all over; what could she do? Would she ever find him again? She felt a constriction of her heart, which nothing relaxed, and which was increasing every day; she no longer knew whether it was winter or summer, sunshine or rain, whether the birds sang, whether it was the season for dahlias or daisies; and she became dejected, absorbed, intent upon a single thought, her eye wild and fixed, as when one looks into the night at the deep black place where an apparition has vanished.

Still she did not let Jean Valjean see anything, except her paleness. She kept her face sweet for him.

These two beings, who had loved each other so exclusively, and with so touching a love, and who had lived so long for each other, were now suffering by each other, and through each other; without speaking of it, without harsh feeling, and smiling the while.

Aid from Below
May Be Aid from Above

WOUND WITHOUT, CURE WITHIN

THERE was left to them but one distraction, and this had formerly been a pleasure: that was to carry bread to those who were hungry, and clothing to those who were cold. In these visits to the poor, in which Cosette often accompanied Jean Valjean, they found some remnant of their former light-heartedness; and, sometimes, when they had had a good day, when many sorrows had been relieved and many little children revived and made warm, Cosette, in the evening, was a little gay. It was at this period that they visited the Jondrette den.

The day after that visit, Jean Valjean appeared in the cottage in the morning, with his ordinary calmness, but with a large wound on his left arm, very much inflamed and very venomous, which resembled a burn, and which he explained in some fashion. This wound confined him within doors more than a month with fever. He would see no physician. When Cosette urged it: "Call the dog-doctor," said he.

Cosette dressed it night and morning with so divine a grace and so angelic a pleasure in being useful to him, that Jean Valjean felt all his old happiness return, his fears and his anxieties dissipate, and he looked upon Cosette, saying: "Oh! the good wound! Oh! the kind hurt!"

Cosette, as her father was sick, had deserted the summer-house and regained her taste for the little lodge and the back-yard. She spent almost all her time with Jean Valjean, and read to him the books which he liked. In general, books of travels. Jean Valjean was born anew; his happiness revived with inexpressible radiance; the Luxembourg, the unknown young prowler, Cosette's coldness, all these clouds of his soul faded away. He now said to himself: "I imagined all that. I am an old fool."

His happiness was so great, that the frightful discovery of the Thénardiers, made in the Jondrette den, and so un-

expectedly, had in some sort glided over him. He had succeeded in escaping; his trace was lost, what mattered the rest!
he thought of it only to grieve over those wretches. "They are
now in prison, and can do no harm in future," thought he,
"but what a pitiful family in distress!"

Spring came, the garden was so wonderful at that season
of the year, that Jean Valjean said to Cosette: "You never
go there, I wish you would walk in it." "As you will, father,"
said Cosette.

And, out of obedience to her father, she resumed her walks
in the garden, oftenest alone, for, as we have remarked, Jean
Valjean, who probably dreaded being seen through the gate,
hardly ever went there.

Jean Valjean's wound had been a diversion.

When Cosette saw that her father was suffering less, and
that he was getting well, and that he seemed happy, she felt
a contentment that she did not even notice, so gently and
naturally did it come upon her. It was then the month of
March, the days were growing longer, winter was departing,
winter always carries with it something of our sadness; then
April came, that daybreak of summer, fresh like every dawn,
gay like every childhood; weeping a little sometimes like the
infant that it is. Nature in this month has charming gleams
which pass from the sky, the clouds, the trees, the fields, and
the flowers, into the heart of man.

Cosette was still too young for this April joy, which resembled her, not to find its way to her heart. Insensibly,
and without a suspicion on her part, the darkness passed
away from her mind. In the spring it becomes light in sad
souls, as at noon it becomes light in cellars. And Cosette
was not now very sad. In the morning, about ten o'clock,
after breakfast, when she had succeeded in enticing her father
into the garden for a quarter of an hour, and while she was
walking in the sun in front of the steps, supporting his
wounded arm, she did not perceive that she was laughing
every moment, and that she was happy.

Jean Valjean saw her, with intoxication, again become
fresh and rosy.

As soon as his wound was cured, he resumed his solitary
and twilight walks.

The End of Which Is
Unlike the Beginning

ENRICHED BY THE COMMENTARIES OF TOUSSAINT

In the garden, near the grated gate, on the street, there was a stone seat protected from the gaze of the curious by a hedge, but which, nevertheless, by an effort, the arm of a passer could reach through the grating and the hedge.

One evening in this same month of April, Jean Valjean had gone out; Cosette, after sunset, had sat down on this seat.

Cosette rose, slowly made the round of the garden.

She returned to the seat.

Just as she was sitting down, she noticed in the place she had left a stone of considerable size which evidently was not there the moment before.

Cosette reflected upon this stone, asking herself what it meant. Suddenly, the idea that this stone did not come upon the seat of itself, that somebody had put it there, that an arm had passed through that grating, this idea came to her and made her afraid. It was a genuine fear this time; there was the stone. No doubt was possible, she did not touch it, fled without daring to look behind her, took refuge in the house, and immediately shut the glass-door of the stairs with shutter, bar, and bolt. She asked Toussaint:

"Has my father come in?"

"Not yet, mademoiselle."

Jean Valjean, a man given to thought and a night-walker, frequently did not return till quite late.

"Toussaint," resumed Cosette, "you are careful in the evening to bar the shutters well, upon the garden at least, and to really put the little iron things into the little rings which fasten?"

"Oh! never fear, mademoiselle."

Toussaint did not fail, and Cosette well knew it, but she could not help adding:

"Because it is so solitary about here!"

"For that matter," said Toussaint, "that is true. We would

be assassinated before we would have time to say Boo! And
then, monsieur doesn't sleep in the house. But don't be
afraid, mademoiselle, I fasten the windows like Bastilles.
Lone women! I am sure it is enough to make us shudder!
Just imagine it! to see men come into the room at night and
say to you: Hush! and set themselves to cutting your throat."

"Be still," said Cosette. "Fasten everything well."

Cosette, dismayed by the melodrama improvised by Toussaint, and perhaps also by the memory of the apparitions of
the previous week which came back to her, did not even dare
to say to her: "Go and look at the stone which somebody has
laid on the seat!" for fear of opening the garden door again,
and lest "the men" would come in. She had all the doors and
windows carefully closed, made Toussaint go over the whole
house from cellar to garret, shut herself up in her room, drew
her bolts, looked under her bed, lay down, and slept badly.

At sunrise—the peculiarity of sunrise is to make us laugh
at all our terrors of the night, and our laugh is always pro-
portioned to the fear we have had—at sunrise Cosette, on
waking, looked upon her fright as upon a nightmare, and
said to herself: "What have I been dreaming about?"

The sun, which shone through the cracks of her shutters,
and made the damask curtains purple, reassured her to such
an extent that it all vanished from her thoughts, even the
stone.

"There was no stone on the bench, any more than there
was a man with a round hat in the garden; I dreamed the
stone as I did the rest."

She dressed herself, went down to the garden, ran to the
bench, and felt a cold sweat. The stone was there.

But this was only for a moment. What is fright by night is
curiosity by day.

"Pshaw!" said she, "now let us see."

She raised the stone, which was pretty large. There was
something underneath which resembled a letter.

Cosette took out of the envelope what it contained, a quire
of paper, each page of which was numbered and contained a
few lines written in a rather pretty hand-writing, thought
Cosette, and very fine.

Cosette looked for a name, there was none; a signature,
there was none. To whom was it addressed? to her probably,
since a hand had placed the packet upon her seat. From
whom did it come? An irresistible fascination took possession of her, she endeavored to turn her eyes away from

these leaves which trembled in her hand, she looked at the sky, the street, the acacias all steeped in light, some pigeons which were flying about a neighboring roof, then all at once her eye eagerly sought the manuscript, and she said to herself that she must know what there was in it.

COSETTE AFTER THE LETTER

DURING the reading, Cosette entered gradually into reverie. It was written in a ravishing hand-writing, thought Cosette; in the same hand, but with different inks, sometimes very black, sometimes pale, as ink is put into the ink-stand, and consequently on different days. It was then a thought which had poured itself out there, sigh by sigh, irregularly, without order, without choice, without aim, at hazard. Cosette had never read anything like it. This manuscript, in which she found still more clearness than obscurity, had the effect upon her of a half-opened sanctuary. What was this manuscript? a letter. A letter with no address, no name, no date, no signature, intense and disinterested, an enigma composed of truths, a message of love made to be brought by an angel and read by a virgin, a rendezvous given beyond the earth, a love-letter from a phantom to a shade. He was a calm yet exhausted absent one, who seemed ready to take refuge in death, and who sent to the absent Her the secret of destiny, the key of life, love.

Now these pages, from whom could they come? Who could have written them?

Cosette did not hesitate for a moment. One single man. He!

Day had revived in her mind; all had appeared again. She felt a wonderful joy and deep anguish. It was he! he who wrote to her! he who was there! he whose arm had passed through that grating! While she was forgetting him, he had found her again! But had she forgotten him? No, never! She was mad to have thought so for a moment. She had always loved him, always adored him.

She fled, went back to the house and shut herself up in her room to read over the manuscript again, to learn it by heart, and to muse. When she had read it well, she kissed it, and put it in her bosom.

It was done. Cosette had fallen back into the profound

seraphic love. The abyss of Eden had reopened.

All that day Cosette was in a sort of stupefaction. She could really conjecture nothing, she hoped while yet trembling, what? vague things. She dared to promise herself nothing, and she would refuse herself nothing. Pallors passed over her face and chills over her body.

THE OLD ARE MADE TO GO OUT WHEN CONVENIENT

WHEN evening came, Jean Valjean went out; Cosette dressed herself. She arranged her hair in the manner which best became her, and she put on a dress the neck of which, as it had received one cut of the scissors too much, and as, by this slope, it allowed the turn of the neck to be seen, was, as young girls say "a little immodest." It was not the least in the world immodest, but it was prettier than otherwise. She did all this without knowing why.

Did she intend to go out? no.

Did she expect a visit? no.

At dusk, she went down to the garden.

She began to walk under the branches, putting them aside with her hand from time to time, because there were some that were very low.

She thus reached the seat.

The stone was still there.

She sat down, and laid her soft white hand upon that stone as if she would caress it and thank it.

All at once, she had that indefinable impression which we feel, though we see nothing, when there is somebody standing behind us.

She turned her head and arose.

It was he.

Cosette, ready to faint, did not utter a cry. She drew back slowly, for she felt herself attracted forward. He did not stir. Through the sad and ineffable something which enwrapped him, she felt the look of his eyes, which she did not see.

Cosette, in retreating, encountered a tree, and leaned against it. But for this tree, she would have fallen.

Then she heard his voice, that voice which she had never really heard, hardly rising above the rustling of the leaves, and murmuring:

"Pardon me, I am here. My heart is bursting, I could not live as I was, I have come. Have you read what I placed there, on this seat? do you recognize me at all? do not be afraid of me. It is a long time now, do you remember the day when you looked upon me? it was at the Luxembourg, near the Gladiator. And the day when you passed before me? it was the 16th of June and the 2nd of July. It will soon be a year. For a very long time now, I have not seen you at all. See, you are my angel, let me come sometimes; I believe I am going to die. If you but knew! I adore you! Pardon me, I am talking to you, I do not know what I am saying to you, perhaps I annoy you, do I annoy you?"

"O mother!" said she.

And she sank down upon herself as if she were dying.

He caught her, she fell, he caught her in his arms, he grasped her tightly, unconscious of what he was doing. He supported her even while tottering himself. He was lost in love.

She took his hand and laid it on her heart. He felt the paper there, and stammered:

"You love me, then?"

She answered in a voice so low that it was no more than a breath which could scarcely be heard:

"Hush! you know it!"

And she hid her blushing head in the bosom of the proud and intoxicated young man.

He fell upon the seat, she by his side. There were no more words. The stars were beginning to shine. How was it that their lips met? How is it that the birds sing, that the snow melts, that the rose opens, that May blooms, that the dawn whitens behind the black trees on the shivering summit of the hills?

When they had finished, when they had told each other everything, she laid her head upon his shoulder, and asked him:

"What is your name?"

"My name is Marius," said he. "And yours?"

"My name is Cosette."

Enchantments and Desolations

NEVER had the sky been more studded with stars, or more charming, the trees more tremulous, the odor of the shrubs more penetrating; never had the birds gone to sleep in the leaves with a softer sound; never had all the harmonies of the universal serenity better responded to the interior music of love; never had Marius been more enamored, more happy, more in ecstasy. But he had found Cosette sad.

It was the first cloud in this wonderful dream.

Marius' first word was:

"What is the matter?"

"See."

Then she sat down on the seat near the stairs, and as he took his place all trembling beside her, she continued:

"My father told me this morning to hold myself in readiness, that he had business, and that perhaps we should go away."

Marius shuddered from head to foot.

Marius awoke. For six weeks Marius had lived outside of life; this word, going away, brought him roughly back to it.

He could not find a word. She said to him in her turn.

"What is the matter?"

He answered so low that Cosette hardly heard him:

"I don't understand what you have said."

She resumed:

"This morning my father told me to arrange all my little affairs and to be ready, that he would give me his clothes to pack, that he was obliged to take a journey, that we were going away, that we must have a large trunk for me and a small one for him, to get all that ready within a week from now, and that we should go perhaps to England."

"But it is monstrous!" exclaimed Marius.

When his eyes were lowered, he saw Cosette smiling upon

226

him. The smile of the woman whom we love has a brilliancy which we can see by night.

"How stupid we are! Marius, I have an idea."

"What?"

"Go if we go! I will tell you where! Come and join me where I am!"

Marius was now a man entirely awakened. He had fallen back into reality. He cried to Cosette:

"Go with you? are you mad? But it takes money, and I have none! Go to England? Why I owe now, I don't know, more than ten louis to Courfeyrac, one of my friends whom you do not know! Why I have an old hat which is not worth three francs, I have a coat from which some of the buttons are gone in front, my shirt is all torn, my elbows are out, my boots let in the water; for six weeks I have not thought of it, and I have not told you about it. Cosette! I am a miserable wretch. You only see me at night, and you give me your love; if you should see me by day, you would give me a sou! Go to England? Ah! I have not the means to pay for a passport!"

He threw himself against a tree which was near by, standing with his arms above his head, his forehead against the bark, feeling neither the tree which was chafing his skin, nor the fever which was hammering his temples, motionless, and ready to fall, like a statue of Despair.

He was a long time thus. One might remain through eternity in such abysses. At last he turned. He heard behind him a little stifled sound, soft and sad.

It was Cosette sobbing.

He caught her hand.

"Cosette, I have never given my word of honor to anybody, because I stand in awe of my word of honor. I feel that my father is at my side. Now, I give you my most sacred word of honor that, if you go away, I shall die."

There was in the tone with which he pronounced these words a melancholy so solemn and so quiet, that Cosette trembled. She felt that chill which is given by a stern and true fact passing over us. From the shock she ceased weeping.

"Now listen," said he, "do not expect me to-morrow."

"Why not?"

"Do not expect me till the day after to-morrow!"

"Oh! why not?"

"You will see."

Marius continued:

"It occurs to me, you must know my address; something may happen, we don't know; I live with that friend named Courfeyrac, Rue de la Verrerie, number 16."

He put his hand in his pocket, took out a penknife, and wrote with the blade upon the plastering of the wall:

16, Rue de la Verrerie.

Cosette, meanwhile, began to look into his eyes again.

"Tell me your idea. Marius, you have an idea. Tell me. Oh! tell me, so that I may pass a good night!"

"My idea is this: that it is impossible that God should wish to separate us. Expect me day after to-morrow."

Where Are They Going?

JEAN VALJEAN

THAT very day, towards four o'clock in the afternoon, Jean Valjean was sitting alone upon the reverse of one of the most solitary embankments of the Champ de Mars. One day, when walking on the boulevard, he had seen Thénardier; thanks to his disguise, Thénardier had not recognized him; but since then Jean Valjean had seen him again several times, and he was now certain that Thénardier was prowling about the *quartier*. Moreover, Paris was not quiet: the political troubles had this inconvenience for him who had anything in his life to conceal, that the police had become very active, and very secret, and that in seeking to track out a man like Pépin or Morey, they would be very likely to discover a man like Jean Valjean. Jean Valjean had decided to leave Paris, and even France, and to pass over to England. He had told Cosette. In less than a week he wished to be gone.

Finally, an inexplicable circumstance which had just burst upon him, and with which he was still warm, had added to his alarm. On the morning of that very day, being the only one up in the house, and walking in the garden before Cosette's shutters were open, he had suddenly come upon this line scratched upon the wall, probably with a nail.

16, Rue de la Verrerie.

It was quite recent, the lines were white in the old black mortar, a tuft of nettles at the foot of the wall was powdered with fresh fine plaster. It had probably been written during the night. What was it? an address? a signal for others? a warning for him? At all events, it was evident that the garden had been violated, and that some persons unknown had penetrated into it.

In the midst of these meditations, he perceived, by a shadow which the sun had projected, that somebody had just stopped upon the crest of the embankment immediately behind him. He was about to turn round, when a folded paper fell upon his knees, as if a hand had dropped it from above his head. He took the paper, unfolded it, and read on it this word, written in large letters with a pencil:

REMOVE.

Jean Valjean rose hastily, there was no longer anybody on the embankment; he looked about him, and perceived a species of being larger than a child, smaller than a man, dressed in a gray blouse, and trousers of dirt-colored cotton velvet, which jumped over the parapet and let itself slide into the ditch of the Champ de Mars.

Jean Valjean returned home immediately, full of thought.

MARIUS

MARIUS left M. Gillenormand's desolate. He had entered with a very small hope; he came out with an immense despair.

He rambled about all day without knowing where; it rained at intervals, he did not perceive it; for his dinner he bought a penny roll at a baker's, put it in his pocket, and forgot it. It would appear that he took a bath in the Seine without being conscious of it. He waited for night with feverish impatience, he had but one clear idea; that was, that at nine o'clock he should see Cosette. This last happiness was now his whole future; afterwards, darkness. At intervals, while walking along the most deserted boulevards, he seemed to hear strange sounds in Paris. He roused himself from his reverie, and said: "Are they fighting?"

At nightfall, at precisely nine o'clock, as he had promised Cosette, he was in the Rue Plumet. When he approached the grating he forgot everything else. It was forty-eight hours since he had seen Cosette, he was going to see her again, every other thought faded away, and he felt now only a deep and wonderful joy.

Marius displaced the grating, and sprang into the garden. Cosette was not at the place where she usually waited for him. He crossed the thicket and went to the recess near the steps. "She is waiting for me there," said he. Cosette was not there. He raised his eyes, and saw the shutters of the house were closed. He took a turn around the garden, the garden was deserted. Then he returned to the house, and, mad with love, intoxicated, dismayed, exasperated with grief and anxiety, like a master who returns home in an untoward hour, he rapped on the shutters. He rapped, he rapped again, at the risk of seeing the window open and the forbidding face of the father appear and ask him: "What do you want?" This was nothing compared with what he now began to see. When he had rapped, he raised his voice and called Cosette. "Cosette!" cried he. "Cosette!" repeated he imperiously. There was no answer. It was settled. Nobody in the garden; nobody in the house.

He sat down upon the steps, his heart full of tenderness and resolution, he blessed his love in the depths of his thought, and he said to himself that since Cosette was gone, there was nothing more for him but to die.

Suddenly he heard a voice which appeared to come from the street, and which cried through the trees:

"Monsieur Marius!"

He arose.

"Hey?" said he.

"Monsieur Marius, is it you?"

"Yes."

"Monsieur Marius," added the voice, "your friends are expecting you at the barricade, in the Rue de la Chanvrerie."

This voice was not entirely unknown to him. It resembled the harsh and roughened voice of Eponine. Marius ran to the grating, pushed aside the movable bar, passed his head through, and saw somebody who appeared to him to be a young man rapidly disappearing in the twilight.

WHILE WAITING

MEANWHILE they had lighted a lamp at the little barricade, and at the large one, one of those wax torches which are seen on Mardi Gras in front of the wagons loaded with masks, which are going to the Comtille.

The torch had been placed in a kind of cage, closed in with paving-stones on the three sides, to shelter it from the wind, and disposed in such a manner that all the light fell upon the flag. The street and the barricade remained plunged in obscurity, and nothing could be seen but the red flag, fearfully lighted up, as if by an enormous dark lantern.

THE MAN RECRUITED IN THE RUE DES BILLETTES

IT was now quite night, nothing came. There were only confused sounds, and at intervals volleys of musketry; but rare, ill-sustained, and distant. This respite, which was thus prolonged, was a sign that the government was taking its time, and massing its forces. These fifty men were awaiting sixty thousand.

Enjolras felt himself possessed by that impatience which seizes strong souls on the threshold of formidable events. He went to find Gavroche who had set himself to making cartridges in the basement room.

Gavroche at this moment was very much engaged, not exactly with his cartridges.

The man from the Rue des Billettes had just entered the basement room and had taken a seat at the table which was least lighted. An infantry musket of large model had fallen to his lot, and he held it between his knees. Gavroche hitherto, distracted by a hundred "amusing" things, had not even seen this man.

When he came in, Gavroche mechanically followed him with his eyes, admiring his musket, then, suddenly, when the man had sat down, the *gamin* arose. Had any one watched this man up to this time, he would have seen him observe everything in the barricade and in the band of insurgents with a singular attention; but since he had come into the room, he had fallen into a kind of meditation and appeared to see nothing more of what was going on. The *gamin* approached this thoughtful personage, and began to turn about him on the points of his toes as one walks when near somebody whom he fears to awake.

It was in the deepest of this meditation that Enjolras accosted him.

"You are small," said Enjolras, "nobody will see you. Go out of the barricades, glide along by the houses, look about the streets a little, and come and tell me what is going on."

Gavroche straightened himself up.

"Little folks are good for something then!" And Gavroche, raising his head and lowering his voice, added, pointing to the man of the Rue des Billettes:

"You see that big fellow there?"

"Well?"

"He is a spy."

"You are sure?"

"It isn't a fortnight since he pulled me by the ear off the cornice of the Pont Royal where I was taking the air."

Enjolras hastily left the *gamin*, and murmured a few words very low to a working-man from the wine docks who was there. The working-man went out of the room and returned almost immediately, accompanied by three others. The four men, four broad-shouldered porters, placed themselves, without doing anything which could attract his attention, behind the table on which the man of the Rue des Billettes was leaning.

Then Enjolras approached the man and asked him:

"Who are you?"

At this abrupt question, the man gave a start. He looked straight to the bottom of Enjolras' frank eye and appeared to catch his thought. He smiled with a smile which, of all things in the world, was the most disdainful, the most energetic, and the most resolute, and answered with a haughty gravity:

"I see how it is——Well, yes!"

"You are a spy?"

"I am an officer of the government."

"Your name is?"

"Javert."

Enjolras made a sign to the four men. In a twinkling, before Javert had had time to turn around, he was collared, thrown down, bound, searched.

They found upon him a little round card framed between two glasses, and bearing on one side the arms of France, engraved with this legend: *Surveillance et vigilance,* and on the other side this endorsement: JAVERT, inspector of police, aged fifty-two, and the signature of the prefect of police of the time, M. Gisquet.

The search finished, they raised Javert, tied his arms behind his back, fastened him in the middle of the basement-room to that celebrated post which had formerly given its name to the wine-shop.

All this was executed so rapidly that it was finished as soon as it was perceived about the wine-shop. Javert had not uttered a cry. Seeing Javert tied to the post, Courfeyrac, Bossuet, Joly, Combeferre, and the men scattered about the two barricades, ran in.

Javert, backed up against the post, and so surrounded with ropes that he could make no movement, held up his head with the intrepid serenity of the man who has never lied.

"It is a spy," said Enjolras.

And turning towards Javert:

"You will be shot ten minutes before the barricade is taken."

Marius Enters the Shadow

FROM THE RUE PLUMET TO THE QUARTIER SAINT DENIS

THAT voice which through the twilight had called Marius to the barricade of the Rue de la Chanvrerie, sounded to him like the voice of destiny. He wished to die, the opportunity presented itself; he was knocking at the door of the tomb, a hand in the shadow held out the key. Marius pushed aside the bar which had let him pass so many times, came out of the garden, and said: "Let us go!"

Marius willed with the will of a man who no longer hopes. He had been called, he must go. He found means to pass through the multitude, and to pass through the bivouac of the troops, he avoided the patrols, evaded the sentinels. He made a detour, reached the Rue de Béthisy, and made his way towards the markets. At the corner of the Rue des Bourdonnais the lamps ended.

After having crossed the belt of the multitude and passed the fringe of troops, he found himself in the midst of something terrible. Not a passer more, not a soldier, not a light; nobody. Solitude, silence, night; a mysterious chill which seized upon him. To enter a street was to enter a cellar.

He continued to advance.

THE EXTREME LIMIT

MARIUS had arrived at the markets.

There all was more calm, more obscure, and more motionless still than in the neighboring streets.

A red glare, however, cut out upon this dark background the high roofs of the houses which barred the Rue de la Chanvrerie on the side towards Saint Eustache. It was the reflection of the torch which was blazing in the barricade of Corinth. Marius directed his steps towards this glare. It led him to the Beet Market, and he dimly saw the dark mouth of the Rue des Prêcheurs. He entered it. The vidette of the insurgents who was on guard at the other end did not perceive him. He felt that he was very near what he had come to seek, and he walked upon tiptoe. He reached in this way the elbow of that short end of the Rue Mondétour, which was the only communication preserved by Enjolras with the outside. Round the corner of the last house on his left, cautiously advancing his head, he looked into this end of the Rue Mondétour.

A little beyond the black corner of the alley and the Rue de la Chanvrerie, which threw a broad shadow, in which he was himself buried, he perceived a light upon the pavement, a portion of the wine-shop, and behind, a lamp twinkling in a kind of shapeless wall, and men crouching down with muskets on their knees. All this was within twenty yards of him. It was the interior of the barricade.

The houses on the right of the alley hid from him the rest of the wine-shop, the great barricade, and the flag.

Marius had but one step more to take.

His gaze wandered into the interior of the barricade. The insurgents were chatting in undertone, without moving about; and that quasi-silence was felt which marks the last phase of delay.

The Grandeurs of Despair

THE FLAG: FIRST ACT

NOTHING came yet. The clock of Saint Merry had struck ten. Enjolras and Combeferre had sat down, carbine in hand, near the opening of the great barricade. They were not talking, they were listening; seeking to catch even the faintest and most distant sound of a march.

Suddenly, in the midst of this dismal calm, a clear, young, cheerful voice, which seemed to come from the Rue Saint Denis, arose and began to sing distinctly to the old popular air, *Au clair de la lune,* some lines which ended in a sort of cry similar to the crow of a cock.

They grasped each other by the hand:

"It is Gavroche," said Enjolras.

"He is warning us," said Combeferre.

A headlong run startled the empty street; they saw a creature nimbler than a clown climb over the omnibus, and Gavroche bounded into the barricade all breathless, saying:

"My musket! Here they are."

A few moments more elapsed, then a sound of steps, measured, heavy, numerous, was distinctly heard from the direction of Saint Leu. This sound, at first faint, then distinct, then heavy and sonorous, approached slowly, without halt, without interruption, with a tranquil and terrible continuity. This tread approached; it approached still nearer, and stopped. They seemed to hear at the end of the street the breathing of many men. They saw nothing, however, only they discovered at the very end, in that dense obscurity, a multitude of metallic threads, as fine as needles and almost imperceptible, which moved about like those indescribable phosphoric networks which we perceive under our closed eyelids at the moment of going to sleep, in the first mists of slumber. They were bayonets and musket barrels dimly lighted up by the distant reflection of the torch.

There was still a pause, as if on both sides they were

awaiting. Suddenly, from the depth of that shadow, a voice, so much the more ominous, because nobody could be seen, and because it seemed as if it were the obscurity itself which was speaking, cried:

"Who is there?"

At the same time they heard the click of the levelled muskets.

Enjolras answered in a lofty and ringing tone:

"French Revolution!"

"Fire!" said the voice.

A flash empurpled all the façades on the street, as if the door of a furnace were opened and suddenly closed.

A fearful explosion burst over the barricade. The red flag fell. The volley had been so heavy and so dense that it had cut the staff, that is to say, the very point of the pole of the omnibus. Some balls, which ricocheted from the cornices of the houses, entered the barricade and wounded several men.

The impression produced by this first charge was freezing. It was evident that they had to do with a whole regiment at least.

"Comrades," cried Courfeyrac, "don't waste the powder. Let us wait to reply till they come into the street."

They heard from without the rattling of the ramrods in the muskets: the troops were reloading.

GAVROCHE WOULD HAVE DONE BETTER TO ACCEPT ENJOLRAS' CARBINE

DURING this time little Gavroche, who alone had not left his post and had remained on the watch, thought he saw some men approaching the barricade with a stealthy step. Suddenly he cried:

"Take care!"

Courfeyrac, Enjolras, Jean Prouvaire, Combeferre, Joly, Bahorel, Bossuet, all sprang tumultuously from the wineshop. There was hardly a moment to spare. They perceived a sparkling breadth of bayonets undulating above the barricade. Municipal Guards of tall stature were penetrating, some by climbing over the omnibus, others by the opening, pushing before them the *gamin*, who fell back, but did not fly.

The moment was critical. It was that first fearful instant of the inundation, when the stream rises to the level of the bank and when the water begins to infiltrate through the fissures in the dyke. A second more, and the barricade had been taken.

Bahorel sprang upon the first Municipal Guard who entered, and killed him at the very muzzle of his carbine; the second killed Bahorel with his bayonet. Another had already prostrated Courfeyrac, who was crying "Help!" The largest of all, a kind of colossus, marched upon Gavroche with fixed bayonet.

Before the bayonet touched Gavroche the musket dropped from the soldier's hands, a ball had struck the Municipal Guard in the middle of the forehead, and he fell on his back. A second ball struck the other Guard, who had assailed Courfeyrac, full in the breast, and threw him upon the pavement.

It was Marius who had just entered the barricade.

THE KEG OF POWDER

MARIUS, still hidden in the corner of the Rue Mondétour, had watched the first phase of the combat, irresolute and shuddering. However, he was not able long to resist that mysterious and sovereign infatuation which we may call the appeal of the abyss. Before the imminence of the danger, all hesitation had vanished, and he had rushed into the conflict, his two pistols in his hands. By the first shot he had saved Gavroche, and by the second delivered Courfeyrac.

Marius had now no arms, he had thrown away his discharged pistols, but he had noticed the keg of powder in the basement room near the door.

As he turned half round, looking in that direction, a soldier aimed at him. At the moment the soldier aimed at Marius, a hand was laid upon the muzzle of the musket, and stopped it. It was somebody who had sprung forward, the young working-man with velvet pantaloons. The shot went off, passed through the hand, and perhaps also through the working-man, for he fell. But the ball did not reach Marius. Marius, who was entering the basement room, hardly noticed it.

The insurgents, surprised, but not dismayed, had rallied.
Enjolras had cried: "Wait! don't fire at random!" In the first
confusion, in fact, they might hit one another. Most of them
had gone up to the window of the second story and to the
dormer windows, whence they commanded the assailants.
The most determined, with Enjolras, Courfeyrac, Jean Prouvaire, and Combeferre, had haughtily placed their backs to
the houses in the rear, openly facing the ranks of soldiers
and guards which crowded the barricade.

All this was accomplished without precipitation, with that
strange and threatening gravity which precedes mêlées.
On both sides they were taking aim, the muzzles of the guns
almost touching; they were so near that they could talk with
each other in an ordinary tone. Just as the spark was about
to fly, an officer in a gorget and with huge epaulets, extended his sword and said, "Take aim!"

"Fire!" said Enjolras.

The two explosions were simultaneous, and everything disappeared in the smoke.

When the smoke cleared away, on both sides the combat-
ants were seen, thinned out, but still in the same places, and
reloading their pieces in silence.

Suddenly, a thundering voice was heard, crying:

"Begone, or I'll blow up the barricade!"

All turned in the direction whence the voice came.

Marius had entered the basement room, and had taken the
keg of powder, then he had profited by the smoke and the
kind of obscure fog which filled the entrenched enclosure,
to glide along the barricade as far as that cage of paving-
stones in which the torch was fixed. To pull out the torch, to
put the keg of powder in its place, to push the pile of paving-
stones upon the keg, which stove it in, with a sort of terrible
self-control—all this had been for Marius the work of stooping
down and rising up; and now all, National Guards, Municipal
Guards, officers, soldiers, grouped at the other extremity of
the barricade, beheld him with horror, his foot upon the
stones, the torch in his hand, his stern face lighted by a
deadly resolution, bending the flame of the torch towards
that formidable pile in which they discerned the broken bar-
rel of powder, and uttering that terrific cry:

"Begone, or I'll blow up the barricade!"

"Blow up the barricade!" said a sergeant, "and yourself
also!"

Marius answered:

"And myself also."

And he approached the torch to the keg of powder.

But there was no longer anybody on the wall. The assailants, leaving their dead and wounded, fled pell-mell and in disorder towards the extremity of the street, and were again lost in the night. It was a rout.

The barricade was redeemed.

"YOU ARE THE CHIEF"

ALL flocked round Marius. Courfeyrac sprang to his neck.

Marius inquired:

"Where is the chief?"

"You are the chief," said Enjolras.

Marius had all day had a furnace in his brain, now it was a whirlwind. It seemed to him that he was already at an immense distance from life. His two luminous months of joy and of love, terminating abruptly upon this frightful precipice, Cosette lost to him, this barricade, himself a chief of insurgents, all these things appeared a monstrous nightmare.

THE AGONY OF DEATH AFTER THE AGONY OF LIFE

A PECULIARITY of this kind of war is that the attack on the barricades is almost always made in front, and that in general the assailants abstain from turning the positions, whether it be that they dread ambuscades, or that they fear to become entangled in the crooked streets. The whole attention of the insurgents therefore was directed to the great barricade, which was evidently the point still threatened, and where the struggle must infallibly recommence. Marius, however, thought of the little barricade and went to it. It was deserted, and was guarded only by the lamp which flickered between the stones.

As Marius, the inspection made, was retiring, he heard his name faintly pronounced in the obscurity:

"Monsieur Marius!"

He shuddered, for he recognised the voice which had called him two hours before, through the grating in the Rue Plumet.

He looked about him and saw nobody.

"Monsieur Marius!" repeated the voice.

This time he could not doubt, he had heard distinctly; he looked, and saw nothing.

"At your feet," said the voice.

He stooped and saw a form in the shadow, which was dragging itself towards him.

The lamp enabled him to distinguish a blouse, a pair of torn pantaloons of coarse velvet, bare feet, and something which resembled a pool of blood. Marius caught a glimpse of a pale face which rose towards him and said to him:

"You do not know me?"

"No."

"Eponine."

Marius bent down quickly. It was indeed that unhappy child. She was dressed as a man.

"How came you here? what are you doing there?"

"I am dying," said she.

"You are wounded! Wait, I will carry you into the room! They will dress your wounds! Is it serious? how shall I take you up so as not to hurt you? Where are you hurt? Help! my God! But what did you come here for?"

And he tried to pass his arm under her to lift her.

In lifting her he touched her hand.

She uttered a feeble cry.

"Have I hurt you?" asked Marius.

"A little."

"But I have only touched your hand."

She raised her hand into Marius' sight, and Marius saw in the centre of that hand a black hole.

"What is the matter with your hand?" said he.

"It is pierced."

"Pierced?"

"Yes."

"By what?"

"By a ball."

"How?"

"Did you see a musket aimed at you?"

"Yes, and a hand which stopped it."

"That was mine."

Marius shuddered.

"What madness! Poor child! But that is not so bad, if that is all, it is nothing, let me carry you to a bed. They will care for you, people don't die from a shot in the hand."

She murmured:

"The ball passed through my hand, but it went out through my back. It is useless to take me from here. I will tell you how you can care for me, better than a surgeon. Sit down by me on that stone."

He obeyed; she laid her head on Marius' knees, and without looking at him, she said:

"Oh! how good it is! How kind he is! That is it! I don't suffer any more!"

She remained a moment in silence, then she turned her head with effort and looked at Marius.

"Do you know, Monsieur Marius? It worried me that you should go into that garden, it was silly, since it was I who had shown you the house, and then indeed I ought surely to have known that a young man like you—"

She stopped, and, leaping over the gloomy transitions which were doubtless in her mind, she added with a heart-rending smile:

"You thought me ugly, didn't you?"

She continued:

"See, you are lost! Nobody will get out of the barricade, now. It was I who led you into this, it was! You are going to die, I am sure. And still when I saw him aiming at you, I put up my hand upon the muzzle of the musket. How droll it is! But it was because I wanted to die before you."

While she was talking she rested her wounded hand upon her breast where there was another hole, from which there came with each pulsation a flow of blood like a jet of wine from an open bung.

Marius gazed upon this unfortunate creature with profound compassion.

"Oh!" she exclaimed suddenly, "it is coming back. I am stifling!"

She seized her blouse and bit it, and her legs writhed upon the pavement.

Marius started.

"Oh! don't go away!" said she, "it will not be long now!"

She was sitting almost upright, but her voice was very low and broken by hiccoughs. At intervals the death-rattle interrupted her. She approached her face as near as she could to Marius' face. She added with a strange expression:

"Listen, I don't want to deceive you. I have a letter in my pocket for you. Since yesterday. I was told to put it in the post. I kept it. I didn't want it to reach you. But you would not like it of me perhaps when we meet again so soon. We do meet again, don't we? Take your letter."

She grasped Marius' hand convulsively with her wounded hand, but she seemed no longer to feel the pain. She put Marius' hand into the pocket of her blouse. Marius really felt a paper there.

"Take it," said she.

Marius took the letter.

"Now for my pains, promise me——"

And she hesitated.

"What?" asked Marius.

"Promise me!"

"I promise you."

"Promise to kiss me on the forehead when I am dead. I shall feel it."

She let her head fall back upon Marius' knees and her eyelids closed. He thought that poor soul had gone. Eponine lay motionless; but just when Marius supposed her for ever asleep, she slowly opened her eyes in which the gloomy deepness of death appeared, and said to him with an accent the sweetness of which already seemed to come from another world:

"And then, do you know, Monsieur Marius, I believe I was a little in love with you."

She essayed to smile again and expired.

GAVROCHE A PROFOUND CALCULATOR OF DISTANCES

MARIUS kept his promise. He kissed that livid forehead from which oozed an icy sweat.

He had not taken the letter which Eponine had given him without a thrill. He was impatient to read it. The heart of man is thus made; the unfortunate child had hardly closed her eyes when Marius thought to unfold the paper. He laid her gently upon the ground, and went away. Something told him that he could not read that letter in sight of this corpse.

He went to a candle in the basement-room. It was a little

note, folded and sealed with the elegant care of woman. The address was in a woman's hand, and ran:

"To Monsieur Marius Pontmercy, at M. Courfeyrac's, Rue de la Verrerie, No. 16."

He broke the seal and read:

"My beloved, alas! my father wishes to start immediately. We shall be to-night in the Rue de l'Homme Armé, No. 7. In a week we shall be in England. COSETTE. June 4th."

Such was the innocence of his love that Marius did not even know Cosette's handwriting.

What happened may be told in a few words. Eponine had done it all. After the evening of the 3rd of June, she had had a thought, to separate Marius from Cosette. She had changed rags with the first young rogue who thought it amusing to dress as a woman while Eponine disguised herself as a man. It was she who, in the Champ de Mars, had given Jean Valjean the expressive warning: *Remove.* Jean Valjean returned home, and said to Cosette: *we start to-night, and we are going to the Rue de l'Homme Armé with Toussaint. Next week we shall be in London.* Cosette, prostrated by this unexpected blow, had hastily written two lines to Marius. But how should she get the letter to the post? She did not go out alone, and Toussaint, surprised at such an errand, would surely show the letter to M. Fauchelevent. In this anxiety, Cosette saw, through the grating, Eponine in men's clothes, who was now prowling continually about the garden. Cosette called "this young working-man" and handed him five francs and the letter, saying to him: "carry this letter to its address right away." Eponine put the letter in her pocket. The next day, June 5th, she went to Courfeyrac's to ask for Marius, not to give him the letter, but, a thing which every jealous and loving soul will understand, "to see." There she waited for Marius, or, at least, for Courfeyrac—still to see. When Courfeyrac said to her: we are going to the barricades, an idea flashed across her mind. To throw herself into that death as she would have thrown herself into any other, and to push Marius into it. She followed Courfeyrac, made sure of the post where they were building the barricade; and very sure, since Marius had received no notice, and she had intercepted the letter, that he would at nightfall be at his usual evening rendezvous, she went to the Rue Plumet, waited there for Marius, and sent him, in the name of his friends, that appeal which must, she thought, lead him to the barricade. She counted upon

Marius' despair when he should not find Cosette; she was not mistaken. She returned herself to the Rue de la Chanvrerie. We have seen what she did there. She died with that tragic joy of jealous hearts which drag the being they love into death with them, saying: nobody shall have him!

Marius covered Cosette's letter with kisses. She loved him then? He had for a moment the idea that now he need not die. Then he said to himself: "She is going away. Her father takes her to England, and my grandfather refuses to consent to the marriage. Nothing is changed in the fatality." Then he thought that there were two duties remaining for him to fulfil: to inform Cosette of his death and to send her a last farewell, and to save from the imminent catastrophe which was approaching this poor child, Eponine's brother and Thénardier's son.

He had a pocket-book with him; the same that had contained the pages upon which he had written so many thoughts of love for Cosette. He tore out a leaf and wrote with a pencil these few lines:

"Our marriage was impossible. I have asked my grandfather, he has refused; I am without fortune, and you also. I ran to your house, I did not find you, you know the promise that I gave you? I keep it, I die, I love you. When you read this, my soul will be near you, and will smile upon you."

Having nothing to seal this letter with, he merely folded the paper, and wrote upon it this address:

"To Mademoiselle Cosette Fauchelevent, at M. Fauchelevant's, Rue de l'Homme Armé, No. 7."

The letter folded, he remained a moment in thought, took his pocket-book again, opened it, and wrote these four lines on the first page with the same pencil:

"My name is Marius Pontmercy. Carry my corpse to my grandfather's, M. Gillenormand, Rue des Filles du Calvaire, No. 6, in the Marais."

He put the book into his coat-pocket, then he called Gavroche. The *gamin*, at the sound of Marius' voice, ran up with his joyous and devoted face:

"Will you do something for me?"

"Anything," said Gavroche. "God of the good God! without you, I should have been cooked, sure."

"You see this letter?"

"Yes."

"Take it. Go out of the barricade immediately (Gavroche,

disturbed, began to scratch his ear), and to-morrow morning you will carry it to its address, to Mademoiselle Cosette, at M. Fauchelevent's, Rue de l'Homme Armé No. 7."

"All right," said he.

And he started off on a run by the little Rue Mondétour.

Gavroche had an idea which decided him, but which he did not tell, for fear Marius would make some objection to it.

That idea was this:

"It is hardly midnight, the Rue de l'Homme Armé is not far, I will carry the letter right away, and I shall get back in time."

The Rue de l'Homme Armé

JEAN VALJEAN, at that very moment, was a prey to a frightful uprising. All the gulfs were reopened within him. He also, like Paris, was shuddering on the threshold of a formidable and obscure revolution. A few hours had sufficed. His destiny and his conscience were suddenly covered with shadow. Of him also, as of Paris, we might say: the two principles are face to face. The angel of light and the angel of darkness are to wrestle on the bridge of the abyss. Which of the two shall hurl down the other? which shall sweep him away?

On the eve of that same day, June 5th, Jean Valjean, accompanied by Cosette and Toussaint, had installed himself in the Rue de l'Homme Armé. A sudden turn of fortune awaited him there.

Jean Valjean had brought Toussaint, which he had never done in his preceding absences. He saw that possibly he should not return to the Rue Plumet, and he could neither leave Toussaint behind, nor tell her his secret. Besides he felt that she was devoted and safe. Between domestic and master, treason begins with curiosity. But Toussaint, as if she had been predestined to be the servant of Jean Valjean, was not curious. She said through her stuttering, in her Barneville peasant's speech: "I am from same to same; I think my act; the remainder is not my labor." (I am so; I do my work! the rest is not my affair.)

In this departure from the Rue Plumet, which was almost a flight, Jean Valjean carried nothing but the little embalmed valise christened by Cosette the *inseparable*. Full trunks would have required porters, and porters are witnesses. They had a coach come to the door on the Rue Babylone, and they went away.

It was with great difficulty that Toussaint obtained permission to pack up a little linen and clothing and a few toilet articles. Cosette carried only her writing-desk and her blotter.

Jean Valjean, to increase the solitude and mystery of this disappearance, had arranged so as not to leave the cottage on the Rue Plumet till the close of the day, which left Cosette time to write her note to Marius. They arrived in the Rue de l'Homme Armé after nightfall.

They went silently to bed.

We are reassured almost as foolishly as we are alarmed; human nature is so constituted. Hardly was Jean Valjean in the Rue de l'Homme Armé, before his anxiety grew less, and by degrees was dissipated.

He slept well. Next morning he awoke almost cheerful. He thought the dining-room charming, although it was hideous, furnished with an old round table, a low sideboard surmounted by a hanging mirror, a worm-eaten armchair, and a few other chairs loaded down with Toussaint's bundles. Through an opening in one of these bundles, Jean Valjean's National Guard uniform could be seen.

As for Cosette, she had Toussaint bring a bowl of soup to her room, and did not make her appearance till evening.

About five o'clock, Toussaint, who was coming and going, very busy with this little removal, set a cold fowl on the dining-room table, which Cosette, out of deference to her father, consented to look at.

This done, Cosette, upon pretext of a severe headache, said good night to Jean Valjean, and shut herself in her bedroom. Jean Valjean ate a chicken's wing with a good appetite, and, leaning on the tables, clearing his brow little by little, was regaining his sense of security.

While he was making this frugal dinner, he became confusedly aware, on two or three occasions, of the stammering of Toussaint, who said to him: "Monsieur, there is a row; they are fighting in Paris." But, absorbed in a multitude of interior combinations, he paid no attention to it. To tell the truth, he had not heard.

He arose and began to walk from the window to the door, and from the door to the window, growing calmer and calmer.

While yet walking up and down, with slow steps, his eye suddenly met something strange.

He perceived facing him, in the inclined mirror which hung above the sideboard, and he distinctly read the lines which follow:

"My beloved, alas! my father wishes to start immediately. We shall be to-night in the Rue de l'Homme Armé No. 7. In a week we shall be in London. COSETTE. June 4th."

Jean Valjean stood aghast.

Cosette, on arriving, had laid her blotter on the sideboard before the mirror, and, wholly absorbed in her sorrowful anguish, had forgotten it there, without even noticing that she left it wide open, and open exactly at the page upon which she had dried the five lines written by her, and which she had given in charge to the young workman passing through the Rue Plumet. The writing was imprinted upon the blotter. The mirror reflected the writing.

There resulted what is called in geometry the symmetrical image; so that the writing reversed on the blotter was corrected by the mirror, and presented its original form; and Jean Valjean had beneath his eyes the letter written in the evening by Cosette to Marius.

It was simple and withering.

Jean Valjean went to the mirror. He read the five lines again, but he did not believe it. They produced upon him the effect of an apparition in a flash of lightning. It was a hallucination. It was impossible. It was not.

Little by little his perception became more precise; he looked at Cosette's blotter, and the consciousness of the real fact returned to him. He understood.

Jean Valjean tottered, let the blotter fall, and sank down into the old armchair by the sideboard, his head drooping, his eye glassy, bewildered. He said to himself that it was clear, and that the light of the world was for ever eclipsed, and that Cosette had written that to somebody.

A circumstance strange and sad, Marius at that moment had not yet Cosette's letter; chance had brought it, like a traitor, to Jean Valjean before delivering it to Marius.

Jean Valjean till this day had never been vanquished when put to the proof. He had been subjected to fearful trials; no violence of ill fortune had been spared him; the ferocity of fate, armed with every vengeance and with every scorn of society, had taken him for a subject and had greedily pursued him. He had neither recoiled nor flinched before anything.

Of all the tortures which he had undergone in that inquisition of destiny, this was the most fearful. Never had such pincers seized him. He felt the mysterious quiver of every latent sensibility. Alas, the supreme ordeal, let us say rather, the only ordeal, is the loss of the beloved being.

His instinct did not hesitate. He put together certain circumstances, certain dates, certain blushes, and certain pallors of Cosette, and he said to himself: "It is he." With his first conjecture, he hit Marius. He did not know the name, but he found the man at once. He perceived distinctly, at the bottom of the implacable evocation of memory, the unknown prowler of the Luxembourg, that wretched seeker of amours, that romantic idler, that imbecile, that coward, for it is cowardice to come and make sweet eyes at girls who are beside their father who loves them.

While he was thinking, Toussaint entered. Jean Valjean arose, and asked her:

"Didn't you tell me just now that they were fighting?"

"Oh! yes, monsieur," answered Toussaint. "It is over by Saint Merry."

There are some mechanical impulses which come to us, without our knowledge even, from our deepest thoughts. It was doubtless under the influence of an impulse of this kind, and of which he was hardly conscious, that Jean Valjean five minutes afterwards found himself in the street.

He was bare-headed, seated upon the stone block by the door of his house. He seemed to be listening.

The night had come.

THE GAMIN AN ENEMY OF LIGHT

THE street was empty. A few anxious bourgeois, who were rapidly returning home, hardly perceived him. Every man for himself in times of peril. The lamplighter came as usual to light the lamp which hung exactly opposite the door of No. 7, and went away. Jean Valjean, to one who had examined him in that shadow, would not have seemed a living man. The tocsin was heard, and vague stormy sounds were heard. In the midst of all this convulsive clamour of the bell mingled with the émeute, the clock of St. Paul's struck eleven, gravely and without haste. The passing of the hour had no effect upon Jean Valjean; Jean Valjean did not stir. However, almost at that very moment, there was a sharp explosion in the direction of the markets, a second followed, more violent still; it was probably that attack on the barricade of the Rue de la Chanvrerie which we have just seen repulsed by Marius. At this double discharge, the fury of which seemed increased by the stupor of the night, Jean Valjean was startled; he looked up in the direction whence the sound came; then he sank down upon the block, folded his arms, and his head dropped slowly upon his breast.

He resumed his dark dialogue with himself.

Suddenly he raised his eyes, somebody was walking in the street, he heard steps near him, he looked, and, by the light of the lamp, in the direction of the Archives, he perceived a livid face, young and radiant.

Gavroche had just arrived in the Rue de l'Homme Armé.

Gavroche was looking in the air, and appeared to be searching for something. He saw Jean Valjean perfectly, but he took no notice of him.

Jean Valjean, who, the instant before, in the state of mind in which he was, would not have spoken nor even replied to anybody, felt irresistibly impelled to address a word to this child.

"Small boy," said he, "what is the matter with you?"

"The matter is that I am hungry," answered Gavroche tartly. And he added: "Small yourself."

Jean Valjean felt in his pocket and took out a five-franc piece.

Jean Valjean approached Gavroche.

"Poor creature," said he, in an undertone, and speaking to himself, "he is hungry."

And he put the hundred-sous piece into his hand.

Gavroche cocked up his nose, astonished at the size of this big sou; he looked at it in the dark, and the whiteness of the big sou dazzled him. He knew five-franc pieces by hearsay; their reputation was agreeable to him; he was delighted to see one so near.

"You are a fine fellow," said Gavroche.

And he put the five-franc piece into one of his pockets.

His confidence increasing, he added:

"Do you belong in the street?"

"Yes; why?"

"Could you show me number seven?"

"What do you want with number seven?"

Here the boy stopped; he feared that he had said too much; he plunged his nails vigorously into his hair, and merely answered:

"Ah! that's it."

An idea flashed across Jean Valjean's mind. Anguish has such lucidities. He said to the child:

"Have you brought the letter I am waiting for?"

"You?" said Gavroche. "You are not a woman."

"The letter is for Mademoiselle Cosette; isn't it?"

"Cosette?" muttered Gavroche, "yes, I believe it is that funny name."

"Well," resumed Jean Valjean, "I am to deliver the letter to her. Give it to me."

"In that case you must know that I am sent from the barricade?"

"Of course," said Jean Valjean.

Gavroche thrust his hand into another of his pockets, and drew out a folded paper.

"Take it."

And he handed the paper to Jean Valjean.

"And hurry yourself, Monsieur What's-your-name, for Mamselle What's-her-name is waiting."

WHILE COSETTE AND TOUSSAINT SLEEP

JEAN VALJEAN went in with Marius' letter.

He groped his way upstairs, pleased with the darkness like an owl which holds his prey, opened and softly closed the door, listened to see if he heard any sound, decided that, according to all appearances, Cosette and Toussaint were asleep, plunged three or four matches into the bottle of the Fumade tinder-box before he could raise a spark, his hand trembled so much; there was theft in what he was about to do. At last, his candle was lighted, he leaned his elbows on the table, unfolded the paper, and read.

In Marius' note to Cosette, Jean Valjean saw only these words.

"——I die. When you read this, my soul will be near you."

Before these two lines, he was horribly dazzled; he sat a moment as if crushed by the change of emotion which was wrought within him, he looked at Marius' note with a sort of drunken astonishment; he had before his eyes that splendor, the death of the hated being.

He uttered a hideous cry of inward joy. So, it was finished.

The end came sooner than he had dared to hope. The being who encumbered his destiny was disappearing. He was going away of himself, freely, of his own accord. Without any intervention on his, Jean Valjean's part, without any fault of his, "that man" was about to die. Perhaps even he was already dead.

All this said within himself, he became gloomy.

Then he went down and waked the porter.

About an hour afterwards, Jean Valjean went out in the full dress of a National Guard, and armed. The porter had easily found in the neighborhood what was necessary to complete his equipment. He had a loaded musket and a cartridge-box full of cartridges. He went in the direction of the markets.

JEAN VALJEAN

War Between Four Walls

FIVE LESS, ONE MORE

"CITIZENS," cried Enjolras, and there was in his voice almost an angry tremor, "the republic is not rich enough in men to incur useless expenditures. Vainglory is a squandering. If it is the duty of some to go away, that duty should be performed as well as any other."

Enjolras, the man of principle, had over his co-religionists that sort of omnipotence which emanates from the absolute. Still, notwithstanding this omnipotence, there was a murmur.

Chief to his finger-ends, Enjolras, seeing that they murmured, insisted. He resumed haughtily:

"Let those who fear to be one of but thirty, say so."

The murmurs redoubled.

"Besides," observed a voice from one of the groups, "to go away is easily said. The barricade is hemmed in."

"Not towards the markets," said Enjolras. "The Rue Mondétour is open, and by the Rue des Prêcheurs one can reach the Marché des Innocents."

"And there," put in another voice from the group, "he will be taken. He will fall upon some grand guard of the line or the banlieue. They will see a man going by in cap and blouse. 'Where do you come from, fellow? you belong to the barricade, don't you?' And they look at your hands. You smell of powder. Shot."

Enjolras, without answering, touched Combeferre's shoulder, and they both went into the basement room.

They came back a moment afterwards. Enjolras held out in his hands the four uniforms which he had reserved. Combeferre followed him, bringing the cross belts and shakos.

"With this uniform," said Enjolras, "you can mingle with the ranks and escape. Here are enough for four."

And he threw the four uniforms upon the unpaved ground.

"Citizens," continued Enjolras, "this is the republic, and

universal suffrage reigns. Designate yourselves those who ought to go."

They obeyed. In a few minutes five were unanimously designated and left the ranks.

"There are five!" exclaimed Marius.

There were only four uniforms.

"Well," resumed the five, "one must stay."

And it was who should stay, and who should find reasons why the others should not stay. The generous quarrel recommenced.

"You, you have a wife who loves you." "As for you, you have your old mother." "You have neither father nor mother, what will become of your three little brothers?" "You are the father of five children." "You have a right to live, you are seventeen, it is too soon."

"Be quick," repeated Courfeyrac.

Somebody cried out from the group, to Marius:

"Designate yourself, which must stay."

"Yes," said the five, "choose. We will obey you."

Marius now believed no emotion possible. Still at this idea: to select a man for death, all his blood flowed back towards his heart. He would have turned pale if he could have been paler.

He advanced towards the five, who smiled upon him, and each, his eye full of that grand flame which we see in the depth of history over the Thermopylæ, cried to him:

"Me! me! me!"

And Marius, in a stupor, counted them; there were still five! Then his eyes fell upon the four uniforms.

At this moment a fifth uniform dropped, as if from heaven, upon the four others.

The fifth man was saved.

Marius raised his eyes and saw M. Fauchelevent.

Jean Valjean had just entered the barricade.

Whether by information obtained, or by instinct, or by chance he came by the little Rue Mondétour. Thanks to his National Guard dress, he had passed easily.

The sentry placed by the insurgents in the Rue Mondétour, had not given the signal of alarm for a single National Guard. He permitted him to get into the street, saying to himself: "he is a reinforcement, probably, and at the very worst a prisoner."

At the moment Jean Valjean entered the redoubt, nobody

had noticed him, all eyes being fixed upon the five chosen ones and upon the four uniforms. Jean Valjean, himself, saw and understood, and, silently, he stripped off his coat, and threw it upon the pile with the others.

The commotion was indescribable.

"Who is the man?" asked Bossuet.

"He is," answered Combeferre, "a man who saves others."

Marius added in a grave voice:

"I know him."

This assurance was enough for all.

Enjolras turned towards Jean Valjean:

"Citizen, you are welcome."

And he added:

"You know that we are going to die."

Jean Valjean, without answering, helped the insurgent whom he saved to put on his uniform.

THE SITUATION GROWS SERIOUS

IT was growing light rapidly. But not a window was opened, not a door stood ajar; it was the dawn, not the hour of awakening. The extremity of the Rue de la Chanvrerie opposite the barricade had been evacuated by the troops.

They saw nothing, but they heard. A mysterious movement was taking place at some distance. It was evident that the critical moment was at hand. As in the evening the sentries were driven in; but this time all.

The barricade was stronger than at the time of the first attack. Since the departure of the five, it had been raised still higher.

They had not long to wait. A piece of artillery appeared. There was intense anxiety in the redoubt.

The gun went off; the detonation burst upon them.

"Present!" cried a cheerful voice.

And at the same time with the ball, Gavroche tumbled into the barricade.

"Proceed," cried Bossuet to the gunners.

COURFEYRAC suddenly perceived somebody at the foot of the barricade, outside in the street, under the balls.

Gavroche had taken a basket from the wine-shop, had gone out by the opening, and was quietly occupied in emptying into his basket the full cartridge-boxes of the National Guards who had been killed on the slope of the redoubt.

"What are you doing there?" said Courfeyrac.

Gavroche cocked up his nose.

"Citizen, I am filling my basket."

"Why, don't you see the grape?"

Gavroche answered:

"Well, it rains. What then?"

Courfeyrac cried:

"Come back!"

"Directly," said Gavroche.

And with a bound, he sprang into the street.

Some twenty dead lay scattered along the whole length of the street on the pavement. Twenty cartridge-boxes for Gavroche, a supply of cartridges for the barricade.

The smoke in the street was like a fog.

Under the folds of this veil of smoke, and thanks to his small size, he could advance far into the street without being seen. He emptied the first seven or eight cartridge-boxes without much danger.

By successive advances, he reached a point where the fog from the firing became transparent.

So that the sharp-shooters of the line drawn up and on the alert behind their wall of paving-stones, and the sharp-shooters of the banlieue massed at the corner of the street, suddenly discovered something moving in the smoke.

Just as Gavroche was relieving a sergeant who lay near a stone-block of his cartridges, a ball struck the body.

"The deuce!" said Gavroche. "So they are killing my dead for me."

A second ball splintered the pavement beside him. A third upset his basket.

The sight was appalling and fascinating. Gavroche, fired at, mocked the firing. He appeared to be very much amused. They aimed at him incessantly, they always missed him. The National Guards and the soldiers laughed as they aimed at him. He lay down, then rose up, hid himself in a doorway, then sprang out, disappeared, reappeared, escaped, returned, retorted upon the volleys by wry faces, and meanwhile pillaged cartridges, emptied cartridge-boxes, and filled his basket. The insurgents, breathless with anxiety, followed him with their eyes. The barricade was trembling; he was singing. It was not a child; it was not a man; it was a strange fairy *gamin*. One would have said the invulnerable dwarf of the mêlée. The bullets ran after him, he was more nimble than they.

One bullet, however, better aimed or more treacherous than the others, reached the Will-o'-the-wisp child. They saw Gavroche totter, then he fell.

MORTUUS PATER FILIUM MORITURUM EXPECTAT

Marius had sprung out of the barricade. Combeferre had followed him. But it was too late. Gavroche was dead. Combeferre brought back the basket of cartridges; Marius brought back the child.

"Alas!" thought he, "what the father had done for his father he was returning to the son; only Thénardier had brought back his father living, while he brought back the child dead."

When Marius re-entered the redoubt with Gavroche in his arms, his face, like the child's, was covered with blood.

Just as he had stooped down to pick up Gavroche, a ball grazed his skull; he did not perceive it.

Courfeyrac took off his cravat and bound up Marius' forehead.

SUDDENLY between two discharges they heard the distant sound of a clock striking.

"It is noon," said Combeferre.

The twelve strokes had not sounded when Enjolras sprang to his feet, and flung down from the top of the barricade this thundering shout:

"Carry some paving-stones into the house. Fortify the windows with them. Half the men to the muskets, the other half to the stones. Not a minute to lose."

The fortress was complete. The barricade was the rampart, the wine-shop was the donjon.

With the paving-stones which remained, they closed up the opening beside the barricade.

He said to Marius: "We are the two chiefs; I will give the last orders within. You stay outside and watch."

Marius posted himself for observation upon the crest of the barricade.

These dispositions made, he turned towards Javert, and said to him:

"I won't forget you."

And, laying a pistol on the table, he added:

"The last man to leave this room will blow out the spy's brains!"

"Here?" inquired a voice.

"No, do not leave this corpse with ours. You can climb over the little barricade on the Rue Mondétour. It is only four feet high. The man is well tied. You will take him there, and execute him there."

There was one man, at that moment, who was more impassable than Enjolras; it was Javert.

Here Jean Valjean appeared.

He was in the throng of insurgents. He stepped forward, and said to Enjolras:

262

"You are the commander?"

"Yes."

"You thanked me just now."

"In the name of the republic. The barricade has two saviors, Marius Pontmercy and you."

"Do you think that I deserve a reward?"

"Certainly."

"Well, I ask one."

"What?"

"To blow out that man's brains myself."

Javert raised his head, saw Jean Valjean, made an imperceptible movement, and said:

"That is appropriate."

As for Enjolras, he had begun to reload his carbine; he cast his eyes about him:

"No objection."

And turning towards Jean Valjean: "Take the spy."

Jean Valjean, in fact, took possession of Javert by sitting down on the end of the table. He caught up the pistol, and a slight click announced that he had cocked it.

JEAN VALJEAN TAKES HIS REVENGE

WHEN Jean Valjean was alone with Javert, he untied the rope that held the prisoner by the middle of the body, the knot of which was under the table. Then he motioned to him to get up.

Javert obeyed, with that undefinable smile into which the supremacy of enchained authority is condensed.

Jean Valjean took Javert by the martingale as you would take a beast of burden by a strap, and, drawing him after him, went out of the wine-shop slowly, for Javert, with his legs fettered, could take only very short steps.

Jean Valjean had the pistol in his hand.

They crossed thus the interior trapezium of the barricade. The insurgents, intent upon the imminent attack, were looking the other way.

Marius, alone, placed towards the left extremity of the wall, saw them pass. This group of the victim and the executioner borrowed a light from the sepulchral gleam which he had in his soul.

Jean Valjean, with some difficulty, bound as Javert was, but without letting go of him for a single instant, made him scale the little entrenchment on the Rue Mondétour.

When they had climbed over this wall, they found themselves alone in the little street. Nobody saw them now. The corner of the house hid them from insurgents. The corpses carried out from the barricades made a terrible mound a few steps off.

Jean Valjean put the pistol under his arm, and fixed upon Javert a look which had no need of words to say: "Javert, it is I."

Javert answered.

"Take your revenge."

Jean Valjean took a knife out of his pocket, and opened it.

"A *surin!*" exclaimed Javert. "You are right. That suits you better."

Jean Valjean cut the martingale which Javert had about his neck, then he cut the ropes which he had on his wrists, then, stooping down, he cut the cord which he had on his feet; and, rising, he said to him:

"You are free."

Javert was not easily astonished, Still, complete master as he was of himself, he could not escape an emotion. He stood aghast and motionless.

Jean Valjean continued:

"I don't expect to leave this place. Still, if by chance I should, I live, under the name of Fauchelevent, in the Rue de l'Homme Armé, Number Seven."

Javert had the scowl of a tiger half opening the corner of his mouth, and he muttered between his teeth:

"Take care."

"Go," said Jean Valjean.

Javert resumed:

"You said Fauchelevent, Rue de l'Homme Armé?"

"Number Seven."

Javert repeated in an undertone: "Number seven." He buttoned his coat, restored the military stiffness between his shoulders, turned half round, folded his arms, supporting his chin with one hand, and walked off in the direction of the markets. Jean Valjean followed him with his eyes.

When Javert was gone, Jean Valjean fired the pistol in the air.

Then he re-entered the barricade and said: "It is done."

SUDDENLY the drum beat the charge.

The attack was a hurricane. A powerful column of infantry of the line, intersected at equal intervals by National Guards and Municipal Guards on foot, and supported by deep masses heard but unseen, turned into the street at a quick step, drums beating, trumpets sounding, bayonets fixed, sappers at their head, and, unswerving under the projectiles, came straight upon the barricade with the weight of a bronze column upon a wall.

There was assault after assault. The horror continued to increase.

Then resounded over this pile of paving-stones, in this Rue de la Chanvrerie, a struggle worthy the walls of Troy. These men, wan, tattered, and exhausted, who had not eaten for twenty-four hours, who had not slept, who had but a few more shots to fire, who felt their pockets empty of cartridges, nearly all wounded, their heads or arms bound with a smutty and blackened cloth, with holes in their coats whence the blood was flowing, scarcely armed with worthless muskets and with old hacked swords, became Titans. The barricade was ten times approached, assaulted, scaled, and never taken.

Bossuet was killed; Feuilly was killed; Courfeyrac was killed; Joly was killed; Combeferre, pierced by three bayonet-thrusts in the breast, just as he was lifting a wounded soldier, had only time to look to heaven and expired.

Marius, still fighting, was so hacked with wounds, particularly about his head, that the countenance was lost in blood, and you would have said that he had his face covered with a red handkerchief.

Enjolras alone was untouched. When his weapon failed, he reached his hand to right or left, and an insurgent put whatever weapon he could in his grasp.

WHEN there were none of the chiefs alive save Enjolras and Marius, who were at the extremities of the barricade, the center, which Courfeyrac, Joly, Bossuet, Feuilly, and Combeferre had so long sustained, gave way.

A final assault was now attempted, and this assault succeeded. The mass bristling with bayonets and hurled at a double-quick step, came on irresistible, and the dense battle-front of the attacking column appeared in the smoke at the top of the escarpment. This time, it was finished. The group of insurgents who defended the center fell back pell-mell.

Marius remained without. A ball had broken his shoulder-blade; he felt that he was fainting, and that he was falling. At that moment, his eyes already closed, he experienced the shock of a vigorous hand seizing him, and his fainting fit, in which he lost consciousness, left him hardly time for this thought, mingled with the last memory of Cosette: "I am taken prisoner. I shall be shot."

PRISONER

MARIUS was in fact a prisoner. Prisoner of Jean Valjean.

Jean Valjean, in the thick cloud of the combat, did not appear to see Marius; the fact is, that he did not take his eyes from him. When a shot struck down Marius, Jean Valjean bounded with the agility of a tiger, dropped upon him as upon a prey, and carried him away.

The whirlwind of the attack at that instant concentrated so fiercely upon Enjolras and the door of the wine-shop, that nobody saw Jean Valjean cross the unpaved field of the barricade, holding the senseless Marius in his arms, and disappear behind the corner of the house of Corinth.

There Jean Valjean stopped; he let Marius slide to the ground, set his back to the wall, and cast his eyes about him.

The situation was appalling.

Jean Valjean looked at the house in front of him, he looked at the barricade by the side of him, then he looked upon the ground, with the violence of the last extremity, in desperation, and as if he would have made a hole in it with his eyes.

Beneath his persistent look, something vaguely tangible in such an agony outlined itself and took form at his feet, as if there were a power in the eye to develop the thing desired. He perceived a few steps from him, at the foot of the little wall so pitilessly watched and guarded on the outside, under some fallen paving-stones which partly hid it, an iron grating laid flat and level with the ground. This grating, made of strong transverse bars, was about two feet square. The stone frame which held it had been torn up, and it was as it were unset. Through the bars a glimpse could be caught of an obscure opening, something like the flue of a chimney or the main of a cistern. Jean Valjean sprang forward. To remove the stones, to lift the grating, to load Marius, who was as inert as a dead body, upon his shoulders, to descend, with that burden upon his back, by the aid of his elbows and knees, into this kind of well, fortunately not very deep, to let fall over his head the heavy iron trapdoor upon which the stones were shaken back again, to find a foothold upon a flagged surface ten feet below the ground, this was executed like what is done in delirium, with the strength of a giant and the rapidity of an eagle; it required but very few moments.

Jean Valjean found himself, with Marius still senseless, in a sort of long underground passage.

There, deep peace, absolute silence, night.

The impression which he had formerly felt in falling from the street into the convent came back to him. Only, what he was now carrying away was not Cosette; it was Marius.

He could now hardly hear above him, like a vague murmur, the fearful tumult of the wine-shop taken by assault.

Mire, But Soul

THE CLOACA AND ITS SURPRISES

IT was in the sewer of Paris that Jean Valjean found himself.

After a few moments, he ceased to be blind. A little light fell from the air-hole through which he had slipped in, and his eye became accustomed to this cave. The passage in which he was earthed, no other word better expresses the condition, was walled up behind him. Before him, there was another wall, a wall of night. The light from the air-hole died out ten or twelve paces from the point at which Jean Valjean stood, and scarcely produced a pallid whiteness over a few yards of the damp wall of the sewer. Beyond, the opaqueness was massive; to penetrate it appeared horrible, and to enter it seemed like being engulfed. He could, however, force his way into that wall of mist, and he must do it. He must even hasten. He had laid Marius upon the ground, he gathered him up, this is again the right word, replaced him upon his shoulders, and began his journey. He resolutely entered that obscurity.

When he had turned the corner of the gallery, the distant gleam of the air-hole disappeared, the curtain of obscurity fell back over him, and he again became blind. He went forward none the less, and as rapidly as he could. Marius' arms were passed about his neck, and his feet hung behind him. He held both arms with one hand, and groped for the wall with the other. He felt a warm stream, which came from Marius, flow over him and penetrate his clothing. Still, a moist warmth at his ear, which touched the wounded man's mouth, indicated respiration, and consequently life.

At a certain moment he felt that he was getting away from under the Paris in which the barricades had suppressed the circulation, and that he was coming beneath the Paris which was alive and normal. He heard suddenly above his head a sound like thunder, distant, but continuous. It was the rumbling of the vehicles.

He had been walking for about half an hour, at least by his own calculation, and had not yet thought of resting; only he had changed the hand which supported Marius. The darkness was deeper than ever, but this depth reassured him.

All at once he saw his shadow before him. It was marked out on a feeble ruddiness almost indistinct, which vaguely empurpled the floor at his feet, and the arch over his head, and which glided along at his right and his left on the two slimy walls of the corridor. In amazement he turned round.

Behind him, in the portion of the passage through which he had passed, at a distance which appeared to him immense, flamed, throwing its rays into the dense obscurity, a sort of horrible star which appeared to be looking at him.

It was the gloomy star of the police which was rising in the sewer.

Behind this star were moving without order eight or ten black forms, straight, indistinct, terrible.

EXPLANATION

DURING the day of the 6th of June, a battue of the sewers had been ordered. It was feared that they would be taken as a refuge by the vanquished, and prefect Gisquet was to ransack the occult Paris, while General Bugeaud was sweeping the public Paris.—

That which was at this moment directed upon Jean Valjean was the lantern of the patrol of the right bank.

Luckily, if he saw the lantern well, the lantern saw him badly. It was light and he was shadow. He was far off, and merged in the blackness of the place. He drew close to the side of the wall, and stopped.

The men of the patrol listened and heard nothing, they looked and saw nothing. They consulted.

The result of this council held by the watch-dogs was that they had been mistaken, that there had been no noise, that there was nobody there.

Before going away, the sergeant, to ease the police conscience, discharged his carbine in the direction they were abandoning, towards Jean Valjean. Some plastering which fell into the stream and spattered the water a few steps from Jean Valjean made him aware that the ball had struck the arch above his head.

JEAN VALJEAN had resumed his advance, and had not stopped again.

This advance became more and more laborious. The level of these arches varies; the medium height is about five feet six inches, and was calculated for the stature of a man; Jean Valjean was compelled to bend so as not to hit Marius against the arch; he had to stoop every second, then rise up, to grope incessantly for the wall. The moisture of the stones and the sliminess of the floor made them bad points of support, whether for the hand or the foot.

It might have been three o'clock in the afternoon when he arrived at the belt sewer.

He was first astonished at this sudden enlargement. He abruptly found himself in the gallery where his outstretched hands did not reach the two walls, and under an arch which his head did not touch. The Grand Sewer indeed is eight feet wide and seven high.

A little beyond an affluent which was probably the branching of the Madeleine, he stopped. He was very tired. A large air-hole, probably the vista on the Rue d'Anjou, produced an almost vivid light. Jean Valjean, with the gentleness of movement of a brother for his wounded brother, laid Marius upon the side bank of the sewer. Marius' bloody face appeared, under the white gleam from the air-hole, as if at the bottom of a tomb. His eyes were closed, his hair adhered to his temples like brushes dried in red paint, his hands dropped down lifeless, his limbs were cold, there was coagulated blood at the corners of his mouth. Jean Valjean tore up his shirt, bandaged the wounds as well as he could, and staunched the flowing blood; then, bending in the twilight over Marius, who was still unconscious and almost lifeless, he looked at him with an inexpressible hatred.

In opening Marius' clothes, he had found two things in his

pockets, the bread which had been forgotten there since the day previous, and Marius' pocket-book. He ate the bread and opened the pocket-book. On the first page he found the four lines written by Marius. They will be remembered.

"My name is Marius Pontmercy. Carry my corpse to my grandfather's, M. Gillenormand, Rue des Filles du Calvaire, No. 6, in the Marais."

By the light of the air-hole, Jean Valjean read these four lines, and stopped a moment as if absorbed in himself, repeating in an undertone: "Rue des Filles du Calvaire, Number Six, Monsieur Gillenormand." He replaced the pocket-book in Marius' pocket. He had eaten, strength had returned to him: he took Marius on his back again, laid his head carefully upon his right shoulder, and began to descend the sewer.

The darkness thickened about Jean Valjean. He none the less continued to advance, groping in the obscurity.

This obscurity suddenly became terrible.

THE FONTIS

JEAN VALJEAN found himself in presence of a fontis.

This kind of settling was then frequent in the subsoil of the Champs Elysées, very unfavorable for hydraulic works, and giving poor support to underground constructions, from its excessive fluidity. When, in 1836, they demolished, for the purpose of rebuilding, the old stone sewer under the Faubourg Saint Honoré, in which we find Jean Valjean now entangled, the quicksand, which is the subsoil from the Champs Elysées to the Seine, was such an obstacle that the work lasted nearly six months.

The fontis which Jean Valjean fell upon was caused by the showers of the previous day. A yielding of the pavement, imperfectly upheld by the underlying sand, had occasioned a damming of the rain-water. Infiltration having taken place, sinking had followed. The floor, broken up, had disappeared in the mire. For what distance? Impossible to say. The obscurity was deeper than anywhere else. It was a mudhole in the cavern of night.

Jean Valjean felt the pavement slipping away under him. He entered into this slime. It was water on the surface, mire at the bottom. He must surely pass through. To retrace his steps was impossible. Marius was expiring, and Jean Valjean exhausted. Jean Valjean advanced. Moreover, the quagmire appeared not very deep for a few steps. But in proportion as he advanced, his feet sank in. He very soon had the mire half-knee deep, and water above his knees. He walked on, holding Marius with both arms as high above the water as he could. The mud now came up to his knees, and the water to his waist. He sank in deeper and deeper. This mire, dense enough for one man's weight, evidently could not bear two. Marius and Jean Valjean would have had a chance of escape separately. Jean Valjean continued to advance, supporting this dying man, who was perhaps a corpse.

The water came up to his armpits; he felt that he was foundering; it was with difficulty that he could move in the depth of mire in which he was. He still held Marius up, and, with an unparalleled outlay of strength, he advanced; but he sank deeper. He now had only his head out of the water, and his arms supporting Marius.

He sank still deeper, he threw his face back to escape the water, and to be able to breathe; he dimly perceived Marius' dropping head and livid face above him; he made a desperate effort, and thrust his foot forward; his foot struck something solid; a support. It was time.

He rose and writhed and rooted himself upon this support with a sort of fury. It produced the effect upon him of the first step of a staircase reascending towards life.

This support, discovered in the mire at the last moment, was the beginning of the other slope of the floor, which had bent without breaking, and had curved beneath the water like a board, and in a single piece. A well-constructed paving forms an arch, and has this firmness. This fragment of the floor, partly submerged, but solid, was a real slope, and, once upon this slope, they were saved. Jean Valjean ascended this inclined plane, and reached the other side of the quagmire.

On coming out of the water, he struck against a stone, and fell upon his knees. This seemed to him fitting, and he remained thus for some time, his soul lost in unspoken prayer to God.

He rose, shivering, chilled, infected, bending beneath this dying man, whom he was dragging on, all dripping with slime, his soul filled with a strange light.

SOMETIMES WE GET AGROUND WHEN WE EXPECT TO GET ASHORE

He resumed his route once more.

He walked with desperation, almost with rapidity, for a hundred paces, without raising his head, almost without breathing, and suddenly struck against the wall. He had reached an angle of the sewer, and, arriving at the turn with his head down, he had encountered the wall. He raised his eyes, and at the extremity of the passage, down there before him, far, very far away, he perceived a light. This time, it was not the terrible light: It was the light of day.

Jean Valjean reached the outlet.

There he stopped.

It was indeed the outlet, but it did not let him out.

The arch was closed by a strong grating, and the grating which, according to all appearance, rarely turned upon its rusty hinges, was held in its stone frame by a stout lock which, red with rust, seemed an enormous brick. He could see the keyhole, and the strong bolt deeply plunged into the iron staple. The lock was plainly a double-lock.

Beyond the grating, the open air, the river, the daylight, the beach, very narrow, but sufficient to get away.

It might have been half-past eight o'clock in the evening. The day was declining.

Jean Valjean laid Marius along the wall on the dry part of the floor, then walked to the grating and clenched the bars with both hands; the shaking was frenzied, the shock nothing. The grating did not stir. Jean Valjean seized the bars one after another, hoping to be able to tear out the least solid one, and to make a lever of it to lift the door or break the lock. Not a bar yielded.

He turned his back to the grating, and dropped upon the pavement, rather prostrate than sitting, beside the yet motionless Marius and his head sank between his knees. No exit. This was the last drop of anguish.

Of whom did he think in this overwhelming dejection? Neither of himself nor of Marius. He thought of Cosette.

THE TORN COAT-TAIL

In the midst of this annihilation, a hand was laid upon his shoulder, and a voice which spoke low, said to him:

"Go halves."

A man was before him.

This man was dressed in a blouse; he was barefooted; he held his shoes in his left hand; he had evidently taken them off to be able to reach Jean Valjean without being heard.

Jean Valjean had not a moment's hesitation. Unforeseen as was the encounter, this man was known to him. This man was Thénardier.

Jean Valjean perceived immediately that Thénardier did not recognise him.

They gazed at each other for a moment in this penumbra, as if they were taking each other's measure. Thénardier was first to break the silence.

"How are you going to manage to get out?"

Jean Valjean did not answer.

Thénardier continued:

"Impossible to pick the lock. Still you must get away from here."

"That is true," said Jean Valjean.

"Well, go halves."

"What do you mean?"

"You have killed the man. For my part, I have the key."

Thénardier pointed to Marius. He went on:

"I don't know you, but I would like to help you. You must be a friend."

Jean Valjean began to understand. Thénardier took him for an assassin.

Thénardier resumed:

"Listen, comrade. You haven't killed that man without looking to what he had in his pockets. Give me my half. I will open the door for you."

And, drawing a big key half out from under his blouse, which was full of holes, he added:

"Would you like to see how the key of the fields is made? There it is."

Thénardier plunged his fist into a huge pocket hidden under his blouse, pulled out a rope, and handed it to Jean Valjean.

"Here," said he, "I'll give you the rope to boot."

"A rope, what for?"

"You want a stone too, but you'll find one outside. There is a heap of rubbish there."

"A stone, what for?"

"Fool, as you are going to throw the *pantre* into the river, you want a stone and a rope; without them it would float on the water."

Jean Valjean took the rope. Everybody has accepted things thus mechanically.

"Now, let us finish the business. Let us divide. You have seen my key, show me your money."

Jean Valjean felt in his pockets.

It was, as will be remembered, his custom always to have money about him. The gloomy life of expedience to which he was condemned, made this a law to him. This time, however, he was caught unprovided. On putting on his national guard's uniform, the evening before, he had forgotten, gloomily absorbed as he was, to take his pocket-book with him. He had only some coins in his waistcoat pocket. He turned out his pocket, all soaked with filth, and displayed upon the curb of the sewer a louis d'or, two five-franc pieces, and five or six big sous.

Thénandier thrust out his under lip with a significant twist of the neck.

"You didn't kill him very dear," said he.

He began to handle, in all familiarity, the pockets of Jean Valjean and Marius. Jean Valjean, principally concerned in keeping his back to the light, did not interfere with him. While he was feeling of Marius' coat, Thénardier, with the dexterity of a juggler, found means, without attracting Jean Valjean's attention, to tear off a strip, which he hid under his blouse, probably thinking that this scrap of cloth might assist him afterwards to identify the assassinated man and the assassin. He found, however, nothing more than the thirty francs.

"It is true," said he, "both together, you have no more than that."

And, forgetting his words, *go halves,* he took the whole.

He hesitated a little before the big sous. Upon reflection, he took them also, mumbling:

"No matter! this is to *suriner* people too cheap."

This said, he took the key from under his blouse anew. "Now, friend, you must go out. This is like the fair, you pay on going out. You have paid, go out."

Thénardier half opened the door, left just a passage for Jean Valjean, closed the grating again, turned the key twice in the lock, and plunged back into the obscurity, without making more noise than a breath.

Jean Valjean found himself outside.

MARIUS SEEMS TO BE DEAD TO ONE WHO IS A GOOD JUDGE

HE let Marius slide down upon the beach.

They were outside!

Jean Valjean could not but gaze at that vast clear shadow which was above him; pensive, he took in the majestic silence of the eternal heavens, a bath of ecstasy and prayer. Then, hastily, as if a feeling of duty came back to him, he bent over Marius, and, dipping up some water in the hollow of his hand, he threw a few drops gently into his face. Marius' eyelids did not part; but his half-open mouth breathed.

Jean Valjean was plunging his hand into the river again, when suddenly he felt an indescribable uneasiness, such as we feel when we have somebody behind us, without seeing him.

He turned round.

As just before, somebody was indeed behind him.

Jean Valjean recognised Javert.

Jean Valjean had passed from one shoal to another.

Javert did not recognise Jean Valjean, who, as we have said, no longer resembled himself. He did not unfold his arms, he secured his club in his grasp by an imperceptible movement, and said in a quick and calm voice:

"Who are you?"

"I."

"What you?"

"Jean Valjean."

Javert put the club between his teeth, bent his knees, inclined his body, laid his two powerful hands upon Jean Valjean's shoulders which they clamped like two vices, examined him, and recognised him.

Jean Valjean stood inert under the grasp of Javert like a lion who should submit to the claw of a lynx.

"Inspector Javert," said he, "you have got me. Besides, since this morning, I have considered myself your prisoner. I did not give you my address to try to escape you. Take me. Only grant me one thing."

Javert seemed not to hear. He rested his fixed eye upon Jean Valjean. At last, he let go of Jean Valjean, rose up as straight as a stick, took his club firmly in his grasp, and, as if in a dream, murmured rather than pronounced this question:

"What are you doing here? and who is this man?"

Jean Valjean answered, and the sound of his voice appeared to awaken Javert:

"It is precisely of him that I wished to speak. Dispose of me as you please; but help me first to carry him home. I only ask that of you."

Javert's face contracted, as it happened to him whenever anybody seemed to consider him capable of a concession. Still he did not say no.

He stooped down again, took a handkerchief from his pocket, which he dipped in the water, and wiped Marius' bloodstained forehead.

"This man was in the barricade," said he in an undertone, and as if speaking to himself. "This is he whom they called Marius."

A spy of the first quality, who had observed everything, listened to everything, heard everything, and recollected everything, believing he was about to die; who spied even in his death-agony, and who, leaning upon the first step of the grave, had taken notes.

He seized Marius' hand, seeking for his pulse.

"He is wounded," said Jean Valjean.

"He is dead," said Javert.

Jean Valjean answered:

"No. Not yet."

"You have brought him, then, from the barricade here?" observed Javert.

Jean Valjean, for his part, seemed to have but one idea.

"He lives in the Marais, Rue des Filles du Calvaire, at his grandfather's—I forget the name."

Jean Valjean felt in Marius' coat, took out the pocket-book, opened it at the page pencilled by Marius, and handed it to Javert.

Javert kept Marius' pocket-book.

A moment later, the carriage, descending by the slope of the watering-place, was on the beach. Marius was laid upon the back seat, and Javert sat down by the side of Jean Valjean on the front seat.

When the door was shut, the fiacre moved rapidly off.

RETURN OF THE PRODIGAL SON—OF HIS LIFE

It was after nightfall when the fiacre arrived at No. 6, in the Rue des Filles du Calvaire.

Everybody in the house was asleep.

Meanwhile Jean Valjean and the driver lifted Marius out of the coach, Jean Valjean supporting him by the armpits, and the coachman by the knees.

Javert called out to the porter in the tone which befits the government, in presence of the porter of a factious man.

"Somebody whose name is Gillenormand?"

"It is here. What do you want with him?"

"His son is brought home."

"His son?" said the porter with amazement.

"He is dead."

Jean Valjean, who came ragged and dirty, behind Javert, and whom the porter beheld with some horror, motioned to him with his head that he was not.

The porter did not appear to understand either Javert's words, or Jean Valjean's signs.

The porter merely woke Basque. Basque woke Nicolette; Nicolette woke Aunt Gillenormand. As to the grandfather, they let him sleep, thinking that he would know it soon enough at all events.

They carried Marius up to the first story, without anybody, moreover, perceiving it in the other portions of the house, and they laid him on an old couch in M. Gillenormand's ante-chamber; and, while Basque went for a doctor and Nicolette was opening the linen closets, Jean Valjean felt Javert touch him on the shoulder. He understood, and went downstairs, having behind him Javert's following steps.

They got into the fiacre, and the driver mounted his box.

"Inspector Javert," said Jean Valjean, "grant me one thing more."

"What?" asked Javert roughly.

"Let me go home a moment. Then you shall do with me what you will."

Javert remained silent for a few seconds, his chin drawn back into the collar of his overcoat, then he let down the window in front.

"Driver," said he, "Rue de l'Homme Armé, No. 7."

COMMOTION IN THE ABSOLUTE

AT the entrance of the Rue de l'Homme Armé, the fiacre stopped, this street being too narrow for carriages to enter. Javert and Jean Valjean got out.

They entered the street. It was, as usual, empty. Javert followed Jean Valjean. They reached No. 7. Jean Valjean rapped. The door opened.

"Very well," said Javert. "Go up."

He added with a strange expression and as if he were making an effort in speaking in such a way:

"I will wait here for you."

Jean Valjean looked at Javert. This manner of proceeding was little in accordance with Javert's habits. Still, that Javert should now have a sort of haughty confidence in him, the confidence of the cat which grants the mouse the liberty of the length of her claw, resolved as Jean Valjean was to deliver himself up and make an end of it, could not surprise him very much. He opened the door, went into the house, cried to the porter who was in bed and who had drawn the cord without getting up: "It is I!" and mounted the stairs.

On reaching the first story, he paused. The window on the landing, which was a sliding window, was open.

Jean Valjean, either to take breath or mechanically, looked out of this window. He leaned over the street. It is short, and the lamp lighted it from one end to the other. Jean Valjean was bewildered with amazement; there was nobody there.

Javert was gone.

Basque and the porter had carried Marius into the parlor, still stretched motionless upon the couch on which he had been first laid. The doctor, who had been sent for, had arrived. Aunt Gillenormand had got up.

On the doctor's order, a cot-bed had been set up near the couch. The doctor examined Marius, and, after having determined that the pulse still beat, that the sufferer had no wound penetrating his breast, and that the blood at the corners of his mouth came from the nasal cavities, he had him laid flat upon the bed, without a pillow, his head on a level with his body, and even a little lower, with his chest bare, in order to facilitate respiration.

The body had not received any interior lesion; a ball, deadened by the pocket-book, had turned aside, and made the tour of the ribs with a hideous gash, but not deep, and consequently not dangerous. The long walk underground had completed the dislocation of the broken shoulder-blade, and there were serious difficulties there. There were sword cuts on the arms. No scar disfigured his face; the head, however, was as it were covered with hacks.

Basque and Nicolette tore up linen and made bandages; Nicolette sewed them, Basque folded them. By the side of the bed, three candles were burning on a table upon which the surgical instruments were spread out. The doctor washed Marius' face and hair with cold water. A bucketful was red in a moment. The porter, candle in hand, stood by.

At the moment the doctor was wiping the face and touching the still closed eyelids lightly with his finger, a door opened at the rear end of the parlor, and a long, pale figure approached.

It was the grandfather.

He perceived the bed, and on the mattress that bleeding young man, white with a waxy whiteness, his eyes closed, his

mouth open, his lips pallid, naked to the waist, gashed everywhere with red wounds, motionless, brightly lighted.

The grandfather had, from head to foot, as much of a
shiver as ossified limbs can have; his eyes, the cornea of
which had become yellow from his great age, were veiled with
a sort of glassy haze; his whole face assumed in an instant
the cadaverous angles of a skeleton head, his arms fell pen-
dent as if a spring were broken in them, and his stupefied
astonishment was expressed by the separation of the fingers
of his aged, tremulous hands; his knees bent forward, showing through the opening of his nightgown his poor naked
legs bristling with white hairs, and he murmured:

"Marius!"

"Monsieur," said Basque, "monsieur has just been brought
home. He has been to the barricade, and——"

"He is dead!" cried the old man in a terrible voice. "Oh!
the brigand."

Then a sort of sepulchral transfiguration made this centen-
arian as straight as a young man.

"Monsieur," said he, "you are the doctor. Come, tell me
one thing. He is dead, isn't he?"

The physician, in the height of anxiety, kept silence.

The old man's white lips moved as if mechanically, and
made way for almost indistinct words, like whispers in a
death-rattle, which could scarcely be heard: "Oh! heartless!
Oh! clubbist! Oh! scoundrel! Oh! Septembrist!"

At this moment, Marius slowly raised his lids, and his gaze,
still veiled in the astonishment of lethargy, rested upon M.
Gillenormand.

"Marius!" cried the old man. "Marius! my darling Marius!
my child! my dear son! You are opening your eyes, you are
looking at me, you are alive, thanks!"

And he fell fainting.

Javert off the Track

JAVERT OFF THE TRACK

JAVERT made his way with slow steps from the Rue de l'Homme Armé.

He walked with his head down, for the first time in his life, and, for the first time in his life as well, with his hands behind his back.

He took the shortest route towards the Seine, reached the Quai des Ormes, went along the quai, passed the Grève, and stopped, at a little distance from the post of the Place du Châtelet, at the corner of the Pont Notre Dame. The Seine there forms between the Pont Notre Dame and the Pont au Change in one direction, and in the other between the Quai de la Mégisserie and the Quai aux Fleurs, a sort of square lake crossed by a rapid.

Javert leaned both elbows on the parapet, with his chin in his hands, and while his fingers were clenched mechanically in the thickest of his whiskers, he reflected.

His condition was inexpressible.

To owe life to a malefactor, to accept that debt and to pay it, to be, in spite of himself, on a level with a fugitive from justice, and to pay him for one service with another service; to allow him to say: "Go away," and to say to him in turn: "Be free;" to sacrifice duty, that general obligation, to personal motives, and to feel in these personal motives something general also, and perhaps superior; to betray society in order to be true to his own conscience; that all these absurdities should be realised and that they should be accumulated upon himself, this it was by which he was prostrated.

One thing had astonished him, that Jean Valjean had spared him, and one thing had petrified him, that he, Javert, had spared Jean Valjean.

Where was he? He sought himself and found himself no longer.

Jean Valjean confounded him. All the axioms which had been the supports of his whole life crumbled away before this man. Jean Valjean's generosity towards him, Javert, overwhelmed him. Other acts, which he remembered and which he had hitherto treated as lies and follies, returned to him now as realities. M. Madeleine reappeared behind Jean Valjean, and the two figures overlaid each other so as to make but one, which was venerable. Javert felt that something horrible was penetrating his soul, admiration for a convict. Respect for a galley-slave, can that be possible? He shuddered at it, yet could not shake it off. It was useless to struggle, he was reduced to confess before his own inner tribunal the sublimity of this wretch. That was hateful.

Unnatural state, if ever there was one. There were only two ways to get out of it. One, to go resolutely to Jean Valjean, and to return the man of the galleys to the dungeon. The other——

The place where Javert was leaning was, it will be remembered, situated exactly over the rapids of the Seine, perpendicularly over that formidable whirlpool which knots and unknots itself like an endless screw.

Javert bent his head and looked. All was black. He could distinguish nothing. He heard a frothing sound; but he did not see the river. At intervals, in that giddy depth, a gleam appeared in dim serpentine contortions, the water having this power, in the most complete night, of taking light, nobody knows whence, and changing it into an adder.

He saw nothing, but he perceived the hostile chill of the water, and the insipid odor of the moist stones. A fierce breath rose from that abyss. The swollen river guessed at rather than perceived, the tragical whispering of the flood, the dismal vastness of the arches of the bridge, the imaginable fall into that gloomy void, all that shadow was full of horror.

Javert remained for some minutes motionless, gazing into that opening of darkness; he contemplated the invisible with a fixedness which resembled attention. Suddenly he took off his hat and laid it on the end of the quai. A moment afterwards, a tall and black form, which from the distance some belated passer might have taken for a phantom, appeared standing on the parapet, bent towards the Seine, then sprang up, and fell straight into the darkness; there was a dull splash; and the shadow alone was in the secret of the convulsions of that obscure form which had disappeared under the water.

The Grandson and the Grandfather

MARIUS, ESCAPING FROM CIVIL WAR,
PREPARES FOR DOMESTIC WAR

MARIUS was for a long time neither dead nor alive. He had for several weeks a fever accompanied with delirium, and serious cerebral symptoms resulting rather from the concussion produced by the wounds in the head than from the wounds themselves.

He repeated the name of Cosette during entire nights in the dismal loquacity of fever and with the gloomy obstinacy of agony. The size of certain gashes was a serious danger, the suppuration of large wounds always being liable to reabsorption, and consequently to kill the patient, under certain atmospheric influences; at every change in the weather, at the slightest storm, the physician was anxious, "Above all, let the wounded man have no excitement," he repeated.

Every day, and sometimes twice a day, a very well-dressed gentleman with white hair, such was the description given by the porter, came to inquire after the wounded man, and left a large package of lint for the dressings.

At last, on the 7th of September, four months, to a day, after the sorrowful night when they had brought him home dying to his grandfather, the physician declared him out of danger. Convalescence began. Marius was, however, obliged still to remain for more than two months stretched on a long chair, on account of the accidents resulting from the fracture of the shoulder-blade. There is always a last wound like this which will not close, and which prolongs the dressings, to the great disgust of the patient.

In proportion as he took new hold of life, his former griefs reappeared, the old ulcers of his memory reopened, he thought once more of the past. Colonel Pontmercy appeared again between M. Gillenormand and him, Marius; he said to himself that there was no real goodness to be hoped for from him who had been so unjust and so hard to his father. And with health, there returned to him a sort of harshness towards his grandfather. The old man bore it with gentleness.

M. Gillenormand, without manifesting it in any way, noticed that Marius, since he had been brought home and restored to consciousness, had not once said to him "father."

A crisis was evidently approaching.

As it almost always happens in similar cases, Marius, in order to try himself, skirmished before offering battle. One morning it happened that M. Gillenormand, over a newspaper which had fallen into his hands, spoke lightly of the Convention and discharged a royalist epiphonema upon Danton, Saint Just, and Robespierre. "The men of '93 were giants," said Marius, sternly. The old man was silent, and did not whisper for the rest of the day.

Marius, who had always present to his mind the inflexible grandfather of his early years, saw in this silence an intense concentration of anger, augured from it a sharp conflict, and increased his preparations for combat in the inner recesses of his thought.

He determined that in case of refusal he would tear off his bandages, dislocate his shoulder, lay bare and open his remaining wounds, and refuse all nourishment. His wounds were his ammunition. To have Cosette or to die.

He waited for the favorable moment with the crafty patience of the sick.

That moment came.

MARIUS ATTACKS

ONE day M. Gillenormand, while his daughter was putting in order the vials and the cups upon the marble top of the bureau, bent over Marius and said to him in his most tender tone:

"Do you see, my darling Marius, in your place I would eat meat now rather than fish. A fried sole is excellent to begin a convalescence, but, to put the sick man on his legs, it takes a good cutlet."

Marius, nearly all whose strength had returned, gathered it together, sat up in bed, rested his clenched hands on the sheets, looked his grandfather in the face, assumed a terrible air, and said:

"This leads me to say something to you."

"What is it?"

"It is that I wish to marry."

"Foreseen," said the grandfather. And he burst out laughing.

"How foreseen?"

"Yes, foreseen. You shall have her, your lassie."

Marius, astounded, and overwhelmed by the dazzling burst of happiness, trembled in every limb.

"Father!" exclaimed Marius.

"Ah! you love me then!" said the old man.

There was an ineffable moment. They choked and could not speak.

At last the old man stammered:

"Come! the ice is broken. He has called me, 'Father.'"

Marius released his head from his grandfather's arms, and said softly:

"But, father, now that I am well, it seems to me that I could see her."

"Foreseen again, you shall see her to-morrow."

"Why not to-day?"

"Well, to-day. Here goes for to-day. You have called me 'Father,' it is well worth that. I will see to it. She shall be brought to you. Foreseen, I tell you."

MADEMOISELLE GILLENORMAND AT LAST THINKS IT NOT IM-
PROPER THAT MONSIEUR FAUCHELEVENT SHOULD COME IN
WITH SOMETHING UNDER HIS ARM

COSETTE and Marius saw each other again.

With Cosette and behind her had entered a man with white hair, grave, smiling nevertheless, but with a vague and poignant smile. This was "Monsieur Fauchelevent;" this was Jean Valjean.

Monsieur Fauchelevent, in Marius' room, stayed near the door, as if apart. He had under his arm a package similar in appearance to an octavo volume, wrapped in paper. The paper of the envelope was greenish, and seemed mouldy.

"Does this gentleman always have books under his arm like that?" asked Mademoiselle Gillenormand, who did not like books, in a low voice of Nicolette.

"Well," answered M. Gillenormand, who had heard her,

in the same tone, "he is a scholar. What then?"

And bowing, he said, in a loud voice:

"Monsieur Tranchelevent——"

Father Gillenormand did not do this on purpose, but inattention to proper names was an aristocratic way he had.

"Monsieur Tranchelevent, I have the honor of asking of you for my grandson, Monsieur the Baron Marius Pontmercy, the hand of mademoiselle."

Monsieur Tranchelevent bowed.

"It is done," said the grandfather.

And, turning towards Marius and Cosette, with arms extended and blessing, he cried:

"Permission to adore each other."

They did not make him say it twice. It was all the same! The cooing began.

The grandfather executed a pirouette upon his ninety-year-old heels, and began to talk again, like a spring which flies back:

"She is exquisite, this darling. She is a masterpiece, this Cosette! She is a very little girl and a very great lady. She will be only a baroness, that is stooping; she was born a marchioness. Hasn't she lashes for you? My children, fix it well in your noodles that you are in the right of it. Love one another. Adore each other. Only," added he, suddenly darkening, "what a misfortune! This is what I am thinking of! More than half of what I have is in annuity; as long as I live, it's all well enough, but after my death, twenty years from now, ah! my poor children, you will not have a sou."

"Mademoiselle Euphrasie Fauchelevent has six hundred thousand francs."

It was Jean Valjean's voice.

"How is Mademoiselle Euphrasie in question?" asked the grandfather, startled.

"That is me," answered Cosette.

"Six hundred thousand francs!" resumed M. Gillenormand.

"Less fourteen or fifteen thousand francs, perhaps," said Jean Valjean.

And he laid on the table the package which Aunt Gillenormand had taken for a book.

Jean Valjean opened the package himself; it was a bundle of bank notes. They ran through them, and they counted them. There were five hundred bills of a thousand francs, and a hundred and sixty-eight of five hundred. In all, five hundred and eighty-four thousand francs.

"That is a good book," said M. Gillenormand.

"Five hundred and eighty-four thousand francs!" murmured the aunt.

As for Marius and Cosette, they were looking at each other during this time; they paid little attention to this incident.

DEPOSIT YOUR MONEY RATHER IN SOME FOREST THAN WITH SOME NOTARY

THE reader has doubtless understood, without it being necessary to explain at length, that Jean Valjean, after the Champmathieu affair, had been able, thanks to his first escape for a few days, to come to Paris, and to withdraw the sum made by him, under the name of Monsieur Madeleine, at M—— sur M——, from Laffitte's in time; and that, in the fear of being retaken, which happened to him, in fact, a short time after, he had concealed and buried that sum in the forest of Montfermeil, in the place called the Blaru grounds. The sum, six hundred and thirty thousand francs, all in banknotes, was of small bulk, and was contained in a box; but to preserve the box from moisture he had placed it in an oaken chest, full of chestnut shavings. In the same chest, he had put his other treasure, the bishop's candlesticks. It will be remembered that he carried away these candlesticks when he escaped from M—— sur M——. Afterwards, whenever Jean Valjean was in need of money, he went to the Blaru glade for it. Hence the absences of which we have spoken. He had a pickaxe somewhere in the bushes, in a hiding-place known only to himself. When he saw Marius convalescent, feeling that the hour was approaching when this money might be useful, he had gone after it.

The real sum was five hundred and eighty-four thousand five hundred francs. Jean Valjean took out five hundred francs for himself. "We will see afterwards," thought he.

The difference between this sum and the six hundred and thirty thousand francs withdrawn from Laffitte's represented the expenses of ten years, from 1823 to 1833. The five years spent in the convent had cost only five thousand francs.

Jean Valjean put the two silver candlesticks upon the mantel, where they shone, to Toussaint's great admiration.

Moreover, Jean Valjean knew that he was delivered from Javert. It has been mentioned in his presence, and he had verified the fact in the *Moniteur*, which published it, that an inspector of police, named Javert, had been found drowned between the Pont au Change and Pont Neuf.

THE TWO OLD MEN DO EVERYTHING, EACH IN HIS OWN WAY, THAT COSETTE MAY BE HAPPY

ALL the preparations were made for the marriage. The physician being consulted said that it might take place in February. This was in December. Some ravishing weeks of perfect happiness rolled away.

The least happy was not the grandfather. He would remain for a quarter of an hour at a time gazing at Cosette.

Jean Valjean did all, smoothed all, conciliated all, made all easy. He hastened towards Cosette's happiness with as much eagerness, and apparently as much joy, as Cosette herself.

As he had been a mayor, he knew how to solve a delicate problem, in the secret of which he was alone: Cosette's civil state. To bluntly give her origin, who knows? that might prevent the marriage. He drew Cosette out of all difficulty. He arranged a family of dead people for her, a sure means of incurring no objection. Cosette was what remained of an extinct family; Cosette was not his daughter, but the daughter of another Fauchelevent. Two brothers Fauchelevent had been gardeners at the convent of the Petit Picpus. They went to this convent, the best recommendations and the most respectable testimonials abounded; the good nuns, little apt and little inclined to fathom questions of paternity, and understanding no malice, had never known very exactly of which of the two Fauchelevents little Cosette was the daughter. They said what was wanted of them, and said it with zeal. A notary's act was drawn up. Cosette became before the law Mademoiselle Euphrasie Fauchelevent. She was declared an orphan. Jean Valjean arranged matters in such a way as to be designated, under the name of Fauchelevent, as Cosette's guardian, with M. Gillenormand as overseeing guardian.

As for the five hundred and eighty-four thousand francs, that was a legacy left to Cosette by a dead person who desired to remain unknown. The original legacy had been five hundred and ninety-four thousand francs; but ten thousand francs had been expended for Mademoiselle Euphrasie's education, of which five thousand francs were paid to the convent itself. This legacy, deposited in the hands of a third party, was to be given up to Cosette at her majority or at the time of her marriage.

Cosette learned that she was not the daughter of that old man whom she had so long called father. He was only a relative; another Fauchelevent was her real father. At any other time, this would have broken her heart. But at this ineffable hour, it was only a little shadow, a darkening, and she had so much joy that this cloud was of short duration. She had Marius. The young man came, the good man faded away; such is life.

She continued, however, to say "Father" to Jean Valjean.

It was arranged that the couple should live with the grandfather. M. Gillenormand absolutely insisted upon giving them his room, the finest in the house. *"It will rejuvenate me,"* he declared. *"It is an old project. I always had the idea of making a wedding in my room."* He filled this room with a profusion of gay old furniture.

M. Gillenormand's library became the attorney's office which Marius required; an office, it will be remembered, being rendered necessary by the rules of the order.

THE EFFECTS OF DREAM MINGLED WITH HAPPINESS

THE lovers saw each other every day. Cosette came with M. Fauchelevent. "It is reversing the order of things," said Mademoiselle Gillenormand, "that the intended should come to the house to be courted like this." But Marius' convalescence had led to the habit; and the armchairs in the Rue des Filles du Calvaire, better for long talks than the straw chairs of the Rue de l'Homme Armé, had rooted it. Marius and M. Fauchelevent saw one another, but did not speak to each other. That seemed to be understood. Every girl needs a chaperon. Cosette could not have come without M. Fauchelevent. To

Marius, M. Fauchelevent was the condition of Cosette. He accepted it.

Marius, inwardly and in the depth of his thought, surrounded this M. Fauchelevent, who was to him simply benevolent and cold, with all sorts of silent questions. In his memory there was a hole, a black place, an abyss scooped out by four months of agony. He was led to ask himself if it were really true that he had seen M. Fauchelevent, such a man, so serious and so calm, in the barricade.

Marius hesitated to believe that the Fauchelevent of the barricade was the same as this Fauchelevent in flesh and blood, so gravely seated near Cosette. The first was probably one of those nightmares coming and going with his hours of delirium. Moreover, their two natures showing a steep front to each other, no question was possible from Marius to M. Fauchelevent. The idea of it did not even occur to him.

Once only, Marius made an attempt. He brought the Rue de la Chanvrerie into the conversation, and, turning towards M. Fauchelevent, he said to him:

"You are well acquainted with that street?"

"What street?"

"The Rue de la Chanvrerie."

"I have no idea of the name of that street," answered M. Fauchelevent in the most natural tone in the world.

The answer, which bore upon the name of the street, and not upon the street itself, appeared to Marius more conclusive than it was.

"Decidedly," thought he, "I have been dreaming. I have had a hallucination. It was somebody who resembled him. M. Fauchelevent was not there."

TWO MEN IMPOSSIBLE TO FIND

The enchantment, great as it was, did not efface other preoccupations from Marius' mind.

During the preparations for the marriage, and while waiting for the time fixed upon, he had some difficult and careful retrospective researches made.

He owed gratitude on several sides, he owed some on his father's account, he owed some on his own.

There was Thénardier; there was the unknown man who had brought him, Marius, to M. Gillenormand's.

Marius persisted in trying to find these two men, not intending to marry, to be happy, and to forget them, and fearing lest these debts of duty unpaid might cast a shadow over his life, so luminous henceforth.

None of the various agents whom Marius employed succeeded in finding Thénardier's track. Effacement seemed complete on that side. The Thénardiess had died in prison pending the examination on the charge. Thénardier and his daughter Azelma, the two who alone remained of that woeful group, had plunged back into the shadow.

As for the other, as for the unknown man who had saved Marius, the researches at first had some result, then stopped short. They succeeded in finding the fiacre which had brought Marius to the Rue des Filles du Calvaire on the evening of the 6th of June. The driver declared that on the 6th of June, by order of a police officer, he had been "stationed," from three o'clock in the afternoon until night, on the quai of the Champs Elysées, above the outlet of the Grand Sewer; that, about nine o'clock in the evening, the grating of the sewer, which overlooks the river beach, was opened; that a man came out, carrying another man on his shoulders, who seemed to be dead; that the officer, who was watching at that point, arrested the living man, and seized the dead man; that, on the order of the officer, he, the driver, received "all those people" into the fiacre; that they went first to the Rue des Filles du Calvaire; that they left the dead man there; that the dead man was Monsieur Marius, and that he, the driver, recognised him plainly, although he was alive "this time;" that they then got into his carriage again; that he whipped up his horses; that, within a few steps of the door of the Archives, he had been called to stop; that there, in the street, he had been paid and left, and that the officer took away the other man; that he knew nothing more, that the night was very dark.

Marius, we have said, recollected nothing. He merely remembered having been seized from behind by a vigorous hand at the moment he fell backwards into the barricades, then all became a blank to him. He had recovered consciousness only at M. Gillenormand's.

He was lost in conjectures.

This man, this mysterious man, whom the driver had seen come out of the grating of the Grand Sewer bearing Marius senseless upon his back, and whom the police officer on the watch had arrested in the very act of saving an insurgent, what had become of him? what had become of the officer himself? Why had this officer kept silence? had the man succeeded in escaping? had he bribed the officer? Why did this man give no sign of life to Marius, who owed everything to him? His disinterestedness was not less wonderful than his devotion. Why did not this man reappear? Perhaps he was above recompense, but nobody is above gratitude. Was he dead? what kind of a man was this? how did he look? Nobody could tell.

In the hope of deriving aid in his researches from them, Marius had had preserved the bloody clothes which he wore when he was brought back to his grandfather's. On examining the coat, it was noticed that one skirt was oddly torn. A piece was missing.

One evening, Marius spoke, before Cosette and Jean Valjean, of all this singular adventure, of the numberless inquiries which he had made, and of the uselessness of his efforts. The cold countenance of "Monsieur Fauchelevent" made him impatient. He exclaimed with a vivacity which had almost the vibration of anger:

"Yes, that man, whoever he may be, was sublime. Do you know what he did, monsieur? He intervened like the archangel. He must have thrown himself into the midst of the combat, have snatched me out of it, have opened the sewer, have drawn me into it, have borne me through it! He must have made his way for more than four miles through hideous subterranean galleries, bent, stooping, in the darkness, in the cloaca, more than four miles, monsieur, with a corpse upon his back! And with what object? With the single object of saving that corpse. And that corpse was I. What was I? An insurgent. What was I? A vanquished man. Oh! if Cosette's six hundred thousand francs were mine——"

"They are yours," interrupted Jean Valjean.

"Well," resumed Marius, "I would give them to find that man!"

Jean Valjean kept silence.

The White Night

THE night of the 16th of February, 1833, was a blessed night. Above its shade the heavens were opened. It was the wedding night of Marius and Cosette. On the previous evening, Jean Valjean had handed to Marius in the presence of M. Gillenormand, the five hundred and eighty-four thousand francs.

A few days before the day fixed for the marriage, an accident happened to Jean Valjean; he slightly bruised the thumb of his right hand. It was not serious; and he had allowed nobody to take any trouble about it, nor to dress it, nor even to see his hurt, not even Cosette. It compelled him, however, to muffle his hand in a bandage, and to carry his arm in a sling, and prevented his signing anything. M. Gillenormand, as Cosette's overseeing guardian, took his place.

JEAN VALJEAN STILL HAS HIS ARM IN A SLING

COSETTE, at the mairie and in the church, was brilliant and touching. Toussaint, aided by Nicolette, had dressed her.

When, at the completion of all the ceremonies, after having pronounced before the mayor and the priest every possible yes, after having signed the registers at the municipality and at the sacristy, after having exchanged their rings, after having been on their knees elbow to elbow under the canopy of white moire in the smoke of the censer, hand in hand, admired and envied by all, Marius in black, she in white, preceded by the usher in colonel's epaulettes, striking the pavement with his halberd, between two hedges of marvelling spectators, they arrived under the portal of the church where the folding-doors were both open, ready to get into the carriage again, and all was over, Cosette could not yet believe it. She looked at Marius, she looked at the throng, she looked at the sky; it seemed as if she were afraid of awaking. Her astonished and bewildered air rendered her unspeakably bewitching. To return, they got into the same carriage, Marius by Cosette's side; M. Gillenormand and Jean Valjean sat opposite. Aunt Gillenormand had drawn back one degree, and was in the second carriage. "My children," said the grandfather, "here you are Monsieur the Baron and Madame the Baroness, with thirty thousand francs a year." And Cosette, leaning close up to Marius, caressed his ear with this angelic whisper: "It is true, then. My name is Marius. I am Madame You."

They returned to the Rue des Filles du Calvaire, to their home. Marius, side by side with Cosette, ascended, triumphant and radiant, that staircase up which he had been carried dying.

Cosette had never been more tender towards Jean Valjean. She was in unison with Grandfather Gillenormand; while he embodied joy in aphorisms and in maxims, she exhaled love and kindness like a perfume. Happiness wishes everybody happy.

She went back, in speaking to Jean Valjean, to the tones of voice of the time when she was a little girl. She caressed him with smiles.

A banquet had been prepared in the dining-room.

Jean Valjean sat in a chair in the parlor, behind the door, which shut back upon him in such a way as almost to hide him. A few moments before they took their seats at the table, Cosette came, as if from a sudden impulse, and made him a low courtesy, spreading out her bridal dress with both hands, and, with a tenderly frolicsome look, she asked him:

"Father, are you pleased?"

"Yes," said Jean Valjean, "I am pleased."

"Well, then, laugh."

Jean Valjean began to laugh.

A few moments afterward, Basque announced dinner.

The guests, preceded by M. Gillenormand giving his arm to Cosette, entered the dining-room, and took their places, according to the appointed order, about the table.

Two large arm-chairs were placed, on the right and on the left of the bride, the first for M. Gillenormand, the second

for Jean Valjean. M. Gillenormand took his seat. The other
arm-chair remained empty.

All eyes sought "Monsieur Fauchelevent."

He was not there.

M. Gillenormand called Basque.

"Do you know where Monsieur Fauchelevent is?"

"Monsieur," answered Basque. "Exactly. Monsieur Fauchelevent told me to say to monsieur that he was suffering a little from his sore hand, and could not dine with Monsieur
the Baron and Madame the Baroness. That he begged they
would excuse him, that he would come to-morrow morning.
He has just gone away."

This empty arm-chair chilled for a moment the effusion of
the nuptial repast. But, M. Fauchelevent absent, M. Gillenormand was there, and the grandfather was brilliant enough
for two. He declared that M. Fauchelevent did well to go to
bed early, if he was suffering, but that it was only a
"scratch." This declaration was enough. M. Gillenormand
had an idea. "By Jove, this arm-chair is empty. Come here,
Marius. Your aunt, although she has a right to you, will allow
it. This arm-chair is for you. It is legal, and it is proper."
Applause from the whole table. Marius took Jean Valjean's
place at Cosette's side; and things arranged themselves in
such a way that Cosette, at first saddened by Jean Valjean's
absence, was finally satisfied with it. From the moment that
Marius was the substitute, Cosette would not have regretted
God. She put her soft little foot encased in white satin upon
Marius' foot.

The arm-chair occupied, M. Fauchelevent was effaced;
and nothing was missed. And, five minutes later, the whole
table was laughing from one end to the other with all the
spirit of forgetfulness.

THE INSEPARABLE

JEAN Valjean returned home. He lighted his candle and went
upstairs. The apartment was empty. Toussaint herself was
no longer there. Jean Valjean's step made more noise than
usual in the rooms. All the closets were open. He went into

Cosette's room. There were no sheets on the bed. The pillow, without a pillow-case and without laces, was laid upon the coverlets folded at the foot of the mattress of which the ticking was to be seen and on which nobody should sleep henceforth. All the little feminine objects to which Cosette clung had been carried away; there remained only the heavy furniture and the four walls. Toussaint's bed was also stripped. A single bed was made and seemed waiting for somebody, that was Jean Valjean's.

Jean Valjean looked at the walls, shut some closet doors, went and came from one room to the other.

Then he found himself again in his own room, and he put his candle on the table.

He had released his arm from the sling, and he helped himself with his right hand as if he did not suffer from it.

He approached his bed, and his eye fell, was it by chance? was it with intention? Upon *the inseparable*, of which Cosette had been jealous, upon the little trunk which never left him. On the 4th of June, on arriving in the Rue de l'Homme Armé, he had placed it upon a candle-stand at the head of his bed. He went to this stand with a sort of vivacity, took a key from his pocket, and opened the valise.

He took out slowly the garments in which, ten years before, Cosette had left Montfermeil; first the little dress, then the black scarf, then the great heavy child's shoes which Cosette could have almost put on still, so small a foot she had, then the bodice of very thick fustian, then the knit-skirt, then the apron with pockets, then the woollen stockings. Those stockings, on which the shape of a little leg was still gracefully marked, were hardly longer than Jean Valjean's hand. These were all black. He had carried these garments for her to Montfermeil. As he took them out of the valise, he laid them on the bed. He was thinking. He remembered. It was in winter, a very cold December, she shivered half-naked in rags, her poor little feet all red in her wooden shoes. He, Jean Valjean, he had taken her away from those rags to clothe her in this mourning garb. The mother must have been pleased in her tomb to see her daughter wear mourning for her, and especially to see that she was clad, and that she was warm. He thought of that forest of Montfermeil; they had crossed it together, Cosette and he; he thought

of the weather, of the trees without leaves, of the forest
without birds, of the sky without sun; it is all the same,
it was charming. He arranged the little things upon the bed,
the scarf next the skirt, the stockings beside the shoes, the
bodice beside the dress, and he looked at them one after
another. She was no higher than that, she had her great
doll in her arms, she had put her louis d'or in the pocket
of this apron, she laughed, they walked holding each other
by the hand, she had nobody but him in the world.

Then his venerable white head fell upon the bed, this old
stoical heart broke, his face was swallowed up, so to speak,
in Cosette's garments, and anybody who had passed along
the staircase at that moment, would have heard fearful sobs.

IMMORTALE JECUR

THE formidable old struggle, several phases of which we
have already seen, recommenced.

Cosette had Marius, Marius possessed Cosette. They had
everything, even riches. And it was his work.

But this happiness, now that it existed, now that it was
here, what was he to do with it, he, Jean Valjean? Should
he impose himself upon this happiness? Should he treat it as
belonging to him? Unquestionably, Cosette was another's;
but should he, Jean Valjean, retain all of Cosette that he
could retain? Should he remain the kind of father, scarcely
seen, but respected, which he had been hitherto? Should he
introduce himself quietly into Cosette's house? Should he
bring, without saying a word, his past to this future? In a
word, should he be, by the side of these two happy beings,
the ominous mute of destiny?

His giddy reverie lasted all night.

He remained there until dawn, in the same attitude,
doubled over on the bed, prostrated under the enormity of
fate, crushed perhaps, alas! his fists clenched, his arms extended at a right angle, like one taken from the cross and
thrown down with his face to the ground. He remained
twelve hours, the twelve hours of a long winter night,
chilled, without lifting his head, and without uttering a

word. To see him thus without motion, one would have said
he was dead; suddenly he thrilled convulsively, and his
mouth, fixed upon Cosette's garments, kissed them; then one
saw that he was alive.

The Last Drop in the Chalice

THE SEVENTH CIRCLE AND THE EIGHTH HEAVEN

THE day after a wedding is solitary. The privacy of the happy is respected. And thus their slumber is a little belated. The tumult of visits and felicitations does not commence until later. On the morning of the 17th of February, it was a little after noon, when Basque, his napkin and duster under his arm, busy "doing his antechamber," heard a light rap at the door. There was no ring, which is considerate on such a day. Basque opened and saw M. Fauchelevent. He introduced him into the parlor, still cumbered and topsy-turvy, and which had the appearance of the battle-field of the evening's festivities.

"Faith, monsieur," observed Basque, "we are waking up late."

"Has your master risen?" inquired Jean Valjean.

"Which? the old or the new one?"

"Monsieur Pontmercy."

"Monsieur the Baron?" said Basque, drawing himself up.

"Monsieur the Baron?" repeated Basque. "I will go and see. I will tell him that Monsieur Fauchelevent is here."

"No. Do not tell him that it is I. Tell him that somebody asks to speak with him in private, and do not give him any name."

"Ah!" said Basque.

And he went out.

Jean Valjean remained alone.

There was a noise at the door, he raised his eyes.

Marius entered, his head erect, his mouth smiling, an indescribable light upon his face, his forehead radiant, his eye triumphant. He also had not slept.

"It is you, father!" exclaimed he on perceiving Jean Valjean; "that idiot of a Basque with his mysterious air! But you come too early. It is only half an hour after noon yet. Cosette is asleep."

That word: Father, said to M. Fauchelevent by Marius, signified: Supreme felicity. There had always been, as we know, barrier, coldness, and constraint between them; ice to break or to melt. Marius had reached that degree of intoxication where the barrier was falling, the ice was dissolving, and M. Fauchelevent was to him, as to Cosette, a father.

"How glad I am to see you! If you knew how we missed you yesterday! Good morning, father. How is your hand? Better, is it not?"

And, satisfied with the good answer which he made to himself, he went on:

"We have both of us talked much about you. Cosette loves you so much! You will not forget that your room is here. We will have no more of the Rue de l'Homme Armé. How could you go to live in a street like that, which is sickly, which is scowling, which is ugly, which has a barrier at one end, where you are cold, and where you cannot get in? you will come and install yourself here. And that to-day. Or you will have a bone to pick with Cosette. She intends to lead us all by the nose, I warn you."

"Monsieur," said Jean Valjean, "I have one thing to tell you. I am an old convict."

Jean Valjean untied the black cravat which sustained his right arm, took off the cloth wound about his head, laid his thumb bare, and showed it to Marius.

"There is nothing the matter with my hand," said he.

Marius looked at the thumb.

"There has never been anything the matter with it," continued Jean Valjean.

There was, in fact, no trace of a wound.

Jean Valjean pursued:

"It was best that I should be absent from your marriage. I absented myself as much as I could. I feigned this wound so as not to commit a forgery, not to introduce a nullity into the marriage acts, to be excused from signing."

Marius stammered out:

"What does this mean?"

"It means," answered Jean Valjean, "that I have been in the galleys."

"You drive me mad!" exclaimed Marius in dismay.

"Monsieur Pontmercy," said Jean Valjean, "I was nineteen years in the galleys. For robbery. Then I was sentenced for life. For robbery. For a second offense. At this hour I am in breach of ban."

It was useless for Marius to recoil before the reality, to refuse the fact, to resist the evidence; he was compelled to yield. He began to comprehend, and as always happens in such a case, he comprehended beyond the truth. He felt the shiver of a horrible interior flash; an idea which made him shudder, crossed his mind. He caught a glimpse in the future of a hideous destiny for himself.

"Tell all, tell all!" cried he. "You are Cosette's father!"

And he took two steps backward with an expression of unspeakable horror.

Jean Valjean raised his head with such a majesty of attitude that he seemed to rise to the ceiling.

"It is necessary that you believe me in this, monsieur; although the oath of such as I be not received."

Here he made a pause; then, with a sort of sovereign and sepulchral authority, he added, articulating slowly and emphasizing his syllables:

"——You will believe me. I, the father of Cosette! before God, no. Monsieur Baron Pontmercy, I am a peasant of Faverolles. I earned my living by pruning trees. My name is not Fauchelevent, my name is Jean Valjean. I am nothing to Cosette. Compose yourself."

Marius faltered:

"Who proves it to me——"

"I. Since I say so."

Marius looked at this man. He was mournful, yet self-possessed. No lie could come out of such a calmness.

"I believe you," said Marius.

Jean Valjean inclined his head as if making oath, and continued:

"What am I to Cosette? a passer. Ten years ago, I did not know that she existed. I love her, it is true. A child whom one has seen when little, being himself already old, he loves. When a man is old, he feels like a grandfather towards all little children. You can, it seems to me, suppose that I have something which resembles a heart. She was an orphan. Without father or mother. She had need of me. That is why I began to love her. Children are so weak, that anybody, even a man like me, may be their protector. I performed that duty with regard to Cosette. Today Cosette leaves my life; our two roads separate. Henceforth I can do nothing more for her. She is Madame Pontmercy. Her protector is changed. And Cosette gains by the change. All is well. As for the six hundred thousand francs, you have not spoken of them to me, but I anticipate your thought; that is a trust. How did this trust come into my hands? What matters it? I make over the trust. Nothing more can be asked of me."

And Jean Valjean looked Marius in the face.

Marius was so stupefied at the new condition of affairs which opened before him that he spoke to this man almost as though he were angry with him for his avowal.

"But after all," exclaimed he, "why do you tell me all this? What compels you to do so? You could have kept the secret to yourself. You are neither denounced, nor pursued, nor hunted. You have some reason for making, from mere wantonness, such a revelation. Finish it. There is something else. In connection with what do you make this avowal? From what motive?"

"From what motive?" answered Jean Valjean, in a voice so low and so hollow that one would have said it was to himself he was speaking rather than to Marius. "From what motive, indeed, does this convict come and say: I am a convict? Well, yes! the motive is strange. It is from honor. I could have lied, it is true, have deceived you all, have remained Monsieur Fauchelevent. As long as it was for her, I could lie; but now it would be for myself, I must not do it. It was enough to remain silent, it is true, and everything would continue. You ask me what forces me to speak? a strange thing; my conscience."

Jean Valjean stopped. Marius listened. Such a chain of ideas and of pangs cannot be interrupted. Jean Valjean lowered his voice anew, but it was no longer a hollow voice, it was an ominous voice.

"You ask why I speak? I am neither informed against, nor pursued, nor hunted, say you. Yes! I am informed against! yes! I am pursued! yes! I am hunted? By whom? by myself. It is I myself who bar the way before myself, and I drag myself, and I urge myself, and I check myself, and I exert myself, and when one holds himself he is well held."

And, with a bitter emphasis, he added:

"Monsieur Pontmercy, this is not common sense, but I am an honest man. It is by degrading myself in your eyes that I

elevate myself in my own. This has already happened to
me once, but it was less grievous then; it was nothing. Yes,
an honest man. I should not be one if you had, by my fault,
continued to esteem me; now that you despise me, I am one.
I am a galley slave who obeys his conscience. I know well
that is improbable. But what would you have me do? it is
so. I have assumed engagements towards myself; I keep
them. There are accidents which bind us, there are chances
which drag us into duties. You see, Monsieur Pontmercy,
some things have happened to me in my life?"

He breathed with difficulty, and forced out these final
words:

"To live, once I stole a loaf of bread; to-day, to live, I
will not steal a name."

"To live!" interrupted Marius. "You have no need of that
name to live!"

"Ah! I understand," answered Jean Valjean, raising and
lowering his head several times in succession.

Then he turned quite round towards Marius:

"And now, monsieur, picture this to yourself: I have said
nothing, I have remained Monsieur Fauchelevent, I have taken
my place in your house, I am one of you, I am in my room, I
come to breakfast in the morning in slippers, at night we all
three go to the theatre, I accompany Madame Pontmercy to
the Tuileries and to the Place Royale, we are together,
you suppose me your equal; some fine day I am there, you are
there, we are chatting, we are laughing, suddenly you hear a
voice shout this name: Jean Valjean! and you see that appalling hand, the police, spring out of the shadow and abruptly tear off my mask!"

He ceased again; Marius had risen with a shudder. Jean
Valjean resumed:

"What say you?"

Marius' silence answered.

Jean Valjean continued:

"You see very well that I am right in not keeping quiet.
Go on, be happy, be in heaven, be an angel of an angel,
be in the sunshine, and be contented with it, and do not
trouble yourself about the way which a poor condemned
man takes to open his heart and do his duty; you have a
wretched man before you, monsieur."

Marius crossed the parlor slowly, and, when he was near
Jean Valjean, extended him his hand.

But Marius had to take that hand which did not offer itself,

Jean Valjean was passive, and it seemed to Marius that he was grasping a hand of marble.

"My grandfather has friends," said Marius. "I will procure your pardon."

"It is useless," answered Jean Valjean. "They think me dead, that is enough."

And, disengaging his hand, which Marius held, he added with a sort of inexorable dignity:

"Besides, to do my duty, that is the friend to which I have recourse; and I need pardon of but one, that is my conscience."

Marius made sure that the door was well closed.

"Poor Cosette!" murmured he, "when she knows——"

At these words, Jean Valjean trembled in every limb. He fixed upon Marius a bewildered eye.

"Cosette! Oh, yes, it is true, you will tell this to Cosette. That is right. Stop, I had not thought of that. People have the strength for some things, but not for others. Monsieur, I beseech you, I entreat you, Monsieur, give me your most sacred word, do not tell her. Is it not enough that you know it yourself? I could have told it of myself without being forced to it, I would have told it to the universe, to all the world, that would be nothing to me. But she, she doesn't know what it is, it would appal her."

He sank into an arm-chair and hid his face in both hands. He could not be heard, but by the shaking of his shoulders it could be seen that he was weeping.

There is a stifling in the sob. A sort of convulsion seized him, he bent over upon the back of the arm-chair as if to breathe, letting his arms hang down and allowing Marius to see his face bathed in tears, and Marius heard him murmur so low that his voice seemed to come from a bottomless depth: "Oh! would that I could die!"

"Be calm," said Marius, "I will keep your secret for myself alone."

"I thank you, monsieur," answered Jean Valjean gently.

He remained thoughtful a moment, passing the end of his forefinger over his thumb-nail mechanically, then he raised his voice:

"It is all nearly finished. There is one thing left——"

"What?"

Jean Valjean had as it were a supreme hesitation, and,

voiceless, almost breathless, he faltered out rather than said:

"Now that you know, do you think, monsieur, you who are the master, that I ought not to see Cosette again?"

"I think that would be best," answered Marius coldly.

"I shall not see her again," murmured Jean Valjean.

And he walked towards the door.

He placed his hand upon the knob, the latch yielded, the door started, Jean Valjean opened it wide enough to enable him to pass out, stopped a second motionless, then shut the door, and turned towards Marius.

He was no longer pale, he was livid. There were no longer tears in his eyes, but a sort of tragical flame. His voice had again become strangely calm.

"But, monsieur," said he, "if you are willing, I will come and see her. I assure you that I desire it very much. If I had not clung to seeing Cosette, I should not have made the avowal which I have made, I should have gone away; but wishing to stay in the place where Cosette is and to continue to see her, I was compelled in honor to tell you all. You follow my reasoning, do you not? that is a thing which explains itself. You see, for nine years past, I have had her near me. I was like her father, and she was my child. I don't know whether you understand me, Monsieur Pontmercy, but from the present time, to see her no more, to speak to her no more, to have nothing more, that would be hard. If you do not think it wrong, I will come from time to time to see Cosette. I should not come often. I would not stay long. You might say I should be received in the little low room. On the ground floor. I would willingly come in by the back-door, which is for the servants, but that would excite wonder, perhaps. It is better, I suppose, that I should enter by the usual door. Monsieur, indeed, I would really like to see Cosette a little still. As rarely as you please. Put yourself in my place, it is all that I have. And then, we must take care. If I should not come at all, it would have a bad effect, it would be thought singular. For instance, what I can do, is to come in the evening, at nightfall."

"You will come every evening," said Marius, "and Cosette will expect you."

"You are kind, monsieur," said Jean Valjean.

Marius bowed to Jean Valjean, happiness conducted despair to the door, and these two men separated.

THE OBSCURITIES WHICH A REVELATION MAY CONTAIN

MARIUS was completely unhinged.

The kind of repulsion which he had always felt for the man with whom he saw Cosette was now explained. There was something strangely enigmatic in this person, of which his instinct had warned him. This enigma was the most hideous of disgraces, the galleys. This M. Fauchelevent was the convict Jean Valjean.

To suddenly find such a secret in the midst of one's happiness is like the discovery of a scorpion in a nest of turtle-doves.

Was the happiness of Marius and Cosette condemned henceforth to this fellowship? Was there nothing more to be done?

Had Marius espoused the convict also?

Another question: Why had this man come into the barricade? For now Marius saw that reminiscence again distinctly, reappearing in these emotions like sympathetic ink before the fire. This man was in the barricade. He did not fight there. What did he come there for? Before this question a specter arose, and made response. Javert. Marius recalled perfectly to mind at this hour the fatal sight of Jean Valjean dragging Javert bound outside the barricade, and he again heard the frightful pistol-shot behind the corner of the little Rue Mondétour. There was, probably, hatred between the spy and this galley-slave. The one cramped the other. Jean Valjean had gone to the barricade to avenge himself. He had arrived late. He knew probably that Javert was a prisoner there. Jean Valjean had killed Javert. At least, that seemed evident.

Finally, a last question: but to this no answer. This question Marius felt like a sting. How did it happen that Jean Valjean's existence had touched Cosette's so long? What

was this gloomy game of providence which had placed this
child in contact with this man? Are coupling chains then
forged on high also, and does it please God to pair the angel
with the demon?

The Twilight Wane

THE BASEMENT ROOM

THE next day, at nightfall, Jean Valjean knocked at the Gillenormand porte-cochère. Basque received him. Basque happened to be in the court-yard very conveniently, and as if he had had orders.

Basque, without waiting for Jean Valjean to come up to him, addressed him as follows:

"Monsieur the Baron told me to ask monsieur whether he desires to go upstairs or to remain below?"

"To remain below," answered Jean Valjean.

Basque, who was moreover absolutely respectful, opened the door of the basement room and said: "I will inform madame."

The room which Jean Valjean entered was an arched and damp basement, used as a cellar when necessary, looking upon the street, paved with red tiles, and dimly lighted by a window with an iron grating.

A fire was kindled, which indicated that somebody had anticipated Jean Valjean's answer: *To remain below.*

Two armchairs were placed at the corners of the fireplace. Between the chairs was spread, in guise of a carpet, an old bed-side rug, showing more warp than wool.

Jean Valjean was fatigued. For some days he had neither eaten nor slept. He let himself fall into one of the arm-chairs.

Basque returned, set a lighted candle upon the mantel, and retired. Jean Valjean, his head bent down and his chin upon his breast, noticed neither Basque nor the candle.

Suddenly he started up. Cosette was behind him.

He had not seen her come in, but he had felt that she was coming.

He turned. He gazed at her. She was adorably beautiful. But what he looked upon with that deep look, was not her beauty but her soul.

"Ah, well!" exclaimed Cosette, "father, I knew that you were singular, but I should never have thought this. What an idea! Marius tells me that it is you who wish me to receive you here."

"Yes, it is I."

"You choose the ugliest room in the house to see me in. It is horrible here."

"You know, madame, I am peculiar, I have my whims."

Cosette clapped her little hands together.

"Madame! Still again! What does this mean?"

Jean Valjean fixed upon her that distressing smile to which he sometimes had recourse:

"You have wished to be madame. You are so."

"Not to you, father."

"Don't call me father any more."

"What."

"Call me Monsieur Jean. Jean, if you will."

"I don't understand anything about it. It is all nonsense; I shall ask my husband's permission for you to be Monsieur Jean. I hope that he will not consent to it. You make me a great deal of trouble. You may have whims, but you must not grieve your darling Cosette. It is wrong. You have no right to be naughty, you are too good."

He made no answer.

She seized both his hands hastily and, with an irresistible impulse, raising them towards her face, she pressed them against her neck under her chin, which is a deep token of affection.

"Oh!" said she to him, "be good!"

And she continued:

"This is what I call being good: being nice, coming to stay here, there are birds here as well as in the Rue Plumet, living with us, leaving that hole in the Rue de l'Homme Armé, not giving us riddles to guess, being like other people, dining with us, breakfasting with us, being my father."

And, growing suddenly serious, she looked fixedly at Jean Valjean, and added:

"So you don't like it that I am happy?"

Jean Valjean grew pale. For a moment he did not answer, then, with an indescribable accent and talking to himself, he murmured:

"Her happiness was the aim of my life. Now, God may

beckon me away. Cosette, you are happy; my time is full."

"Ah, you have called me Cosette!" exclaimed she.

And she sprang upon his neck.

Jean Valjean, in desperation, clasped her to his breast wild-ly. It seemed to him almost as if he were taking her back.

"Thank you, father!" said Cosette to him.

The transport was becoming poignant to Jean Valjean. He gently put away Cosette's arms, and took his hat.

"Well?" said Cosette.

Jean Valjean answered:

"I will leave you, madame; they are waiting for you."

And, from the door, he added:

"I called you Cosette. Tell your husband that that shall not happen again. Pardon me."

Jean Valjean went out, leaving Cosette astounded at that enigmatic farewell.

OTHER STEPS BACKWARD

THE following day, at the same hour, Jean Valjean came.

Cosette put no questions to him, was no longer astonished, no longer exclaimed that she was cold, no longer talked of the parlor; she avoided saying either father or Monsieur Jean. She let him speak as he would.

It is probable that she had had one of those conversations with Marius, in which the beloved man says what he pleases, explains nothing, and satisfies the beloved woman. The curiosity of lovers does not go very far beyond their love.

Every succeeding morrow brought Jean Valjean at the same hour. He came every day, not having the strength to take Marius' words otherwise than to the letter. Marius made his arrangements, so as to be absent at the hours when Jean Valjean came.

Several weeks passed thus. A new life gradually took pos-session of Cosette; the relations which marriage creates, the visits, the care of the house, the pleasures, those grand af-fairs. Cosette's pleasures were not costly; they consisted in a single one: being with Marius. Going out with him, staying at home with him, this was the great occupation of her life. Jean Valjean came every day.

The disappearance of familiarity, the madame, the Monsieur Jean, all this made him different to Cosette. The care which he had taken to detach her from him succeeded with her. She became more and more cheerful, and less and less affectionate. However, she still loved him very much, and he felt it.

He still lived in the Rue de l'Homme Armé, unable to resolve to move further from the *quartier* in which Cosette dwelt.

At first he stayed with Cosette only a few minutes, then went away.

Little by little he got into the habit of making his visits longer. One would have said that he took advantage of the example of the days which were growing longer: he came earlier and went away later.

One day Cosette inadvertently said to him: "Father." A flash of joy illuminated Jean Valjean's gloomy old face. He replied to her: "Say Jean." "Ah! true," she answered with a burst of laughter, "Monsieur Jean." "That is right," said he, and he turned away that she might not see him wipe his eyes.

ATTRACTION AND EXTINCTION

DURING the last months of the spring and the first months of the summer of 1833, the scattered wayfarers in the Marais, the storekeepers, the idlers upon the doorsteps, noticed an old man neatly dressed in black, every day, about the same hour, at night-fall, come out of the Rue de l'Homme Armé, in the direction of the Rue Sainte Croix de la Bretonnerie, pass by the Blancs Manteaux, to the Rue Culture Sainte Catherine, and, reaching the Rue de l'Echarpe, turn to the left, and enter the Rue Saint Louis.

There he walked with slow steps, his head bent forward, seeing nothing, hearing nothing, his eye immovably fixed upon one point, always the same, which seemed studded with stars to him, and which was nothing more nor less than the corner of the Rue des Filles du Calvaire. As he approached the corner of that street, his face lighted up; a kind of joy il-

luminated his eye like an interior halo, he had a fascinated
and softened expression, his lips moved vaguely, as if he were
speaking to some one whom he did not see, he smiled faintly,
and he advanced as slowly as he could. However long he succeeded in deferring it, he must arrive at last; he reached the
Rue des Filles du Calvaire; then he stopped, he trembled, he
put his head with a kind of gloomy timidity beyond the
corner of the last house, and he looked into that street, and
there was in that tragical look something which resembled the
bewilderment of the impossible, and the reflection of a for-
bidden paradise. Then a tear, which had gradually gathered
in the corner of his eye, grown large enough to fall, glided
over his cheek, and sometimes stopped at his mouth. The old
man tasted its bitterness. He remained thus a few minutes,
as if he had been stone; then he returned by the same route
and at the same pace; and, in proportion as he receded, that
look was extinguished.

Little by little, this old man ceased to go as far as the
corner of the Rue des Filles du Calvaire; he stopped half way
down the Rue Saint Louis; sometimes a little further, sometimes a little nearer.

Every day, he came out of his house at the same hour, he
commenced the same walk, but he did not finish it, and, perhaps unconsciously, he continually shortened it. His whole
countenance expressed this single idea; What is the use? The
eye was dull; no more radiance. The tear also was gone; it no
longer gathered at the corner of the lids; that thoughtful eye
was dry. The old man's head was still bent forward; his
chin quivered at times; the wrinkles of his thin neck were
painful to behold. Sometimes, when the weather was bad, he
carried an umbrella under his arm, which he never opened.
The good women of the *quartier* said: "He is a natural." The
children followed him laughing.

Supreme Shadow, Supreme Dawn

PITY FOR THE UNHAPPY, BUT INDULGENCE FOR THE HAPPY

MARIUS as we have explained, before his marriage, had put no questions to M. Fauchelevent, and, since, he had feared to put any to Jean Valjean. He did nothing more than gradually to banish Jean Valjean from his house, and to obliterate him as much as possible from Cosette's mind.

Marius did what he deemed necessary and just. He supposed he had, for discarding Jean Valjean, without harshness, but without weakness, serious reasons, which we have already seen, and still others which we shall see further on. Having chanced to meet, in a cause in which he was engaged, an old clerk of the house of Laffitte, he had obtained, without seeking it, some mysterious information which he could not, in truth, probe to the bottom, from respect for the secret which he had promised to keep, and from care for Jean Valjean's perilous situation. He believed, at that very time, that he had a solemn duty to perform, the restitution of the six hundred thousand francs to somebody whom he was seeking as cautiously as possible. In the meantime, he abstained from using that money.

THE LAST FLICKERINGS OF THE EXHAUSTED LAMP

ONE day Jean Valjean went down stairs, took three steps into the street, sat down upon a stone block, upon that same block where Gavroche, on the night of the 5th of June, had found him musing; he remained there a few minutes, then went upstairs again. The next day, he did not leave his room. The day after he did not leave his bed.

A week elapsed, and Jean Valjean had not taken a step in his room. He was still in bed. The portress said to her husband: "The goodman upstairs does not get up any more, he does not eat any more, he won't last long. He has trouble, he has. Nobody can get it out of my head that his daughter has made a bad match."

The porter replied, with the accent of the marital sovereignty:

"If he is rich, let him have a doctor. If he is not rich, let him not have any. If he doesn't have a doctor, he will die."

"And if he does have one?"

"He will die," said the porter.

The portress began to dig up with an old knife some grass which was sprouting in what she called her pavement, and, while she was pulling up the grass, she muttered:

"It is a pity. An old man who is so nice! He is white as a chicken."

She saw a physician of the *quartier* passing at the end of the street, she took it upon herself to beg him to go up.

The physician saw Jean Valjean, and spoke with him.

When he came down, the portress questioned him:

"Well, doctor?"

"Your sick man is very sick."

"What is the matter with him?"

"Everything and nothing. He is a man who, to all appearance, has lost some dear friend. People die of that."

"What did he tell you?"

"He told me that he was well."

"Will you come again, doctor?"

"Yes," answered the physician. "But another than I must come again."

A PEN IS HEAVY TO HIM WHO LIFTED
FAUCHELEVENT'S CART

ONE evening Jean Valjean had difficulty in raising himself upon his elbow; he felt his wrist and found no pulse; his breathing was short, and stopped at intervals; he realized that he was weaker than he had been before. Then, undoubtedly under the pressure of some supreme desire, he made an effort, sat up in bed, and dressed himself. He put on his old working-man's garb. As he went out no longer, he had returned to it, and he preferred it. He was obliged to stop several times while dressing; the mere effort of putting on his waistcoat, made the sweat roll down his forehead.

He opened the valise and took out Cosette's suit.

He spread it out upon his bed.

The bishop's candlesticks were in their place, on the mantle. He took two wax tapers from a drawer, and put them into the candlesticks. Then, although it was still broad daylight, it was in summer, he lighted them. We sometimes see torches lighted thus in broad day, in rooms where the dead lie.

Each step that he took in going from one piece of furniture to another, exhausted him, and he was obliged to sit down.

One of the chairs upon which he sank, was standing before that mirror, so fatal for him, so providential for Marius in which he had read Cosette's note, reversed on the blotter. He saw himself in this mirror, and did not recognize himself. He was eighty years old; before Marius' marriage, one would hardly have thought him fifty; this year had counted thirty. What was now upon his forehead was not the wrinkle of age, it was the mysterious mark of death.

Night had come. With much labor he drew a table and an old arm-chair near the fireplace, and put upon the table pen, ink, and paper.

Then he fainted. When he regained consciousness he was thirsty. Being unable to lift the water-pitcher, with great effort he tipped it towards his mouth, and drank a swallow.

Then he turned to the bed, and, still sitting, for he could stand but a moment, he looked at the little black dress, and all those dear objects.

Suddenly he shivered, he felt that the chill was coming; he leaned upon the table which was lighted by the bishop's candlesticks, and took the pen.

As neither the pen nor the ink had been used for a long time, the tip of the pen was bent back, the ink was dried, he was obliged to get up and put a few drops of water into the ink, which he could not do without stopping and sitting down two or three times, and he was compelled to write with the back of the pen. He wiped his forehead from time to time.

His hand trembled. He slowly wrote the few lines which follow:

"Cosette, I bless you. I am going to make an explanation to you. Your husband was quite right in giving me to understand that I ought to leave; still there is some mistake in what he believed, but he was right. He is very good. Always love him well when I am dead. Monsieur Pontmercy, always love my darling child. Cosette, this paper will be found, this is what I want to tell you, you shall see the figures, if I have the strength to recall them, listen well, this money is really your own. This is the whole story: The white jet comes from Norway, the black jet comes from England, the black glass imitation comes from Germany. The jet is lighter, more precious, more costly. We can make imitations in France as well as in Germany. It requires a little anvil two inches square, and a spirit-lamp to soften the wax. The wax was formerly made with resin and lamp-black, and cost four francs a pound. I hit upon making it with gum lac and turpentine. This costs only thirty sous, and it is much better. The buckles are made of violet glass, which is fastened by means of this wax to a narrow rim of black iron. The glass should be violet for the iron trinkets, and black for gold trinkets. Spain purchases many of them. That is the country of jet——"

Here he stopped, the pen fell from his fingers, he gave way to one of those despairing sobs which rose at times from the depths of his being, the poor man clasped his head with both hands, and reflected.

"Oh!" exclaimed he within himself (pitiful cries, heard by God alone), "it is all over. I shall never see her more. She is a smile which has passed over me. I am going to enter into the night without even seeing her again. Oh! a minute, an instant, to hear her voice, to touch her dress, to look at her, the angel! and then to die! It is nothing to die, but it is dreadful to die without seeing her. She would smile upon me, she would say a word to me. Would that harm anybody? No, it is over, forever. Here I am, all alone. My God! my God! I shall never see her again."

At this moment there was a rap at his door.

THAT very day, or rather that very evening, just as Marius had left the table and retired into his office, having a bundle of papers to study over, Basque had handed him a letter, saying: "the person who wrote the letter is in the antechamber."

He broke the seal eagerly, and read:—

"Monsieur Baron,—If the Supreme Being had given me the talents for it, I could have been Baron Thénard, member of the Institute (Academy of Ciences), but I am not so. I merely bear the same name that he does, happy if this remembrance commends me to the excellence of your bounties. The benefit with which you honor me will be reciprocal. I am in possession of a secret concerning an individual. This individual conserns you. I hold the secret at your disposition, desiring to have the honor of being useful to you. I will give you the simple means of drivving from your honorable family this individual who has no right in it, Madame the Baroness being of high birth. The sanctuary of virtue could not coabit longer with crime without abdicating.

"I atend in the entichamber the orders of Monsieur the Baron.—With respect."

The letter was signed "THÉNARD."
"Show him in," said Marius.
Basque announced:
"Monsieur Thénard."
A man entered.
"I commence gratis," said the stranger. "You will see that I am interesting."
"Go on."
"Monsieur Baron, you have in your house a robber and an assassin."

Marius shuddered.

"In my house? no," said he.

The stranger, imperturbable, brushed his hat with his sleeve, and continued:

"Assassin and robber. Observe, Monsieur Baron, that I do not speak here of acts, old, by-gone, and withered, which may be cancelled by prescription in the eye of the law, and by repentance in the eye of God. I speak of recent acts, present acts, acts yet unknown to justice at this hour. I will proceed. This man has glided into your confidence, and almost into your family, under a false name. I am going to tell you his true name. And to tell it to you for nothing."

"I am listening."

"His name is Jean Valjean."

"I know it."

"I'm going to tell you, also for nothing, who he is."

"Say on."

"He is an old convict."

"I know it."

"You know it since I have had the honor of telling you."

"No. I knew it before."

Marius' cool tone, that double reply, *I know it*, his laconic method of speech, embarrassing to conversation, excited some suppressed anger in the stranger.

The stranger resumed with a smile:

"I do not permit myself to contradict Monsieur the Baron. At all events, you must see that I am informed. Now, what I have to acquaint you with, is known to myself alone. It concerns the fortune of Madame the Baroness. It is an extraordinary secret. It is for sale. I offer it to you first. Cheap. Twenty thousand francs."

"I know that secret as well as the others," said Marius.

The person felt the necessity of lowering his price a little.

"Monsieur Baron, say ten thousand francs, and I will go on."

"I repeat, that you have nothing to acquaint me with. I know what you wish to tell me."

There was a new flash in the man's eye. He exclaimed:

"Still I must dine to-day. It is an extraordinary secret, I tell you. Monsieur the Baron, I am going to speak. I will speak. Give me twenty francs."

Marius looked at him steadily:

"I know your extraordinary secret; just as I knew Jean Valjean's name: just as I know your name."

"My name?"

"Yes."

"That is not difficult, Monsieur Baron. I have had the honor of writing it to you and telling it to you. Thénard."

"Dier."

"Eh?"

"Thénardier."

"Who is that?"

"Thénadier, I have told you your name. Now your secret, what you came to make known to me, do you want me to tell you that? I too have my means of information. You shall see that I know more about it than you do. Jean Valjean, as you have said, is an assassin and a robber. A robber, because he robbed a rich manufacturer, M. Madeleine, whose ruin he caused. An assassin, because he assassinated the police-officer, Javert."

Thénardier cast upon Marius the sovereign glance of a beaten man, who lays hold on victory again, and who has just recovered in one minute all the ground which he had lost. But the smile returned immediately; the inferior before the superior can only have a skulking triumph, and Thénardier merely said to Marius:

"Monsieur Baron, we are on the wrong track."

"What!" replied Marius, "do you deny that? These are facts."

"They are chimeras. The confidence with which Monsieur the Baron honors me makes it my duty to tell him so. Before all things, truth and justice. I do not like to see people accused unjustly. Monsieur Baron, Jean Valjean never robbed Monsieur Madeleine, and Jean Valjean never killed Javert."

"You speak strongly! how is that?"

"For two reasons."

"What are they? tell me."

"The first is this: he did not rob Monsieur Madeleine, since it is Jean Valjean himself who was Monsieur Madeleine."

"What is that you are telling me?"

"And the second is this: he did not assassinate Javert, since Javert himself killed Javert."

"What do you mean?"

"That Javert committed suicide."

"Prove it! prove it!" cried Marius, beside himself.

Thénardier took from his pocket a large envelope of grey paper, which seemed to contain folded sheets of different sizes.

"I have my documents," said he, with calmness.

And he added:

"Monsieur Baron, in your interest, I wished to find out Jean Valjean to the bottom. I say that Jean Valjean and Madeleine are the same man; and I say that Javert had no other assassin than Javert; and when I speak I have the proofs. Not manuscript proofs; writing is suspicious; writing is complaisant, but proofs in print."

While speaking, Thénardier took out of the envelope two newspapers, yellow, faded, and strongly saturated with tobacco. One of these two newspapers, broken at all the folds, and falling in square pieces, seemed much older than the other.

"Two facts, two proofs," said Thénardier. And unfolding the two papers, he handed them to Marius.

One, the oldest, a copy of the *Drapeau Blanc*, of the 25th of July, 1823, established the identity of M. Madeleine and Jean Valjean. The other, a *Moniteur* of the 15th of June, 1832, verified the suicide of Javert, adding that it appeared from a verbal report made by Javert to the prefect that, taken prisoner in the barricade of the Rue de la Chanvrerie, he had owed his life to the magnanimity of an insurgent who, though he had him at the muzzle of his pistol, instead of blowing out his brains, had fired into the air.

Marius read. There was evidence, certain date, unquestionable proof; these two newspapers had not been printed expressly to support Thénardier's words. The note published in the *Moniteur* was an official communication from the prefecture of police. Marius could not doubt. The information derived from the cashier was false, and he himself was mistaken. Jean Valjean, suddenly growing grand, arose from the cloud. Marius could not restrain a cry of joy:

"Well, then, this unhappy man is a wonderful man! all that fortune was really his own! he is Madeleine, the providence of a whole region! he is Jean Valjean, the saviour of Javert! he is a hero! he is a saint!"

"He is not a saint, and he is not a hero," said Thénardier. "He is an assassin and a robber."

Robber, assassin; these words, which Marius supposed

were gone, yet which came back, fell upon him like a shower of ice.

"Again," said he.

"Still," said Thénardier. "Jean Valjean did not rob Madeleine, but he is a robber. He did not kill Javert, but he is a murderer."

"Will you speak," resumed Marius, "of that petty theft of forty years ago, expiated, as appears from your newspapers themselves, by a whole life of repentance, abnegation, and virtue?"

"I said assassination and robbery, Monsieur Baron. And I repeat that I speak of recent facts. What I have to reveal to you is absolutely unknown.

"Monsieur Baron, on the 6th of June, 1832, about a year ago, a man was in the Grand Sewer of Paris, near where the sewer empties into the Seine, between the Pont des Invalides and the Pont d'Iéna."

Marius suddenly drew his chair near Thénardier's. Thénardier noticed this movement, and continued with the deliberation of a speaker who holds his interlocutor fast, and who feels the palpitation of his adversary beneath his words:

"This man, compelled to conceal himself, for reasons foreign to politics, however, had taken the sewer for his dwelling, and had a key to it. It was, I repeat it, the 6th of June; it might have been eight o'clock in the evening. The man heard a noise in the sewer. Very much surprised, he hid himself, and watched. It was a sound of steps, somebody was walking in the darkness; somebody was coming in his direction. Strange to say, there was another man in the sewer beside him. The grating of the outlet of the sewer was not far off. A little light which came from it enabled him to recognise the newcomer, and to see that this man was carrying something on his back. He walked bent over. The man who was walking bent over was an old convict, and what he was carrying upon his shoulders was a corpse. Assassination *in flagrante delicto,* if ever there was such a thing. As for the robbery, it follows of course; nobody kills a man for nothing. This convict was going to throw his corpse into the river. It is a noteworthy fact, that before reaching the grating of the outlet, this convict, who came from a distance in the sewer, had been compelled to pass through a horrible quagmire in which it would seem that he might have left the corpse; but, the sewer-men working upon the quagmire might, the very next day, have found the assassinated man, and that was not the assassin's game. He preferred to go through the quagmire with his load, and his efforts must have been terrible; it is impossible to put one's life in greater peril; I do not understand how he came out of it alive."

Marius' chair drew still nearer. Thénardier took advantage of it to draw a long breath. He continued:

"Monsieur Baron, a sewer is not the Champ de Mars. One lacks everything there, even room. When two men are in a sewer, they must meet each other. That is what happened. The resident and the traveller were compelled to say good-day to each other, to their mutual regret. The traveller said to the resident: *"You see what I have on my back, I must get out, you have the key, give it to me."* This convict was a man of terrible strength. There was no refusing him. Still he who had the key parleyed, merely to gain time. He examined the dead man, but he could see nothing, except that he was young, well dressed, apparently a rich man, and all disfigured with blood. While he was talking, he found means to cut and tear off from behind, without the assassin perceiving it, a piece of the assassinated man's coat. A piece of evidence, you understand; means of getting trace of the affair, and proving the crime upon the criminal. He put this piece of evidence in his pocket. After which he opened the grating, let the man out with his encumbrance on his back, shut the grating again and escaped, little caring to be mixed up with the remainder of the adventure, and especially desiring not to be present when the assassin should throw the assassinated man into the river. He who was carrying the corpse was Jean Valjean; he who had the key is now speaking to you, and the piece of the coat——"

Thénardier finished the phrase by drawing from his pocket and holding up, on a level with his eyes, between his thumbs and his forefingers, a strip of ragged black cloth, covered with dark stains.

Marius had risen, pale, hardly breathing, his eye fixed upon the scrap of black cloth, and, without uttering a word, without losing sight of this rag, he retreated to the wall, and, with his right hand stretched behind him, groped about for a key which was in the lock of a closet near the chimney. He found this key, opened the closet, and thrust his arm into it without looking, and without removing his startled eyes from the fragment that Thénardier held up.

Meanwhile Thénardier continued:

"Monsieur Baron, I have the strongest reasons to believe that the assassinated young man was an opulent stranger drawn into a snare by Jean Valjean, and the bearer of an enormous sum."

"The young man was myself, and there is the coat!" cried Marius, and he threw an old black coat covered with blood upon the carpet.

Then, snatching the fragment from Thénardier's hands, he bent down over the coat, and applied the piece to the cut skirt. The edges fitted exactly, and the strip completed the coat.

Thénardier was petrified.

Marius rose up, quivering, desperate, flashing.

He felt in his pocket, and walked, furious, towards Thénardier, offering him and almost pushing into his face his fist full of five hundred and a thousand franc notes.

"You are a wretch! you are a liar, a slanderer, a scoundrel. You came to accuse this man, you have justified him; you wanted to destroy him, you have succeeded only in glorifying him. And it is you who are a robber! and it is you who are an assassin. I saw you, Thénardier, Jondrette, in that den on the Boulevard de l'Hôpital. I know enough about you to send you to the galleys, and further even, if I wished. Here, there are a thousand francs, braggart that you are!"

And he threw a bill for a thousand francs to Thénardier.

"Ah! Jondrette Thénardier, vile knave! Take these five hundred francs, and leave this place! Waterloo protects you."

"Waterloo!" muttered Thénardier, pocketing the five hundred francs with the thousand francs.

"Yes, assassin! you saved the life of a colonel there——"

"Of a general," said Thénardier, raising his head.

"Of a colonel!" replied Marius with a burst of passion. "I would not give a farthing for a general. And you came here to act out your infamy! I tell you that you have committed every crime. Go! out of my sight! You will start tomorrow for America, with your daughter, for your wife is dead, abominable liar. I will see to your departure, bandit, and I will count out to you then twenty thousand francs. Go and get hung elsewhere!"

"Monsieur Baron," answered Thénardier, bowing to the ground, "eternal gratitude."

And Thénardier went out comprehending nothing, astounded and transported with this sweet crushing under sacks of gold and with this thunderbolt bursting upon his head in bank-notes.

Let us finish with this man at once. Two days after the events which we are now relating, he left, through Marius' care, for America, under a false name, with his daughter Azelma, provided with a draft upon New York for twenty thousand francs. Thénardier, the moral misery of Thénardier, the broken down bourgeois, was irremediable; he was in America what he had been in Europe. With Marius' money, Thénardier became a slaver.

As soon as Thénardier was out of doors, Marius ran to the garden where Cosette was still walking:

"Cosette! Cosette!" cried he. "Come! come quick! Let us go. Basque, a fiacre! Cosette, come. Oh! my God! It was he who saved my life! Let us not lose a minute! Put on your shawl."

Cosette thought him mad, and obeyed.

In a moment, a fiacre was at the door.

Marius helped Cosette in and sprang in himself.

"Driver," said he, "Rue de l'Homme Armé, Number 7."

The fiacre started.

"Oh! what happiness!" said Cosette. "Rue de l'Homme Armé! I dared not speak to you of it again. We are going to see Monsieur Jean."

"Your father! Cosette, your father more than ever. Cosette, I see it. You told me that you never received the letter which I sent you by Gavroche. It must have fallen into his hands. Cosette, he went to the barricade to save me. As it is a necessity for him to be an angel, on the way, he saved others; he saved Javert. He snatched me out of that gulf to give me to you. He carried me on his back in that frightful sewer. Cosette, after having been your providence, he was mine. Only think that there was a horrible quagmire, enough to drown him a hundred times, to drown him in the mire, Cosette! he carried me through that. I had fainted; I saw nothing, I heard nothing, I could know nothing of my own fate. We are going to bring him back, take him with us, whether he will or no, he shall never leave us again. If he is only at home! If we only find him! I will pass the rest of my

life in venerating him. Yes, that must be it, do you see, Cosette? Gavroche must have handed my letter to him. It is
all explained. You understand."

Cosette did not understand a word.

"You are right," said she to him.

Meanwhile the fiacre rolled on.

NIGHT BEHIND WHICH IS DAWN

AT the knock which he heard at his door, Jean Valjean turned
his head.

"Come in," said he feebly.

The door opened. Cosette and Marius appeared.

Cosette rushed into the room.

Marius remained upon the threshold, leaning against the
casing of the door.

"Cosette!" said Jean Valjean, and he rose in his chair, his
arms stretched out and trembling, haggard, livid, terrible,
with immense joy in his eyes.

Cosette stifled with emotion, fell upon Jean Valjean's
breast.

"Father!" said she.

Jean Valjean, beside himself, stammered:

"Cosette! she? you, madame? it is you, Cosette? Oh, my
God!"

And, clasped in Cosette's arms, he exclaimed:

"It is you, Cosette? you are here? You forgive me then!"

Marius, dropping his eyelids that the tears might not fall,
stepped forward and mumured between his lips which were
contracted convulsively to check the sobs:

"Father!"

"And you too, you forgive me!" said Jean Valjean.

Marius could not utter a word, and Jean Valjean added:
"Thanks."

Cosette took off her shawl and threw her hat upon the bed.

"They are in my way," said she.

And seating herself upon the old man's knees, she stroked
away his white hair with an adorable grace, and kissed his
forehead.

Jean Valjean faltered:

"How foolish we are! I thought I should never see her

again. Only think, Monsieur Pontmercy, that at the moment you came in, I was saying to myself: It is over. There is her little dress, I am a miserable man, I shall never see Cosette again, I was saying that at the very moment you were coming up the stairs. But we reckon without God. God said: You think that you are going to be abandoned, dolt? No. Come, here is a poor goodman who has need of an angel. And the angel comes; and I see my Cosette again! and I see my darling Cosette again! Oh! I was very miserable!"

For a moment he could not speak, then he continued:

"I really needed to see Cosette a little while from time to time. A heart does want a bone to gnaw. Still I felt plainly that I was in the way. I gave myself reasons: they have no need of you, stay in your corner, you have no right to continue for ever."

And Cosette continued again:

"How naughty to have left us in this way! Where have you been? Why did not you let us know? Do you know that you are very much changed. Oh! the naughty father! he has been sick, and we did not know it! Here, Marius, feel his hand, how cold it is!"

"So you are here, Monsieur Pontmercy, you forgive me!" repeated Jean Valjean.

At these words, which Jean Valjean now said for the second time, all that was swelling Marius' heart found an outlet, he broke forth:

"Cosette, do you hear? that is the way with him! he begs my pardon, and do you know what he has done for me, Cosette? he has saved my life. He has given you to me. And, after having saved me, and after having given you to me, Cosette, what did he do with himself? he sacrificed himself. There is the man. And, to me the ungrateful, to me the forgetful, to me the pitiless, to me the guilty, he says: Thanks! Cosette, my whole life passed at the feet of this man would be too little. That barricade, that sewer, that furnace, that cloaca, he went through everything for me, for you, Cosette! He bore me through death in every form which he put aside from me, and which he accepted for himself. All courage, all virtue, all heroism, all sanctity, he has it all, Cosette, that man is an angel!"

"Hush! hush!" said Jean Valjean in a whisper. "Why tell all that?"

"But you!" exclaimed Marius, with a passion in which

veneration was mingled, "why have not you told it? It is your fault, too. You save people's lives, and you hide it from them! You do more, under pretence of unmasking yourself, you calumniate yourself. It is frightful."

"I told the truth," answered Jean Valjean.

"No," replied Marius, "the truth is the whole truth; and you did not tell it. You were Monsieur Madeleine, why not have said so? You had saved Javert, why not have said so? I owe my life to you, why not have said so?"

"Because I felt that you were right. It was necessary that I should go away. If you had known that affair of the sewer, you would have made me stay with you. I should then have had to keep silent. If I had spoken, it would have embarrassed all."

"Embarrassed what? embarrassed whom?" replied Marius. "Do you suppose you are going to stay here? We are going to carry you back. Oh! my God! when I think it was by accident that I learned it all! You are her father and mine. You shall not spend another day in this horrid house. Do not imagine that you will be here to-morrow."

"To-morrow," said Jean Valjean, "I shall not be here, but I shall not be at your house."

"What do you mean?" replied Marius. "Ah now, we shall allow no more journeys. You shall never leave us again."

"This time, it is for good," added Cosette. "We have a carriage below. I am going to carry you off. If necessary, I shall use force."

And laughing, she made as if she would lift the old man in her arms.

Jean Valjean listened to her without hearing her. He heard the music of her voice rather than the meaning of her words; one of those big tears which are the gloomy pearls of the soul, gathered slowly in his eye. He murmured:

"The proof that God is good is that she is here."

"Father!" cried Cosette.

Cosette took both the old man's hands in her own.

"My God!" said she, "your hands are colder yet. Are you sick? Are you suffering?"

"No," answered Jean Valjean. "I am very well. Only——" He stopped.

"Only what?"

"I shall die in a few minutes."

Cosette and Marius shuddered.

"Die!" exclaimed Marius.

"Yes, but that is nothing," said Jean Valjean.

Cosette uttered a piercing cry:

"Father! my father! you shall live. You are going to live. I will have you live, do you hear!"

Jean Valjean raised his head towards her with adoration.

"Oh yes, forbid me to die. Who knows? I shall obey perhaps. I was just dying when you came. That stopped me, it seemed to me that I was born again."

"You are full of strength and life," exclaimed Marius. "Do you think people die like that? You have had trouble, you shall have no more. I ask your pardon now, and that on my knees! You shall live, and live with us, and live long. We will take you back. Both of us here will have but one thought henceforth, your happiness!"

"You see," added Cosette in tears, "that Marius says you will not die."

Jean Valjean continued to smile.

"If you should take me back, Monsieur Pontmercy, would that make me different from what I am? No; God thought as you and I did, and he has not changed his mind; it is best that I should go away. Death is a good arrangement. God knows better than we do what we need."

There was a noise at the door. It was the physician coming in.

The physician felt his pulse.

"Ah! it was you he needed!" murmured he, looking at Cosette and Marius.

And, bending towards Marius' ear he added very low: "Too late."

Jean Valjean, almost without ceasing to gaze upon Cosette, turned upon Marius and the physician a look of serenity.

Suddenly he arose. These returns of strength are sometimes a sign of the death-struggle. He walked with a firm step to the wall, put aside Marius and the physician, who offered to assist him, took down from the wall the little copper crucifix which hung there, came back, and sat down with all the freedom of motion of perfect health, and said in a loud voice, laying the crucifix on the table:

"Behold the great martyr."

Then his breast sank in, his head wavered, as if the dizziness of the tomb seized him.

Jean Valjean, after this semi-syncope, gathered strength,

shook his forehead as if to throw off the darkness, and became almost completely lucid once more. He took a fold of Cosette's sleeve, and kissed it.

"He is reviving! doctor, he is reviving!" cried Marius.

"You are both kind," said Jean Valjean. "I will tell you what has given me pain. What has given me pain, Monsieur Pontmercy, was that you have been unwilling to touch that money. That money really belongs to your wife. I will explain it to you, my children, on that account I am glad to see you. The black jet comes from England, the white jet comes from Norway. All this is in the paper you see there, which you will read. For bracelets, I invented the substitution of clasps made by bending the metal for clasps made by soldering the metal. They are handsomer, better, and cheaper. You understand how much money can be made. So Cosette's fortune is really her own. I give you these particulars so that your minds may be at rest."

The portress had come up, and was looking through the half-open door. The physician motioned her away, but he could not prevent that good, zealous woman from crying to the dying man before she went:

"Do you want a priest?"

"I have one," answered Jean Valjean.

And, with his finger, he seemed to designate a point above his head, where, you would have said, he saw someone.

It is probable that the Bishop was indeed a witness of this death-agony.

Cosette slipped a pillow under his back gently.

From moment to moment, Jean Valjean grew weaker. His breath had become intermittent; it was interrupted by a slight rattle. He had difficulty in moving his wrists, his feet had lost all motion, and, at the same time that the distress of the limbs and the exhaustion of the body increased, all the majesty of the soul rose and displayed itself upon his forehead. The light of the unknown world was already visible in his eye.

He motioned to Cosette to approach, then to Marius; it was evidently the last minute of the last hour, and he began to speak to them in a voice so faint it seemed to come from afar, and you would have said that there was already a wall between them and him.

"Come closer, come closer, both of you. I love you dearly.

Oh! it is good to die so! You too, you love me, my Cosette. I knew very well that you still had some affection for your old goodman. How kind you are to put this cushion under my back! You will weep for me a little, will you not? Not too much. I do not wish you to have any deep grief. You must amuse yourselves a great deal, my children. I forgot to tell you that on buckles without tongues still more is made than on anything else. A gross, twelve dozen, costs ten francs, and sells for sixty. That is really a good business. So you need not be astonished at the six hundred thousand francs, Monsieur Pontmercy. It is honest money. You can be rich without concern. You must have a carriage, from time to time a box at the theatres, beautiful ball dresses, my Cosette, and then give good dinners to your friends, be very happy. I was writing just now to Cosette. She will find my letter. To her I bequeath the two candlesticks which are on the mantle. They are silver; but to me they are gold, they are diamond; they change the candles which are put into them, into consecrated tapers. I do not know whether he who gave them to me is satisfied with me in heaven. I have done what I could. My children, you will not forget that I am a poor man, you will have me buried in the most convenient piece of ground under a stone to mark the spot. That is my wish. No name on the stone. If Cosette will come for a little while sometimes, it will give me pleasure. You too, Monsieur Pontmercy. I must confess to you that I have not always loved you; I ask your pardon. Now, she and you are but one to me. I am very grateful to you. I feel that you make Cosette happy. If you knew, Monsieur Pontmercy, her beautiful rosy cheeks were my joy; when I saw her a little pale, I was sad. There is a five hundred franc bill in the bureau. I have not touched it. It is for the poor. Cosette, do you see your little dress, there on the bed? do you recognise it? Yet it was only ten years ago. We have been very happy. My children, do not weep, I am not going very far, I shall see you from there. You will only have to look when it is night, you will see me smile. Cosette, do you remember Montfermeil? You were in the wood, you were very much frightened; do you remember when I took the handle of the water-bucket? That was the first time I touched your poor little hand. It was so cold! Ah! you had red hands in those days. Mademoiselle, your hands are very white now. Those Thénardiers were wicked. We must forgive them. Cosette, the time has come to tell you the name of your mother. Her name was Fantine. Fall on your knees whenever you pronounce it. She suffered much. And loved you much. Her measure of unhappiness was as full as yours of happiness. Such are the distributions of God. He is on high, he sees us all, and he knows what he does in the midst of his great stars. So I am going away, my children. Love each other dearly always. There is scarcely anything else in the world but that: to love one another. You will think sometimes of the poor old man who died here. O my Cosette! it is not my fault, indeed, if I have not seen you all this time, it broke my heart; I went as far as the corner of the street, I must have seemed strange to the people who saw me pass, I looked like a crazy man, once I went out with no hat. My children, I do not see very clearly now, I had some more things to say, but it makes no difference. Think of me a little. You are blessed creatures. I do not know what is the matter with me, I see a light. Come nearer. I die happy. Let me put my hands upon you dear beloved heads."

Cosette and Marius fell on their knees, overwhelmed, choked with tears, each grasping one of Jean Valjean's hands. Those august hands moved no more.

He had fallen backwards, the light from the candlesticks fell upon him; his white face looked up towards heaven, he let Cosette and Marius cover his hands with kisses; he was dead.

GRASS HIDES AND RAIN BLOTS OUT

THERE is, in the cemetery of Père Lachaise, in the neighborhood of the Potters' field, far from the elegant *quartier* of the city of sepulchers, far from all those fantastic tombs which display in presence of eternity the hideous fashions of death, in a deserted corner, beside an old wall, beneath a great yew on which the bindweed climbs, among the dog-grass and the mosses, a stone. This stone is exempt no more than the rest from the leprosy of time, from the mould, the lichen, and the droppings of the birds. The air turns it black, the water green. It is near no path, and people do not like to go in that direction, because the grass is high, and they would wet their feet. When there is a little sunshine, the lizards come out. There is, all about, a rustling of wild oats. In the spring, the linnets sing in the tree.

This stone is entirely blank. The only thought in cutting it was of the essentials of the grave, and there was no other care than to make this stone long enough and narrow enough to cover a man.

No name can be read there.

B-9